Beneath the Surface

Beneath the Surface

FIONA NEILL

MICHAEL JOSEPH
an imprint of
PENGUIN BOOKS

MICHAEL JOSEPH

UK | USA | Canada | Ireland | Australia
India | New Zealand | South Africa

Michael Joseph is part of the Penguin Random House group of companies
whose addresses can be found at global.penguinrandomhouse.com

First published 2019
001

Set in 13.75/16 pt Garamond MT Std
Typeset by Jouve (UK), Milton Keynes
Printed and bound in Great Britain by Clays Ltd, Elcograf S.p.A.

A CIP catalogue record for this book is available from the British Library

HARDBACK ISBN: 978–0–718–18978–5
OM PAPERBACK ISBN: 978–0–718–18979–2

www.greenpenguin.co.uk

MIX
Paper from
responsible sources
FSC® C018179

Penguin Random House is committed to a
sustainable future for our business, our readers
and our planet. This book is made from Forest
Stewardship Council® certified paper.

For Phil Robertson

No man ever steps in the same river twice, for it's
not the same river and he's not the same man.

Heraclitus

Prologue

It was Mia who found it. She came across the blue and white cardboard box in one of the storage crates stacked in the garage. *Strictly speaking*, it was inside its packaging, inside a box that was inside the crate, a bit like the set of Russian dolls on the bookshelf in her bedroom. *Whoever put this here didn't want it to be found but neither did they want it to be lost.* Later she would say it was as if it was waiting to be discovered. Later still, she would claim that it called out to her. Because how else could you explain the mysterious way the pregnancy test revealed itself amid the chaos of thousands of family belongings?

Mia pulled the plastic dipstick out of its packaging. She might be only ten years old but she had watched enough *Pretty Little Liars* with her older sister over the summer to understand that the blue line in the little window indicated that the person who had peed on the dipstick was going to have a baby. Her knowledge of the mechanics of sex was a muddle of what she had learnt from David Attenborough and sex education classes at school, but she knew that, *strictly speaking*, the thin blue line meant this person had mated and, *strictly speaking*, the sex had led to reproduction. 'Strictly speaking' was her favourite new expression that summer. But suddenly it seemed to have vaguely sexual connotations, as did the word 'dipstick' and the salty taste of sweat she licked from her upper lip. She felt intoxicated, as if she'd drunk black coffee or dived into freezing cold water.

She gingerly held the pregnancy test between the tips of her thumb and index finger as if it might be contagious, which in a sense it was, although not in ways she could possibly imagine. She was half wondering if she should take it to school when the new term started. 'You have to have a currency at school,' Lilly had tried to explain recently, when Mia had told her she felt like a nothing. 'Something that makes you special.' It was easy for her older sister to say that. Lilly was both clever and pretty. Whereas until the beginning of year five, when her new friend Tas had appeared at the desk beside her, clutching his red rucksack with the broken zip, Mia could go for whole days without anyone talking to her. As far as currencies went, it didn't get much better than owning a positive pregnancy test. Surely it would make her more interesting, even to the girls who ignored her.

It was time to get Lilly involved. It felt grown-up and sisterly to be in a position to share something so intimate, a glimpse of how one day the seven years that separated them might no longer feel like such a chasm. Mia longed for a life of eternal bonds in a world where nothing seemed permanent. She had attended three different schools, had endured five different special-needs teachers, lost three grandparents and, until she'd met Tas, had never had a friendship that lasted longer than a few weeks.

She spotted the top of Lilly's head emerging from a cardboard box beside the door into the garden. All she could see of her was the messy blonde bun that was held together with pencils. But even that looked cool.

'Look what I've found!' Mia tried to sound casual rather than excited. Unlike Tas, Lilly didn't respond well to her mood surges.

'Just a minute.' That was Lilly's favourite phrase that summer. Especially when it came to Mia. She never said it unkindly. Lilly was always patient with her. But neither did she ever get back to her once Mia had counted to sixty in her head.

They weren't meant to be in the garage that afternoon. It was full of precariously stacked crates and boxes, packed in haste a couple of weeks earlier so the builders could get started on the damp, which seemed to seep out of the very pores of their new home. But when Lilly had sensed a pre-lunch row brewing between her parents, uncle and aunt she had dragged Mia away from the barbecue into the hot, stuffy garage.

This was not an act of selflessness to protect Mia from conflict. It was because Lilly knew that if they stayed outside the adults would be more guarded, and the garage was the perfect vantage point to observe what unfolded. Besides, she needed to unearth a rucksack for a music festival on the last weekend of the holidays. She had bought the ticket without telling her mum because Grace would never agree to her going. The dates clashed with a pre-term advanced English course at school and her mum was obsessed with Lilly being 'ahead of the game' when it came to academic achievement. Until the toilet walls had grown mushrooms, they had been covered with her certificates and awards. Uptight didn't really cover it.

Lilly knew trouble was brewing because earlier in the week she had overheard her dad describing his brother, Rob, as an 'A-grade fuck-wit', a phrase he used so rarely that he made it sound as if he was grading an essay by one of his A-level students. Her aunt Ana, who normally had to try really hard to find Lilly's parents interesting,

3

had improbably asked to come and see them because she needed some advice.

Lilly felt she had the right to know the reason behind all the tension. She wanted to hear the raw, unfiltered version of what was going on. She wanted to witness Wild Passions and Total Loss of Control. Not least because, over the past couple of months, she had got involved with a boy from school and was going through some emotional extremes of her own. She felt that if they dug deep, underneath the good manners and bad jokes, her parents, uncle and aunt were capable of great drama.

So, she had convinced her little sister they should go and search for Lilly's collection of gemstones in the storage boxes, promising that if they found them she would give half to Mia for her birthday, including the fool's gold and agate geode. Lilly knew her sister would find this an irresistible bribe. She liked to consider herself a collector. Her room was filled with bizarre objects: feathers, Allen keys in different sizes, bulldog clips. Her current prize possession was an eel she had found at the end of the garden during the spring floods, who lived in a bucket beside her bed.

'Look at this – you won't believe it,' said Mia, a little more desperately.

'In a minute, Mimi,' Lilly replied languidly, without bothering to look up. It was hot and humid in the garage, and when she wasn't with Cormack, she felt overwhelmed with a languor that only he could dissipate. *I'm like an inert gas. I only react with him.* She had seen him almost every weekend since June because they both had a Saturday shift at the same punting company in the centre of Cambridge. Her mum had reluctantly agreed that it would sound good on her university application to prove she could manage a job alongside her school work. Although Grace hadn't said so, Lilly knew the extra spending money would come in handy: family finances were obviously tight or why would they have moved to this dump?

But today Grace had insisted she stay at home to have lunch with Rob and Ana. Lilly imagined herself entwined around Cormack in the cool waters at Earith Sluice. That was all that mattered. Everything that used to count – exam results, university entrance, Insta likes, Hayley – had faded into the background. She thought about him all the time. *What used to be in that space in her head that he now took up? Or was it some new space he had opened?*

Lilly was half-heartedly examining the contents of a box behind the door, pretending to search for the gemstones, while keeping an ear open for what was going on outside. The box was full of musty-smelling children's books. *Dr Seuss. Goodnight Moon. Legends of the Fens.* Comforting, familiar titles that she had read to Mia years ago when she relished playing mother to her younger sister. She pulled out the Best Friends For Ever diary that she and Hayley had kept from year six to year eight and flicked through the pages. *Our favourite colours. Our best swimsuits.* A Polaroid of the two of them having their ears pierced. A ticket to Glee Live. She pressed the notebook to her face and inhaled. It smelt like the rest of the house, a thick musty odour that made her feel heavy-headed.

According to her dad, the reason for the smell was that the dodgy construction company that had sold them the house on the new-build estate in Black Fen Close last November had 'forgotten' to do a proper damp-proof course. Her mother, in classic Debbie Downer mode, declared that it was because the marshland beneath was reclaiming territory that was rightfully its own. 'Did you know the North Sea used to come as far as Cambridge?' she kept telling them.

When they had first moved in and her mum could still joke about the damp because it was confined to one room, Grace had teased Patrick that it was an act of vengeance on him for his Dutch ancestors who had drained the Fens to turn them into farmland.

'Lil, look!'

'Have you found the gemstones?'

'It's a pregnancy test,' said Mia, keeping her tone deliberately even. 'With a clear blue line.' She was trying to knot her long, curly auburn hair into a bun like Lilly's, but it was too thick and unruly.

This time there was no 'Just a minute.' Lilly looked up straight away, her face a gratifying picture of astonishment. Finally Mia had her total attention. Lilly hastily negotiated a route through the storage crates towards Mia, tripping over her sister's foot in her eagerness to reach her.

'Why do you always wear those big black boots?' she asked impatiently, as she took the pregnancy test from Mia's hand and held it up to the light for closer inspection.

'They make me feel strong,' said Mia, with a shrug.

'Show me where you found this, Mimi.'

Mia pointed at a large silver tin with llamas embossed on the lid. 'There's loads of hippie clothes too,' she said, holding up a brown suede waistcoat fringed with long tassels. She sniffed it. 'Smells weird. Sort of sickly.'

Lilly handed back the pregnancy test, removed the lid of the tin and started examining what, in Mia's opinion, were far less interesting objects, including pieces of torn-up postcard and a notebook with 'The Certainties' handwritten in black felt-tip pen on the front.

'Why would anyone keep a pregnancy test?' Mia asked, trying to refocus Lilly's attention.

'Because it means something. Because it represents part

of how you have become who you are. Because it's your history.'

'Weird, huh? I'm going to ask Mum about it,' declared Mia. She stood up and brushed down her bare legs, sending a flurry of dust into the air. Her denim skirt had shifted around her narrow boyish hips so that the zip was at the side instead of the front. She shunted it back and put the pregnancy test into her pocket.

'Wait,' said Lilly, abruptly. 'You can't do that.'

'Why not?'

Lilly frowned so intently that her eyebrows met in the middle. There was a long silence during which Mia tried and failed again to tie her long curly hair into a bun.

'Because it's mine.'

'I found it first.'

'You don't understand. It belongs to me.'

For a split second Mia suspected Lilly was winding her up. Then she saw the expression on her face. The last time she had looked so worried was the day she'd got her GCSE results. Even then Mia hadn't taken her anxiety seriously because everyone except Lilly was certain she would get the highest grades. This, however, was different.

'You're pregnant?' Mia asked. She wasn't sure what to do. Should she hug Lilly or give her a high five? What did people do on TV? But as she stepped forward Mia accidentally trod on an electronic globe that she had taken out of the box where she'd found the pregnancy test. It started parroting the population rate of different countries around the world: 'Mexico 132 million. Indonesia 269 million.' She would have asked Lilly if this was a good example of irony, a grammatical point she was struggling with at school, if she hadn't been so concerned about what she had just learnt. When Lilly didn't react, she kicked the globe with her leather boot and it started playing the national anthem.

Mia suddenly felt tearful without understanding why. At first she thought it was the realization that Lilly would always do everything before her and she would never catch up. But it was more than that and worse than that. Mia knew right away that she could never compete for attention with a newborn baby, which made her feel bad about herself. She would be expected to learn to change nappies, prepare bottles, babysit and generally assume responsibilities as an aunt that she didn't feel ready to take on. And what if Lilly died in childbirth?

'Past tense. Was pregnant,' Lilly said. 'I had an abortion.'

Abortion didn't feature in David Attenborough or on the school sex-ed curriculum and at first Mia didn't understand what Lilly was talking about. It sounded as though she had either hidden the baby somewhere or given it away. As usual, Mia was playing catch-up. 'What do you mean?'

'I went to a special clinic and took a special pill so I wouldn't have the baby.'

This was even more cataclysmic. Now Mia felt regret for the niece she would never know (she had no doubt it would have been a girl) and the ten-year-old aunt she would never be. The baby might have grown up to become her closest friend after Tas. They could have gone on holiday together and taken the train to London to go shopping. A period to mourn the loss properly would be required. As Grace often observed about Mia, being contrary was a terrible affliction.

'Does Cormack know?'

Unlike her parents, Mia knew all about Lilly's secret boyfriend. A few weeks ago, after a lot of negotiation with Grace, Tas's mum had arranged for Mia to spend the day at the Travellers' site where they lived in a caravan. But after lunch, knowing Grace would be at work, the two of them had caught the bus home to release her pet eel, Elvis, for a swim in the pond at the bottom of the garden. Unusually, they were arguing as they carried the bucket across the lawn. The time when the eels would leave the Fens to swim back to the Sargasso Sea was approaching and Tas thought Elvis should be released back into the wild while Mia wanted to keep him through the winter. 'That's cruel,' Tas argued, as they walked down the garden. 'And unnatural. Like preventing Travellers from travelling.'

Rationally, Mia knew he had a point but emotionally she couldn't bear to part with her eel. She had felt weary over this dilemma: the pull between doing the right thing and what you wanted to do in your heart gave her an idea of how it might feel to be adult. Because their voices were raised they didn't hear Lilly and Cormack, who were lying in the long grass close to the pond. Mia tripped over a bare leg, the bucket tipped on its side, and Elvis slithered over Cormack's bare buttock through the grass towards the pond.

'What the fuck?' said Cormack, jumping up to wipe eely slobber from his leg. The water from the bucket stank of old fish, pondweed and the fear of trapped eel.

Lilly hugged her arms around her bare breasts, while Cormack tried to hide his penis with his hands. Mia was too distressed about losing her eel to worry about their nudity. She ran towards the pond, with Tas in hot pursuit. The dust and the long dry grass stuck to Elvis's slimy skin and slowed him down. Mia caught him just as he slid into the water. His glassy eyes were full of tears as she'd put him back into the bucket and fixed the grille on top.

'No. You're the only person who knows,' Lilly replied.

'You didn't tell Hayley?'

'Hayley doesn't know about me and Cormack yet.'

'Why not?'

'We want to keep it low key.'

Mia looked up at her older sister and smiled. Lilly had had sex, got pregnant and had an abortion. The distance between them should have been wider than ever but the fact that Lilly had confided in her alone made it feel as though there was a new closeness in their relationship. Lilly smiled back.

'Not a word to anyone,' she said firmly. 'It's never to be mentioned again.'

'I promise,' said Mia. She paused for a moment. 'Was it awful?' She couldn't help it. Strictly speaking, this might be her last chance to ask any questions.

'Was what awful?'

'Getting rid of the baby. Did it hurt? What did they do with the body?'

'It was the size of a tadpole, Mia. I don't want to talk about it. Ever. Again.'

Fortunately at this point they were distracted by the sound of raised voices in the garden. They drifted towards the noise to hear what was going on. Through the gap in the side of the door, they observed their parents, aunt and uncle out by the barbecue.

'You promised you wouldn't drink. You are so full of shit.' That was all it took. It was difficult for Lilly to read the expression on Ana's face because she was sitting in a deckchair under the shade of a rambling rose, wearing a wide-brimmed straw hat and sunglasses, but there was no mistaking the menace in her tone. Unlike Patrick and Grace, whose marriage was boringly monotone, Rob and Ana had always been fantastically, compellingly volatile. Small words sparked like matches between them, transforming tiny flames into incendiary bonfires. Mia gripped Lilly's arm with the curious mixture of trepidation and exhilaration that defined the essence of her personality.

'The Medusa has spoken,' proclaimed Rob, theatrically. He stood stock still in front of Ana and held the bottle upside down so the beer poured on to the desiccated yellow lawn.

'Gosh, why's he doing that?' Mia asked in astonishment, elbowing Lilly out of the way to get the best view through the doorjamb.

'Ana's turned him to stone,' said Lilly.

'Really?' Mia gripped her arm. 'Like Mr Tumnus? What do we do now? Is there an antidote?'

'You're so gullible.' Lilly giggled.

Rob remained immobile.

Grace ignored them and instead furiously tossed the salad, sending a flurry of rocket and radicchio on to the table before turning with equal focus to the business of picking up every last piece and nonchalantly throwing it back into the bowl. Her T-shirt was splattered with spots of dressing.

It still wasn't completely clear to Lilly why her aunt and uncle were even in their garden, ruining the hottest day of the summer so far and derailing her plans to meet Cormack. It wasn't that Rob and Ana didn't get on with her parents. It was more that Rob was a big-shot music producer with better places to go for the weekend than their ugly new-build estate six miles from the city centre on the wrong side of Cambridge. Lilly didn't hold this against them. She would never have chosen to come here either unless she was forced to. It was like Toytown. Everything was fake: the houses, the hedges and even the trees had been transplanted on to the wild, bleak landscape.

'God, you're pathetic!' said Ana, spitting out the words, like watermelon pips. Verbal warfare had always been part of Rob and Ana's relationship. In the past Lilly had seen them squall over anything from song lyrics to whether manatees really existed, and the last time they'd all spent Christmas together, they had argued for two days about whether *Die Hard* could be defined as a Christmas film. *How could anyone care about this stuff so much?* Lilly wondered. It was exhausting and compelling at the same time.

She watched as her mum tried to catch her dad's attention. But Patrick didn't look up. He was applying the same ferocious focus as Grace had to her salad to the business of methodically flipping the steaks, sausages and veggie burgers on his new barbecue. Because he was an art-history teacher he had a strong visual sense of how everything should look. He bent down to scrutinize the layout from different angles and made a few subtle adjustments.

'What's Dad really thinking about?' Mia asked. It was a constant puzzle to them both. They never called it right. When they thought he was thinking great thoughts about Anglo-Saxon manuscripts it turned out he was reviewing sell-by dates on the spice rack. And when they saw him lining up the spice rack in alphabetical order it turned out he was pondering the Codex Amiatinus.

'Cycling, probably,' Lilly whispered, because usually at this time on a Saturday afternoon Patrick would be trying to beat his personal best on his favourite thirty-nine-mile route through Black Fen.

'And Mum?'

'That's easy. She'll be worrying about how exactly I'm going to re-jig my revision schedule to make up for the time I've lost today and how you haven't done your extra spellings,' said Lilly, distractedly, trying to piece together the jigsaw of torn postcard.

'Are you actually talking to the sausages?' they heard Rob ask Patrick, as he put down the empty beer bottle beside the barbecue.

'Don't be ridiculous.' Patrick bristled, pointedly moving the bottle on to the garden table.

'I swear I heard you say the words "peak torque",' Rob teased. 'Or was it "teak pork"? Those chops do look a bit overcooked.' He prowled around Patrick, rubbing his hands through his dark hair until it stood on end, and took a sausage from the middle of his brother's carefully ordered arrangement. 'You are so easy to read.' He laughed, and took a tentative bite.

Lilly could tell her dad was simmering from the way he gripped the barbecue tongs to manoeuvre the sausages until symmetry had been restored. In the background Grace was telling Ana how Lilly had been picked by her English teacher to join an elite class for Oxbridge candidates and how she could recite chunks of *Beowulf* by heart. She wondered what her mum would do if she told her that she could read Cormack's body as well as her own, and was not only familiar with his every scar and dimple but could tell from the rise and fall of his breath exactly when he was about to come.

'Please, Mum,' Lilly muttered. She was saved from further embarrassment by her uncle, who pulled a packet of cigarettes out of the back pocket of his jeans.

'I don't bloody believe it!' exploded Ana, interrupting Grace, who was in the middle of recounting how Lilly had recorded the fastest times for 100-metres breaststroke in the county and how this would make her stand out from the crowd on her university application because it spoke of focus and drive.

'I only smoke when I'm tense and you make me tense,' said Rob, dismissively.

'Why can't you ever show any self-restraint?' Ana asked.

'Because that would make me boring.'

'Think of your sperm!'

'I am,' said Rob drily. 'At the weekend they love nothing more than kicking back with a bottle of Brewdog and a fag.'

'Can someone please remind me why I married him?' Ana turned to Patrick and Grace for back-up.

Lilly saw her parents exchange looks. Her dad wiped his face with his hand, leaving a streak of charcoal across his cheek as Rob increased his pace around the barbecue. He had circled the same route so many times that there was now a trodden-down circle of dry grass. Patrick bent down on one knee and unthinkingly combed the grass upright.

'God, you're so fucking suburban.' Rob laughed again. 'You're beginning to remind me of Mum and Dad. I bet you've even got a Flymo.'

'This is going to be a bad one, isn't it, Lil?' Mia asked eagerly, at the unusual prospect of an argument involving all four of them. Even in the dappled light, Lilly could see her eyes were as wide as saucers.

'It is,' Lilly confirmed, trying to sound more composed than she felt.

'Don't put your shit on Patrick!' Ana shouted. 'It's not fair.'

'Come on, Ana, I've done everything you ordered,' Rob said, his voice getting louder, as if someone was turning up the volume, 'and still it's not enough. I stand here in loose-fitting shorts, wearing no pants, keeping my bollocks at a steady thirty-four point five degrees to optimize my fertility. I've stopped wanking, eating red meat and drinking coffee. I go to work every day, I earn half a million pounds a year. I fulfil my potential. And you can't let me have one beer with my brother? You're such a ball-breaker.'

Inside the garage, Lilly watched Mia stuff a fist into her mouth as if she wanted to push back emotions she didn't comprehend. She evidently didn't fully understand what Rob was implying, but there was enough tension and swearing for her to understand that this was A Very Big Moment.

'Lil?' she whispered. 'Lil?'

Lilly turned to her, anticipating a difficult question. There was a long pause. *Which would it be*, she wondered, *'bollocks', 'wanking' or 'fucking', and how much detail should she supply in her response?* Would too much honesty get her into trouble with her parents? And too little mean that Mia would ask them anyway?

'What's a Flymo?'

'It's a lawnmower,' Lilly explained, trying to keep a straight face.

'What's wrong with Dad having a lawnmower?'

The argument in the garden continued to rage.

'There's something I want to say,' said Ana, her voice trembling.

'Is it because lawnmowers are bad for the environment?' Mia persisted.

'Sssh.' Lilly nudged her. Another of Mia's worst traits was missing the point because she was obsessing about the wrong thing. 'Ana's about to reveal the real reason they're here.'

Ana removed her hat and sunglasses. Her long dark hair cascaded around her face. Her gaze darted between Grace and Patrick, who instinctively drew towards one another in a sideways crab walk between the barbecue and the garden table until their shoulders were touching.

'Rob doesn't like to talk about it.'

'Please, Ana,' Rob begged. Lilly saw him glance at Grace. It was a look somewhere between panic and despair. Neither were characteristics she associated with her confidently upbeat uncle. She could tell he wanted her mum to intervene. Grace, however, equally uncharacteristically for someone who spent her life sorting out other people's problems, remained silent.

Ana took a deep breath, as if she was trying to summon the right words. 'We've been trying to have a baby for almost two years. We've done everything we can. Organic food. Ovulation calendars. Cutting out caffeine and alcohol. But nothing works.'

'This has nothing to do with Grace and Patrick,' Rob interrupted.

'We need to try IVF. But Rob won't even talk about it. He keeps saying if we relax it will just happen. But I'm almost forty and time is running out.'

Patrick stepped forward, as if he was about to mediate. Mia clung to Lilly's arm so tightly that it started to go numb. Five sets of eyes looked to him to bring them back from the brink. Lilly's stomach ached with the nervous anxiety of a daughter who desperately wanted her dad to say the right thing but already doubted he could do justice to the emotional intensity of the occasion.

'I was wondering, Ana, in light of this, if you still like your steak cooked medium rare?'

'Oh, Dad,' said Lilly, in disappointment.

Ana's head dropped. Tiny damp patches formed on her yellow linen dress until there were so many they turned into one giant stain. It took a moment for Lilly to realize she was crying.

'Can you convince him, Grace? He always listens to you,' Ana pleaded, in between sobs.

'I can't get involved in something so personal to you both,' said Grace, cautiously.

Lilly was riveted. She tried to disentangle herself from Mia so she could concentrate on the nuances. The way her dad was scuffing his feet in the grass; her mum's inability to meet Ana's gaze; Rob's failure to comfort Ana and his attempt to catch Grace's eye. Was this how adults behaved when children weren't around? It was so unexpectedly raw. Lilly wished she had her phone with her so she could film it. That was what Cormack would have done.

'It's a shame we didn't know about this before,' whispered Mia.

'What do you mean?' asked Lilly, impatient with her constant interruptions.

'You could have given them your baby.'

Lilly gripped Mia's shoulder and bent down until she was the same height as her little sister. 'If you mention that again I'll tell Mum and Dad about the secret hiding place behind your radiator.'

Outside the argument continued to rage.

'All I want is an ordinary life,' shouted Ana.

'If you wanted ordinary you should have married Patrick, not me,' Rob yelled back.

Lilly tucked the confetti of torn-up postcard inside the notebook and slipped it into the back pocket of her jeans. She inspected the pregnancy test, like her dad might examine an ancient artefact, and stuffed it into a plastic bag. She felt strangely light-headed and blamed it on the stale air in the garage and the musty sweetness of the suede waistcoat. When she turned round to tell Mia she didn't feel so good, she saw that her little sister had unexpectedly burst out of the garage into the garden and was running over to Rob and Ana.

'Would you like to see my eel?' she heard her ask them. 'Strictly speaking, they reproduce by having orgies. I'm not sure what that means but it might help.'

'Sounds like a great strategy,' said Rob.

PART ONE

I

Two months later

It begins with a tremor. Just like it did last time. Lilly lifts
the hand that is meant to be writing notes and holds it in
front of her face, fingers splayed. But it's completely still, as
she'd known it would be. The sensation is coming from
inside, more tingle than tremble, as if someone is passing
an electrical current through the fleshy centre of her hand.

She closes her eyes for a moment and breathes in deeply.
Why is this happening again? There is the same heady
odour, a drift of some old-fashioned sickly scent, like faded
roses or violet creams, that makes her feel instantly nauseous. She scans the classroom for a rotting vase of flowers
or a half-open window that might explain the smell. But
even in the muggy heat the teacher insists the windows
should be closed to avoid any distraction from the outside
world, and the only plants in the room are Mr Galveston's
cactus collection.

She looks past the cacti out of the window and thinks
about how the view has remained the same but the perspective has changed over her seven years at St Edith's, as she
has got taller and moved up a floor each year. *Is this how life
works?* she wonders. A gradual unfolding? The first couple

of years she could only see across the playground to the modern houses on the other side of the road. Now on the top floor her view stretches beyond the housing estate to the dyke, straight as a parting, running behind it and then to the dark grid of fields and the new wind-turbine farm scything slowly through the sky beyond. The land is as flat as the sea from which it was stolen. It's all about the sky here. Today it is almost completely still, apart from two swans paddling serenely upriver. They look so unruffled.

The tingling in her hand creeps up into her forearm. Still staring out of the window, Lilly massages her inner wrist and half wonders if her artery is conducting the current. Out of the corner of her eye she sees Cormack crossing the playground with a girl who isn't her. The way he moves, smooth and relaxed, thick hair, black as the peat soil, rucksack flung over his shoulder: it's the familiarity that hurts the most. He turns his face towards the girl and she can see he is smiling the same smile that he used on her.

She should have done what he did. Shrugged her shoulders and agreed it was a fling. But it wasn't like her to treat life so casually. She had gone through all their messages and photos at the weekend and still couldn't understand how, less than a month ago, they had shared each other's bodies, worn each other's clothes and sucked on the same cigarette, discussing whether they thought their parents still had sex or when they should tell their friends they were seeing each other. Now she doesn't even get a walk-on role on his Instagram stories.

She feels the tears start to prick and tries to distract herself by tracing a line with her eyes as far as she can along the dyke to where it connects with the River Cam and the smaller waterways beyond. She loves the geometry of all the straight lines, the monotone fields, the man-made dykes and ditches that frame them. They could have been drawn with a ruler. Which they probably were: almost everything about this landscape was designed by her Dutch ancestors.

Shadowy thoughts play in Lilly's head, so she focuses on the cacti and forces herself to think of the good things she has done so that she doesn't dwell on the bad: *I gave my entire collection of gemstones to Mia without her asking for them; I joined Mr Galveston's English class to placate Mum, because she wants me to do Oxbridge, even though every lesson makes me feel sick with nerves; I made cakes to raise money for the Syrian refugees. I'm nice to the new girl. Unlike Hayley.*

Lilly looks around to check if anyone else is watching. But, thankfully, her classmates are oblivious. This is the advantage of being chosen for Mr Galveston's English group. Or twice chosen, as he likes to say. 'Once to be in the class and twice to stay.' He demands and generally inspires total focus, especially when it comes to the current text, *Beowulf*, which he can apparently recite from memory, although no one has been brave enough to challenge him. It's a class joke that even when he speaks normally he uses Anglo-Saxon metre.

Fortunately for Lilly, he's reached the apex of the lesson, as he reveals in a voice stiff with emotion that there is good evidence *Beowulf* has its cultural roots in a village less than an hour from the Cambridge classroom where they now sit. He points out of the window and tells them the Fens were the haunt of Beowulf's nemesis, Grendel, and that 'fen' is an Old English word meaning marsh, dirt or mud that is used all over northern Europe because that was where the Anglo-Saxons came from. He announces that he will be organizing a trip to the British Museum sometime soon to see the burial masks that were dug up there. There is a silence he mistakes for awe.

'Fuck that,' mutters Jordy, Mr Galveston's most reluctant recruit. Lilly knows it's for her benefit and normally she would laugh but she's too focused on the way saliva is pooling in her throat to respond. Being sick in front of everyone would complete the humiliation of the past three weeks. Jordy elbows her in the ribs and she's grateful for the distraction. He quickly loses interest, because while he has one of the most agile minds in the class he is hotwired to lose focus. At least, that is what Mr Galveston claims. Lilly tries to remember what he says about her. Something about how she needs to be more of a risk-taker. Dare to think her own thoughts instead of regurgitating other people's. *Are we who we think we are or who other people think we are?* It was the sort of conversation she used to have with Cormack. He is one of the few people she knows who is the same in real life as he is on social media. She searches for him again in the playground but he's disappeared.

Lilly stares at Mr Galveston, wondering whether he takes risks, intellectual or otherwise. She has always thought of him as ancient but in reality he's probably not much older than his students. It's just the way he looks, beardy and encased in tweed, that ages him, as well as his tendency to get excited that the Anglo-Saxons had four different words for 'friend'. 'Shoulder companion. Lord and friend. Friend of old. And intimate friend.' Right now Lilly would choose a shoulder companion, Jordy definitely being friend of old – they were born two days apart in the same hospital – but her shoulder companion of choice, Hayley, has chosen a different seat at the front of the class, leaving Lilly stuck between Jordy and the new girl. The Anglo-Saxons don't have a word for fickle friends. They would probably have sorted it out with a good old-fashioned fight. She had hoped

Hayley might have moved on from what happened in the summer. But apparently not.

Jordy keeps taking notes, glancing over at Lilly's neat looped handwriting to make sure he hasn't missed anything that could lose him points in an exam or the edge in a university interview. Because, according to Mr Galveston, success in life is all about 'having the edge'. She notices crusty red blotches of eczema creeping below Jordy's shirtsleeve on the inside of his wrist and around his collar. *So he isn't immune from the pressure either.* This should make her feel better, but if Jordy is feeling the heat it means the pressure is real, not simply in her head. She pulls out a tissue from her bag and discreetly spits into it. For a moment her throat clears.

Meanwhile Mr Galveston switches off the lights and plays his usual end-of-lesson slide show. Jordy calls this part the money shot. Today a battle mask flashes up on the whiteboard. He starts to compare it to the battle mask described in *Beowulf*. He flicks through the sequence so fast that, if she didn't know him so well, she would mistake his excitement for impatience.

'Look at the similarities. The images of boars.' Flick. 'The way the upper crest is bound with wire. *Wirum bewunden.*' Flick. 'The emblem of the stag.' Flick. There's a glint of gold each time the slide changes.

Lilly blinks whenever the screen flashes with a new image. The electrical charge that started in her hand hares up her arm, across her shoulders and down into her right hand. She wants to tell Jordy that she feels weird but when she opens her mouth she finds she can't speak. She can locate the words in her head but they're stuck in her throat.

Jordy keeps writing. He's left-handed and presses too hard on the paper. The nib makes a scratching noise that gets louder and louder until it's the only thing she can hear. She realizes he's taking advantage of the darkened room to get ahead with his homework, a quiz set by Mr Galveston on kennings, which he likes to describe as the Anglo-Saxon equivalent of cryptic crossword clues. So the word for 'river' is 'swan road', 'sea' is a 'whale road', and 'death' the 'sleep of the sword'. *Right now, I would like the sleep of the sword.*

'Lilly!' calls Mr Galveston, turning on all the lights.

She attempts to nod but the most she can manage is a polite bob of her forehead.

'Can you remind us, what are the most important lessons of Hrothgar's last sermon?'

No one bothers to look round. Lilly always has the right answers to all the questions. It is so obvious that she is Mr Galveston's favourite that it doesn't even bother anyone. And this is an easy one. Basic. You don't have to have made notes on any of the books on Mr Galveston's three-page reading list to know the answer to this one. Her body freezes, yet inside it feels as though someone has set off a million chemical reactions. She needs to find something clever and articulate to say to avoid being accused of cliché.

Something catastrophic is happening inside her. But no one seems to notice. A trickle of sweat slides down a channel from her forehead, past her nose and mouth. The damp tissue drops on to the floor beside her. She regrets wearing Cormack's pale blue T-shirt under her school shirt, because she's so hot there are damp patches under each arm.

'Lilly?' His gravelly voice grows louder. 'Can I remind you that my classes require all of your attention and full brain capacity? For most of you, even you, Lilly, that won't be enough.'

Her head lolls forwards as if she is defeated by his question. A hand shoots up in the back row. As far as gestures go, it's trivial, yet everyone in the class understands it represents the passing of one era and the dawning of another. There is no rejoicing because everyone likes Lilly and is suspicious of Freya, who turned up unannounced at the beginning of the Easter term, the first student Mr Galveston had ever allowed to join his class in the middle of the school year. Mostly people get thrown out for not fulfilling their potential.

'Freya. Queen of the goddesses.' Mr Galveston points at the new girl. 'Please enlighten us.'

Everyone turns to stare at the girl sitting at the far corner of the back row. Head bowed, Lilly's gaze edges towards Freya. Her pupils shudder and ache with the effort but at least they are obedient to her command, unlike the rest of her body. Freya has one of those faces in which every feature is a challenge. Silver hair, with an aggressively straight fringe cut too high on her forehead. Sharp nose. Dark, almond-shaped eyes. She looks like a raven. A swan of blood, as Mr Galveston might posit ('posit' being one of his favourite verbs) on account of the way ravens were always the first to arrive to pick over the dead bodies after battles. She radiates the kind of self-assured cool that Lilly wishes she possessed. 'Hrothgar's sermon highlights the value of creating stability in an unsafe and chaotic world,' says Freya, confidently. 'He talks about the temptations of pride. That great joy is always followed by great sorrow. That fame is folly.'

Lilly waits for Mr Galveston to accuse her of lack of originality.

'Very good, Freya,' he booms instead. 'Something we would all be wise to heed in this uncertain world, where nothing can be taken for granted, artificial intelligence is going to steal our jobs and global warming destroy our environment. Do not believe the people who say you can be what you want to be just because you wish for it. You can't. Everything requires hard work and sometimes that's not enough. Otherwise why would I be here standing in front of you and not at the university up the road? Could have, should have, would have. What do you call this kind of verb?'

'The modals of lost opportunities,' says Freya. She has a curious, precise way of speaking as if everything she says has been rehearsed.

'Correct,' says Mr Galveston. 'Don't let your life be contaminated by the modals of lost opportunities.'

Lilly feels herself slide off the stool. She anticipates pain as her legs buckle and her torso sinks to the floor but she feels nothing. Almost simultaneously, as if he, too, has become liquid, Jordy sinks down on his knees beside her. She notices the rip in the left leg of his jeans and the hair that sprouts through the hole, like a weed.

'Lilly! Lilly!' he whispers in her ear. His tone is surprisingly tender for someone who usually hurls himself at the world and his breath tickles her neck. He gently shakes her shoulder, strokes her cheek with his fingers and holds her hand, like he used to when they were little, except he's squeezing it so tight that it hurts. She wants to tell Jordy that she's glad they grew up together, that he's the closest thing on earth she has to a brother, that she misses wrestling with him, and that it was helpful they had used each other for kissing practice a couple of years ago, even if there was no chemistry. They had adopted the same methodical approach as they had to build Lego models together at primary school, deciding to touch tongues and count to twenty. But the way Jordy kept sweeping his tongue backwards and forwards across her gums reminded Lilly of windscreen wipers and she had burst out laughing. Jordy claimed she had destroyed his confidence but the following week he had got with Hayley, who declared him to be a reasonable kisser.

Mr Galveston rushes towards them and slides across the floor on his knees, as if he's performing a sequence he's learnt from *Strictly Come Dancing*. She's never seen him move this fast. Lilly hears him speak but it's as if she's floating above her own body, looking down at the fracas below. It's a strangely comfortable sensation, like conscious sleeping. 'Detachment is liberation,' Mr Galveston says, and now she finally understands what he means.

'She feels really cold,' Jordy panics. 'Look how pale she is!'

'Can you speak, Lilly?' Mr Galveston booms. The words form in her brain but they don't reach her mouth. She hears herself emit a strange gurgling sound. *Don't you think I would if I could?*

He shakes her more vigorously so the back of her head bumps uncomfortably on the wooden floor. *Why so angry?* she wonders.

'Jordy, call nine-nine-nine,' barks Mr Galveston. 'Right now.' Somehow he knows that Jordy will be the one student who has disobeyed his rule about not bringing electronic devices into the classroom. Jordy pulls out his phone and it starts playing loud music.

'Nice one, Jordy,' someone mutters.

Lilly recognizes the song. 'Creature Comfort' by Arcade Fire. It's the band who played at the festival she went to with Cormack. The phone slips through Jordy's fingers and hits the floor. She tries to focus on the words, something about making it painless. She waits for Mr Galveston to tell them this is a good example of irony. Someone giggles hysterically.

'Make it stop, Jordy, make it stop,' the voice says. She recognizes Emma Vickers's voice. Lilly doesn't hold the giggling against her. She would laugh too if she could.

'Shut that music up, Cormack,' barks Mr Galveston. Why is Cormack in the room? He mustn't see her like this.

Out of the corner of her eye Lilly sees Freya grab the phone from Jordy's hand, turn off the music and coolly take over.

'Ambulance service, please,' she says. 'St Edith's School, Goodwin Way.'

Lilly suddenly gasps for breath. For at least ten seconds her chest remains still. Then she gulps again. She sees herself diving into the river at Earith. She feels as if she's underwater.

'She's drowning, Mr Galveston! She's drowning!' Jordy is panicking again.

'Like a fish out of water, like a fish out of water,' Hayley whispers.

'Maybe we should put her in the recovery position,' someone else suggests.

Why is everyone saying everything twice? Lilly wonders. They all watch as her head unexpectedly rears back, the crown slamming against the wooden floor.

For a split second Lilly is still. Then her arms and legs stiffen and her back arches so violently that the short blue T-shirt rides right up her stomach to reveal the thick elastic hem of a white bra gone grey. This sudden revelation of flesh in front of Mr Galveston is almost as shocking as the cruel contortions of her body. His hand hovers above Lilly's breasts. He pulls down her top so that the bra is concealed, looking worried that he's being inappropriate. But no sooner has he protected her dignity than the same convulsive movement starts again.

'Is she dying?' Jordy repeats, over and over again.

Mr Galveston asks if Lilly suffers from epilepsy. Or asthma. Or allergies. Or anything that could explain what is happening. Someone mentions an Epipen. Freya tips up Lilly's bag. Out tumble mascara, stray Tampax, a Polaroid of her with Cormack taken at the festival in the summer, and a packet of cigarettes followed by revision cards on *Beowulf.* The notebook she found in the garage lands spine down on the floor by her feet. Lilly notices Jordy pick it up and stuff it into his pocket, checking to make sure no one else has noticed. *Good boy.* Then she closes her eyes as her brain catches fire again.

The force of the next fit propels Lilly across the floor a couple of feet, to rest against the table with the cacti. Her legs beat with such strength against the table that the cacti topple to the floor. Soil spills on to Lilly's face. She feels someone sweep it away from her eyes and nostrils.

'It's Mr Galveston, Lilly. Can you hear me? Can you hear me?'

After a final bout of shaking and trembling, Lilly's body falls still. Everyone crowds around.

'She's dead,' wails Hayley. 'She's dead.'

Lilly wants to tell them that, on the contrary, she has returned to her body and it's a good feeling, like lying in the sun after swimming.

'Get Hayley out of here, now,' orders Mr Galveston, removing his tweed jacket for the first time ever. He rests his head on Lilly's chest. It is heavy with medieval Britain, she thinks, with kennings and battle masks and mead halls. The weight feels comforting rather than embarrassing. No sooner has she adjusted to this intimacy between them than he sits up again and roughly squeezes her earlobe. It's painful and she tries to cry out. This time she can make nothing move, not even her eyes. All she hears is the gurgle in her throat.

When there is no reaction Mr Galveston puts his hand on Lilly's sweaty forehead, tilts her chin towards the window and bends over so close that she can feel his breath on her face. It smells of Rich Tea biscuits and roll-up cigarettes and she wants to turn away but she can't. The last thing Lilly feels is his fingers pinching her nose and the sensation of his lips on her own. She tries to imagine that it's Cormack but Mr Galveston's beard chafes her chin, like corn on bare legs. He blows in and puts his ear close to her mouth.

'Tell them there's no pulse, Freya,' she hears him shout.

'They say to try chest compressions,' Freya shouts back.

Mr Galveston breaks into the chorus of 'Staying Alive' by the Bee Gees. She waits for her classmates to laugh but there is silence. Once he has found his rhythm he presses his hands to her chest and pushes hard to the beat of the song. He sings the same line eight times. Then he stops and puts his ear so close to her mouth that it touches her lips.

'He's totally lost it this time,' Jordy mutters.

'It's the right rhythm for CPR,' explains Freya coolly, as he starts up again.

I am dying, Lilly realizes, when she can't feel the painful punch of the compressions on her heart. *I am dying*. She remembers when Cormack told her they couldn't see each other any more because they were too similar. 'We are the same,' he had said.

No, we're not. We just did a bad thing together, she wanted to say. Now no one will ever know what really happened.

2

As Grace pulls into the street where she picks up Mia from primary school, an ambulance speeds out of the car park of the adjacent secondary school, sirens blaring, forcing her into a neck-straining manoeuvre to reverse back into the busy main road. She thinks nothing of it shrieking past, beyond guilty irritation that it's using a narrow street that bisects the only two schools in the area as a rat run to the hospital.

There's not even the flicker of anxiety that has come upon her lately in the face of the unexpected, like the way she has woken up every morning this week to find the house mysteriously coated with a fine red dust or how Hayley's mum, Nuala, unexpectedly humiliated her at book club last week by accusing her of choosing an A-level English text as their next read so she could write Lilly's essays for her. 'Why don't you nominate *Battle Hymn of the Tiger Mother* instead?' Nuala had teased amid raucous laughter.

Instead Grace is preoccupied because she's already fifteen minutes late for her first meeting of the school year with Mia's new teacher. But just as she was trying to escape from work, her boss, the editor of the local newsletter where she works as chief reporter, had asked her to find someone to interview for a splash on an upsurge of crime in an isolated Fenland village. 'Can't you ask the deputy chief reporter to help?' she asked mischievously. It was a joke against herself. There was no deputy. For the past fifteen years it had been just her and Tony churning out their monthly account of mostly non-notable events in north Cambridge. It wasn't a bad job for someone who had never gone to university. But the office above the fish shop wasn't exactly where Grace had dreamt her journalistic career would begin and end.

Feeling guilty at mocking their set-up, Grace had then tried to convince Tony that, although it wasn't inaccurate to say crime had doubled in the past twelve months, this was because only one incident had been recorded the previous year. The headline had proved too tempting, however, and at the last minute he insisted she track down an elderly woman who had had two miniature ponies stolen from her back garden. It had been treated as two separate crimes, which made the whole story even more absurd, but Grace knew it was pointless to argue with him when he was in that kind of mood. 'Ponies make good click bait,' he said, as if he was running a national newspaper and she headed up an award-winning investigative team. 'Simples.'

As soon as she left the office she turned off her phone to avoid any more calls from Tony. *Why would anyone keep miniature ponies in their garden?* Grace wonders, as she searches for a parking space as close as possible to the school. She remembers the picture on Facebook of the ponies standing in the woman's sitting room watching television with her. Apparently their favourite programme was *Dancing on Ice*, which had a strange logic.

The urge to get to the bottom of all human behaviour is probably her best and worst trait. Her husband firmly believes most people are motivated by the hunt for comfort. According to Patrick, life is really that straightforward. That was partly why she fell in love with him. For his certainty.

As she parks in a space opposite Lilly's school, Grace catches sight of herself in the rear-view mirror. She rubs underneath her eyes to even out the eye-liner and pinches her lips to give them colour. Her eyes are the same shape as Mia's and they share the same bow mouth, but that's where their similarities begin and end. She combs her long brown hair with her fingers to give it some volume. It's lank with sweat and dust from the building work that started at home six weeks ago. After a heroic battle with the developers who had built Black Fen Close, Patrick had become the first resident to get them to agree to fund work on the damp, although as he points out it hardly counts as repairs when the problems were there from the day they moved in.

'You'll do.' Grace addresses her reflection in the mirror, then wishes she hadn't because it's a phrase her mother used when she had a hangover and looked like shit.

She gets out of the car and spots Lilly's headmaster in fevered conversation with her tutor, Mr Galveston, in the car park of the secondary school. It must be hot because Mr Galveston has removed the tweed jacket that he keeps on all year round and his shirt tail is hanging out. Usually he's immaculately dressed. He repeatedly runs his fingers through his beard. Ordinarily Grace would stop for a chat or at least wave hello but she's late and they're oblivious, locked in discussion, possibly about the students Mr Galveston wants to recommend for Oxbridge, which reminds her that Lilly really needs to get a move on with her personal statement. She doesn't doubt that Lilly will be one of his chosen ones. *No doubt.* She sets an alert on her phone, *Prepare potential interview questions on Beowulf,* then forces her thoughts back to Mia.

Unlike Lilly, her younger daughter is a riddle that needs deconstructing to strangers. Lilly has never been the subject of an unexpected phone call from school, whereas being called in to discuss Mia is such a familiar routine that she barely has to rehearse what she needs to say.

'There are seven years between my two children, so Mia can sometimes appear more grown-up than she really is.'

'In some ways Mia resembles an only child, which accounts for why she observes more than she participates.'

'Mia has a tendency to take things too literally, so other children can find her a little strange.'

'Mia has a vivid imagination and finds it easier to express herself through drawings than words.'

'*If only all parents could be as honest about their children,*' Grace imagines the teacher saying in the staffroom later. It doesn't occur to her that the teacher might think she's trying to find interesting excuses for challenging behaviour, or that quirky eccentricity isn't necessarily endearing when there are twenty-seven other children in the class.

The year-six classroom is just inside the main gate and, through the window, she catches sight of Mia sitting at her desk, staring resolutely into the middle distance. She is playing one of her favourite roles, that of child abandoned by her parents, pulling what Lilly calls her SpongeBob face, an expression that involves opening her eyes as wide as possible while chewing her lower lip, as if she's trying her hardest to be brave. Ever since she was little, people have commented on Mia's aptitude for drama. It's a trait Grace prefers to ignore because it reminds her too much of her mother.

Mia sits bolt upright in her chair, back straight as a ballerina's, frizzy hair tamed into a thick single plait with a toggle at the bottom that emphasizes her posture like an exclamation mark. Any sense of grace, however, is undermined

36

by her huge feet – size six and still growing – which turn out at ungainly right angles, even when she's sitting down. Grace heads into the classroom without knocking, sees Mia's teacher at her desk and realizes she can't remember her name.

'Miss Swain,' the teacher says, holding out her hand and giving a quick, efficient, lipsticked smile, which makes it difficult to judge how annoyed she is. 'I don't think we've met before. Thanks for coming in at short notice. I didn't want to wait. I never like things to fester.'

'Quite,' says Grace, who guesses that Miss Swain is one of those slightly over-zealous newbie teachers, who loves nothing more than a knotty child to disentangle. In which case she will enjoy Mia. As she walks towards the desk Grace glances at the classroom wall and sees a large, neat display that includes cards with each letter of the Anglo-Saxon alphabet, laminated pictures of coins, and a chronology of events from AD 400 to 1066.

'Wow,' says Grace, enthusiastically, pointing at the display. 'I'm impressed. Especially so early in the term.' The teacher gives a tight smile that indicates she doesn't do small-talk.

'Please, take a seat.' The only place to sit is in a low chair beside Mia, which gives Miss Swain immediate psychological advantage.

'Hi, Mum,' says Mia, betraying nothing. She hugs Grace, nestling her head into her right shoulder for a moment. Even as a baby Mia preferred not to be held, and Grace still relishes any spontaneous affection.

Miss Swain clears her throat and flicks a strand of her long hair away from her face. 'Mia? Can I please have your attention?'

'Yes, Miss Swain,' says Mia, turning impassively towards

her. Her calm, oval face is as still as the photocopy of the Anglo-Saxon mask on the display board, but Grace notes the fury in her clenched fists.

'We've been talking a lot today about the importance of honesty, haven't we, Mia?' says Miss Swain, all kindly tone and steely stare.

Neither of them blinks. Grace winces. It's the wrong strategy to adopt with her stubborn daughter. Mia is not one for backing down. She has never been the sort of child you can bend to your will. This is something she will also need to explain – Mia requires a more thoughtful and col-laborative approach.

'*You* have,' says Mia, without breaking her gaze. Grace doesn't like the way she emphasizes the pronoun. It doesn't bode well. Now Grace is as stiff-backed as Mia.

'And what did we learn?'

'I learnt that you think my truth is a lie,' says Mia, flatly. 'I don't know what you learnt, Miss Swain.' To her credit, Miss Swain remains composed and smiles at Mia, although the smile doesn't reach her eyes. Grace can't help noticing a tiny scale of lipstick on the teacher's tooth. This bothers her more than it should. It suggests that she hasn't had time to look in the mirror, which probably means she's tired and in no mood to be emollient. And it also means that Miss Swain and Mia have probably been sitting here in silence since school ended half an hour earlier. It's unbearably hot and stuffy. Grace pulls out her notebook and starts fanning herself.

'Do you want to tell your mum what we did today?'

Mia turns to her mother and begins to talk animatedly. 'We went to visit the archaeologists who are digging up the Travellers' site.'

'Wow!' says Grace. 'How amazing.'

'They're excavating the remains of an Anglo-Saxon girl and her baby. She's buried facing north–south rather than east–west, which means she had probably done something bad.' She frowns, searching for the right word, and turns to her mother. 'She might have been deviant.'

'Deviant? Wow!' says Grace, brightly, wondering why she keeps saying 'wow'. She sounds as though she's speaking in cartoon speech bubbles. 'Sounds like quite a trip.' *She's done it again.* School always makes her nervous. It's a legacy from a childhood spent waiting for her parents to say and do the wrong thing.

'They're running a "Be an archaeologist for a day programme" for primary-school children as part of the curriculum,' explains Miss Swain. 'I sent out a letter to parents.'

'Oh, Lord! I forgot to do the packed lunch, didn't I?' says Grace, as if this might be the reason for the meeting or at least might prove a useful sidetrack. 'Did someone share with you, Mia?'

'Tas's mum gave me something. She was in her caravan.'

'That's very kind, isn't it?' says Grace to Miss Swain.

Miss Swain doesn't respond. 'What did the archaeologists tell us, Mia?' she continues.

'They said the girl's spine is deformed, which meant she was probably a servant who had been forced to carry heavy loads and that she most likely died during childbirth. Her mouth was frozen in a scream of agony. And there's a tiny skeleton of a baby between her legs that was born after she died.'

'How can a baby be born after someone is dead?' Grace asks. She's glad the teacher can see that, even though Mia struggles to get her thoughts down on paper, she has an almost photographic memory.

'Two or three days after she died, the mother's body

started decomposing and produced gases that expelled the baby.' She turns to Grace. 'The archaeologist said the baby would have been born dead but how does he know? What if the baby was born and then suffocated? He called it a coffin birth. But maybe it was a coffin death.'

'That's very well remembered,' says Miss Swain, who appears unmoved by Mia's graphic description.

'Wow! It sounds a little gruesome,' says Grace, forcing a laugh. She can't yet see where all this is leading.

'It was a small part of the whole day,' says Miss Swain, abruptly. She turns to Mia again. 'What else can you remember?'

'That the Anglo-Saxons believe a baby's soul enters its body for the first time when a mother feels it kicking. That women had more rights in Anglo-Saxon times than in Victorian times.'

'Anything else?'

'Tas kept crying.'

'Why?' asks Grace.

'He thinks his family won't be allowed to live there any more because the archaeologists keep finding more graves and taking away land from the Travellers.'

'That isn't what I meant, Mia, although I agree that was upsetting for the whole class,' says the teacher. She turns to Grace to explain. 'Unfortunately no one had thought to warn me that Tas's family live on that Travellers' site. My bad.' She gives a quick smile and Grace can't help noticing that the fleck of lipstick has moved.

'Tas says they are angering the spirits of the dead by digging them up,' says Mia. 'He says no good will come from disturbing them.' Grace assumes Miss Swain will address this issue, which so quintessentially reflects Mia's character that she finds herself smiling.

'What else did you see, Mia?' the teacher continues.

'The skeletons of other children. They were buried apart, all on their own. They had really bad teeth because they never had enough food. They were inside pots. Little pots for little people. That's what the archaeologist said.' She pauses, her eyes cloud with tears, and she leans forward towards Miss Swain to repeat the phrase: 'Little pots for little people. Poor, tiny, innocent babies taken before their time.'

Miss Swain is having none of it. 'What else was in the pots, Mia?'

'Coins. Jewellery and belt buckles.'

'And what was the unfortunate news that the head archaeologist had to tell us about the jewellery when we all got on the bus to leave?'

'The unfortunate news was that a ring had gone missing from the table where the jewellery was laid out by the grave,' says Mia, as if she's answering a comprehension test. She anticipates the next question. 'It was object number twenty-one and it was made of gold with a red garnet and had Anglo-Saxon letters on the inside.'

Miss Swain turns to Grace. Grace turns to Mia. *Now she understands.*

'I didn't take it, Mum,' says Mia, shaking her head so vigorously that her plait wags from side to side, like a dog's tail.

'He also mentioned that you were the last person to look at the ring, didn't he, Mia?' says Miss Swain, her voice getting quieter and quieter. Unlike Mia's.

'I did not take that ring!' Mia protests loudly.

'Did you touch it at all?' Miss Swain asks.

'Lots of people touched it. We were all told to touch it and imagine the woman who had owned it. I could feel it belonged to the girl with the baby and that the person

41

who made her deviant might have given it to her. To show he still loved her even after everything that had happened.'

'How could you feel that?' asks Grace, surprised by Mia's insight into the complexities of human relationships.

'I felt a surge of energy shoot through my body,' says Mia, green eyes flashing. 'Like electricity.'

Grace does a quick, cool journalistic calculation in her head even as images of the random objects she has found in Mia's bedroom drift into focus: the feathers, the owl pellet, the watch. But the facts are these: the ring has gone; it's most likely been taken by one of the children; if Mia is telling the truth then someone else has it. Possibly Tas. Because he and Mia were in a pair and were lagging behind the others. The teacher doesn't want to accuse the Traveller child because it would play into stereotypes that the school spends a lot of money and time trying to eradicate. She's not convinced of her daughter's innocence but neither must she give Miss Swain any impression that she thinks Mia could be responsible.

'Was anyone else at the site, apart from the children and the archaeologists?' Grace asks calmly. 'Just out of interest.'

'No,' says Miss Swain. 'Only the regular professionals.'

'If you didn't take it, do you know who did?' Grace asks Mia.

'No,' says Mia. 'And if I did, I wouldn't say who.'

'Are you questioning any other parents about this incident?' Grace turns to Miss Swain again.

'Mia was the last to get back on the bus. Someone even saw her try the ring on her finger. I was hoping for a swift and discreet resolution to the problem. If Mia gives the ring back I will return it and no further questions will be asked.'

'I didn't do it,' says Mia, more vehemently, sitting on her hands as if to hide the fingers that touched the ring.

'Perhaps someone knocked it off the table on to the ground,' suggests Grace.

'It could have fallen back into the grave and got covered in soil again,' adds Mia, hopefully. 'I put it close to the edge of the table. Maybe the archaeologists need to start digging again. They said it's really important to get all the facts together before jumping to any quick conclusions, didn't they, Miss Swain?'

'I think that is a highly unlikely scenario,' replies Miss Swain.

'But it could have fallen off the table,' says Grace.

'There was a big sheet of tarpaulin beneath it. If it had fallen off someone would have found it there.'

'The archaeologist could be telling an untruth,' suggests Mia.

'Adults don't generally lie about that kind of stuff,' says Miss Swain.

'Adults lie a lot,' says Mia.

'I don't think you mean that,' Grace smoothly intervenes.

'What do you mean, then?' interrupts Miss Swain.

'Apart from the obvious lies?' asks Mia.

'What on earth are the obvious lies?' the teacher questions.

'Father Christmas, the Tooth Fairy . . . I mean, you know they're not real because parents wouldn't allow strangers into their children's bedrooms, would they, because they might be paedophiles?'

Miss Swain nods but it's clear she's losing control of the conversation.

'My uncle says he'd do anything to have a baby with my aunt but he's lying. He says he loves her and it's not true.'

Grace is too taken aback to speak.

'My dad says that our ancestors were heroes for draining the marshes but actually they caused an environmental disaster,' Mia continues. 'The Fens are sinking. That's why some of the roads are higher than the fields. And they made water people become land people. Which goes against their nature. Like forcing Tas's family to be settled instead of travelling around.'

The teacher tries a completely new tack, praising Mia for the work she has put into her upcoming performance as a swan in the class play, her kindness towards her classmates and for keeping one of the best Anglo-Saxon diaries in the class. 'Your writing shows real promise,' she says. 'Especially because I know you find it difficult to get things down on paper. And the drawings are fabulous.' She pushes Mia's diary towards Grace, who opens it. The first page is all about the Anglo-Saxon god Woden. The second is Mia's name in runic letters.

ᛗᛁᚠ

On the next page there is a drawing of an Anglo-Saxon girl with a sad face. It is full of detail, down to the buckle on her leather belt. Grace notices she's wearing a ring with red stones. But it's the fact that she's noticeably pregnant that captures her attention. On the opposite page are three lines of writing. She can tell from the way the pen has pressed deep into the paper that this part was hard work for Mia.

I am loved by the wrong person.
I am in love with the wrong person.
I am pregnant.

'It's a very sad story,' comments Miss Swain. 'And a very good one.'

'That doesn't work on me,' Mia politely intervenes. 'I know that you're trying to use praise as a way of making me feel comfortable so that I admit doing something I haven't done.'

'I'm simply trying to say that, apart from this incident, your behaviour has been very good and I will take this into account if you admit to me now what happened to the ring.' She wants to wind this up and looks to Grace for support.

'I didn't do it,' says Mia, ferociously, placing her hands palms down on the desk and leaning as far forwards towards Miss Swain as she can without leaving her chair.

'It seems a little strange that you were the last person seen holding the ring,' says Miss Swain.

'I was the last in the queue.' Mia shrugs.

'I'll give you one more chance to tell the truth, Mia.'

'It wasn't me.'

Miss Swain looks at Grace again.

'I believe my daughter.'

'Would you mind if we took a look through your bag, Mia?' asks Miss Swain.

Grace feels mildly affronted, as if her opinion about her daughter's good character counts for nothing.

'Sure. Let's go right ahead,' says Mia. She slowly undoes each zip until every compartment and pocket is open, without once losing eye contact with Miss Swain. Then she stands up, carries the bag to the teacher, and tips out the entire contents on to her desk. Exercise books, pens, lids, rulers, crisps, stickers, key rings, all fall out. A compass skids along the desk towards Miss Swain and slides into her lap, where they all stare at it, uncertain what to do next. Mia's face reveals nothing.

'I think perhaps we need to arrange an appointment with the school counsellor to resolve some of the issues surrounding this incident,' says Miss Swain, eventually. She locks the compass in her desk drawer. 'Mia seems to have some problems managing anger. Are you in agreement?'

'Of course,' says Grace, trying to rein in her own irritation. 'If you think that is appropriate.'

They leave the classroom in silence.

'That didn't go too badly, did it, Mum?' Mia comments, as they enter the revolving door at the entrance of the primary school. They step inside, and when it reaches the midpoint, Grace puts her foot against the bottom of the door, trapping them both inside.

'Did you steal that ring?' she asks sternly, turning to face her daughter. 'Or was it Tas? If you tell me the truth now, we might be able to resolve this.'

'I didn't take it, Mum,' says Mia, her gaze unflinching. Grace releases the door and switches on her phone.

She needs to speak to Patrick. Just outside the school gates, she spots Catriona Vickers, the only other parent with children in the same year at both schools, trotting towards her in wedge sandals, with her clipboard, in a showy way that reminds Grace a little of the stolen miniature ponies. She looks cool and composed in the late-afternoon heat, in a summer dress that matches the unchipped nail varnish on her fingers and toes.

'All good, Grace?' Catriona asks, with barely concealed curiosity about why Grace and Mia are here out of hours.

'All very good,' Grace confirms.

'Have you managed to sort out the problems with your new home? I was driving past the other day and saw the scaffolding.'

'Yes, thanks. The developers finally admitted responsibility.'

'You've done well. My sister-in-law says no one else has seen a penny yet.'

46

'It's all down to Patrick.' She deflects further questions by asking about the petition and hurriedly signs her name without really listening to Catriona's long-winded explanation about wind farms causing mystery illnesses because her phone has started buzzing with messages. 'Young lives are at risk. We owe it to our children to put a stop to this. Perhaps you could do a piece for your newsletter,' Catriona says.

Grace doesn't respond. She's reading Patrick's messages in reverse order. 'We have to go. Right now,' she says to Mia. 'Sorry!' she calls back to Catriona, as she drags Mia through the school gate. 'Something has come up.'

3

Lilly collapsed in class, a panicked voice at the end of the phone had explained to Patrick a couple of hours ago. Just four words and everything he had taken for granted slipped away. *Is this how it happens?* he asks himself, as he sits in the emergency assessment room holding his teenage daughter's hand, like he used to when she was a small child. *Is the space between a blessed and cursed life really so fragile?*

It seems incredible that only this morning his biggest worries were that the cost of sorting out the damp in their new home had ballooned to twice the initial budget and one of his A-level students had catastrophically muddled his slides on twentieth-century sculpture. Wasn't it bloody obvious that Rodin came before Henry Moore, he had chided. Look at the shape of the women! Then he had worried that mentioning body shape to a female student might be considered inappropriate. *What luxury to get worked up about such trivia.*

Some people take a while to process bad news but Patrick understood straight away that everything had changed. Even the molecular structure of the world around him feels altered. Since the phone call he can take only small, shallow gulps of air. Which is exactly how the teacher described what had happened to Lilly during her English class.

The only thing Patrick got wrong was that the call came from Lilly's school, not Mia's. Phone calls from school are always about Mia. Especially at the beginning of term. Mr Galveston had nervously corrected him a couple of times on that front. *Lilly is on her way to hospital . . . We've tried to get hold of your wife to tell her about Lilly, but she's not picking up her phone . . . I performed CPR on Lilly . . .*

Patrick let him speak. Lilly's teacher was clearly in shock, but all Patrick wanted to know was whether she had recovered. When Mr Galveston couldn't give a straight answer he had hung up and got a cab to the hospital without even going back into his classroom to instruct his students to wind up their discussion on the historical context of Rachel Whiteread's Holocaust memorial. They will be disappointed. It's no secret that he's their favourite teacher. When the school tried to cut art history from the curriculum last year they had staged a protest until he was reinstated, albeit with fewer teaching hours.

His gaze darts back and forth from Lilly's cold hand to her face as he wills her to wake up and tell him she's fine, stop being clingy. Her eyes are closed, her face is waxy and pale, and her lips stuck tight so she resembles the effigy of the Earl of Shrewsbury, one of his favourite sculptures in the Fitzwilliam. 'Don't stop breathing. Don't stop breathing,' he says repeatedly, to the rhythm of the rise and fall of her chest. It's more incantation than prayer. He's not religious. But he's convinced himself that as long as he doesn't stop, Lilly will keep breathing. The words remind him of her favourite song as a child, the ridiculously cheesy 'Don't Stop Believing'. His voice falters. He wipes his nose and pulls his phone out of his pocket. Nothing. *Where the hell is Grace?*

In the space between Mr Galveston's first call and

arriving here he must have sent a dozen messages to her, each shorter and tauter than the last, as he struggled to find the words to articulate what was happening. He's spoken to her boss, Tony, phoned his mum, texted Nuala, called their Polish builder and, in desperation, even phoned Ana, who suggested Grace was most likely interviewing someone and had got sidetracked trying to sort out their problems. 'You know how she collects disasters, Patrick.' He does. It's an unkind comment, particularly given Grace's role in helping to resolve Ana and Rob's marital crisis a few years ago.

He is plagued by wildly irrational thoughts: it is impossible for Lilly to die in the same hospital where she was born; if her monitor keeps beeping in the opposite rhythm to the one connected to the woman in the neighbouring cubicle everything will be fine; as long as he doesn't tell anyone, this isn't really happening. 'Human beings are at their most superstitious when they feel most out of control,' he finds himself telling the nurse when she checks Lilly. It's one of the best lines from his lecture on the history of sculptures designed to ward off evil spirits, but it's the first time he really understands what it means. He chews his knuckle, like Mia does to stop herself crying. The nurse looks worried and offers to bring him a cup of tea.

In between checking his phone, like a teenager, he keeps watch over Lilly for signs that she is regaining consciousness. Sometimes her eyelids twitch and once or twice he is almost certain that she is trying to squeeze his hand. At one point her lips start to move. It looks as though she is saying words but when he puts his ear to her mouth, no sound comes out, just the faintest breath. He touches her lips with his sweaty fingers and they feel dry and cracked, as if the lifeblood is being sucked from her body.

He checks all the monitors without understanding what

they mean and resumes his vigil. He hasn't watched his daughter so intently for years. He notices tiny pink veins in her eyelids, the brown birthmark on her shoulder, and the chickenpox scar by her earlobe that Grace slathered in vitamin E cream every morning and evening for months. She didn't cry when she was born, or when she had chickenpox. Lilly has always been an easy child. A thought flashes through his head: *I wish it was Mia lying here, not Lilly.* His face burns hot with shame. He's not thinking straight. He loves both his children but Lilly has always been easier to love.

Mia was tricky from the moment she was born. She refused to breastfeed, and for the first two years of her life, she woke through the night crying until Grace discovered that she would go back to sleep if one of them walked her around in the sling. Patrick called it his straitjacket. He could never work out how the straps were meant to tie around his body and thought there was too much emphasis on happy babies and not enough on happy parents. They went for eight months without sex. His penis was on display as often as the ancient fertility symbols he was occasionally allowed to borrow from the basement at the Fitzwilliam for one of his evening lectures to parents.

He feels his phone buzzing in his pocket. He doesn't want to leave Lilly alone to answer it. So he cups his hand around the phone to muffle his voice and gets up to face the window. He's been here for less than two hours but already he has internalized the unwritten rules of the emergency department: relatives make calls in the corridor, not on the ward, because it is enough for them to absorb the emotion of their own lives without overhearing other people's; they don't ask each other questions, rather they wait for information to be divulged; they speak quietly. They have the wisdom of people who have suddenly recalibrated life's priorities and found its true meaning.

'Grace,' he whispers into the phone. 'Thank God.'

'Tell me, tell me,' she says breathlessly.

'She had a seizure. She's unconscious but stable. They've sedated her and she's on a drip.'

'Oh, my God! Is she going to be okay?'

'I don't know yet. They don't know yet.'

'I'm on my way. Mia is with me.'

'Is that a good idea?' he asks, but she has already gone. He stares out of the window at the countryside beyond, the sun hammering against his skull, and thinks about how, centuries ago, when Cambridge was a great port, he might have seen a ship sailing past. A nurse comes to tell him Lilly is going to be moved to the neurology ward. Even the word 'neurology' gives him the chills because it suggests there is something wrong with her brain. He looks at his watch. He can't believe he's been here only two hours. Time plays tricks in hospital, like it's compressed and all the things that have happened should stretch over days instead of hours.

When Mia first catches sight of Lilly she wonders fleetingly if they are too late. Her heart jumps to her mouth and back again. Grace half runs towards the bed, pulling her by the hand, but the closer they get, the more reluctant Mia is to approach. Eventually she grinds to a halt in the middle of the ward and stares at the bed where Patrick is sitting, head bowed over the rails as if he's worshipping Lilly. *Which he does*, thinks Mia. *We all do.* When he looks up and tries to smile at her, his face crumples as though it's melting. She wants to hug him but she is transfixed by Lilly.

The bottom half of her sister's body is covered with a

white hospital sheet. Her blonde hair is scraped off her face in a high ponytail, a style she hates, her face is swollen, and she is wearing a baggy grey and white hospital gown that has been cut open at the front to make room for three wires stuck around the heart that missed a beat, which is how her mother described what had happened to Lilly during the tense car journey to the hospital. There are other wires attached to her middle finger, both arms and her neck. Her face is so pale that it is almost translucent, in contrast to the ugly grey and yellow bruises all over her torso. She doesn't move or make any noise.

Mia can't help being reminded of the Anglo-Saxon girl with the tiny skeleton of the baby between her legs. She was probably the same age as Lilly when she died. And she was pregnant. She thinks about the little pots for little people and makes a promise to herself that if Lilly doesn't make it she will bury all the gemstones in a pot in her grave because by rights they belong to her. Maybe she should include the iPhone she borrowed from Bea Vickers last year, so that Lilly can speak to her from Heaven. The thought of losing Lilly is so devastating that Mia is convinced she feels her own heart miss a beat.

Mia adjusts her wonky school skirt and fiddles with a loose shirt button. *Anything to avoid approaching the bed.* 'Is she going to die?' she asks loudly. Adults have a nasty way of trying to avoid difficult subjects and she wants to know the truth. Her voice echoes around the room, over the sound of all the monitors, voicing the unspoken fear of everyone in the unit. She has always had an uncanny knack for articulating what is on people's minds. 'I don't want to be an only child.'

'She's in a very deep sleep,' explains Patrick, who speaks as though he's sucking on a very large sweet. 'The nurse says it's important we talk to her because she knows we're here even if she can't communicate.' He stretches out his arm towards Mia. 'Come here, Mimi.'

Grace presses the small of her back to coax her forward. 'Why don't you tell her about your day?' she whispers. 'Perhaps miss out the gory bits.'

Mia wants to be brave but she's too scared for Lilly. Death was a way of life for the Anglo-Saxons, the archaeologist told them this morning. Half of all pregnant women died during childbirth and only a quarter of children made it to their second birthday. She thinks about what she learnt at the beginning of the summer and wonders if Lilly's illness has anything to do with her lost baby. After the argument she had gone back into the garage and found the pregnancy test stuffed into a plastic bag. It was too big a find to risk losing and is now hidden behind the radiator in her room, along with the iPhone.

From now on, Mia resolves to be more courageous and less hostage to her wild emotions. She feels her mother's fingers squeezing her hand. She's holding it so tightly that her nails are digging uncomfortably into Mia's flesh. The pain galvanizes her. She approaches the empty chair on the opposite side of the bed to Patrick, sits down and gently takes Lilly's hand.

'When exactly did Lil's heart stop beating?' she asks him in a whisper.

'Just before lunch,' Patrick whispers back. Mia does a quick calculation in her head and realizes that the seizure must have happened at exactly the same time as the archaeologist lifted the tarpaulin to show her class the skeleton of the deviant girl and her baby. She thinks of Tas's words and shivers. *They'll bring trouble down on us all.*

*

Grace walks round the bed towards Patrick, who stands up so abruptly that the polystyrene cup collapses in his hand and hot tea stains his trouser leg.

'She's stable,' he whispers, as if speaking too loudly might break the spell being woven between all the machines that are keeping her alive. 'They say stable is good.'

He holds out his arms to hug Grace but her focus is on Lilly. She shakes her head in disbelief that this is the same child who walked out of the house that morning, her blue rucksack overloaded with books and headphones full of music, warning that she would be late because she had an extra English class.

'Oh, my God,' Grace whispers, pulling the chair as close to Lilly as possible.

She puts a hand on Lilly's forehead to check her temperature, pushes away some stray hairs from her face and tucks them behind her ear. Then she tenderly strokes her cheek before starting the same process all over again. She turns her attention to Lilly's torso and gasps when she sees the bruising around her ribs. 'It looks like she's been attacked,' she cries.

'It's from the chest compressions,' Patrick explains. 'Mr Galveston performed CPR.'

'I saw Mr Galveston in the car park, just after the ambulance left. He looked awful. Thank God he knew what to do. Imagine if it had happened when she was on her own or on the bus home or –'

'Enough,' says Patrick, gently, 'No what-ifs.' He puts up his hand to stop her.

Grace goes back to the beginning, as people do whenever they're frightened of endings. It feels like time travel. She remembers the early stages of her pregnancy when Lilly was no bigger than a lemon and the hospital asked her to come back for a repeat scan because they couldn't find the fourth chamber of her heart. But all was fine. She remembers when she started bleeding in the twenty-fourth week of pregnancy and Patrick had come straight from work for an emergency scan. But all was fine. She remembers how Lilly was born yellow and had to be blasted with ultraviolet light. She fast-forwards through her childhood ailments: fevers, growing pains, a dislocated shoulder, a fainting episode a year ago. But all was fine. Until now. Every day ordinary lives are turned upside down. Why should they be spared? What about the boy in year seven who was diagnosed with leukaemia the same week his mother started chemotherapy for breast cancer? Or her sister-in-law, Ana, discovering Rob had been unfaithful? Again. Or Tas's mother, worrying she will have to move home just months after his father died?

'We need to talk to the teacher and Lil's friends to get an idea of exactly what was going on before the seizure.' Patrick interrupts her frenzied thoughts. 'The doctor said it could help with the diagnosis. He wants to know about Lil's medical history too.'

Grace nods. She gently kisses Lilly's forehead.

'Why don't you grab a coffee before the doctor gets here?' suggests Patrick, who is nibbling a limp egg sandwich.

She feels enraged with him for his ability to do something so mundane and for encouraging her to leave their daughter. How can he even eat? Then she feels bad because he's only trying to be kind by giving her a moment to come to terms with the shock.

'Did Mr Galveston really give Lilly the kiss of life?' Mia asks, from the other side of the bed. Grace nods.

'Did he actually put his lips on hers?'

57

'He did,' Grace confirms.

'Isn't that going to be really embarrassing when she goes back to school?' Mia asks, but no one takes any notice. *At least it might make Cormack jealous and then he might fall in love with Lil again and they can make another baby.* She wonders if she should tell her parents what Lilly had told her in the garage and glances anxiously at Grace. She sees her mum's mouth is a straight line and knows she mustn't say anything. She's beginning to understand that although adults obsess about telling the truth it's mostly something they don't want to hear. Besides, she can't betray Lilly's trust, especially when this is the first secret she has ever properly confided in her.

'Can I sing her a song?' Mia asks suddenly.

Grace looks startled as if she had forgotten Mia was there. 'As long as you do it really quietly,' she warns, wincing as Mia noisily scrapes the legs of her chair across the floor to get as close as possible to Lilly.

Patrick and Grace fall into whispered conversation, trying to make sense of what has happened, attempting to assemble the jumble of facts in the correct chronological order and prioritize questions they want to ask the doctor.

'The Anglo-Saxons came by Sea,/from the Netherlands, Denmark and Germany,/When was this? 410 AD,' Mia sings softly into Lilly's ear. She touches the clothes-peg-style clip that leads from Lilly's finger to one of the machines. If Lilly is conscious, surely she'll wake up to savage the ridiculous rhyme scheme. That is what she would usually do. She sings the chorus again. It's the same song her class had sung in the bus on the way to the archaeological site this morning. But not on the journey back because Mia and Tas had been made to sit at the front where the teachers could keep an eye on them. Mia had called them the Seats of Shame, which made Tas giggle for the first time that day. It was the best sound in the world. She loved the way he threw his head back when he laughed so she could tickle the soft fleshy part under his chin.

At that stage she was in double trouble. First because she was the prime suspect in the case of the missing ring, but also because when the archaeologist asked if anyone had any questions she had stuck up her hand and asked why the living should lose their homes to make way for the dead, causing much throat-clearing and shuffling of feet but no good answers. All that would be forgotten now. Her teacher will have to be nice to her because she is the sister of someone who is *gravely sick*. It is the phrase Miss Swain had used to describe the girl who died during childbirth.

Mia keeps a close eye on her parents, and when she is sure their attention is elsewhere, she slowly reaches down inside her grey ankle sock with the hand that isn't holding Lilly's. She feels the ring there, nestling neatly against her anklebone. Just touching it makes her feel better. She traces a line around its edge to feel the indentations of the tiny carved symbols. The archaeologist had explained that the pattern on the outside of the ring was most likely designed in a magic sequence to protect its owner from shit happening. Actually, the last part was what Tas had said. And it was at that exact moment that she had resolved to take the ring. To help him. So the good spirits would protect his family and prevent them from having to leave their home. But now she realizes that perhaps its powers can also be called upon to help Lilly.

She slips the ring on to her index finger and it fits as snugly as if it was made for her. She closes her eyes and waits to see if she feels any different. She tries to imagine Lilly as the Anglo-Saxon girl but can't decide how she would be dressed.

Tunic and under-dress? Cloak with hood? Belt and brooch? Unlike her, Lilly was born with an innate sense of style.

Her parents are distracted by the arrival of the doctor, who introduces himself as Dr Santini, a consultant neurologist who specializes in brain disorders. He's all rolled-up sleeves and calm efficiency. *There's nothing wrong with Lilly's brain other than the fact that it's bigger than everyone else's*, thinks Mia. She should save him the trouble and put him right on that front straight away. Although her mum can normally be relied upon to do that.

'The positive news is that so far all the tests have come back normal. The heart trace and blood tests aren't showing any abnormalities, apart from a slight increase in her white cell count, which could have been caused by the seizure. Her pulse and blood pressure are normal.'

'That's good news, isn't it? That's good news?' The words get tangled in Grace's throat.

Mia is alarmed. She tries to remember the last time she saw her mum cry. It was probably last year when Grace discovered that Mia was the only person in the entire year not to be invited to Bea Vickers's birthday party. Mia had kept trying to convince her that she didn't really mind. Parties are a nightmare of noise and competitive games that she can never win. But her mum has always been obsessed about her having a group of friends, even though she doesn't seem to have one herself. Grace sticks magnets on the fridge that say things like 'A good friend is like a four-leaf clover: hard to find and lucky to have', or 'The only way to have a good friend is to be one', as if she thinks it's Mia's fault that no one, apart from Tas, wants to hang out with her.

'It is, but there are some other tests we need to run when the sedative wears off,' the doctor explains.

'What sort of tests?' Patrick asks. Even he sounds worried.

60

'We're considering a lumbar puncture and some basic neurological tests, to check Lilly's motor abilities and mental function. I'd like to do an MRI scan and EEG to measure Lilly's brainwaves.'

'What does that involve?' Grace and Patrick ask simultaneously.

'We attach small metal discs to Lilly's head to record her brainwaves over a period of time. Our brains all have an electrical pattern and it's possible to pick up any abnormalities. Has anything like this happened before?'

'No,' says Grace. 'Lilly's hardly ever ill. She swims for the county. She's in the top set at school for every subject. She's on track for Cambridge. She's a very focused student.' Her mum speaks as if these facts can somehow protect Lilly from catastrophe.

'Is there any history of allergies in the family?'

'None,' says Grace.

'And do you just have the two children?'

'Yes. Just two girls.'

Mia puts the hand with the ring beneath Lilly's and places her other hand on top so that the ring presses into Lilly's palm. She glances to the other side of the bed. Her parents are still asking endless questions. No one is taking any notice of her. She needs to think up a charm. She wishes Tas was with her because he would be good at this part. 'Fear not flying fish,' she whispers in Lilly's ear, remembering the example of alliteration that Miss Swain had used in yesterday's English lesson. 'Fear not flying fish.' She's torn between embarrassment and the urge to laugh hysterically. In contrast to Lilly, she is really bad at English. At least the words fit with the other fact the archaeologists had told them about finding a fossilized dolphin in the Fens, which proved the region had once belonged to the sea.

'Fear not flying fish,' she says again, a little louder and more seriously. 'Fear not flying fish.' The words might be ridiculous but the overall effect is miraculous because at that moment Lilly's eyes half open and she turns her head towards her parents and the doctor. *This is what it must have felt like to be Jesus.* Mia looks at her parents, half expecting them to sob with gratitude to her for bringing about this miracle or at least give a nod of acknowledgement but they are totally focused on Lilly.

'Where am I?' she asks groggily.

'You collapsed at school. You're in hospital,' says Grace.

'I'm so thirsty,' Lilly says, as the doctor leans over to shine a light into her eyes. Grace and Patrick clash heads as they both lurch for the plastic beaker of water at the same time. The doctor introduces himself to Lilly.

'Where's my book?' Lilly rasps, trying to move her head.

'Don't think about work, darling,' says Grace, stroking her hand. Mia sees her mum give the doctor the same 'I told you so' look she uses on her dad.

'Are you actually old enough to be a doctor?' Mia questions him suspiciously. He does look incredibly fresh-faced and his name makes him sound more like a magician.

'Mia,' warns Patrick.

'I'd like to ask your sister a couple of questions, if that's okay with you, Mia?' the doctor says.

There's a faint tease in his tone. Mia seethes. She doesn't like it when people don't take her seriously. He doesn't seem to realize that if it weren't for her Lilly would still be unconscious.

'Do you remember what happened, Lilly?'

'I collapsed in my English class,' she says throatily. 'Everything went black.'

'Well done,' says the doctor. 'Has anything like this ever happened to you before?'

'No,' Grace answers for her.

'I'm sorry, Mrs Vermuyden, but I would like as far as possible for Lilly to answer for herself,' he says gently.

'Never,' Lilly croaks.

'Have you ever had an allergic reaction? To food, for example, or insect bites?'

'Never,' says Grace again. Patrick nudges her.

'Did you eat anything unusual before the seizure? We're trying to work out why this might have happened to you.'

Lilly shakes her head.

'Well done. We'll talk some more tomorrow. It's important you rest as much as you can,' he says, then turns to Patrick and Grace. 'We'd like to keep her in for observation and to run those tests. She'll need to stay here at least until the end of the week in case she has any more seizures. Do you have any immediate questions?'

'I think you've covered everything,' says Patrick. 'Thank you.'

Mia sticks up her hand. 'Have you considered that Lilly might have caught the Ague?' she suggests, giving the doctor a long, hard stare, as if he might be deliberately withholding information. She remembers something else Miss Swain had said during the school trip. 'The Fens can be a pestilent place.'

The doctor laughs, which is not the response Mia is hoping for, and although Patrick and Grace have no idea why this is funny or what Mia is talking about, they laugh too. Even Lilly manages a sandpapery rasp.

'There's nothing funny about people dying,' says Mia, incensed by this reaction. 'A doctor should know that.'

'Of course not,' says the consultant, realizing his mistake. 'You're right. The Ague was no laughing matter. But it died out hundreds of years ago.'

'Can someone please tell me what you're talking about?' asks Grace, trying to curb the exasperated tone she often finds herself using with Mia. She feels exhausted. She's certainly in no state to unpick one of Mia's flights of fantasy. Even at the best of times, only Patrick has the patience for that.

'The Ague was a type of malaria that was endemic in the Fens until the marshland was drained. It caused fevers and seizures,' the doctor explains to her. 'They called it marsh fever.'

'But if you dig up the dead, couldn't it be released from the soil and come back?' asks Mia. 'Like the Black Death?'

The doctor smiles again. 'Do you know how the Ague was cured?' he asks. Mia shakes her head. 'People used to treat it by boiling the heads of white poppies in sweetened water. Virtually every man, woman and child consumed poppy tea. They even gave it to babies to help them sleep and to pregnant mothers to help them go into labour. There was a huge problem with opium addiction in this area because, of course, opium is made from poppies.'

'Where on earth have you learnt about the Ague?' Patrick asks Mia.

Grace can't help feeling irritated by her younger daughter's unnerving ability to absorb everyone's attention, even at a moment like this.

'We're doing the Anglo-Saxons at school. They lived in houses on stilts above the water and had webbed feet. I thought Lilly might have inhaled miasma when she went swimming in the river at Earith Sluice during the summer holidays. And that's what has made her ill.'

'What are you talking about? Lilly has never been swimming at the sluice,' says Grace, sharply. 'She was working in the city centre all summer.'

64

'Yes, she has,' insists Mia, indignantly. 'She went with Hayley, Jordy and that boy every afternoon.'

'What boy?'

Mia looks nervously at Lilly. Grace sees Lilly almost imperceptibly shake her head.

'Cormack,' whispers Mia. 'He's called Cormack.'

4

Nurses come and go. Shifts change. Lights are dimmed. It's almost like being on a long-haul flight, except Grace can't concentrate enough to read anything. Not even a text message. Patrick has sent two: one to say he got home safely with Mia and another at midnight to say he has put her to bed. He wants to know how Lilly has been since he left. *Asleep*, she tries to write back but can't type the right letters. Now she has cotton-wool fingers as well as cotton-wool mouth. She picks up the glass of water from the bedside table and forces herself to take tiny sips as if she's the one who is sick.

Her phone is alive with messages and missed calls. Rob, Ana, her mother-in-law, Nuala, Catriona Vickers, Mr Galveston, Miss Swain. She ignores them all. It's not that she doesn't want to speak to anyone. It's more that she feels, if she does, every emotion she has ever felt might burst to the surface at once.

At half past midnight the nurse instructs Grace to go home. Tells her that the best thing she can do is get a good night's sleep, and presses a plastic bag containing Lilly's phone into the hand that isn't holding her daughter's. Grace explains that it feels wrong to stop watching, and that as long as she is vigilant nothing bad can happen. It's the inverse of her own childhood where no one looked out for her and everything went wrong. 'A mother's instinct is everything, isn't it?' she tells the nurse with a fleeting smile, as she strokes Lilly's hand. When the people who are meant to protect you don't, it leaves a hole in your soul and Grace isn't going to let this happen to her children. Every day is a struggle to compensate for her faulty DNA. She knows how quickly things can unravel if you let the drift settle in.

She remembers Patrick asking about her childhood shortly after they first met at one of the early gigs Rob organized in London. *Classic Seventies Shambolic Bohemian Hippie*, she had responded glibly, with the same quick smile she had just used on the nurse. *A compilation album of all the worst features of that era.* Her strategy was always to make it sound more glamorous and comical than it was. 'My dad was an artist and my mother a poet. They split up when I was fifteen.' When this didn't completely satisfy his curiosity, she described what it wasn't. 'No mealtimes. No bedtimes. No weekly shop. No time where you had to be home. No need to say where you were staying. No day you knew your clothes would get washed. No swimming lessons.' She never mentioned the teacher at school who had brought in a sandwich for her every day or the neighbour who had let her do homework at her kitchen table.

For some reason people always fixated on the lack of swimming lessons. Then at least she didn't have to explain that when her father left her mother it didn't matter because a different man moved in the same night and that seemed normal. Or how she learnt that the best way to deflect unwanted interest from men twice her age was to ask questions.

'You can't swim?' Patrick had quizzed her.

'No.'

'I'll teach you. I grew up surrounded by water. I swam before I could walk.'

That was when he had explained how his ancestors came to East Anglia from Holland in the seventeenth century to transform forty thousand acres of marsh into farmland. He spoke of ditches, dykes, washes, sluices and lodes. The terminology was alien but the concept of a family that could trace its history back to the same place for three hundred years was instantly appealing, even if the swimming lessons, like so many of Patrick's plans, never quite materialized.

'I'm scared of water,' Grace had explained. 'Someone I once knew drowned.' She changed the subject. 'Tell me more about you. What do you do?' Unlike her, Patrick was good at not asking questions. Little wonder she was so happy to be absorbed into his world. After staying with his parents, Beth and Lawrence, for the first time she knew she wanted to be excised from her life and grafted on to his. 'They're the perfect combination of warmth and orderliness,' Grace had declared, when Patrick anxiously asked how she was enjoying the weekend at their house in Ely. He had mistaken her reticence for cool; her nervousness when they had sex for lack of experience; and her long flowery dress as evidence of a Bohemian sensibility.

She still remembers the sense of awe when she opened Beth and Lawrence's fridge and saw neat drawers of vegetables from the garden and shelves of home-cooked food in colour-coordinated plastic containers. Patrick had caught her staring and apologized for his parents' dullness. 'It's not dull, it's dazzling,' she countered.

'You're turned on by the fridge?' he had teased, raising an eyebrow and pulling her towards him. He had laughed because he liked the way she was so tolerant of his parents and their sterile routines, and she had laughed because he couldn't understand how extraordinary this was to her. It was only much later that it occurred to Grace they were already talking at cross-purposes.

Within three months of meeting Patrick she was pregnant. She couldn't believe her luck when he wanted to get married. Suddenly life was all about their future and the beautiful family they would create together. His parents' caution about marrying a woman with no history dissolved as soon as Lilly emerged with all the classic Vermuyden characteristics – the pale eyes, the blonde hair, and the same phlegmatic temperament.

'You need to go. For your own sake,' the nurse insists, putting a kindly hand on her shoulder. Grace explains that she doesn't want Lilly to wake up and find herself alone. The nurse says he will keep a close eye on her and promises to get in touch if there is any change. Grace leans over the metal bedrail, the flesh on her stomach absorbing its cold hardness, and plants a slow kiss on Lilly's cheek. Her own daughter no longer smells familiar. She is infused with the thick, cloying fug of antiseptic and industrially washed sheets, although there is a hint of something sweet and sickly that reminds Grace of her childhood. *Why didn't you tell me about the boy?* she whispers in Lilly's ear. *What else haven't you told me? I don't want there to be any secrets between us.* Lilly doesn't stir.

Grace takes the long road from the hospital, heading away from the city through open countryside to drive home. She grips the steering wheel as tightly as she can to stop her hands shaking and opens all the car windows. The warm wind blows the acidy smell of leeks and baked mud through the car. The repetitive monotony of the straight roads, empty apart from the occasional lorry lumbering vegetables from farms to supermarkets, makes her feel less wired.

She puts on the radio. *The Shipping Forecast* has started, which means it must be almost one o'clock in the morning. *Dogger. Fisher. German Bight.* She hears without listening, unable to stop thinking about Lilly. The nurse said there would be no more news until tomorrow. But what if she has another seizure? She worries about the heart that missed a beat. She thinks about all the processes that have to take place at exactly the right time, every second of the day, for it to work properly. She can't believe how she has taken this for granted for so many years. She imagines the valves opening and shutting. The pumps working in perfect synchronicity. The arteries flooding the capillaries with exactly the right amount of blood.

It reminds her of all the sluices, drains, dykes and pumps working round the clock to stop the Fens flooding. During the heavy rains in the spring, that system had also failed and a muddy pond had appeared at the end of their garden. She had warned Patrick when they bought the house that it was built below sea level. Against nature. He argued that his family had tamed this land and that the developers wouldn't have been given permission to build a new estate where there was a flood risk. In the end they had had to make a quick decision.

Almost exactly a year ago Patrick had revealed to Grace that his teaching hours had been cut and he could no longer cover his share of the mortgage and bills. They needed to buy a cheaper flat but prices in Cambridge had gone through the roof. So Grace reluctantly agreed that it would be better to move to one of the new-build estates north of the city so the children didn't have to change schools and they could commute to work.

Her thoughts turn to the boy Mia mentioned. *Cormack.* She says his name out loud. She's never heard Lilly mention him. She's not even sure if he's at school with her. Now his name is inextricably linked to today's events and suddenly it seems imperative to find out more about him. As she pulls up outside the house she casts her mind back to the summer holidays. For the first time in years they had stayed at home all summer. Usually they would visit Beth, who had moved to Brighton to live with her sister after Lawrence died, but the damp caused by the spring floods was creeping up through the house. The reprieve Patrick had anticipated because of the heatwave hadn't materialized. There was mould on the skirting boards; a two-centimetre gap had opened up between the bottom of the patio doors and the floor; and every morning Grace found slimy slug trails across the kitchen floor and woodlice in the toaster and electricity sockets.

It occurs to her now that Lilly had seemed truly happy that summer. She had stopped complaining about moving house and had settled into a rhythm of doing school work during the week and working at the punting company over the weekend. She ended up spending most Saturday nights at Hayley's house because she lived more centrally. This reminds her that at least three of the missed calls are from Hayley's mum, Nuala. She reluctantly resolves to speak to her in the morning. They haven't met for coffee since an awkward encounter in the middle of the holidays when Nuala had casually asked if Lilly was going to a music festival with Hayley. Grace had countered that she didn't approve of festivals and that Lilly hadn't even mentioned it because it wasn't her scene and, in any case, she had been invited to attend Mr Galveston's pre-term English course for potential Oxbridge candidates. Flaky doesn't really sum it up when it comes to Nuala.

After a tussle with the front door, which no longer fits

properly in its frame, Grace locks it behind her and heads into the kitchen, expecting to find Patrick. All the downstairs lights are turned on but he's not there. *That's how you can tell if someone grew up in a household where money wasn't a worry*, decides Grace, swatting at switches until only one light remains on. The builders have finished injecting silicone into the brickwork and switched on blow heaters to dry out the room as quickly as possible. It's oppressively hot and every surface is coated with a new film of red dust. Sample pots taunt her from the kitchen table. She wishes she could go back in time to the moment when she left the house this morning and her biggest problem was deciding what colour to paint the walls.

The contents of the kitchen cupboards have been unpacked by the builders into an archipelago of neat mounds hidden with dustsheets and Grace knows that somewhere she will find a bottle of vodka. She wants to pour a shot into a glass with some orange squash and drink it down in one go with her eyes closed before she has time to start ruminating on everything that has happened in the past twelve hours. She scrabbles beneath the dustsheets. There's no logic to the mounds. Kitchen knives are mixed with herbs, plates with dishcloths, tinned tomatoes with phone chargers. Which reminds her that she has Lilly's phone. She retrieves the charger and plugs it in so that she can take it to her when she goes back to the hospital in the morning.

Upstairs she finds Patrick spreadeagled across their bed, arms and legs splayed, hands gripping the edge of the mattress as if he's sailing through rough seas. She switches on the light. He doesn't flinch. His sweat has mingled with the red dust so the crumpled sheet resembles a crime scene. She used to view his ability to sleep through any upheaval with wonder, as an indication of his calm and constancy.

73

Now it makes her irritated. *Christ, he's even wearing pyjamas. Hasn't it crossed his mind that we could be called back to the hospital at any minute?* Jangly-nerved, she yanks the curtains shut so the rings screech against the metal rail but Patrick still doesn't stir.

She goes up to the loft to check on Mia. Her bedroom is opposite Lilly's at the top of the stairs. The rooms are unimaginatively identical, except that Lilly's looks out on to the road at the front of the house, while Mia's faces open countryside. Lilly had been given first refusal on the basis that she was the one who had least wanted to move here. She had argued hard to stay in Pretoria Road without realizing that moving out of the city centre was a financial necessity rather than a lifestyle choice. She chose the room because there were streetlights on that side of the estate and she could see the bus stop with the route back to their old home. 'Suburbia is terrifying, Mum,' she had said, until she saw the eerie, empty view from Mia's room where the recently ploughed fields stretched black as far as the horizon.

Lilly's door is closed. Grace's hand hovers over the handle. She can't decide whether she will find consolation inside or drown in her daughter's absence. She has an overwhelming urge to lie on Lilly's bed and wrap herself in her duvet to wait for sunrise, when she can go back to the hospital. She recalls a midwife once showing them how to calm Mia when she was a baby by swaddling her, and Patrick's frustration that he could never perform the correct origami with a blanket. She wants to do the same now. She imagines Lilly's contempt at her mawkishness and it makes her smile. Sleep is out of the question. Even if she could doze off, Grace doesn't want to because then she will have to wake up and remember what has happened all over again.

As she starts to turn the handle, she hears a noise coming

from Mia's room and turns to see a thin line of light at the bottom of the door. It's a quiet, low sound, more hum than song. She gently pushes open the door and finds Mia standing completely still, back to the door, staring out of the open window, her long white cotton nightie billowing around her knees in the warm breeze. Her frizzy hair is loose and cascades around her arms and shoulders like a cape. Her arms hang stiffly by her side and her fists are curled. She goes quiet, then starts muttering the same unintelligible words all over again. For a moment Grace wonders if she's sleepwalking. Not that she's ever done so before but it's not uncommon after a distressing event. *Why on earth did Patrick leave her up here alone? Especially after the drama involving the missing ring.* Then she remembers she forgot to mention anything about it to him.

Grace stands just inside the bedroom door, unsure what to do. She doesn't want to startle her. Even if Mia gets back into bed, she's not going to leave her alone in a bedroom with an open window. Not now. Not after what has happened to Lilly. Children don't always walk past open windows. Her gaze floats to the bed where she notices Lilly's duvet and pillow lying on top of Mia's. It's not often that she sees herself in her younger daughter and she feels tears prick as she realizes they are both engaged in the same hunt for comfort. Perhaps they could lie down on top of Lilly's duvet together. She could steal up beside her like she used to do when Mia was a little girl and couldn't get to sleep unless someone was in the room with her.

Mia starts to speak again. Grace steps into the middle of the room, dodging Elvis's bucket, so she can see her in profile. It's like she's reciting a nursery rhyme, but although individually some of the words make sense, when put together they sound like gibberish.

'One-ery, two-ery, ickery Ann,
Filoson, followson, Nicholas, Jan,
Weavy, squeavy, squaavy, squoavy,
Zinctum, zanctum, zorum, buck.'

She emphasizes the last word of each line and, at the end of the rhyme, startles Grace by throwing her arms into the air and leaning out of the window.

'Mia . . .' Grace warily asks. 'What are you doing?'

Unperturbed, Mia turns to face her, as if she already knew she was there. She's wide awake. Her skin is bleached pale, yet there is a film of sweat above her upper lip. She doesn't smile or seem particularly surprised to find her mum in her bedroom at two o'clock in the morning. She clasps her hands behind her and straightens her back, like she's standing to attention.

'I'm trying to stop what has started by saying Tas's rhyme,' she says in a matter-of-fact tone.

'What are you talking about? What has started?' asks Grace, in confusion. She can't cope with Mia's histrionics tonight.

'It's like Tas said. The bad spirits have escaped from the ground and we need them to go back.'

'There is no such thing as bad spirits. Just bad people.'

'Those archaeologists are going to bring trouble down on us all, Mum!'

'Don't be ridiculous, Mia. Archaeology is possibly one of the most harmless professions in the world,' says Grace, laughing.

'What about Indiana Jones?'

'He's not a real person, is he? Besides, he's more looter than archaeologist.'

'What's a looter?'

'Someone who steals artefacts from archaeological sites,' Grace explains.

Mia's right eye narrows. 'Something woke me up, Mum. I could feel it sitting on my chest, crushing me until I could hardly breathe. I had to use all my strength to throw it off. It escaped out of the window and wanted me to go with it.'

'You were having a nightmare, darling,' says Grace, her tone softening. 'Because of what happened to Lil. Because she couldn't breathe.' She wraps her arms around Mia. She feels so small and spindly-limbed. Her arms are cold but her body is clammy. 'It's because you love her too.'

'You always try and explain your way out of everything but Tas says most of life's questions have no answers.'

'Tas comes at things from a different angle,' says Grace, as Mia pulls away.

'Why?'

'He comes from another culture,' says Grace, carefully.

'I can see them dancing in the river beyond the dyke,' Mia says, one hand pointing out of the window into the darkness beyond as she presses herself into Grace's softness. 'They're trying to get me to follow them. I'm so scared, Mum. I don't want to leave you and Dad.' Mia's grip around her waist tightens.

'Do you think I'd let you sleep alone in this room if I truly believed there were bad spirits trying to steal you away?' says Grace, stroking the top of her head and cursing Tas for putting ideas into her head. He's a nice boy but he's as prone to mad imaginings as Mia.

Mia unfurls from her. 'Look out of the window and you'll see them.'

Grace glances at the open window, then back at Mia, trying to gauge whether caving in will give too much credence to her fears or resolve them. There's no logic to anything that has happened today and she no longer trusts her instincts. How could the ambulance have driven past without her realizing Lilly was inside? Why didn't she know about that boy? Or that Lilly had been swimming at Earith every weekend?

'I'll take a look as long as you promise to go back to bed. You've got school tomorrow,' she says finally.

'Strictly speaking, they can't make me go to school if my sister's gravely ill in hospital, can they?'

'I'll be with Lilly all day. You'll get bored. And you need to look after Tas. Remember how upset he was yesterday?' It feels manipulative but she knows that argument will work.

'Will you take me, then?'

Grace hesitates. She wants Patrick to deal with Mia so that she can concentrate on Lilly.

'Please, Mum.'

'I have to get back to the hospital.'

'I'm begging you, Mum. You need to tell Miss Swain what's happened. So she doesn't pick on me again. Dad won't do it as well as you. She doesn't like me. I can tell. She thinks I'm a – a fantasist.'

'A fantasist?'

'I heard her say that to the counsellor.'

'Okay.' Grace sighs. She would never have let Lilly get away with this kind of emotional blackmail.

'What is a fantasist, Mum?'

'Someone who confuses what is make-believe with what is real.'

'Do you think I do that?'

'I think we're all the sum of our own stories,' says Grace, sidestepping Mia's question.

She pushes the window as wide as it will open and looks outside. Her eyes slowly adjust to the dark. It's the last weekend of September and the placid light of a harvest moon illuminates the landscape. It's a warm, balmy night. The scaly edges of the furrows of the recently ploughed field and even the usually sullen water of the dyke glimmer in the distance. Everything is still.

'Can you see anything, Mum?' asks Mia, anxiously, cowering behind her.

'Like what?' asks Grace.

'Strange lights dancing in the river. Like human figures but with blurry outlines. As if they're on fire.'

'Fire and water don't generally mix,' Grace points out.

'It's the will-o'-the-wisps,' Mia whispers. 'They were trying to get me to follow them into the water so I would drown with all my secrets.'

Grace bursts out laughing again. The noise carries out of the window across the garden, the hedge and into the field beyond. Mia might absorb more of her attention than any other member of the family but she also makes her laugh more than anyone else.

'Sssh, Mum, they'll hear you and then they'll be even angrier,' pleads Mia, but Grace sees a hint of a smile start to curl her upper lip.

'Honestly, Mia! Where on earth have you learnt about will-o'-the-wisps?'

'Miss Swain read a story about them.'

'They're an old legend from years ago, when the Fens were still marshland. People think that gases trapped in the peat were released and self-ignited. I bet Miss Swain didn't tell you that.'

'No. Maybe that bit isn't part of the curriculum.'

'If you'd read my piece on local legends in the last issue of the newsletter you would have known,' she says, with mock reproach.

Grace resolves to arrange another meeting with Miss Swain when they know what's going on with Lilly. Until then, life is on hold. As she stares out of the window she wonders if Lilly is still asleep and whether the nurse really will have time to check on her. A pheasant's cry explodes from the long grass by the river, and there is a brief skirmish. There are so many foxes around since they banned hunting. Dark shapes move along one of the furrows. Hares, most likely. On the edge she spots thc white outline of two swans roosting in the long grass on the headland. She points them out to Mia. 'Look. Whooper swans.'

'I don't want to look out again in case I see the lights.'

'They've flown all the way from Iceland on their own. Twelve hours without rest,' says Grace. 'If they can do that, then the least you can do is look out of the window at them.'

Mia takes her hand and leans out beside her. In the distance the swans flap their wings and the noise sounds like drums beating. 'How do you know they're whoopers?'

'The Bewicks come later because they've got even further to travel.'

'I think I'm ready to go back to sleep, Mum,' Mia says.

Grace closes the window and the two of them lie on top of Lilly's duvet. She puts out her hand and wraps it around Mia's clenched fist until her fingers start to relax. Occasionally now, she feels sorry for her own mother, that she never learnt the simple pleasure of soothing a child.

'I'm telling the truth,' says Mia, sleepily.

'Tell me your truth and I will tell you mine,' Grace says.

'What does that mean?'

'That people don't always share the same point of view.'

Mia snuggles into her side and Grace puts her arm around her. She lies on her back and stares at the ceiling. The stains seem to have got bigger. There used to be only one but it has reproduced and now there are patches like small footprints across the sagging ceiling. It's the same in

Lilly's room. The irony that Patrick's Dutch ancestors invented this system, yet he can't stop the damp in his own home, is not lost on her. Or him. She thinks of the marshland beneath. It's more like living in a boat that has sprung a leak than a house. Especially in the winter when the fog drifts from the fields to hang over the house all day and the garden turns to bog.

Maybe the spores from the mould have made Lilly sick. The doctor mentioned environmental factors. Heart racing, Grace picks up her phone and googles bathroom mould. Within minutes she is an expert. She diagnoses *Penicillium* – it's the greenish hue that clinches it – but there are more than two hundred species. She locates a mould expert in Cambridge with seventy-three five-star reviews and sends an email requesting an emergency appointment, forgetting that it is three o'clock in the morning. Mia stirs beside her.

'Don't worry. I've seen Lilly's death and this isn't it,' Mia says sleepily.

At that exact moment Lilly wakes up and gulps in the hot dry air as if she's breaking to the surface after swimming underwater at Earith, except instead of the sweet smell of bog myrtle it reeks of antiseptic. *Where am I?* she wonders. *What am I doing here?* Then she remembers. She half waits for the tingling in her fingers to start and when it doesn't she reaches for the pocket where her phone should be, forgetting she's dressed in a hospital gown and unfamiliar pyjama bottoms. She tries to get out of bed but, like a dog on a lead, she can only roam as far as the wires allow her. 'I want to go home,' she says, surprised by the clarity of her voice. No one responds.

The knot in her stomach is still there. She remembers how the school counsellor had advised her to picture herself in the place she felt happiest whenever she felt anxious. So she lies down again, closes her eyes against the jaundiced fluorescent light and thinks about the game they had invented over the summer.

Cormack had borrowed his dad's pick-up and every Saturday, after they had finished their shift at the punting company, he drove her, Jordy and Hayley to swim in the river at Earith. They all sat in the front of the truck, no seatbelts, sweaty legs and arms stuck together, singing to Arcade Fire at full volume with the windows wound down, as Cormack drove too fast, one hand on the steering wheel, along the endlessly straight Fenland roads. When they reached Earith they stripped down to their underwear, climbed up the lock gates and jumped into the deep water the other side of the sluice. *My time has come*, Lilly remembers thinking, the first time she threw herself over the edge, eyes tight shut, into the dark water below. The next time she shouted it out loud and they all laughed as if it was the funniest thing anyone had ever said. For so long she had been waiting for her life to start and then suddenly it wouldn't stop.

'You've become so reckless,' Hayley commented in surprise.

'It's because this is my land.' Lilly laughed, opening her arms with the sheer joy of a freedom she had never experienced before.

'Explain,' said Cormack.

So Lilly told him how her family had drained the Fens to turn the marshes into agricultural land and described the old map of the waterways that hung on the wall at home. 'Old Bedford River. Counter Wash Drain. New Bedford River. Welche's Dam. Sixteen Foot Drain. And my favourite, Vermuyden's Drain, because it's named after my family.' She recited the names, like a mantra. 'He built Earith Sluice and created the Old Bedford River and the Hundred Foot Drain to divert water from the Ouse when the water level gets too high,' she said proudly.

'Your family dug the rivers where we're swimming?' Jordy had asked incredulously.

'You're made from mud, Lilly Vermuyden,' Cormack teased, giving her hair a gentle tug.

'I didn't come here for a history lesson,' said Hayley, abruptly. 'Let's swim.'

The game had started by accident. On their second or third trip, one of them, Jordy most likely, had kicked down hard through the water and discovered he could stop himself floating back to the surface by holding on to the slimy green weeds growing on the riverbed. Soon they were all competing to see who could hold their breath longest. The four of them clung to the weeds with their eyes open, pulling faces in the glimmering water to make each other laugh. The first to give up had to perform a dare devised by the others. At first the dares were predictable – jump into the water naked, do a back flip off the lock, eat a live insect – and they posted pictures and videos of them on their Snapchat group. But as time went on Cormack de-cided these dares were too ordinary. *Boredom is a kind of death*, he kept saying. He wanted total escape. And so too did Lilly. Things got out of hand. By then everything had changed between them in ways they couldn't fully know or comprehend until much later.

The first time Cormack's hand glided across her but-tocks under water Lilly had assumed the glimmer of limbs entwined beneath the surface was an accident. There were often currents that buffeted them against each other. She didn't move away. But neither did she move closer. She noticed later, when they lay on their backs in the reeds smoking weed and debating whether there was anything emptier and purer in life than the blue sky above them, that Cormack's hand had drifted to the side of her thigh and stayed there where the others couldn't see. She wanted him to touch her so much that she couldn't speak. She watched her ribcage rise and fall as her breathing altered and waited for Hayley to notice and say something to embarrass her. Afterwards she spent hours trying to re-create the scene in her head, wondering if she had imagined that he was touching her on purpose.

This was not the way it was meant to be. Hayley's plan was that she would get with Cormack and Lilly would get with Jordy. 'You're my sideman,' she kept telling Lilly. Hayley wasn't concerned that Lilly didn't fancy Jordy. She was obsessed by Cormack and talked about him all the time. Whether he was sending a subliminal message by playing Cigarettes After Sex whenever he picked her up in his truck; how he wondered who she was going to share a tent with at the music festival at the end of the holidays; the fact he always wanted to know if Lilly was staying over at her house to check if Hayley was alone. Hayley never felt on the edge of anything. It was inconceivable to her that Cormack might be more interested in Lilly's whereabouts than her own. Just once, Lilly had commented that Cormack looked like an otter when his head broke the surface and he shook the water from his hair, and Hayley ignored her for the rest of the day.

As the summer drifted by it became obvious that the breath-holding competition was between Lilly and Cormack and that it was about much more than who had the biggest lung capacity. The weed made Jordy more and more paranoid that a pike with razor-sharp teeth was waiting for him in the water, and after a seal once emerged beside them

Haylcy refused to go back in. Lilly and Cormack would stay under the surface, limbs entwined as they trod water, eyes half open, challenging each other to stay down for longer and longer until the blood vessels in their temples started pounding and their chests felt as if they would explode. When they finally surfaced, blue-lipped and dizzy, among the lily pads and dragonflies, she would flip on to her back to float until her breathing returned to normal while Cormack cradled her head. She had never felt so reckless. 'I need you,' he had whispered in her ear, at the end of the first week. That was how it all began. And how it ended. No one had warned her that need wasn't the same as love or that he might feel neither. But, given what she had discovered about her mother at the beginning of the summer, it wasn't an uncommon experience.

5

Patrick wakes with a lurch. Something is wrong. The curtains are open and the early-morning sun glows unpleasantly in his face, like a naked light bulb. His body is sticky with sweat, and when he scratches his balls half-moons of red sludge from the builder's dust get stuck beneath his nails. He drowsily puts out his arm to reach for Grace but she isn't there and he wonders if this accounts for his unease. He likes to joke that she might disappear from his life as quickly as she appeared in it. *We belong.* She always smiles when he says this. *We beautifully belong.* But he can't get over the feeling that whatever he is doing with her, whether it's gardening, fucking or testing paint colours, part of her is closed off to him. In the seventeen years they have been together he has never felt she needs him as much as he needs her.

He's out of bed now, standing in front of the mirror in a state of confusion, and it all comes back. *Lilly!* He snatches his phone from the bedside table and reads Grace's last message from the hospital. *Erlop zz.* What on earth does she mean?

He feels simultaneously depleted and wired. Putting Mia to bed last night had been frazzling. For the first time in years she had pleaded with him to read a story, which ostensibly was a good plan to distract them both from worrying about Lilly. But as always with Mia there was a catch. She only wanted him to read 'The Dauntless Girl', a tale from an old anthology of Fenland legends that had belonged to him as a child. He remembered Grace had hidden the book in one of the boxes in the garage after Mia had become obsessed with it. By the time he gave up foraging for the book he was covered with dust and it was close to eleven. So he ended up recounting from memory the tale of a girl who fearlessly crosses the Fens to fetch ale for her father, scaring away all the bad spirits she encounters along the way. His recall was hazy and Mia interrupted to correct him every time he got a detail wrong, which meant it took for ever. 'It's boggles and blogarts, not hobgoblins'; 'And a skull not a skeleton.' No sooner had he finished than she wanted him to start all over again. Her room smelt of damp and old eel but she refused to let him open the window.

Mia's mood had been peculiar, her earlier anxiety over Lilly subsumed by a manic intensity, as if everything was imbued with mysterious meaning. She kept asking morbid questions about babies: 'Is Ana pregnant yet and if she is could she die during childbirth?'; 'If a baby dies, how can you be certain it's really dead when it's buried?'; 'Why is it that people who want babies can't have them and people who don't want them get pregnant?' He holds Rob and Ana responsible for this exhausting line of questioning because of the argument Mia had overheard in the summer.

He was furious with Rob after that weekend, but he couldn't afford to betray his feelings because his little brother had done him a big favour. Although Patrick had told Grace that the developer was paying for repairs to the house, the reality was that the warranty was worthless and compensation could take years. He realized this as soon as he searched online and saw there were nine pages alone relating to complaints about damp in new-build homes on Snagging.org.

He couldn't bring himself to tell Grace. He told himself he just wanted to put things right without worrying her, but it was more that he didn't want to reopen the debate about the risks of buying a house built on marshland or prompt her to ask awkward questions about their increasingly perilous financial situation. He had avoided telling her about his teaching hours being cut last year for as long as possible because he couldn't face her disappointment. And when eventually he broke the news, he still didn't admit the full extent of the loans he had taken out on different credit cards, the missed payments and ramped-up debts. So when the builders threatened to walk because he owed them money, Patrick asked Rob for a loan to cover the bills. 'Just for a couple of weeks.' A month ago, an envelope in his name, marked Private, had arrived in the post with a cheque from Rob for fifteen thousand pounds.

He pulls off his pyjamas, throws on yesterday's clothes, and goes downstairs two at a time, leaving a trail of red dust from the carpet in his slipstream. He wants to speak to his brother as soon as possible to tell him what has happened, not least to elicit sympathy because he needs to ask Rob for more money.

Tracking the reversal in their fortunes over the years makes Patrick almost breathless with incredulity. He was the son who had chosen the righteous path. Head boy at school. First-class degree. Institute of Education. He was the one who followed the rules to lead a restrained and regimented life. Steady self-improvement was his mantra. But then 2008 happened. Their costs spiralled. History of art became less and less popular as an A-level subject. Two classes became one and instead of a salary he was paid by the hour. He kept telling himself that something would turn up but, beyond establishing an evening course for parents, he couldn't find anything. Rob, on the other hand, had flunked his A levels and dedicated his life to the pursuit of hedonism before going into the music industry. By the age of thirty he had reinvented himself as a big-cheese producer, his mantelpiece groaning with awards.

Still, he wouldn't have met Grace if he hadn't gone to a gig by the band that made Rob's name. Patrick remembers with absolute clarity the first time he saw her, standing beside his brother at the bar, looking cool and unapproachable in her short black dress. But then she ordered a pint of orange squash and he was so intrigued by this contradiction that he had started talking to her. 'Sweet tooth?' he asked.

She shook her head and gave him a quick smile. 'I wasn't allowed sugar as a child.'

He's relieved to find Grace at the kitchen table, crouched over her mobile phone. Every so often she stops scrolling through messages to write something in a notebook. Notebooks are one of her things. Along with orange squash. If there were bad news she would have woken him up. She certainly wouldn't be working. Relieved, Patrick hugs her from behind and she leans back into him.

'Any update from the hospital?' he asks, kissing the top of her head.

'I just spoke to the nurse. Lil slept through the night. All her vital signs are normal.'

'What does that mean?'

'Her temperature, blood pressure, heart rate and breathing are all fine.'

'Thank God,' he says, sitting down beside her, grateful that he can always count on Grace to be on top of everything.

'She's even eaten breakfast. They're running more tests this morning. They said we should go back after midday. I'm not going to work, so I can take Mia to school.'

'Why don't you let me do that? You must be knackered.'

'You know what she's like. It was part of a negotiation.'

He raises an eyebrow. 'Don't get into that again,' he cautions, remembering Mia's diktat over the bedtime story. 'Even now. Especially now. If you give her an inch –'

'I know,' she interrupts. 'She had a problem with her new teacher yesterday. It needs sorting out. Before it mushrooms.'

'What kind of problem?'

Grace explains about the missing ring. Patrick smiles and shakes his head in mock despair. 'Why would she want some rusty old ring?' He snorts. He's trying hard to make everything feel normal: it's his guiding principle that if you pretend something long enough it becomes true, and there's an impatient and feverish edge to Grace's tone that reminds him of troubles past.

'My thoughts exactly.'

'So why did the teacher think it was her?' asks Patrick.

'Probably because she was the last one seen with the ring. It's the same in murder investigations,' says Grace. 'The first person to be investigated is always the last person to see the victim alive.'

He laughs but Grace doesn't. He squints down at the notebook, trying to decipher her tiny spidery writing. There are three names underlined in black ink: Cormack. Hayley. Jordy. Beside each there are a few words in quotation marks.

'What are you doing?' he asks, frowning as he recognizes the dark blue phone case. 'Isn't that Lil's phone?'

'I'm taking a look at the messages that have come through for her,' she explains breezily, snapping the notebook shut.

'How do you know her password?' he asks.

'I don't. The new messages flash up on her screen. I thought I should take a look.'

'Why?'

'We need to know what's been going on,' she says emphatically. 'I'm looking for clues, Patrick.'

'Clues to what?'

'I'm trying to work out who this boy Cormack is and what Lilly was doing with him at Earith Sluice.'

'Cormack?' he asks, in confusion. As usual he's off the pace with his wife.

'The boy Mia mentioned when we were in the hospital last night,' she says impatiently.

'What boy?'

'Mia said Lilly had been seeing a boy.'

'So what?'

'She's been seeing him behind our backs.'

'Grace,' he says firmly, trying to prise Lilly's phone from her hand. 'She's almost eighteen. That's a major invasion of her privacy.'

'Bollocks to major invasion of privacy. Why didn't she tell us?' Grace counters.

'Come on, when has Lil shown bad judgement? Keep the faith. We all do things we'd like to keep to ourselves, don't we?' He's trying to cajole her out of her mood because this strategy has worked in the past. 'She doesn't have to tell us every detail about her private life.'

'Listen to what some of these messages say and then draw conclusions.'

'I don't want to,' says Patrick, getting up abruptly from the table. 'It doesn't feel right.'

'Jordy sent this one after she went to hospital. Look at the time. Fourteen thirty-seven.' She reads from her notebook

'*Got your back.* Why would he send a message like that right after her seizure?'

'Why not? Jordy's one of her oldest friends. He cares about Lil.'

'What do you think he's implying?'

'It's difficult to tell from three words, Grace.' He tries and fails to distract her with details about what time the builders are arriving and the best technique for clearing up the red dust.

'It could mean something really practical, like he's picked up her school books,' she continues.

'It could.'

'Or it could mean he'll always look out for her.'

'Yeah.'

'Or it could mean that he's keeping a secret on her behalf.'

'That too,' he says, in an aggressively ambivalent tone. He knows Grace won't let it go. It's the same quality that makes Mia so uncompromising.

'Then, a few minutes later, there's a message from someone called cmack that says, *RUOK?* That's him.'

'He's asking how she is. Lilly has friends who worry about her when she's ill. What's wrong with that? I don't understand the point of all this.' Now it's his turn to sound exasperated.

'It's from him, isn't it? That's the point.'

'From who?'

'Cormack. There's another one ten minutes later. *Keep it low.* What does that mean? And what about this? *Two minutes thirty seconds, u win.*'

Patrick tries to grab Lilly's phone from her hand. There is a brief tussle, and the phone falls to the floor.

'Shit,' they say simultaneously.

'Lil doesn't like anyone touching her phone,' says Mia, sternly. They didn't hear her come into the kitchen and have

93

no idea how long she has been standing by the door. She's dressed in school uniform but, as she comes over to pick up the phone, Patrick notices that once again her jumper is on back to front so the V is at the back and, even though he's sitting in a T-shirt and shorts, she's wearing her black leather boots and grey woollen knee socks. Her bony knees are scabby with playground accidents and her face is even paler than usual. He feels a sudden wrench of emotion for his younger daughter. It's not that she doesn't try to blend in, it's that she can't. No wonder she's ended up being such close friends with the only other outsider in the class, the curly-haired Roma boy from the Travellers' site.

'I hope you didn't have any bad dreams about hobgoblins,' he teases.

'You mean boggles, Dad.' She throws him a supercilious glance and puts the phone face up on the kitchen table so they can see the tiny crack in the corner of the screen. 'Can you take me to school, please, Mum? I don't want to get into trouble for being late, and you need to speak to Miss Swain about being kind to me because my sister is gravely sick.'

Mia takes the ring to school hidden in her sock. She knows it's high risk, but the closer it is to Tas, the more likely its energy will help him, too. To her mind, the ring's powers were conclusively proven last night when she roused Lilly from her coma simply by touching her with it. Moreover, when she woke up this morning Mia noticed the house was coated with a red dust the exact same colour as the garnet.

She isn't remotely surprised by this turn of events. The archaeologists had explained how Anglo-Saxon warriors wore garnets to protect themselves against death and injury,

94

and the ancient Egyptians thought they could ward off the evil eye. She believes what the archaeologists say, even if she doubts their ability to appreciate the harm they have unleashed by stirring up the spirits of the dead. She bends down to touch the ring and its energy makes her feel invincible. For once, she's not worried about going to school.

Although Mia is convinced that the ring will somehow prevent Tas and his family's eviction from their home on the Travellers' site, she has no firm idea about how exactly this might come about. She mulls it over as she walks along the pavement holding Grace's hand. *Outcome (a): the archaeologists will be forced to abandon the dig because they will catch the Ague. Outcome (b): a natural disaster, like a mudslide or lightning strike, will destroy the site and bury everything that has been uncovered so far. Outcome (c): the spirits of the dead mothers and babies will drive them away.* The last, in Mia's view, is the least likely because, *strictly speaking*, mothers and babies lack the warrior spirit that she now possesses. Having babies makes you weak. She had once heard her mum telling Nuala that she hadn't known what anxiety was until she had children.

There is plenty of time to think because Grace is completely distracted and has addressed barely a word to her since they left home. She had started driving with Mia's packed lunch on the roof of the car and kept pulling over to have tense phone calls about mould on the bedroom ceiling, which hardly seems the priority when Lilly is in hospital. For the first time in the history of school runs, she didn't make her do spellings or times tables in the car. It's as if Mia is wearing an invisibility cloak.

She glances up at her mum and can't help noticing the way the skin is pulled so tight over her face that the outline of her skull is visible beneath. She thinks of the Anglo-Saxon girl and wonders how it is possible that bone survives

95

for thousands of years while flesh starts to rot within days. Grace's distress makes Mia feel conflicted. She is almost certain her sister's seizure has something to do with the pregnancy test but, remembering how angry Lilly looked when she mentioned Cormack's name in hospital, she knows her life won't be worth living if she says anything.

She stops again to rub the tip of her right boot against the inside of her left ankle, where the ring nestles in the soft flesh just below her anklebone. Each time she does this, she feels a mysterious warmth surge through her body.

'Please stop dawdling,' says Grace. She shoots Mia a quick smile but it fades before it has settled. 'Remember, the early bird catches the worm.'

'But the early worm gets caught by the bird,' Mia responds, with a puzzled frown. So little of what adults say or do makes any sense.

She glances across to the secondary school to check if the boys who call Tas names are there. She will definitely call on the power of the ring if they do it today. They always accuse him of being dirty, even though the caravan where he lives with his mother, Rawnie, and his two older sisters is immaculate. They don't even use the toilets and shower in their trailer because they're not allowed to cook and wash in the same space. 'It's *mochadi*.' Tas had shrugged when she asked him to explain. 'Unclean.'

'Why?'

'It's our way.' He always says the same thing. She can't understand why people are so mean to Tas but, given how much is stacked against him, he's definitely someone who needs her protection.

Grace tightens her grip around Mia's hand and pulls her towards a shoal of uniformed teenagers drifting along

96

the pavement, white shirt tails flapping in the breeze, like washing on a line, heads bowed reverentially in worship of their mobile phones. She wants to get Mia off to school without a fuss so she can go back to Lilly as quickly as possible.

Although she would never admit it to anyone, this feeling of needing to escape Mia isn't completely unfamiliar. She remembers being furious with Patrick when he recently compared parenting their younger daughter to bailing out a boat with a constant leak. 'All anger is fear disguised,' he had argued. He was right on both counts. The prospect of a life of perpetual worry about Mia is overwhelming. It doesn't help that no one has come up with an accurate diagnosis. The educational psychologists can identify what she isn't. But they can't decide what she is, beyond a random cluster of contradictory symptoms.

She takes a long time to get anything down on paper, yet has the vocabulary of someone three years older; she can't ride a bicycle but she's just won her yellow belt at the after-school karate club; she has no friends who are girls but is popular with boys.

Sometimes Grace feels as trapped as Mia's pet eel. She remembers Elvis rearing up towards her, like a charmed snake, when she was cleaning Mia's room this week, skin mottled with green algae, to fix her with his glassy eyes, opening and closing his mouth as if pleading to be set free. He had swum three thousand miles from the exotic waters of the warm Sargasso Sea to the Fens to end up living in a bucket. Like her, he had once known freedom. She suppresses that thought before it takes root.

'Did you hear what happened?' shouts the girl in front of them over her headphones. Grace knows right away she is talking about Lilly.

'I saw it all,' a voice replies. It's Hayley. Grace has forgotten that Lilly and Hayley usually meet outside the car park every morning to go into school together. It's a ritual that started in their first week at St Edith's. At the beginning it had been an uneven relationship. Lilly was too much in thrall to Hayley and couldn't believe she had chosen her to be a friend. She copied Hayley's fringe even though it made her face look fat and gave her spots on her forehead, and wore skimpy tops that drew attention to her childish pot-belly. By the time they were sixteen, however, Lilly's puppy fat had disappeared, she had been promoted to the top set for every subject and developed her own thrift-store style, courtesy of online second-hand stores.

'I can't get the image of her lying so still on that stretcher out of my head. I thought . . . I really thought –' Hayley continues.

'Don't say it,' Freya interrupts.

Grace hasn't really considered the impact of what has happened to Lilly on her friends, who witnessed the seizure. She has spent most of the past eighteen hours hermetically sealed in her own private torment. Now she hears the fear in Hayley's voice and walks a little faster, hoping she might catch up in time to reassure her that Lilly had a good night.

'I couldn't stop crying last night,' says Hayley. 'I won't forgive myself if something happens to Lil. I think I've got PTSD from the shock of it all. Every time I close my eyes I see her face and think of the way her mouth hinged open so wide that I thought her jaw would actually dislocate. She was looking at me the entire time. I could see the terror in her eyes. It was like watching someone drown.'

Lilly couldn't breathe. *Just like the eel*, Grace thinks. She admonishes herself for spending the whole night worrying about Lilly's heart without considering the problem might be her lungs. It fits with her theory about spores from the mould. She checks her phone to see if any of the mould companies have got back to her.

'Shut up, Hayley,' someone says.

'Sounds like some weird shit went down,' says another boy.

'She had a kind of fit.' Grace recognizes Jordy's voice. Little fingers tighten around her own, and she gives them a reassuring squeeze. She picks up pace, ready to overtake them.

'Were you actually there?' a girl at the end of the row asks.

'Yeah,' says Jordy. 'I thought we were going to lose her. It was really fucking scary.' He speaks fast, running his hand through his red curly hair over and over again. 'Even Mr Galveston was worried. He didn't mention *Beowulf* for almost an hour.'

'And then what did he say?'

'He told us that life comes out of nowhere and floats into nowhere so you'd better make it count,' says Jordy. 'Upbeat as always.'

'Do you think she might have brain damage, Freya?' Jordy turns to the girl beside him in the black trousers.

'She wasn't unconscious for long enough. Mr Galveston started the CPR right away. It takes about a minute for brain cells to really start dying,' Freya says, putting her arm around Jordy. She's so tall that when Jordy leans towards her, his head rests somewhere close to her elbow. 'Don't worry, Jords.' She pats his head and he melts in the heat of her attention.

Grace tenses at the mention of brain damage. She has written the same question on her list for the consultant, above the one about allergy testing and below a couple on the damage to her ribcage from Mr Galveston's chest compressions. But the unease also comes from Freya's intimacy with Lilly's group of friends. She suddenly notices how Hayley's hair is dyed black and cut into the same short, sharp bob as Freya's and how she has abandoned the school skirt that was usually hiked so high she earned a weekly detention, in favour of black trousers. 'Freya doesn't have to work. She just knows it,' Lilly had said last week, when she was crying over an English essay. It occurs to her that, with Lilly in hospital, the path is clear for Freya to outperform her completely. She's worrying about this as Mia splutters to another abrupt halt and bends down to scratch her left ankle with the hand that isn't holding her packed lunch.

'Come on, Mia,' Grace says impatiently, tugging her by the hand.

'Is there any question you can't answer, Freya?' teases the boy to her left. He's obviously taking the piss out of Jordy by imitating his long, flat Fenland vowels. 'Does the shadow of death hunt in the darkness, for example?'

'Shut up, Cormack,' chaffs Hayley.

Grace stiffens. She can't see much of him from behind, but it's not difficult to decode the cocky swagger of his gait and the self-regard of his floppy hair. She recognizes his type. He's the kind of boy who peaks in the upper sixth, when skateboarding skills and poetic nihilism hold maximum appeal. That's why Lilly didn't say anything about him. Grace feels instantly threatened by Cormack. But the real threat is to her dreams for Lilly. She watches as he leans towards Jordy, mouth too close to his ear, and patronizingly ruffles his hair. Then he does a perfect rendition of Jordy reciting *Beowulf*, although he exaggerates his Fenland accent.

'Till the monster stirred, that demon, that fiend
Grendel who haunted the moors, the wild
Marshes, and made his home in a hell
Not hell but hell on earth. He was spawned
    in that slime.'

'Leave it out, Cormack,' Jordy orders.

'What's he talking about?' Mia whispers.

'It's from a book,' Grace explains.

'Is he talking about the monsters in the Fens?' Mia asks fearfully.

'It's make-believe,' Grace snaps. 'There are no monsters.'

'The school counsellor is going to speak to everyone today. If you have something to say, Cormack, talk to her,' says Freya, sharply.

'How do you know that?' asks Jordy, sounding impressed.

'Because I'm on the school council, Jords,' Freya explains. 'And I can tell you that Mrs Vickers has gone bat-shit crazy about what happened to Lilly and got the school really worked up. She's emailed every parent to get them to demand therapists to speak to anyone who is traumatized by what happened. She thinks the school needs to investigate whether it's something contagious. Like meningitis.'

'The only thing that's contagious is Mrs Vickers,' jokes Jordy. 'She's always been loco. No wonder her poor daughter is such a fruit loop.' He looks around waiting to land a laugh but the mood has soured.

'Isn't meningitis the illness where you turn purple and they amputate your leg and then you die?' panics Hayley. 'If it's contagious, I'll definitely get it.'

'You haven't sat next to Lil since the beginning of term,' Jordy points out. 'I'm far more likely to catch something.'

Grace doesn't like the sound of this. It smacks of hysteria.

She remembers the five missed calls from Catriona Vickers and regrets not speaking to her because she could have explained that Lilly's blood tests indicate there is no infection. Then she resents worrying about Catriona when all her attention should be focused on Lilly.

'Apparently Mrs Vickers thinks it's more likely connected to something bad in the environment,' says Freya.

Mia nudges Grace in the ribs when she hears this.

'Like what?' Jordy asks.

'There's shit everywhere, isn't there?' says Hayley. 'The food we eat, the air we breathe, the water we drink. They even found micro beads in the Antarctic, didn't they? Maybe Lil caught something swimming in the sluice.'

'That's because it's next to the archaeological site, Mum,' whispers Mia. 'I told you they've brought trouble upon us.'

'Why aren't we all affected, then?' Grace replies.

'Maybe it will come for us all,' says Mia.

'You saved Lilly's life,' says Hayley, linking her arm through Freya's. 'You were as cool-headed as Mr Galveston. Unlike me.' Cormack tries to put an arm around Hayley but she shakes him off.

'I saw her foaming at the mouth,' someone else chips in.

'Foaming? For real?'

'Like a rabid dog.'

'That's what happens if you can't swallow,' says Freya.

'Lilly swallows all right. Lilly does everything.'

There is some edgy laughter.

'Fucking fuck off, Cormack,' says Jordy.

'What does he mean, Mum?' Mia asks. 'What does he mean about Lilly swallowing?'

'Just ignore them. It's boys being silly,' says Grace, in a forced bright tone. 'Let's try to overtake so we can speak to Miss Swain before the other parents arrive.'

'Don't tell me you haven't thought about it, Jordy boy,' shouts Cormack, dancing backwards away from Jordy so that Grace can see his face. He's good-looking. She'll grant him that. Not far from the kind of boy she went for at the same age. But she'd thought Lilly would make better decisions than her. *You're so fucking obvious*, she wants to tell him.

'I've seen the way you look at her.'

'Have some respect, road man,' says Jordy. He puts his head down and runs at Cormack, barrelling into his stomach, like a ram.

Although Cormack is taller and more muscular, Jordy has the advantage of surprise. The force pushes Cormack against the wall of the car park. Winded, he buckles over, gasping for air. 'You got me there, Jordy,' he pants.

Grace urges Mia through the throng, evil-eyeing Cormack as they accelerate past. The group of teenagers falls silent.

'Isn't that Lil's little sister?' someone asks.

'Awkward,' mutters Freya, looking down at her black leather boots.

Jordy stiffly waves his hand in greeting.

'Hi, Mrs Vermuyden. Hi, Mia,' he says, blushing so red that even the tips of his ears are burning. He's wearing heart-shaped purple sunglasses, which remind Grace of times gone by when he and Lilly used to play dressing up. He pushes them up on to his head. Grace knows he wants to ask about Lilly but understands that he's too flustered – they must have heard what just happened – to form a sensible sentence. *I've got your back.* Grace remembers the message as she waves to him. Maybe Patrick is right. There's nothing in it. He's a good kid.

'How's your eel, Mia?' Cormack pants on the pavement as he rubs his stomach.

103

Mia looks back at him over her shoulder. 'He's good,' she says confidently.

'I'll have to come and see him again,' says Cormack, turning into the car park of the secondary school with the rest of them. He doesn't give Grace a second glance.

'Have you met that boy before?' Grace questions Mia, as they head across the road.

'Cormack, you mean?' Grace nods. 'Of course,' says Mia, as she surges forward, with a hint of swagger in her stride.

'Where?'

'At our house,' Mia says smugly, evidently relishing the shock value of this information. She glances back at Grace.

'How come?' Grace tries to keep her voice steady so that Mia can't detect how much she wants to know.

'If I tell you, will you do a story in your newsletter about what's happening to Tas's family?'

'I can't do that, Mia,' says Grace. 'It's not the kind of thing we put in the newsletter.'

'Why?'

'It's too political.'

'Then I won't tell you about Lilly and Cormack,' says Mia, stubbornly. 'Strictly speaking, I don't need you to come into school with me any more.' She marches across the playground in her clumpy boots, head held high, as if she has suddenly discovered that being the younger sister of Lilly Vermuyden means she is no longer invisible.

By the time she turns into the hospital car park a chill of apprehension has settled in Grace's bones. It reminds her of the sudden mists that roll in from the Fens and hang over the house, like a veil, so that even the air you breathe inside is cold. It's the feeling of her childhood. The nerve-jangling sense that something bad can happen at any moment and she is powerless to do anything about it.

I'm losing perspective.

Again.

Impetuously, she decides to give Nuala a call before she goes into the hospital.

Nuala picks up after one ring as if she's been expecting her. 'Grace,' she says warmly. 'I've been thinking about you so much. How's Lil doing?'

Grace gives her an update. She hears herself speak and thinks her tone sounds shrill so she tries to slow down and ends up too guarded. 'As well as can be expected. They're pleased with her progress so far. But it's early days.'

'How long do you think she'll be in hospital?'

'We'll know more this morning. I'm on my way to see her right now.'

There's a lull in conversation. There was a time when Grace and Nuala used to have easy chats over coffee together a couple of times a month. They took Lilly and Hayley to London to see Glee Live and lived close enough to help each other out during the school holidays; a couple of years ago they had even gone to Center Parcs for a family weekend together. But Patrick struggled with Nuala's husband, George, a property developer, who always drank at lunchtime and became belligerently opposed to anything from paying taxes to migrants, even though most of his workforce was East European. 'Nothing like a good debate, Patrick.' The last time they had seen each other, he had argued that history of art should be struck off the A-level curriculum and accused Patrick of lacking a sense of humour when he angrily pointed out it would leave him without a job. After that she had seen Nuala alone or at book club.

Now they don't see each other often enough to slip

into easy familiarity but there is the awkwardness of once having been intimate. Grace imagines Nuala sitting at her desk at the law firm where she works as a paralegal, winding strands of her long straight hair around her finger with the hand that isn't holding the phone, and wishes she were the one going to work instead of visiting her daughter in hospital. She's even missing Tony and his aphorism of the week, which he writes on the whiteboard every Monday morning.

How could this happen to us?

'Are you still there?'

She looks at the phone lying in her lap and is almost surprised to hear Nuala's voice speaking to her. 'Of course I'm still here,' Grace says smoothly.

'I was just saying we're here to help,' says Nuala, nervously. 'You don't have to go through this alone, Grace.'

'That's very kind of you. And thanks for having Lilly to stay so much in the summer holidays.' Grace allows herself a brief moment of self-congratulation for splicing the question she really wants to ask so effortlessly on to their exchange. Nuala's answer is contained in the silence that follows. Grace guesses that she is doing a quick calculation to work out the appropriate ratio of honesty and lie.

'She didn't stay with us much,' Nuala says finally. 'No more than a couple of nights. But it was always lovely to see her.'

'That's what I meant. Thanks for putting her up until she'd got the bus route sorted. It was a big help.'

'I'm not sure if you know,' Nuala tentatively adds, 'but Hayley and Lilly have had a falling-out. Over a boy. You know I try to stay out of these things, but I think it all came to a head at that festival they went to at the end of the holidays. Hayley wouldn't tell me the details. Sometimes it's best not to know.' She gives an overwrought laugh.

'In my experience, it's never best not to know,' says Grace, imperiously. 'Lil didn't go to the festival. She was at Mr Galveston's extra-English course.'

'I don't want to make anything more difficult for you, Grace, because I know how you get worked up about these things. And I didn't say anything because I didn't realize until after they'd left that Lilly hadn't told you, but a group of them all went together and shared a tent.'

'Who?' asks Grace, abruptly.

'Lilly, Hayley, Jordy and the boy they fell out over. Cormack.'

As Grace walks into the hospital, brief vignettes of Lilly's life flash past. She remembers teaching her to read and the way she tore words apart with such savage intent that Patrick described it as a crime against consonants. She finished the entire series of Biff and Chip in less than a month and was appalled at how boring their life seemed, which, perhaps, was a clue to some part of Lilly's personality that Grace had overlooked. With Mia it was completely different. Patrick patiently drew the letters in the air like a conductor. 'B is big stick down, circle away from my body.' But even after months she still couldn't recognize the second letter of the alphabet.

Any setbacks only renewed Grace's determination to give both her girls every opportunity that she had missed out on. She took Lilly to swimming lessons almost as soon as she could walk, before she could intuit Grace's own terror of water. When Lilly declared that she felt more at home in water than on dry land, Grace cried so much that she had to pretend she was overcome with chlorine fumes. She was elated. *History would not repeat itself.* For years they got up together at six o'clock in the morning three times a week so that Lilly could train in the pool before school. Mia lacked Lilly's co-ordination but not her energy. Her crawl was frenetic but unproductive, as if she was swimming on the spot. 'I'll never be as good as Lilly at anything,' Mia used to sob. Grace urged patience, promising Mia that one day she would make her mark.

When Lilly was little, Grace used to record everything, from what she ate to how many hours she slept. No one had worked harder to make life secure and predictable for her children. Patrick teased her that there were schedules of schedules. Repeat orders of repeat orders. Direct debits of direct debits. And still it wasn't enough. Because when it came to the big stuff, like Lilly's first boyfriend, Grace hadn't even clocked his existence, let alone that she had obviously spent every Saturday night at his house throughout the entire summer holiday.

She needs to apply the same level of forensic attention to Lilly's life now as she did when she was a baby. She resolves to find out everything that has been going on. Who Lilly has been spending time with. Where they have been hanging out. She needs to know everything about Lilly that she doesn't know.

6

Lilly feels like a fraud. She's the only person in the room who doesn't have a proper illness. The curtains that close around each cubicle give the illusion of privacy but she can hear everything that is said. So she knows the woman in the bed next to her has an incurable disease that makes her speech slurred and her eyelids droop like a bloodhound's; the girl opposite became paralysed over a two-week period, like she was being slowly encased in plaster of Paris (her words); and the teenager in the corner can't stand up without falling over. Two other women are unable to speak because they have holes cut in their throats in order to breathe. Unlike these patients, *who are literally dying*, she's lounging in bed, wondering where her mobile phone is; worrying about the *Beowulf* essay – 'Morality is a veil that can be dropped at any second' – that she was meant to hand in this morning, especially because her grades have tanked this term; and imagining the swimming gala next week where she's doing front crawl and butterfly.

She wants to message Hayley about the weird illnesses she has seen on the neurology ward. She knows she would be irresistibly interested because Hayley loves a bit of gore. She remembers when Emma Vickers once sliced her finger to the bone with a scalpel during a DT class and Hayley held the two flaps of skin together, squealing until the first-aider arrived, whereupon she pretended to faint in Jordy's arms.

Now she's stuck in here, Lilly misses her more than ever. She's hoping her collapse might make Hayley feel sorry for her or at least soften the hard shell she has built around herself. The way Hayley cried yesterday when she thought she was dying gives her hope. Lilly half wonders whether, if she told her everything, Hayley might find a way to forgive her. But no matter how she tries, Lilly can't get Cormack out of her mind, which means that whatever she said would be a lie and there are already too many of those.

She can still remember the exact expression on Hayley's face when she discovered what had been going on between her and Cormack at the end of the holidays. It was the final evening of the music festival and they had slipped away from Jordy and Hayley before the end of Waze and Odyssey to go back to their four-man tent. *Why not four-woman? And why man and not men?* Lilly kept asking. Every time she said this they all giggled as if she were the main act on *Saturday Night Live*. The laughs came easily because they were all baked on some weed Cormack had scored from the pub and she no longer cared if Grace found out she had ditched Mr Galveston's holiday course.

Now she finds it difficult to explain why she went along with Cormack's insistence that no one should know about their relationship or how they managed to keep it under wraps. Usually at St Edith's even the most inconsequential hook-up made headlines. At first it seemed immaterial. Lilly couldn't believe Cormack was interested in her, and she convinced herself that the inevitable end would be less humiliating if no one else knew. Besides, she quickly learnt that the secrecy heightened the excitement.

Lilly couldn't quite believe that she could simultaneously

deceive her mother into thinking she was spending the night at Hayley's, while Hayley assumed Cormack was dropping her home. It was so easy. She never felt bad about misleading her parents. Especially her mum. There were very good reasons not to be home that summer. But as the weeks turned into months she felt increasingly guilty and anxious that Hayley didn't know. Then it became too late to say anything. At least, this was Cormack's view. The realization that he got off on the deception crept up slowly. He would Snapchat her when they were all together, sending her filthy messages that turned her into a hot mess; touch her when the others weren't looking; and put her on edge by revealing things about her that only Hayley should know.

That night they hadn't bothered to zip up the tent. This oversight was less about risk-taking and more about when they had sex the rest of the world receded, until it almost felt as if they were visible only to each other. Lilly had always imagined she would share every detail of her first boyfriend with Hayley but there was something so mysterious about the pleasure they could give each other that she didn't want to put it into words.

Hayley came back to look for them all before the end of the DJ set. Her head poked round the tent flap. Cormack was on top of Lilly, his back to Hayley, jeans and pants halfway down his thighs. Lilly's dress was ruched up around her waist. The soft familiar features of Hayley's face, the smudge of lips, the almond-shaped eyes and snub nose that usually worked in flattering unity fragmented as she took in the scene until she was all flashing eyes, twisted mouth and flared nostrils. Cormack turned round, saw her, and kept going. Lilly tried to push him off. She thinks he asked Hayley to join in. 'Fuck you. Fuck both of you,' Hayley said.

Those were the last words she had addressed to Lilly until yesterday. Hayley left and they kept going.

Lilly's mind turns to the present. She starts prioritizing everything she needs to do. She's behind on her background reading for English and hasn't revised for her biology test on homeostasis. Going to university is more important than ever now that there is nothing else left. She has to escape. From her mum. From Hayley. From the new house with no history. And from Cormack because there's too much history. The knot in her stomach tightens. She can't afford to waste any more time in here. She looks at the clock on the wall and estimates that she has already lost seven hours of study time. She needs her phone. She wants to contact Jordy to check if he has the notebook. And she wants to reiterate to her little sister that if she mentions the pregnancy test to anyone, she will definitely tell her parents Mia stole the iPhone from Bea Vickers.

Yesterday, Mia had waited until Grace and Patrick went to the hospital shop to tell her that half of Anglo-Saxon women died during childbirth. 'Is that why you had an abortion? Were you scared you might die?' she asked.

'No,' Lilly had hissed. 'But you'll be dead if you mention it again.'

Lilly spots Grace and Patrick hovering in the side room, waiting for the afternoon ward round to finish. She is dreading seeing them. Her dad waves through the glass window and she gives a half-hearted wave back. She can almost tolerate his false cheer and effort to pretend everything is normal. Her mum, however, is a different prospect. She could tell yesterday that she was itching to ask her questions, which was why she pretended she needed to get some more sleep. Some kind of inquisition about Cormack is inevitable. She could kill Mia for opening her mouth about that.

Luckily, the consultant, Dr Santini, leaves her till last. Even though the medical students who accompany him are embarrassingly close to her in age, Lilly tries to be as interesting as possible so that they don't want to leave. When one asks whether she could sense the seizure was about to happen she goes into a long description about the sickly-sweet smell and the sensation of being dragged backwards into a dark tunnel. In hospital you're only as interesting as your illness, and in the hierarchy of disease on this ward, Lilly realizes she is definitely at the bottom of the ladder. Dr Santini simply lists the tests she is due to have today. But just as he finishes herding his students towards the door there is a reprieve: he unexpectedly turns back towards her. 'I'd like a quick word, Lilly, in private, before I speak to your parents. Is that okay?' He smiles. He has no hair on his face and his skin is as smooth and burnished as the Etruscan statues her dad lectures about. She fights the urge to reach out and stroke his cheek.

'Sure,' she says.

'I'd like to know exactly what was going on in the hours before the seizure. Describe everything. I'm interested in all the details. Even if they seem boring to you.' He sits on the chair, pen poised. 'In my experience, the first time an event like this occurs is always the most illustrative.' He stares at her for a beat too long.

Lilly describes the classroom, the discussion about *Beowulf* and the heat. She mentions the feeling of nausea, the electric-shock sensation in her arms and legs and the feeling of detachment. The doctor commends her precision. He lets her talk. It's like writing an essay, really. Point, evidence, conclusion. When she finishes, he puts the lid on the pen, tucks it into his pocket and lays down the medical notes on the bed beside her. She waits for him to congratulate her because hospital seems to be the one place you get praised for everything. Even peeing into a bottle. He pauses again.

'Lilly, do you understand what patient confidentiality is?' he asks.

'It's like being a Catholic priest and hearing confession, isn't it?'

He laughs. 'Something like that. It means that anything you say to me is completely private. You're seventeen years old and I don't need to tell your parents everything you tell me. The reason I'm asking is that I want you to feel that you can be completely honest with me.'

'Fire away.' She shrugs. 'In the interests of honesty.'

'Has anything like this happened to you before?'

She stares into his dark eyes. His eyebrows are now arranged in a sorrowful shape so they arch up in the middle and down at the sides. He licks his lips nervously. She knows right away that he knows.

'No.' He looks disappointed and she feels bad because she wants to please him.

'Are you sure about that?' he doggedly continues.

'I am.'

'It's just I can see you received medical treatment at a festival in the summer. Six weeks ago, I think. The notes are a little sketchy, but if that was your first seizure, it would be even more useful if you tell me about what happened then.' His face is so kind that she is almost tempted to tell him everything. He wouldn't be judgemental. She remembers Jordy recounting his favourite Buzzfeed story during an English class when they were meant to be composing kennings. A series of X-rays titled, 'Objects people have lost in their arse', including a Buzz Lightyear figure and a light bulb. *Gives new meaning to infinity and beyond*, she had joked, making Jordy laugh so hard that Mr Galveston sent him out into the corridor. There's nothing that can shock a doctor.

'There must be a mistake. And please don't mention the festival in front of my parents. They don't know I went.'

'I'm not here to judge you. I'm here to give you the best possible treatment. And to give you the best possible treatment, I need you to tell me everything.' He looks at her so earnestly that she feels sorry for him. It must be terrible to care so much about people you don't even know. It's painful enough caring about the people you do know. Like her mum.

She glances at the window of the small side room attached to the neurology ward where her parents are waiting and sees Grace staring at her. It will take too long to explain to him and Grace will get suspicious and ask questions. Besides, Lilly is almost positive her mother can lip-read. She can certainly read documents upside-down because she once told her it was a key journalistic skill, albeit not very relevant when your main beat is lost cats and giant marrows. That's another thing she's never going to do that her mother has done: step back from her career and live through her children. Grace has crushed her with the weight of her expectation.

'This isn't the first time this has happened, is it?' Dr Santini asks one last time.

Lilly doesn't reply. Instead she picks at the loose thread in the hospital sheet and twists it into the letter C.

Grace and Patrick have been waiting for Dr Santini to give the signal to come in for almost an hour. Patrick has made the most of his time to write up revision notes on potential exam questions for his A-level students; he has exchanged a series of messages with his mum about Lilly's progress; and has turned to news about the Indian summer. More of the same. Roads melting in the heat. Rails buckling. River levels at an all-time low. Fish suffocating from lack of oxygen. At least it means the house might dry out properly. By winter everything will be sorted. He's hoping that, caught up in the vortex of IVF, Rob might even forget the money Patrick owes him.

'Are you worrying about Lilly?' Grace asks him.

'No.' He sees the intent expression on her face and knows he's better off answering the question in the affirmative. 'Yes.'

They've already had a skirmish over her outlandish theory that Lilly's seizure could have been triggered by mould in the upstairs bathroom. Especially after Grace revealed that she had unilaterally contracted a company in the city that is going to charge more than a thousand pounds to test spores that will disappear as soon as the damp-proofing is finished and the extractor fan properly connected. He sighs and goes back to his phone.

His composure irritates Grace, who restlessly paces up and down the room beside the window, alternating between checking if Dr Santini is ready for them and googling anything from photos of mould to the symptoms of multiple sclerosis on her phone. She doesn't want to allow any space for bad thoughts to worm in or time for thinking.

She looks around the room again. She can tell from the décor that this is a place where bad news is routinely delivered. There are four hard plastic chairs uncomfortably arranged around a low table scattered with out-of-date magazines, an empty tissues box, and a number for the hospital chaplain. Her stomach churns again.

She returns to the subject of what she overheard outside school two days earlier. The horrible way Cormack spoke about Lilly; the incontrovertible truth that they were sleeping with each other; how all the talk was about Lilly's seizure and the way she foamed at the mouth. Patrick, meanwhile, has put aside his phone and is slouched over a three-year-old copy of *Country Life*.

'I don't trust him,' she says.

'Good headline, don't you think?' he asks, holding up the magazine cover in front of his face for her to see. '*Little Owl. Big Attitude*. You couldn't have come up with anything better yourself.'

'Why do you always do that?' she asks.

'Do what?'

'Change the subject whenever something difficult comes up.'

'I don't.'

'You do.'

'You're losing perspective, Grace. I told you the first time you mentioned that boy. Our priority right now is Lilly's health. Not a relationship that is already over. I'm not going to feed your anxiety.'

'She lied to us about the festival too.'

'She isn't the first teenager to keep a secret from her parents. Especially when she knew that you would never agree to her going.'

'We,' says Grace emphatically. 'We didn't want her to go. Not just me.'

'Actually, I told her I thought it would be nice for her to hang out with her friends when she mentioned Hayley was going. You were the one who was so opposed to the whole thing.'

'Well, why didn't you tell me that?'

117

'I did. But you never want to listen.' He puts down the magazine. 'How about we deal with the festival later? Please.'

'That's what you say about everything. So nothing gets dealt with until it's too late.'

Her discontent feels cosmic, like a black hole that is about to swallow her. She turns her back on Patrick and skim-reads a red and white poster outlining the symptoms of sepsis. *Sepsis takes the lives of eighteen children every day*, it says. She notes that one of the symptoms is seizures and feels certain that the doctor is about to tell them that this is Lilly's diagnosis. She remembers her cutting her foot at the swimming pool a couple of weeks ago and refusing to wear a plaster.

Grace closes her eyes and breathes deeply to calm her nerves. When she opens them, her attention is drawn to another poster on the opposite wall that she hadn't noticed before. Three sub-headings. 'SAD' reads the acronym down the side. Sex. Alcohol. Drugs. *Lilly does everything*, it reads across the top in big letters. She blinks a couple of times. The poster blurs until it disappears. She moves closer to the wall where she saw it hanging but there is nothing there, only the dusty outline of where a picture might once have been. Her heart pounds and her face grows hotter and hotter. There was a period in her life before she met Patrick when Grace Did Everything. She wonders if Patrick's goodness is as limitless as her badness. And whether badness is genetic.

'He's calling us in,' says Patrick. When Grace doesn't move he leans over and gently touches her knee. 'Are you okay?' he asks.

Their mighty prince, the storied leader, sat stricken and helpless, humiliated by the loss of his guard, bewildered and stunned, staring aghast. The quote that Lilly can never remember from *Beowulf* comes to her as soon as she sees her mum stutter into the ward. She looks awful, as if she's slept in her clothes or, rather, hasn't slept. Her jaw is set fast with tension, like a pug with an underbite. She's not wearing make-up. Her mouth is a pale pink straight line, her skin is blotchy and red, and there are dark circles under her eyes. Lilly is shocked but she refuses to feel sorry for her. *This is all her fault.* She's unnerved by the certainty of her reaction.

As Grace reaches the bed she stumbles. She rights herself on the arm of the chair but the entire CD collection of Seamus Heaney reciting *Beowulf* falls from her handbag on to the floor, closely followed by a wedge of A-level biology practice papers and medical documents on seizures that she has printed out. Dr Santini bends down to pick everything up while Grace embraces Lilly. 'How are you feeling, darling? Did you have a good sleep? Can I get you anything?'

Lilly quickly disentangles herself. 'Do you know where my phone is, Mum? I really need it.'

'The nurse gave it to us to take home. It was out of charge. He thinks you should have a digital detox.'

'You've been doing your homework, Mrs Vermuyden,' jokes the doctor, as he hands back piles of papers.

God, she's so embarrassing!

'And Lilly's too, by the look of it,' jokes Patrick, as he puts the *Beowulf* CDs in the right order.

'I read that a third of all seizures have an underlying cause,' says Grace, undeterred by their teasing. 'Intracranial haemorrhage, head injury, excessive alcohol, brain infection, meningitis, encephalitis . . . How can you know exactly what has caused it?'

'You're quite right,' says Dr Santini. 'But the MRI results

from this morning mean we can rule out some of those and we don't think her clinical features would make any of the others very likely. It's a process of elimination.'

'That's great news,' says Patrick. 'Isn't it, Grace?'

The doctor continues. 'I've done a very thorough neurological investigation and I can't find anything to worry about. Lilly's reflexes are good, her eyesight is normal and there is no loss of strength in any of her muscles.'

'Wonderful. Isn't that good, Lil?' gushes Patrick, who is being embarrassing in his own way by trying to overcompensate for Grace's anxiety. 'You're making such good progress.'

She evil-eyes him. *I wish they'd both leave and never come back.*

Dr Santini is unerringly patient and kind. It strikes Lilly that patience is one of the most underrated human qualities. She thinks of Jordy and the way he flits from screen to screen, from biology to English, from loving swimming to hating swimming, skating over the surface of life, without ever stopping to examine what lies beneath. Maybe if she's patient Cormack will want her again.

'The only elements we're keeping an eye on at the moment are her temperature, which is slightly raised, as well a borderline increase in her white cell count that I'm going to re-test. But these could both be caused by the stress of yesterday's seizure. The EEG will hopefully tell us a lot more about the electrical activity in Lilly's brain. It's one of the best ways of spotting abnormalities.'

He flashes a smile and goes into a brief description of the EEG and how the worst thing about it is trying to pick off the glue left by the electrodes stuck to one's scalp when it's over.

'When will you know the results?' Lilly asks.

'If there's an anomaly, almost immediately,' he says. He

turns towards her parents. 'We've been trying to build a picture of exactly what was happening just before Lilly's seizure. It seems she was feeling a little stressed by her English teacher.'

'What do you mean?' asks Grace, in astonishment. 'Lilly loves Mr Galveston. She's his star student.'

'It sounds like a very competitive class,' he says.

'Not when you're at the top of it, like Lil,' says Grace, unequivocally.

'Not any more, Mum,' says Lilly. It gives her pleasure to see the disappointment on Grace's face. 'The seizure happened after Mr Galveston gave back my essay. I was reading his notes at the bottom. He says I'm too unsure about my own opinions.'

'That doesn't sound like a very sensible strategy for building confidence,' observes Dr Santini.

'She's a straight-A student,' Grace interjects. 'He has understandably high expectations.'

'Is this important to you, Mrs Vermuyden?' He turns towards Grace. 'I noticed that you said something similar the other day. About Lilly's grades.' His tone is curious rather than challenging.

'Anything that is important to Lilly is important to me,' says Grace, haughtily.

'What exactly did he say at the bottom of the essay?' Patrick asks.

'He said that mediocrity is self-inflicted and genius is self-bestowed,' says Lilly. 'He thinks I'm not working hard enough. But I can't put in any more hours unless I stay up through the night.'

'Lilly tells me that she's been feeling a lot of anxiety at school this term,' Dr Santini says, turning to Grace and Patrick. 'She's feeling the pressure from her teacher and she's anxious that you might be disappointed if she doesn't get the results you're hoping for.'

'She's been preparing for some important exams,' says Grace, brightly. 'It's a very demanding process.'

'I'm wondering if her test results are fine, and she goes back to school, whether it might be a good idea to move her out of this class to reduce the potential for further stress.'

'There's no evidence this has got anything to do with her illness,' says Grace, tightly. Her phone starts to ring. She looks down at the number. 'I'm sorry but I need to get this,' she says apologetically. 'It's Mia's school.'

Miss Swain's face kaleidoscopes on the other side of the revolving door as teachers and children pour out of school so it's impossible to get a fix on her expression, although Grace is pleased to see she has a protective arm around Mia. The atmosphere is uncharacteristically subdued: swollen-eyed kids, who would usually sling school bags on to the ground and race noisily to queue at the ice-cream van, instead allow their parents to hold them close. Everyone knows that, for the second time in less than a week, a child from a local school who arrived perfectly healthy has left unconscious in an ambulance. Less than an hour ago, a paramedic had carried Tas through this same door and gently lifted him on to a stretcher waiting in the playground, where he lay on his side in the foetal position, staring into space. It was rumoured that the whites of his eyes had turned blood red.

Teachers are careful to avoid the searching gaze of parents as they leave and hurry away, eyes fixed on the ground. They have been instructed to stick to the facts: a boy in year six collapsed (*don't* mention seizures); he has been taken to hospital (*just* as a precaution); they are aware of a similar case at the neighbouring secondary school (*no one* can be sure they are connected); head teachers from both schools are co-ordinating a response with the help of health officials (but they can't agree on what to say).

'What if Catriona is right and it's something contagious?' Grace panics, scarcely able to take in that another family is going through the same trauma as them. 'Lilly and Tas have obviously got the same illness. What happens if Mia catches it too?'

'Let's not jump to conclusions until we've got all the facts lined up,' says Patrick. But Grace can tell he's already jumped from the way he keeps shifting nervously from one foot to the other.

'Do you think mould could be growing in Tas's caravan?'

'Have you been inside? It's immaculate.' There's a note of impatience in his tone.

Many of the children stop to speak to Mia before they leave. Some even give her a hug, including a couple of the girls who had spent the best part of last year tormenting her by setting up an Instagram account solely dedicated to discussing her choice of school shoes. At one point an arc of smaller children crowds around while Mia answers their questions. She gives some of them a reassuring pat on the head. Grace notes a couple are wearing their sweaters back to front in Mia's honour.

'She's being so brave, isn't she?' Grace whispers to Patrick. 'She's had to cope with so much over the past week.'

'Mia is made of tough stuff,' agrees Patrick.

When everyone has gone they eagerly cram into the same compartment of the revolving door. Grace finds herself pressed up against Patrick's back as they take shuffling baby steps to push the door forward. Her cheek sticks to his shirt. They must look ridiculous. When they emerge in the atrium Mia surges forward and wraps her arms around both of them. 'How's Lil?' she whispers.

'She's doing great. More importantly, how are you?' asks Patrick, tilting her chin up towards him to plant a kiss on her forehead. Her face is pale, bringing into relief the unruly constellation of freckles on her nose and cheeks.

'Did you hear what happened?' Mia asks.

'That's why we're here, Mimi,' says Grace, stroking her hair. 'We came as soon as we were told.'

'Tas is gravely ill,' she says, nodding sagely. 'Gravely.'

Miss Swain steps forward and shakes hands with Patrick and Grace, her attempt at reassuring efficiency undermined by smudged mascara and the dark circles of sweat under the armpits of her pale grey silk shirt. 'Thank you for coming,' she says, squeezing Grace's forearm. 'Especially when your other daughter is in hospital. It must be a very stressful time for you both.'

She leads them to the year-six classroom, explaining that she wants to ask Mia some questions in order to pass on a formal account to the headmistress and the public-health authorities, who have been called in to investigate the mystery illness.

'It's classed as an outbreak if two students have the same illness,' she explains. 'Mia is the only person who was there from the beginning of Tas's seizure. She is the main witness.'

'I will do anything to help Tas,' Mia says, her voice quivering with emotion. 'He is the kindest friend I have ever had.'

For the second time in a week, Grace finds herself in Mia's classroom. A lonely rucksack and lunchbox sit next to her daughter's desk in the front row.

'They belong to Tas,' Mia says solemnly, touching the bags with her fingertip, as though they're sacred objects, as she walks past.

This time Miss Swain has arranged an arc of adult-sized

chairs around her desk. 'First of all,' says Miss Swain, urging them to take a seat, 'I want to tell you how incredibly courageous Mia has been. We've all been so impressed by her maturity and quick thinking.' She shoots an approving glance at Mia, who almost imperceptibly nods, as if to indicate that she will, on this occasion, deign to accept Miss Swain's compliment. Miss Swain looks grateful.

Grace can see that the balance of power has completely tilted on its axis since the beginning of the week.

'Is there anything I can get you before we start, Mia?' Miss Swain asks. 'Would you like a glass of water?'

'Can I have a double ice cream with two chocolate Flakes and sprinkles, please?' Mia replies. She stares beatifically into the distance, knowing full well that Grace is in no position to deliver her usual spiel on how sugar is poison and makes her hyperactive.

'Of course,' says Miss Swain, with an indulgent smile. She phones through to the school office and instructs someone to fetch an ice cream from the van outside.

'Shall I start?' Mia asks.

'Take your time,' says Miss Swain, opening her notebook and picking up a pen. 'And if you need a break at any point, please tell me straight away. You've been through a very tough experience.'

Three heads turn towards Mia. She sits completely erect, lips moving, as though she's replaying the scene in her head. When she finally starts speaking her voice is loud and clear.

'It's afternoon break. I'm playing Anglo-Saxons with Tas. He's my horse and I'm getting him ready him for a race so I put a skipping rope around his waist to train him. We run up and down the playground until he starts to get really sweaty.'

Grace nudges Patrick. Why is she speaking in the present

tense? Miss Swain doesn't seem concerned because she's too busy trying to record everything, but Grace worries that Mia might be suffering from shock. There is a lot of extraneous detail. Mia describes how she picks a scab from her knee and shares it with Tas because the Anglo-Saxons suffered from iron deficiency. The school bell makes the horse jump and she calms him down by saying a prayer to Woden.

'Woden?' Patrick asks in confusion.

'He's the king of the Anglo-Saxon gods,' Mia explains. 'Shall I recite it?'

'I don't think that's absolutely necessary,' says Miss Swain, who is obviously struggling to keep up. She shakes the pen because the ink isn't flowing fast enough.

'Once we finish Tas's training I take him to his stable,' she says. Miss Swain looks perplexed. 'We use the playhouse underneath the climbing frame,' she explains. 'I pick grass to put on the ground so it's nice and soft for him. We sit cross-legged in the stable and share a snack. But Tas only takes the smallest bites.'

'Why is that?' asks Grace.

'Because he's too worried to eat,' Mia says impatiently. 'Someone from the council came to see his mum and her family yesterday to tell her they need to start looking for somewhere else to live. The archaeologists think there is an entire Anglo-Saxon village buried underneath the caravans. Tas wants to stay there and the stress of it all is making his mum ill.'

'Surely this can't be right,' exclaims Patrick. 'That Travellers' site has been there since I was a kid.'

'Tas's mum says that the *gorjas* care more about the eels going extinct than they do about them losing their home.' She turns to Grace. 'It's true, Mum. You wrote a story about the eels but you wouldn't write anything about Tas's family.'

'What exactly did you feed your horse?' asks Miss Swain. 'Was it something you found on the playing field? A wild plant, perhaps? Or even a mushroom?'

'Don't be silly. It was Manriklo.'

'That doesn't sound very Anglo-Saxon,' Patrick intervenes.

'Is it horse food?' asks Grace.

'No.' Mia snorts. 'It's a kind of bread with pork inside that Rawnie makes. I eat half of it and nothing happens to me so I doubt it's got anything to do with Tas's illness.' She starts to tell Patrick and Grace how the only animals the Anglo-Saxons raised to eat were pigs because they produce piglets so quickly. Sheep were used for wool. Cows for milk. And when they died they used their fat for oil lamps. 'The smell of melting animal fat must have been truly awful,' Mia says. Miss Swain puts down her pen and rubs her fingers. 'A live eel smells bad enough. Did you know, Miss Swain, that I keep a pet eel in my bedroom?'

'I don't think I did know that, Mia.' She sounds exhausted.

'In the Middle Ages there were so many eels in the Fens that they became a currency known as fish silver,' Mia explains. 'That's why the town where my grandparents used to live is called Ely. It was paid for with eels. My other grandparents died in mysterious circumstances. We don't even have any photos of them.'

'That's very interesting,' says Miss Swain.

'And then what happened?' Grace asks. She's desperate for clues that might link Tas's illness with Lilly. More than anything, she wants a diagnosis. The uncertainty is nerve-shredding.

'We sipped mead,' says Mia.

'You drank alcohol on the school premises?' asks Miss Swain.

'Of course not.' Mia tuts at Miss Swain's stupidity. 'It was Coca-Cola mixed with water.'

'When exactly did you first notice there was something wrong with Tas?'

Mia waits for a beat. 'It happens like this. Tas holds up his hands in front of him and asks if I can see anything wrong with them. He says it feels like the flesh inside has been stung by a thousand stinging nettles. I take his hands in my own and tell him not to worry, that he actually has pins and needles.' Miss Swain writes this down and underlines it in red ink. 'When I touch his fingers, they're boiling hot. It's the same with his face. He's burning up. I pour the mead over his head to cool him down and ask him if he wants me to fetch you, Miss Swain, but he says he doesn't want to be left alone. That he wants to stay with me for the rest of our lives but his mother won't let him marry a *gorja* and if he has to move we'll never see each other again.'

'A *gorja*?' Miss Swain asks.

'Someone who isn't Roma. A settled person. Like us,' Grace explains.

For the first time since she started, Mia's lower lip starts to wobble. 'I should have got help straight away. That was my big mistake.'

Miss Swain stops writing and looks up at her. 'Tas wanted you to stay. That's what a good friend does.'

'You don't have to talk about this now unless you want to, Mia,' says Grace, gently. 'It's too soon.'

Mia closes her eyes for a moment. When she opens them they are brimming over with tears. 'Does it help Tas if I go on?' she asks.

'The more the doctors know, the easier it is to get the right help for him,' says Miss Swain.

'And for Lilly,' Grace adds. 'It sounds as though they

have been through a very similar experience.' She doesn't want to call it an illness to avoid making Mia even more worried.

'Very well,' says Mia. She gets out of her chair, puts her hands behind her back and sticks out her chest. 'Tas looks as though he's trying to get up. He opens and closes his mouth but no words come out. Like Elvis. His face goes deathly pale and his eyes turn as red as garnets. I put my hand in front of his mouth to feel his breath but there's not even a whisper.' Her voice lowers. 'I lean over, hold his nose and put my mouth on his and blow as hard as I can, like Mr Galveston did for Lilly. Then just as I think I've lost him, his body suddenly jerks and twitches so violently that he knocks over the table.' Everyone jumps as Mia bangs her hand on Miss Swain's desk to demonstrate the crash of the table in the playhouse toppling to the floor.

Patrick glances at his daughter. On the one hand, her account of what happened, with its well-judged changes in tempo, pregnant pauses and variation in tone, is congruent with her innate sense of drama. On the other, there is something almost rehearsed about her delivery. And yet it is less than a couple of hours since Tas fell ill so she can't have had much time to think about what happened. Mia is still staring straight ahead. He traces her gaze to the display board. A huge sign saying 'The Anglo-Saxons' runs across the top. Beneath are different areas describing medieval life. The first is about the Anglo-Saxon love of horses; the second describes the most common illnesses, including iron deficiency; the third is a list of Anglo-Saxon gods, including Woden.

7

Grace wakes up to find herself fully dressed in the wrong bed in the wrong bedroom. She takes a couple of deep breaths and a thick, sickly-sweet smell fills her lungs and nostrils. She swallows and tries to clear her throat but the odour hangs in the air. She recognizes it immediately: it is the smell of her childhood. Patchouli mixed with violet creams and the fug of stale marijuana.

She is transported back to the bedroom of her teenage years. The old survival strategies kick in. She looks round nervously to check whether she has barricaded the door with her chest of drawers and locked the window, then puts out her arm to check on her little brother. But there is no chest of drawers; the bedroom isn't on the ground floor; and Luca is long gone. *I am in Lilly's bed. I am safe. Lilly is in hospital. She is safe.* The smell fades but the nausea lingers, making her feel dizzy. She remembers Lilly's description of her symptoms before the seizure and wonders if she might have caught the same illness. After all, there's no guarantee that adults are protected. *Pull yourself together, Grace. If you get ill, who will look after Lilly?*

It seems incredible now, but when she was pregnant with Lilly, Grace's biggest terror was that she wouldn't be able to love her. She never told anyone, because even articulating this fear seemed deviant. 'I love you, I love you, I love you,' she would tell the bump that was to become Lilly, in the hope that she could conjure up love simply by saying it enough times. She was petrified that if she confided in Patrick, the little he knew about her childhood would breathe oxygen into her anxiety, and his inability to be anything other than sweetly honest would make it impossible for him to disguise his true opinion: that she was damaged and therefore incapable of maternal love.

How do you look after your own children when neither your mother nor your father possessed the parenting gene? This was the question that stalked Grace's first pregnancy. The anxiety was twofold: not only might she have inherited a rogue gene that could predispose her to neglecting her baby, she had no parenting template to follow or reject. Most of her friends ended up tweaking the routines and rituals handed down from their own happy childhoods. They laughed at how their parents left them to cry, tethered in a baby harness, in a pram at the end of the garden, and joked about how it would now be considered child abuse. But they were loved. And Grace wasn't. It would require a superhuman effort to make good the wrongs of her childhood.

'My parents are dead,' she nonchalantly told the other women in her baby group before she gave birth to Lilly. 'It's fine. It was a long time ago.' She had told Patrick, whom she had known for less than a year, the same version of her life story. In some ways it felt like the truth. She hardly knew her father and hadn't seen her mother, Olwyn, since she was fifteen and had barely thought about her again until she was pregnant. It was so much easier than explaining that Olwyn lived in a commune in Devon, in thrall to a guru, who believed he had the power to talk to women's ovaries and that most of life's problems could be cured through vaginal massage. Because she didn't want pity, she quickly added that Patrick's mother, Beth, was 'a complete natural and absolutely on board', which was also true – but her mother-in-law's limitless competence only inflated her own insecurities.

Intuiting her anxiety, Beth kept saying, 'Grace, babies have shared the same priorities since the beginning of time: sleep, feed and nappy change. It will all be A Breeze. A Breeze.' Beth always spoke in capital letters. She couldn't comprehend how Grace had no instincts. Nothing was intuitive. Every element would have to be carefully thought out and learnt.

During one of these exchanges Patrick's father, Lawrence, had looked up over his newspaper. 'You're resilient, Grace,' he declared. 'That's the most important quality in a parent. And a child.' Somehow he understood without knowing.

Her response was to read everything she could about being a parent. She believed that knowledge could compensate for her lack of instinct. Every week throughout her pregnancy and the first year of Lilly's life, new books arrived in the post. She learnt about attachment theory, healthy brain development, co-parenting, conscious parenting and creative parenting. She could cite the latest research on cot death; explain why child mortality rates in the UK were twice those of Sweden; and obsessively dwelt on the fact that drowning was the second highest cause of accidental death in children under the age of five.

At first Patrick was patient. He assumed that all first-time mothers behaved like this and he could hardly criticize Grace for wanting to do the right thing by Lilly. Then when Lilly was born she started buying books for him. *Being a Good Dad in the 21st Century. Dads and Daughters. Making Men into Fathers.* 'Do you think I'm a bad dad?' he asked indignantly. She couldn't see the irony that she was pressing these books into his hands just as he was making up a bottle or changing Lilly's nappy.

When she finally accepted that she couldn't breastfeed after months of trying, Grace manically googled articles that suggested this would undermine her bond with Lilly, jeopardize her IQ and make her obese. Initially Patrick tried to prove the opposite with research of his own. Grace remained unconvinced. Patrick flippantly suggested that a loosening of the bond might be a good thing because she was 'being, er, perhaps, a little obsessive'. Grace had freaked out, accusing him of not wanting the best for their daughter. The following day she woke up to find Patrick burning all the books and research in the garden of their old home.

What none of the literature told her was that it was possible to love too much. From the moment Lilly was born, Grace lurched between a state of complete ecstasy and utter terror. As time went by, the peaks and troughs diminished but the sensation endured that nothing would go wrong as long as she was in control. And that strategy had worked. Until now.

Grace sits up, still confused at how she came to be in Lilly's bed. The nausea and dizziness have passed. Bleary-eyed, she swings round her legs to the edge of the mattress and plants her feet firmly on the floor, shaking her head to wake herself up. It feels humid underfoot. Surely the floor can't be damp as well. She stares at the carpet, remembering how Lilly point-blank refused to choose a colour from the screen of options at the developers' a year ago. It was her protest against moving house. It took them by surprise because Lilly had always been so easy about everything. In the end Grace had decided for her. The colour had appeared neutral beige on the computer screen but when it arrived it was a horrible jaundiced yellow that Lilly called 'bile-duct beige with flecks of vomit'. *Is this where it started?* Grace wonders. *Was this the moment she began to pull away?*

They had tried so hard to be positive to the children about designing their new house, enthusing over the choice of gaudy tiles, the fake Shaker taps and the cheap finish on the engineered wood floor. 'What's not to love?' Patrick kept saying, extolling the virtues of the open-plan kitchen, huge garden and garage. The reality was that none of them, apart from Mia, wanted to leave their old home and she was only excited because of the new house's proximity to the Travellers' site, which was why it was affordable. Everything has gone wrong since they moved here. Grace blames the house. And then she blames Patrick for the poor financial decisions that drove them out of the city centre. If only he had told her earlier about his teaching hours being cut, they might have been able to do something about it. Their maisonette in Pretoria Road had been the perfect home. Grace still misses the old Victorian bay windows, which looked out on to the garden, and their elderly neighbours upstairs, who always bought Christmas presents for Lilly and Mia. Best of all, it was ten minutes' walk from the city centre and four minutes from the nearest shop. No wonder Lilly had cried when they left.

Now fully awake, Grace looks around Lilly's room and is bewildered to see that most of the yellow carpet is obscured by heaps of clothes, shoes, books and papers. Everything has been removed from the wardrobe, even the boxes and old clothes from the uppermost shelves that can only be reached from a chair; the chest of drawers is completely empty; and Lilly's books and files have all been taken out of the bookshelf. Her wallet has been emptied and her school bag tipped upside down. It is as if someone has come in during the night and turned the bedroom inside out.

Heart pounding, Grace assesses the piles of socks, knickers, T-shirts, trousers and dresses. She notices how the drawers from Lilly's desk are piled in the corner and their contents laid out on top of the bookshelf: papers, hole-punch, fluorescent pens, hair ties, Post-it notes, nail varnishes, Tampax. This isn't the usual teenage mess: the room looks as though it has been professionally searched. *Who has done this?* Grace knows the answer to this question even before she has finished asking it. *It must have been me. I must have done it in my sleep.*

Anxiously she casts her mind back to the stressful sequence of events the previous evening. They had brought Mia home from school and had dinner together, during which they heaped praise on her for how she'd reacted when Tas had fallen ill and her apparent ability to move on from the trauma of the day's events. After dinner Grace had phoned Rawnie, who told her that she was in hospital with Tas, waiting for further tests. 'That's exactly what they did with Lil,' Grace tried to reassure her. She asked Rawnie if Tas ever went swimming in the water at Earith in case both he and Lilly had caught some waterborne disease. 'Weil's disease can cause seizures and red eyes,' Grace explained. Rawnie said this was impossible because Tas couldn't swim. Then she told Grace that another girl from the secondary school, two years below Lilly, had been brought into hospital a couple of hours after Tas, suffering from similar symptoms.

When they turned on the television to watch the local news Grace and Patrick were horrified to see a news report on how children from local schools in north Cambridge were coming down with a mystery illness whose symptoms involved severe nausea, nerve damage and seizures. An image of both schools flashed up on screen. Public Health

England was investigating, the reporter explained. Lilly's headmaster was interviewed, saying there was no evidence as yet to link the three cases, and parents and children should carry on with life as normal. A parent from Mia's school, whom Grace didn't recognize, told the reporter that she would be keeping both of her children at home until someone had 'got a grip' on what was going on. 'No one is telling us anything,' she said. Her fear was almost palpable. Grace felt nauseous with anxiety that Lilly's illness was no longer a private issue and that, contrary to Dr Santini's diagnosis, it was clearly infectious.

The last thing she can remember with absolute clarity is getting into bed with Patrick. It was too hot and humid for sleep. They had talked late into the night, lying side by side without touching, discussing plausible explanations for the contagion. Grace settled on the idea that Tas was a regular visitor to their house and could have breathed in the same spores from the mould caused by the damp. Patrick pointed out that if the mould had triggered the seizures they would all have been affected, their neighbours too. Grace wondered if the secondary-school girl who had been taken to hospital lived in Black Fen Close. She tried to call Rawnie to ask her for more details but she didn't pick up.

Maybe we'll all get ill, Grace panicked. She told Patrick how Catriona Vickers had told Nuala that the water supply in north Cambridge must have been contaminated by pollution from the new wind farm out on Black Fen. She checked her social media for updates and saw news of what had happened was all over Facebook and Twitter.

Grace wanted to show Patrick the emails Catriona had sent to parents about the wind farm but Patrick said he couldn't be bothered to read them. He reminded Grace that Catriona's husband worked for a news organization that specialized in spreading anti-climate-change propaganda. Grace was disbelieving until he showed her the man's nonsensical website: *There is no radiative greenhouse effect; why CO_2 has nothing to do with temperature. The climate is always changing, it has nothing to do with humans.*

'The world's gone mad.'

'Yes, the world *has* gone mad.'

This was one of the few things they could agree on.

They had then argued ferociously over what the doctor had said about Lilly's anxiety over her school work. Dr Santini suggested that, whatever the diagnosis, Lilly needed time and space to recuperate. Patrick wanted her to delay applying to university for a year to ease the pressure. Grace insisted that watching from the sidelines while her friends planned their future would make Lilly feel worse.

'She's done so much work to get to this point. She'll be really disappointed, especially when the others start to get offers,' Grace said. She was thinking of Freya.

'*You* will be disappointed,' he said archly. 'Lilly might be relieved.'

'Let's have a chat with her when she's feeling better.'

'She can't be honest with you, Grace. She wants to please you too much. She knows you want this as much as she does.'

'The seizure has nothing to do with school work. Otherwise Tas wouldn't have had one too.' Grace struggled to keep her voice even. 'Please back me up on this one.'

Patrick closed his eyes and lay on his back, perfectly still. Just as she was about to poke him in the side, he opened his eyes and turned to face her.

'Answer me this. What has gone wrong with your own life that makes you so anxious about Lilly making the right decisions for her own? Who is it you don't trust? Her? You? Or me?'

His questions unsettled her. Patrick usually preferred to skim the surface of life and avoided confrontation at all costs. He was rarely prone to overthinking. His lightness of being was one of the qualities that had first attracted Grace to him because it spoke of an optimistic view of human nature that she couldn't share. Last night, however, he had intimated truths about her personality that lie so deeply buried she doesn't even admit them to herself. She would have liked to tell him that she knows everything that is given can be taken away. That life can be diverted from its course in an instant. But she couldn't explain to him how she needs to protect herself from memories of her childhood and her feelings about them because, since Lilly has fallen ill, they are threatening to drag her under again.

'Going to university was my big dream. But my parents died and I messed up my A levels so I had to get a job. That's why I've ended up working for a pissy local newsletter, writing about lost cats and giant marrows. I might have had a proper career otherwise.' It's a half-truth rather than a complete lie.

'No one is suggesting Lil shouldn't go to university,' said Patrick, giving her a long, hard stare.

He was so close she could feel his breath on her face. She could have defused the row then and there if she had reached out and touched his cheek. 'I don't want her to repeat my mistakes. I want Lil to fulfil her potential.'

'You are completely different people. She has us looking out for her and you didn't have anyone.'

'I don't want her to mess things up because of that boy. This is the most important year of her life. Everything has been leading up to this moment.' She could hear the fear in her voice. 'You have no idea how things can fall apart.'

'You're totally losing perspective,' he warned her.

'I want Lilly to have all the opportunities that I didn't.'

Patrick paused. 'What exactly is it that is missing from your life, Grace?'

She tried to distil everything into a response that was neither evasive nor provocative. 'I want Lilly's life to be more than making do.'

'You sound just like Rob talking about Ana. And we all know that's never a good comparison.'

Grace can't recall anything that happened after that. She tries to visualize herself going up the stairs and opening the door into Lilly's room. She imagines herself dragging the chair across to the wardrobe to reach the highest cupboards. She pictures herself going through the essays and notes in the lever arch files and turning socks inside out. But she remembers nothing. A new thought takes shape as she looks around Lilly's bedroom. *Patrick mustn't see this.* It's not that he won't understand. He'll understand too well. The bone-aching tiredness that makes her feel lead-limbed and foggy-headed is superseded by a growing panic that at least infuses her with a sense of purpose.

She turns her attention to the files and textbooks splayed face down on top of each other to the left of her feet. Lilly is fanatical about her work being arranged properly. *Fanatical.* Everything is organized thematically and colour-coded. She gathers up the stray papers: *DNA and protein synthesis; genetic diversity; adaptation.* Then she realizes there are two different biology files, one for last year and one for this year. She puts the papers at the front of one, resolving to sort them out properly when she has more time. She turns her attention to the socks. Each has been separated from its partner and turned inside out so the seam is the wrong way round. She starts to marry up the obvious pairs and leaves the outliers in a pile on Lilly's chair.

Her attention is diverted by a small pile of papers and seemingly random objects on the bedside table that she must have assembled during her search. She unfurls a wrinkled A-level English essay that has been folded into four, noticing how closely Lilly's neat, upright handwriting resembles her own, and starts to read. By the fifth line she realizes that the essay is no more than the same five sentences repeated on three sides of A4. 'Drowning. I love you, I'd give my two breasts to hold you. Sky-rider, when your dream lets you down, drown with me in the vague haar of my hair on this blue beneath you. Do you doubt me? Here's my tear shadow.'

She reads the strange words out loud and understands their sense without understanding their meaning. Images flash through her mind of loves lost and loves gone by until her body feels heavy with memories. She folds the paper over and over again to make the words disappear. Beneath the essay is a receipt from a pub that Grace doesn't recognize and a ticket from the festival that conclusively proves Nuala was right. The idea that flaky Nuala knows more about what Lilly has been up to than she does makes Grace feel even more panicky. Then she picks up an envelope with Lilly's name on the front and pulls out a card. She recognizes Mr Galveston's overblown, baroque handwriting right away:

Lilly. I am worried about you. Your focus and drive are ebbing. Your essays this term are so far removed from your usual standards that I can only conclude there is something very wrong. Please come and see me if you would like to talk anything over.

Best wishes,
Peter Galveston

It seems that everyone knew there was something wrong with Lilly apart from her. Even head-in-the-clouds Mr Galveston, who apparently didn't notice when Jordy spent an entire lesson hidden under a pile of coats. Only a few weeks ago she was criticizing Nuala for not realizing that Hayley had gone on the pill even though she didn't have a regular boyfriend. And Catriona Vickers for allowing Bea to get into a situation on the computer where she was googling 'daisy chain' and accidentally accessed hardcore gay porn. In reality she is the Bad Mother, not them.

She jumps as the window in Lilly's bedroom suddenly bangs open, hitting the outside wall of the house. A welcome breeze sweeps through the room, lifting Mr Galveston's card from the table and on to the floor, but instead of refreshed Grace feels hot and clammy. She recognizes the sensation straight away although she hasn't experienced it for years. It's the same sense of shame that she used to feel as a teenager about her own mother.

She tries to focus on the wall of photos above Lilly's bed. But wherever she looks she sees her mother's face: the watery blue eyes, brimming with self-pity; the dyed blonde hair with its ragged centre parting and dark roots, always the wrong side of long; and her slightly doughy face, flushed pink by too much drink or drugs or sex. The sickly smell drifts back into the room. *There's nothing that can't be cured by a hug, Grace.* She hears her mother's voice pleading with her.

'Go away,' she commands. 'Go away, Olwyn.'

'Who on earth are you talking to?' Grace turns round in confusion to see Patrick standing at the edge of the room on a small patch of carpet that Grace has cleared. 'Who is Olwyn?'

Grace springs back with such intensity that she knocks

thc bedside lamp from the table. The sun casts shadows across Patrick's face so it seems to be daubed with war-paint. His gaze darts around the room from the wardrobe, to the chest of drawers, to Lilly's desk. 'Did you do all this?' he asks incredulously. 'Why?'

'I can't remember,' Grace says.

He shoots her a disbelieving look. 'Don't be ridiculous,' he says. 'It looks like a forensic team has combed the room.'

'See how she's written the same thing over and over again. It's not right,' Grace says, holding up the essay and waving it in his face. 'We need to know what's bcen going on.'

Patrick takes the essay and looks at it more closely. 'It's a love poem. Lilly is obviously nursing a broken heart. Don't you remember what that's like?'

She shows him the note from Mr Galveston. 'Even he thinks something's wrong.'

'Dropping a few grades isn't the end of the world,' says Patrick, trying to reassure her. 'We mustn't get this out of proportion.'

'Lilly hasn't been honest about what's going on in her life. She's shut me out.'

'Come on, Grace, all teenagers lead double lives to some extent. If my mother had watched my every move, I would have done the same. You need to give her some breathing space. What were you up to at her age?'

He stomps out of the room and goes into Mia's bedroom to tell her she needs to get out of bed. Grace checks the time and realizes she has been up for thrce hours already.

Patrick offers to take Mia to school. It sounds like rap-prochement but in reality he's anxious to get Mia out of the house in case she heads back upstairs and sees what

Grace has done to Lilly's bedroom. Even he's freaked out by her behaviour. 'Come on, Mia,' he says impatiently. He also wants to leave before the builders arrive. Marius, the head man, seems to relish delivering bad news about the damp, painting the bleakest picture possible so that even the tiniest progress requires accolades involving at least ten adjectives. He sets Grace on edge with his vision of apocalyptic doom, as if they're on board *Titanic*, rather than victims of a shitty house-building company. And he might mention that Patrick is four weeks late in paying his last bill.

In the kitchen Mia cleaves to Grace's side, asking questions about Tas that are impossible to answer. Is he still in hospital? Can she visit him? If Tas is sick, does it mean his family won't have to leave the Travellers' site? Patrick puts on the radio and switches it off when the third item has to do with the illness sweeping through schools in north Cambridge. He notices that Mia keeps bending down to adjust her left sock and wonders if it's a tic related to her self-consciousness over her feet. Although it occurs to him that if she was really worried about the size of her feet she wouldn't wear the same oversized leather boots to school all year round.

Pondering this, he makes Mia a piece of toast and regrets it because she always takes ages to eat and has a particularly maddening routine with toast in which she takes tiny bites from around the edge until only a small square is left at the centre that has to be shaped into the letter M.

'Eat up, sweetheart,' he mutters. She looks up and stops chewing, staring at him with her big sorrowful eyes, as though he is the one missing the point.

'There's no point in rushing her,' Grace warns under her breath. 'It's counterproductive.'

'She's right, Dad,' says Mia, apologetically, in between nibbles.

While he's waiting for Mia, Patrick paces up and down the kitchen, dishcloth in hand, systematically wiping every surface in a futile attempt to get rid of the red dust. But, as he rubs, the water from the cloth turns it into a viscous glaze that proves even harder to remove. He washes his hands again under the tap, scrubbing his nails with a brush, trying to work out if he's more unnerved by what Grace has done or that she can't remember doing it. The stress is getting to them all.

'I'll let you take me as long as we go by bus,' Mia suddenly proposes.

He wonders at her ability to turn even the most mundane decision into a debate. He's torn between his instinct not to give in to her and the sense that it would be petty not to indulge her after what happened yesterday. They haven't caught the bus to school since they moved here because Lilly has to register almost an hour before Mia and the journey takes too long. So Grace usually drops them on her way to work.

'If I learn the route it'll make it easier for you and Mum now that Lilly lives in hospital,' she says. 'Tas always comes on the bus. Strictly speaking, when he's better, we could travel together.'

'Lilly will be home very soon,' Patrick reassures her.

'Not now that Tas has the same illness,' says Mia, seriously.

She's right, of course, he thinks, as he watches her head to the front door to wait for the bus. From behind Patrick notices that her pigtail is tucked inside the back of her shirt and her feet are splayed at right angles. He can tell from the uneven way her shirt tail hangs across the back of her skirt that the buttons at the front are done up wrongly. His heart lurches. At least the little Romany boy doesn't care about her clumsy limbs and her dishevelled uniform. He just cares that Mia makes him laugh.

'Do you think they allow eels to visit hospital?' Mia suddenly asks.

'I don't think there will be a specific rule but turning up with Elvis isn't a good idea. There'll be a health and safety issue.' He puts out his hand to stroke her hair, then remembers she doesn't like it when people touch her unexpectedly.

Grace doesn't get up from the kitchen table to say goodbye. She's too busy on her computer, trying to work out which pub the receipt came from so she can find out where Lilly had been with that boy. She makes careful notes in her blue book. Two pages have been filled today, although admittedly one is taken up with Lilly's essay. He already hates that notebook. He's filled with an urge to put his arms around Grace and reassure her that in a few weeks this will be over and they will be laughing about it. But her phone pings with yet another message, and simmering irritation that a new round of rumour-mongering has begun on social media dissolves his goodwill.

The bus trundles along the ruler-straight road that runs parallel to Black Fen towards Cambridge. Patrick finds the landscape instantly soothing. It isn't simply that it is so familiar to him from his childhood. It's the way, in contrast to everything else that has happened over the past week, it holds no nasty surprises. In a land where the sky is king, the weather announces itself hours in advance; the fields, ditches and dykes have a Mondrian-like geometry that repeats itself with utter predictability as far as the horizon; and you can see anyone approaching for miles.

It never ceases to amaze Patrick that his ancestors created this landscape. Who would have dared to dream that water could be drained from an area that is effectively a basin? Was it arrogance or delusion that made Cornelius Vermuyden think he could divert the strength of the mighty River Ouse back into the sea by digging two huge artificial channels that ran for twenty-two miles either side? That he could force his will on it by carving out dykes and drains, lodes and leams. Patrick wishes he had the same self-belief. Rob got that gene. Not him. He can't even prevent his own garden from flooding in the rain. Or his wife slipping away from him again.

He opens his briefcase and takes out a file. On the side it says 'Animal Totems of Burkina Faso' in big black letters. He came up with a title that he knew Grace would find totally boring so she wouldn't be tempted to look inside, because it contains details of estimates and unpaid bills that he doesn't want her to see. He takes out the revised budget that Marius calculates will be necessary to fix the problems on the top floor of the house and feels almost nauseous when he sees it comes to over fifteen thousand pounds. He reads through it, trying to work out where they might be able to cut corners. If they did their own plastering and painting they could save a couple of thousand pounds. Perhaps he could teach himself to tile. Or maybe this part of the process could wait for a year, until everything is more settled.

He will need to sound out Marius without revealing his financial problems. He's used up Rob's loan and still owes the builder seven thousand pounds for the work he has already completed. Patrick half wonders if he could ask his mother for money. But that would require a trip to Brighton and he can't leave Lilly. Marius had told him in a surprisingly gentle tone at the beginning of last week that they wouldn't buy any more materials until he had paid at least half of his outstanding debt. Then Lilly had had her seizure and he hasn't mentioned anything since, so maybe Patrick has inadvertently bought himself some time. He snaps shut the file and shakes his head. Mia puts out her hand and tries to smooth the lines on his forehead but ends up cack-handedly nicking his skin with her fingernail.

'Don't worry. Lilly will be fine, Dad. And so will Tas.' She rests her head on his shoulder and starts questioning him about the bus route. She wants to know the name of the stop by the Travellers' site; whether it's quicker for Tas to travel clockwise or anti-clockwise to Cambridge; and how long it takes between each stop. Patrick welcomes the diversion. He tells her that this is one of his favourite cycling routes and that perhaps one day they could do a circuit together.

'You're forgetting one thing, Dad,' says Mia, cheerfully.

'What's that?'

'I'm useless at cycling.'

Mia stares at the map on the wall in front of them and tries to memorize the names of every stop on the route, saying them out loud until she can remember them with her eyes closed. 'Cottenham, Histon, Impington, Arbury, Chesterton.'

'What do you do when you go to Tas's home?' he asks.

'Do you want to know what we really do or what I tell Mum we do?' She gives him a wicked grin.

'The truth.'

'Last time we rode one of Tas's horses bareback. Guit. He's a piebald cob.'

'Did you like it?'

'I told Tas it was like being on a rocking chair and we laughed so much that we fell off.'

Patrick laughs. 'That sounds like fun.'

'We play games in the yard too.'

'Like what?'

'Don't laugh. It's not very imaginative. We play Travellers.'

He suppresses a smile.

She explains that they sit in the yard on an old leather seat that came out of a truck and pretend they're driving around different countries of the world. 'Our favourite trip is to the Australian outback. We're going there together one day. When we get bored with that we tunnel underneath the caravan looking for treasure.'

Patrick raises an eyebrow. 'What kind of treasure?'

'Tiles, bricks, bales of hay, spray paint, boxing gloves. Last time Tas found a blowtorch and melted a tyre. Definitely don't tell Mum that.'

'I won't,' he promises.

'Would you like to see my Anglo-Saxon diary?' Mia suddenly asks. She pulls it out of her rucksack before he's even answered.

'Sure,' Patrick says.

He admires the cover. Mia has drawn the runic alphabet around the title: 'Diary of a Deviant Anglo-Saxon Girl'.

'Deviant?' Patrick asks, a little surprised.

'The Anglo-Saxons had special graves for bad people who didn't live by the rules. Like girls who got pregnant before they were married. And "deviant" was on the SATs uncommon vocab list,' explains Mia. 'Which means I get an extra mark from Miss Swain. Clever, huh?'

'Very.' Patrick chuckles. 'You're learning how to work the system.'

He flicks through the next couple of pages, praising her drawings of huts on stilts and her menu for an Anglo-Saxon meal. *Leek and split-pea soup. Spit roast. Griddle cakes.* He can tell how hard Mia has tried to write neatly and spell everything correctly from the smears due to using a rubber too many times. In some places she has pressed so hard with her pencil that she has almost scored through to the other side of the paper. The effort she has put into her work fills Patrick with unexpected emotion because it reveals a desire to please that he rarely sees in Mia and a sense of her daily struggle to express herself on paper. He finds himself blinking away tears.

He turns to the next page and is amused to see a drawing of a heavily pregnant Anglo-Saxon girl. There are two lines of description beneath. 'I am seventeen years old. I love someone but they don't love me back. My days are filled with tears.' He reads the words out loud. Miss Swain has written a short note at the bottom encouraging Mia to write more words and draw fewer pictures. *Why can't she simply congratulate her on her work?* he wonders.

'That's a very sad story,' he says indulgently, wanting to compensate for Miss Swain's sour comment. But his good mood dissipates when he sees that Mia has transposed a small photo of Lilly's face on to the drawing of the girl. He's not sure what to think. It's simultaneously creepy and eye-catching. He stares at it without speaking for a little while. Then he asks: 'Why have you done this?'

'I wanted to imagine what it would be like if Lilly had a baby.' She turns to the next page. He's startled to see an A4 photocopy of a skeleton lying in a shallow grave with another tiny skeleton between its legs. The woman lies on her front, head to the side, mouth wide open in a rictus scream. She must have died in agony.

'What's going on here?' Patrick asks in shock.

'It's my girl,' explains Mia. 'She died during childbirth. Her body decomposed and then the baby was expelled. It's called a coffin birth. And now the archaeologists have dug her up and I'm pretty certain she's come to get Lilly.'

8

Patrick has never seen so many people outside Mia's primary school, not even on the last day of term. Cars and vans are haphazardly double parked, bumper to bumper, in the street and on pavements. In the playground, parents and children form dense, irregular groups that seamlessly cluster together and drift apart as if their movements are choreographed. A BBC Cambridge television van with a satellite dish on its roof has even been allowed to park inside the playground. He counts three television cameras, four microphones and as many people with notebooks. *How on earth has this happened?*

Bewildered, he grips Mia's hand and hesitates for a moment outside the entrance, wondering what is going on. He finds a crumpled copy of the *Cambridge News* under his left foot. When he bends down to pick it up he is stunned to see Lilly smiling radiantly up at him from the front page under the headline 'Health Emergency as School Children Struck by Mystery Contagion'. He recognizes the photo from her Facebook page. He traces a circle around her face with his index finger and skim-reads the first couple of paragraphs, '*first victim . . . dangerous seizure . . . battery of tests . . . a second child . . . official investigation . . .*'

He doesn't have to ask how the media has identified

Lilly: in the far corner of the playground, Catriona Vickers holds court in front of an arc of journalists.

He quickly stuffs the newspaper into his bag and anxiously checks on Mia, hoping she might suggest they turn tail and head home. After all, she had spent much of year five reaching this point and refusing to go in. But, in typically contrary fashion, she emphatically hikes up her school skirt, pulls back her shoulders and takes a couple of deep breaths, urging him towards the fray with a determined push to the base of his spine.

'Come on, Dad,' Mia shouts up at him. 'All things are difficult before they are easy.' It's the same phrase he used with her last year when she was refusing to go into school. The irony doesn't make him smile. The diary with the creepy photomontage of Lilly is still fresh in his memory and he shivers in spite of the sultry heat rising from the tarmac. Her composure unsettles him. It's not natural. He buries the thought before it has taken shape. He can only worry about one child at a time. Instead he wipes his forehead and imagines himself on his bike, legs pumping as he speeds along Black Fen Drove, the only noise the sound of his breath. *Inhale three strokes, hold for two strokes, exhale six strokes. Ten breaths per minute.* He hasn't been on a ride all week and he's missed it.

The febrile atmosphere washes over them as they walk towards the back of the crowd. He keeps a tight grip on Mia's hand, worrying about what she makes of it all. It's so noisy he can hardly hear himself think. He glances down but, to his surprise, she smiles serenely. 'It's started,' she says, staring up at him with her strange watery green eyes. Or, at least, that's what he thinks she says, because her voice is lost in the general din. Unlike Patrick, she doesn't seem in the least unnerved by what is unfolding in her playground.

People he doesn't recognize are wielding professional-looking placards with angry messages: 'We demand answers! Now!'; 'Wind turbine syndrome – get the facts!'; 'Who will be next?' Every so often a chant ripples through the crowd, although he notices not everyone joins in. He's faintly reassured to see that many of them look as disturbed as he feels. He can't believe that all this has been triggered by what has happened to his daughter. *Thank God Grace didn't come! Thank God Lilly is in hospital without her phone! Thank God for Mia's resilience!*

He ruffles Mia's hair affectionately as they push forwards. Everyone is talking too fast and too loudly. Sentences hang in the air, only half formed. Patrick is reminded of the word game he sometimes plays with Mia where she has to fill in the gaps. 'I heard that she's been put in an . . .' There are three options: 'isolation ward', 'induced coma', 'intensive care'.

He can't stand the way people seem to relish the drama of his family's situation. 'I hear she's been given the all-clear and sent home,' Patrick wants to shout back at them. Except no one will listen. Besides, it's not true: he's just read Grace's last message (she's sent eight since he left home), saying the hospital has phoned and they want to do some tests that involve Lilly being locked away in a room for three days while a machine monitors her brainwaves and a video camera records her every movement. It sounds as creepy as an episode of *Black Mirror.*

Mia surges into the crowd, Patrick trailing behind her. The gossip changes course. 'I heard the gypsy boy stole . . .': 'a ring', 'an iPhone', 'a swan'.

Mia stops to correct them. 'Not true, not true, not true,' she yells, but no one takes any notice. Patrick tells her to ignore them and urges her forward. Everyone seems to have forgotten that children are witnessing this craziness. *Why on earth don't the parents get them into school where calm and order will surely prevail?*

He looks up at the first-floor window and sees the head-mistress, Miss Swain and other teachers staring down at them all, no doubt trying to work out what they can do to quell the growing hysteria. Patrick pauses to plot the best route to the revolving door. He sees Mia look up at her form teacher and wave. To his surprise, Miss Swain waves back and even gives a stiff smile. She must have been watching them all the time.

Mia weaves through the crowd. Patrick follows, head down, cycling style, breathing in the heady fug of sweat, fear and adrenalin, hoping no one recognizes them because they are now infamous as the tragic family. He had wanted to get to school early, specifically to avoid the gaze of other parents, but going by bus had scuppered that plan because it took so long. He knew their well-meant but anxious enquiries about Lilly and Mia would have unsettled his younger daughter and upset him. And he has enough self-insight to know he would have been unable to distinguish between genuine concern and someone fishing for information to be shared with one of the multiple WhatsApp groups that have sprouted like weeds over the past week to analyse every aspect of what is going on.

There are already three different groups for the parents in Mia's class. One for those Grace describes as 'the voices of reason', a second, established by Catriona, for the conspiracy theorists, and a third by Miss Swain to keep in touch with parents. The teacher's messages are limited to practicalities, reminding them school is open as usual, that she will be doing an extended weekly session of Show and Tell, to take pupils' minds off their missing classmate, and providing updates about Tas. 'He's as well as can be expected,' read her last message, a phrase that sounded faintly ominous and fuelled renewed speculation on Catriona's group chat that information was being withheld from them.

There are two separate groups for Lilly's class but Grace had been excluded from one, a gesture she reads as hostile but Patrick argues is humanitarian because it was set up by Nuala, who is a proper friend, to deliver updates to concerned parents of students in Mr Galveston's class so that they don't bother Grace with too many questions. 'Watch out, she's working against our daughter,' Grace had warned him. She'd said the same thing about Miss Swain. Her paranoia frightens him. She doesn't trust anyone.

When he couldn't sleep last night, he had taken a look at Catriona's WhatsApp group on Grace's phone and seen that it contained links to spurious articles about wind-turbine syndrome, including an interview with a woman who claimed that she had seizures due to the noise from turbines. 'How Infrasound Has Blighted My Life,' read the headline. He now regrets that, in a fit of pique, he had added a link from Grace's phone to a piece in the *Guardian*: 'How to Catch Wind-turbine Syndrome From Hearing Someone Talk About It'. He wrote a long message about how infrasound is emitted by surf, storms, wind, heartbeat and respiration, and suggested that perhaps Catriona should also start a campaign to ban the air they breathe. Catriona's husband then posted a series of links to various climate-change-denial websites.

Finally Nuala had waded in to advise parents to expend positive energy supporting each other rather than engaging in 'petty political point scoring'. Grace was furious with them all, but especially Patrick, because he had made it seem she was more focused on fake news than on Lilly. He's beginning to realize that, apart from worrying about Lilly, Grace's biggest fear is people thinking she is a bad mother.

He feels Mia pulling at his arm. 'I want to go and see the television cameras,' she shouts up at him. Before he can answer, her slippery hand has slithered through his fingers.

'Mia,' he shouts, 'come back! There isn't time.' Patrick is desperate to get her away from the playground and into school so he can go to the hospital. He tries to push after her but he treads on someone's foot and stops to apologize. When he looks round she has been swallowed by the crowd.

'Steady on, mate.' A man he doesn't recognize puts his hand firmly on his shoulder to hold him back.

'Sorry, I've lost my daughter,' Patrick explains breathlessly, as he turns to face him.

'You need to slow down,' the man says, tightening his grip.

'You don't understand,' says Patrick, who is less worried about Mia getting lost than what she might say to other people.

The man leans forward so his mouth almost touches Patrick's ear. He feels spots of saliva spray his cheek as he speaks. 'We're all worried. Just imagine if you were the father of the poor girl lying in a coma and no one was telling you the truth because of a cover-up.'

'She's not in a coma,' says Patrick, angrily. But the man isn't listening because the headmistress has opened a window on the first floor and is leaning out to address everyone through a megaphone.

'Testing, testing, testing,' she says, clearing her throat. 'Please can you move back to let our pupils get into the school building. We are open as normal.'

'Why aren't you telling us the truth?' someone shouts up at the window.

'We have told you everything we know and are posting regular updates on the school messaging system.' Her voice reverberates round the playground.

'Is it true another pupil has fallen ill?' another voice yells.

'As soon as we have more news, we will inform you,' she reiterates. Her responses sound rehearsed, as if she's reading from a script given to her by the Department of Health.

While everyone's attention is on the headmistress, Patrick takes advantage of the space that has opened up to sidestep in the direction of the television van. To his relief he comes across a familiar face fighting her way towards him. 'Hey,' he shouts. 'Hey, Nuala!' He's never been so pleased to see her.

'Hey, Patrick!' she shouts back.

'Have you seen Mia anywhere?' he asks, as she gets closer.

'Yes.' She nods and points in the general direction of the BBC van.

He's relieved to see she's not with her husband. Patrick now realizes that one of the reasons so many people are here is that entire families are milling around the playground, trying to decide whether to send their children into school. He would have no patience with George's urge to play the maverick on a day like this.

Nuala tacks towards him, making steady progress, her long tent dress swaying from side to side, like a sail, as she glides effortlessly between people, while he is relentlessly buffeted by sharp shoulders and elbows. When she finally reaches him, he's taken aback as she throws her suntanned arms around his neck to give him an emotional hug. 'I can't imagine what you're going through,' she says in his ear. 'Such terrible times.' Her curly dark hair tickles his face and lips. 'How's Lil?'

'We measure the days in good nights and she's had another good one. It's strange, but when we're with her you wouldn't know there's anything wrong. But as soon as we leave, all I can think about is whether she's going to have another seizure. Thanks for asking.'

'That's great news. Hayley is still very affected by it all. And Mia? I heard about what happened yesterday.'

'She is strangely fine. Emphasis on strangely. We're very proud of her.' He forces a laugh and she smiles. Nuala doesn't pull away from him. He notices how her hair smells of coconut and, beneath the fabric of her dress, she feels as small and scrawny as a sparrow. His hand rests on the bony cartilage at the top of her spine. He gives her a re-assuring hug. One that says, 'I'm fine and I hope you're fine, and these people are the mad and we are the sane.' But instead of feeling like the arbiter of calm, he is momentarily possessed by the image of Nuala up against the wall in the derelict waste-ground at the end of the road, palms resting against the crumbling brickwork, as he falls to his knees, slowly lifts her dress, and parts her legs to press his face into the warmth between her thighs. The pressure and the heat are getting to him. *Thinking is not doing*, he reminds himself. '*But if you think, you might as well do,*' he imagines his brother saying, while laughing at him.

He tries to unravel himself from Nuala's embrace before she can feel him growing hard through his shorts. They dis-entangle and she leans towards him again until her mouth is so close to his left ear that he can feel her breath cooling his cheek. 'Is Grace okay? She seems a little on edge.'

'What happened yesterday evening was my fault,' he says, assuming she's referring to the WhatsApp spat. 'I sent the *Guardian* piece from Grace's phone. I wanted to inject a bit of sanity into the debate. Wind-turbine syndrome is com-plete bunkum. I can't believe that theory has gained any traction. And Catriona's husband works for a company that peddles misinformation about climate change.'

'I understand,' says Nuala.

'Grace is furious with me.' He feels disloyal saying it but

the urge to connect with someone amid this madness over-whelms his usual reticence.

'She's furious with me too,' says Nuala. 'She's under a lot of pressure.'

'It's all got so out of hand so quickly,' he says, sweeping his hand around the playground, then resting it on her shoulder.

'It's terrifying how it's taken on a life of its own. Not that I told you that. Otherwise Catriona will accuse me of being a collaborator.'

'Where have all these people come from?' Patrick asks. 'They can't all be parents.'

'Social media rent-a-mob.' Nuala shrugs. 'Twitter is aflame. It's the usual fact-phobics.'

'Is it true another child has been taken to hospital?' Patrick asks.

She nods. 'She's from the secondary school. That's all I know. Year ten. There's no obvious connection between her, Lilly and Tas.' She flounders. 'Perhaps it is something contagious. Not necessarily the wind turbines, but perhaps something else has got into the groundwater. Maybe we'll all be infected.'

'It's always tempting to read too much into coincidence,' he says, placing a reassuring arm around her shoulders.

Mia has found her way to the far corner of the playground where a group of adults and children cluster around jour-nalists interviewing Catriona Vickers. Even Mia can tell Catriona dressed for attention when she got up this morn-ing. While everyone else is in shorts and T-shirts, she is wearing a bright yellow sundress, belted tightly in the mid-dle, red lipstick and high-heeled shoes. She looks like a giant inflatable balloon, except instead of gas she is pumped up with her own importance.

The journalists fire questions at her. 'Have there been any other cases of wind-turbine syndrome in the UK?'; 'What is the science behind the theory?'; 'Is there a range of symptoms?' Catriona holds forth. She goes on and on about how wind turbines cause pollution, sleeplessness and put chickens off laying eggs until even the journalists start to look bored. 'We need a new angle,' Mia hears one of them mutter.

She can't believe that no one is asking the right questions, still less that Catriona has wangled her way centre stage to hijack what should have been *her* show. *They should be interviewing me! I'm the one who knows what's going on. I'm the one who was with Tas.* Less than twenty-four hours ago, everyone wanted Mia's opinion. Pupils and teachers alike were tripping over to congratulate her, but today she has become invisible again. She scuffs the toes of her leather boots on the asphalt in frustration. Nobody has even noticed that she's here.

This is not what was meant to happen. At the end of yesterday's meeting with Miss Swain, when the headmistress and the school counsellor had come into the classroom to speak to Mia and her parents, she had been quite clear about the reasons for the illness sweeping the school. It was so obvious that Mia couldn't believe they hadn't already worked it out for themselves: by digging up the Anglo-Saxon burial site, the archaeologists had angered the spirits of the dead and released a medieval illness that had been buried for centuries. Lilly had swum near the site all summer and Tas lived next door. This was obviously the common denominator they kept searching for.

'Strictly speaking, the dead have come to claim the living,' she calmly told them.

Although she couldn't say this, she knew Lilly had been targeted because she was a deviant woman, like the girl with her baby in the grave: Lilly had got pregnant without being married. Her mum was on the right track when she argued with her dad that Lilly might have done something that brought on the seizure.

Mia had watched as everyone carefully made notes. She noticed her parents exchanging worried looks with the headmistress and was pleased that at last they were paying proper attention to her warning. There was a long silence as they absorbed the seriousness of the situation. Then Miss Swain asked her a typically annoying question. 'So why do you think you haven't fallen ill, Mia?'

'Perhaps I am protected,' she said dreamily, pressing her calves together so she could feel the ring digging into her ankle. 'Or perhaps I will be next. Or maybe you will.' She gave Miss Swain her best death stare and she stopped asking questions.

Yet, observing the hoo-ha in the playground this morning, it seems her theory has been forgotten or completely ignored. Instead of people demanding that the archaeologists suspend their dig right away and the Travellers be allowed to stay on their site, the focus has moved to some wind farm she hadn't even heard of until today.

Catriona's interference has changed everything. The possibility that the council will force the Travellers to leave to make way for the archaeologists to excavate the entire site remains a real possibility. No one will object because no one cares about the Travellers. She can tell that from the way Rawnie has to go to the toilet and shower in an unheated outside washroom even in the winter, and because she relies on Tas for reading and writing. And she overheard her parents talking about the reason their new home was so cheap was because it was near the Travellers' site.

Her stomach somersaults as she imagines Rawnie

packing up her caravan. Tas had told her the day before he got ill that his mum mentioned they might have to move north to Lincolnshire because they had family there and a pitch had come up on a site near Boston. They had searched for Boston on a map and quickly grasped that it would be impossible for Tas to stay at the same school. They would probably never see each other again.

Mia needs to win back momentum fast. She bends down and takes out the ring from the inside of her sock and carefully puts it on her finger. She has made a promise to Tas that he won't ever have to leave his home. She will do anything in her power to keep her word. She wishes he were here with her now because they could work out a new plan together. Mia is good at coming up with ideas. But there are always so many crowding her head that she finds it difficult to decide which one to choose. Tas knows which is the best. But it's impossible to get in touch with him because he's in hospital.

As she watches Catriona answer more questions – she's even talking about Lilly now, describing how her symptoms match those of a woman who caught wind-turbine syndrome in Australia – Mia imagines all the things she will never do again if Tas leaves: she will never eat biscuits from the plate with the fancy pink drawings of ladies with parasols; she will never trot so fast round the field on Guit's back that she feels her actual internal organs bounce inside her stomach; she will never hear Tas's older sisters tease him that his wife has arrived when Mia appears at the gate. Even worse, Tas seems to have grown more accepting of the situation. He kept saying he didn't want to do anything that might make things even more difficult for his family and that he's already had to move schools five times, twice because he was bullied for being a gypsy.

When Mia suggested that maybe he and his mum could move into a house closer to Cambridge he had burst out laughing. 'Mum settled in a house? You're having a laugh, Mia. It's not our way.'

'Would you ever live in a house?' she had asked him, with curiosity. He shook his head vigorously.

'Even if it meant we could be together?' she asked.

'It's not my world, Mia,' he said. But then he had kissed her cheek for the first time. 'I don't want to be settled.'

Think, Mia, think. Her mind darts back to the beginning of term when the school had introduced a weekly after-school class called 'The Power of Positive Thinking'. It was a project Miss Swain had come up with to impress the headmistress. Mia tries to remember the lessons in case there is something that might prove useful. She has begun to appreciate that Miss Swain is someone who generally manages to turn life to her advantage and that this is a skill she would do well to learn herself.

She casts her mind back to the first session. It focused on the importance of life-affirming messages. Miss Swain had asked everyone in the class to write positive messages about themselves on Post-it notes. 'I am clever'; 'I am unique'; 'I like myself the way I am.' They then had to repeat these out loud. When Miss Swain went round the class asking them how they felt afterwards, Mia said she felt just the same. She pointed out that the phrases had no meaning if everyone said the same thing. 'We can't all be unique, we can't all be clever and we can't all like ourselves the way we are. There are always winners and losers in life.' This was a concept she had experienced at first hand.

The second session was on 'How to Be a Good Friend'. Mia and her classmates all had to fill in a chart on a piece of A4. On the left side they were asked to list good choices about friendship and on the right bad choices. A prize was awarded for the child who came up with the best ideas. Bea Vickers had won. Her good choices included 'asking someone if they need help when they are crying'; 'sharing the giant bricks'; 'helping with spellings'. Her bad choices involved 'cyber bullying someone for the way they look'; 'leaving someone out of a game' and 'not sharing sweets'.

Not only had Bea inflicted all these 'bad choices' on Mia, she had also set up an Instagram poll asking people to vote on whether or not they thought Mia was an ugly freak. Eighty-nine people said yes and three said no, which meant that Mia had one more friend than she had previously thought. It was after this that Mia had confiscated Bea's phone. After awarding the prize, Miss Swain had asked if anyone wanted to discuss what they had learnt during the session. Mia had stood up. She could remember exactly what she said because Miss Swain had kept her back at the end of class and warned her about being intimidating. These words come back to her now. She steps out towards Catriona and the journalists and claps her hands, like Miss Swain does when she wants everyone's attention. She stands upright, hands clasped behind her back, heels together and boots sticking out at right angles.

'Just because she says something doesn't make it true,' she announces, pointing at Catriona Vickers.

It has the desired effect. Suddenly everyone's attention is on her. Even the man holding the camera swings it round so that its big eye is watching her. But instead of asking her name and her opinion on everything that has happened, the television reporter bursts out laughing, which makes the other journalists laugh too. 'That's the most sensible thing I've heard all morning.' He guffaws. 'What do you know, young lady?'

'I know a lot of stuff,' says Mia, defiantly, remembering how her dad always says to stick to the facts. 'I know that thousands of years ago you could walk all the way to Russia from here, and that pole-vaulting was invented in the Fens to get over the dykes and rivers. And I have a pet eel that took four years to swim here from the Sargasso Sea. And one day he will go back. For an orgy.'

Laughter ripples through the crowd. Mia feels her face burn with shame and darts back into the throng. When she touches her cheeks they are wet with tears of frustration. She doesn't stop running until she reaches Patrick again.

9

The hours drag so slowly on the neurological ward that Lilly swears time itself has stood still. She's now been here for over a week but the atmosphere is so stultifying that whenever she forces herself into action, trying to reread *The Merchant of Venice* or learn about gene expression for her next biology test, she finds herself falling asleep. Even in a heatwave, the radiators on the ward are left on all day and the window won't open more than a couple of inches. When Lilly complains to the nurse that she can't stay awake, Juan insists it's a sign her brain needs to rest. 'What if it's a sign I'm dying of boredom?' she jokes. Grace has banned her from all screens and there's no television on the ward.

To pass the time she drags the uncomfortable plastic chair to the window and settles down to watch a tractor working in the vast field beyond the hospital car park. It's the best place to sit because an occasional breath of fresh air skims her face. Besides, there's something hypnotic about watching the parched yellow stubble turn black by degrees as the plough churns the soil into neat furrows. The way the tractor goes up and down in perfect straight lines at the same steady speed reminds Lilly of how she cuts up and down the pool during swimming squad. She closes her eyes for a minute and remembers her technique for front crawl. *Left arm, right arm, left arm, breathe in, right arm, left arm, right arm, breathe out.* She's missed yet another training session this morning.

Lilly used to curse the way Grace made her get up three times a week to swim before breakfast but now she longs to be back in the water. She feels like Mia's eel, lethargically chasing its tail around its plastic prison, longing for a freedom it remembers less and less each day. If she doesn't get out of here soon, she'll likely lose her place in Mr Galveston's English class as well as in swimming squad, and Cormack will have forgotten her. Also, she's growing to like the doctor too much to be able to keep lying to him about when she had her first seizure.

There's a commotion at the door of the ward. Her eyelids feel almost too heavy to open. Visiting hours must officially have started, which means her parents will soon be here. Her mood dips further. Sometimes she feels as if she will buckle under the weight of their scrutiny. It's like being under surveillance. Her dad literally jumps out of his seat every time the monitor hits a bum note, even though Juan has explained a hundred times that this is completely normal, and her mum is hypersensitive to everything she says.

A pattern has developed whereby Grace makes a sinew-quivering effort to rein herself in for most of the visit, but just as she's on the point of leaving she can't contain herself any longer and starts interrogating every detail of what Lilly has said, until the duty nurse intervenes and tells them it's time to go home. If only she could apply the same degree of analysis to herself. Sometimes Lilly wishes she had kept the pregnancy test to bring it out at the end of one of these inquisitions just to shock Grace into silence. *Here. Now do you get it?* she would demand.

She can't believe she's spent so much of her life striving

to please her mother and meet her exacting standards, when Grace apparently has so few of her own. In a quiet moment yesterday, the doctor had mentioned how a traumatic experience can change people's perspective on life and Lilly has already come to one very definite conclusion: keeping Grace happy is no longer her responsibility. Her dad is the one who should have been doing that.

'Lilly!' squawks a familiar voice at the end of the room. She turns to see Hayley, Cormack and Jordy following Juan into the ward.

'You came!' she says, her voice a high-pitched squeal. 'I knew you'd come. I knew it.' She's completely elated by their unexpected arrival and jumps up from the chair, arms outstretched to hug them all. She feels a sudden burst of optimism that what has happened to her might bring them all together again. Maybe Cormack will want to go out with her publicly this time and Hayley won't mind because she will accept that they are destined to be together.

'Sssh. I'm letting them in against my better judgement,' the nurse teases Lilly. 'I thought you needed cheering up.'

She observes them as they approach. The further they come into the ward the slower they walk. She can't maintain her open-armed pose until they reach her so she drops her hands to her sides and waits awkwardly by the window. She notices how they gawk at the other patients and remembers doing the same when she first came round after her seizure. It requires a lot of self-control not to stare.

Lilly never thought she would feel lucky about what had happened to her until she started to compare her situation to her fellow patients on the ward: she hasn't had a stroke aged twenty-four like the girl opposite (who can't walk and has a plastic tube coming out of her skull to drain fluid from her brain); she isn't trapped in her body with Guillain-Barré syndrome, like the woman to the right of the door that leads into the ward (who breathes through a tube in her throat). Lilly can balance on one leg; her knee kicks in the air when they test her reflexes; the tuning fork feels cold against her skin; she can feed herself the disgusting hospital food and, most importantly, she can communicate.

She smooths down her top to give herself something to do with her hands, wishing there had been some advance warning so she could have changed out of the frayed tartan pyjama bottoms she has worn since she was twelve and the blue T-shirt that belongs to Cormack, which hasn't been washed since she arrived. She doesn't want him to think she's wearing it because of him. At least the delay gives her the chance to gather herself and gauge their mood.

Jordy is a familiar shade of ghostly pale, the harsh yellow lighting giving him a more liverish tone than usual. Lilly can tell he's anxious by the way he sucks his lower lip with his teeth. He flings a protective arm around Hayley, who likes to pretend she's squeamish for maximum effect. The deeper she gets into the ward, the more she shrinks into Jordy's shoulder until her head is almost pressed into his armpit. It's been just over a week since Lilly last saw her, but Hayley looks different. She's had a short asymmetric haircut and, for the first time since Lilly can remember, she's wearing trousers for school and has done up the top button of her shirt. The differences are subtle but deliberate, to emphasize her new alliance with Freya. It's no more than she deserves. Hayley looks up at Lilly and opens her mouth to speak but no sound comes out.

Lilly saves the best till last: Cormack prowls behind the other two, all hunched slouch, so it's not until they are almost within touching distance that she sees him properly. Right away she feels the familiar kick in the stomach as she traces a line up his arms, tanned and muscular from punting, across his broad shoulders, before finally reaching his face and his eyes, which look everywhere but at her. By the time the three of them reach her cubicle, an awkward silence has opened up. Lilly understands. She wants to tell them that you can get used to the horrible things you see on the ward and what really counts is not what they say but the fact they are here.

'Next time it will be easier,' she says, immediately regretting her words because she shouldn't assume they will come again and doesn't want them to think she's going to be here much longer in case they get too used to life without her.

There's so much to talk about but she's unsure where to start. It occurs to her that this is the first time the four of them have been alone together since the festival and wonders if they are having the same thought at the same time.

'How's it all going?' Jordy eventually asks. You can count on Jordy to put an awkward silence to rest. He lifts up his hand to do a fist bump. It's a routine that started when they were at primary school. But then he notices Lilly's finger is attached to a wire and hastily lowers his arm where it remains stiffly glued to his side.

'It's all good,' says Lilly, cheerily. 'Apart from being spaced out all the time, I feel completely normal. There's a couple more tests and then maybe I can come home and get back to school.'

She waits for Jordy to express enthusiasm at the prospect, or at least give one of those broad smiles that make his pointy chin bob up, but he says nothing. The ease between them has ebbed away. He's nervous and jumpy and can't look her in the eye. Hayley steps into the vacuum and leans in for a hug but pulls away before Lilly feels any warmth.

'It was fucking mental watching you freak out like that,' Jordy says, sitting down in the chair closest to her. 'One minute you were beside me on that stool, the next you were thrashing around the floor and foaming at the mouth. Mr Galveston's cactus collection still hasn't recovered.' He goes on like this for a minute or two, and the more he speaks the more ashamed Lilly feels about so many people witnessing her seizure. When he describes how it looked like Mr Galveston was kissing her, and Cormack laughs, she wonders how she will ever face her English class again.

'I don't think I'll ever get over the shock,' says Hayley, sitting down to share Jordy's chair. Cormack hangs back behind her bed, checking his phone. 'I've had proper nightmares about it.'

'It was probably worse for you than it was for me,' says Lilly, trying to regain her composure and avoid staring at Cormack. 'It was the weirdest thing, like the connection between my brain and body had broken. I knew what was going on but I couldn't do anything about it.'

Even as she speaks she gets annoyed with herself for behaving as if Hayley is the one who thought she was going to die. *Why does everything always have to be about her?* And then she remembers the way she lied to Hayley and is oppressed by the idea that she will have to atone for that for ever.

'It was even worse than when –'

'Shut up, Jordy,' Hayley says, nudging him in the ribs.

He was about to mention what had happened at the festival and Lilly wishes more than anything that the four of them could talk about it together. But instead of taking Jordy's cue she makes an inane comment about how tanned Hayley is and asks Jordy why he's wearing a long-sleeved top when the weather is so hot. Self-consciously, he pulls down his sleeves over his hands but not before she's clocked the weeping red manacles of eczema around his wrists. Hayley and Cormack notice too and Lilly feels bad for drawing attention to them.

'It's a cool top,' she says. He gives a grateful smile. But it's too late.

'What the fuck is that?' Cormack asks, pointing at Jordy's wrists. 'You should keep them covered in case you're contagious too.' Cormack looks at Lilly properly for the first time.

She's puzzled by his comment. 'Contagious?' she asks. 'What do you mean?'

'She doesn't know,' says Jordy, nervously. 'It's obvious.'

'You haven't heard?' Cormack asks. Finally he's spoken to her. He walks around the bed and sits on the windowsill behind her. She can feel the heat from his thigh and hopes the heart monitor doesn't give away how he makes her feel. He makes no attempt to touch her but Lilly assumes he's being sensitive to Hayley. 'It's all over social media. My parents even saw it on the news.'

'I don't get to hear anything,' says Lilly. She's been so caught up in her own troubles that she hasn't really contemplated life outside Ward D3. She tries not to betray her anxiety, remembering one of the reasons Cormack fell for her in the first place was because he thought she was cool. She turns to face him. His expression reveals nothing. His eyes remind her of the black water at Earith. They betray nothing of what lies beneath the surface. She remembers how they swam along the riverbed, their bodies twisting and turning around each other, like otters, and how they lay entwined in the long grass by the riverbank afterwards, their naked bodies coated in a blend of sweat, semen and river slime. She wonders if he ever thinks about this too. It's terrifying how something can mean so much to one person and nothing to another.

'It's gone fucking mental,' says Jordy. 'You're on the front page of the *Post*. Good photo, though.'

Lilly is incredulous. The last time she was in the local paper was when she got a perfect score in her maths GCSE. Now she's become some pitiful tragic figure and she can't handle it. 'What does it say? How did they get a picture of me?' she gabbles.

Hayley leans conspiratorially towards Lilly and holds her hand in sympathy. 'Facebook.'

Lilly recalibrates her expectations: everything will be fine if only she can be friends with Hayley again. She wants to tell her that she has kept the entire history of their friendship in a box in her bedroom: the woven bracelet Hayley made for her, the joint diary they kept in year six, the Polaroid of them getting their ears pierced together, the ticket from the festival, and the receipt from the pub where they had gone with Cormack that evening he scored the pills.

'Two other kids have had seizures. One of them is the boy from the Travellers' site who is friends with Mia.'

'Tas?'

Hayley nods. 'Apparently he cried red tears, like he'd been possessed by the devil. The other is a girl from year ten. She was a complete nobody until it happened. No one saw what happened to her because she was at home.'

Lilly doesn't understand. She had assumed her illness was somehow connected to Mia's discovery of the pregnancy test. Now people think she has a contagious illness. *Was this why Jordy didn't want to hug her? How is it possible that someone I have never met has the same disease and Tas has been infected but not Mia?* But what is most troubling is that all this makes it less likely she will be allowed home soon, which means Cormack will get with someone else. He's never without a girlfriend for long.

'There's health officials swarming over the school, taking water samples, checking the air-conditioning and food from the canteen. Some people thought it might be the HPV vaccine, but when Tas had a seizure they ditched that theory pretty quickly because he's a boy,' says Hayley, the words tumbling out so fast that Lilly's brain struggles to keep up. 'There are rumours that the archaeologists who are digging up that Anglo-Saxon burial ground on the Travellers' site have released some medieval illness on us all.'

'Like the Black Death,' says Jordy, eagerly.

'Maybe the boils on Jordy's wrists are buboes,' jokes Cormack.

'That's impossible. The Black Death didn't happen until the fourteenth century,' Lilly says, without thinking. Jordy smiles. For a moment everything feels normal.

'That's your sister's theory, anyway,' says Hayley. 'Because Tas lives there and he had a seizure the same week as their class visited the Anglo-Saxon burial site.'

'Why does anyone care what Mia thinks?' asks Lilly, in astonishment.

'She saved the boy's life,' says Jordy. 'Your sister is a hero.'

Lilly is simultaneously floored by this news and enraged with her parents for not telling her any of it.

'Emma Vickers's mum has gone crazy. She's organizing a big campaign against the wind farm. She reckons the noise from the blades interferes with brainwaves and causes seizures. But your dad is in a big argument with her because apparently Emma Vickers's dad hates wind farms because he's trying to win a fracking contract.'

'If it was the wind turbines, then lots of people would be affected and it would have happened before somewhere else,' says Lilly.

'That's exactly what my mum says,' Hayley replies.

'All I know is that it's completely wack,' says Jordy. 'That's why we're not at school. No one cares or notices. Not even Mr Galveston. He's furious because no one listens in class any more.'

'Yesterday Cormack and I went swimming at the sluice in the middle of the day and didn't bother going back,' says Hayley. 'We didn't even get a detention.'

'But you hate swimming there, don't you?' asks Lilly, immediately regretting the note of desperation in her tone. 'I thought you were scared of the seals?'

'Not any more.' Hayley smiles.

'Did you go too?' Lilly turns to Jordy, willing him to say yes. Jordy shakes his head and focuses on plucking out bright red hairs from his big toe. Lilly's guts twist. She can hardly mind. It's not as though they're going behind her back, like she did with Cormack. Hayley is being completely open with her. But swimming there was something she shared with Cormack. Distracted by these thoughts, Lilly at first doesn't notice that the doctor has appeared on the other side of her bed. He scans the results of her latest blood tests.

'Very good, very good, Lilly,' Dr Santini congratulates her, as though she is personally responsible for producing the right number of red blood cells, platelets and iron. He smiles broadly and his eyes crinkle until they almost shut.

'You can always guarantee Lilly will get the highest scores,' Jordy teases.

'So I hear, so I hear,' says Dr Santini, laughing. 'She's a model student as well as a model patient.'

Lilly introduces him to her friends and finds herself long-windedly describing how long she has known each of them, what A levels they're studying and where they live because adults like such facts so they don't have to face up to life's more difficult questions like *How can you tell if someone truly loves you? And what is the point of living?* She apologizes because she knows there aren't enough doctors in the hospital to waste his time on trivia and, according to Cormack, one of her worst traits is being a people-pleaser. He listens attentively as if she is his only patient. Lilly is about to start telling him that they all did the same summer job together when he takes a couple of steps towards her friends.

'Since you're here, perhaps you wouldn't mind clearing up a few mysteries for me,' he says. 'It would be most helpful.'

'Sure,' says Jordy, with an obliging shrug of his shoulders. 'Anything to help Lil.'

'I knew you'd want to be useful.' He sits on the edge of the bed, arms crossed, like he has all the time in the world. 'Were any of you present when Lilly had her first seizure?' he asks casually. He picks up her biology textbook from the table and flicks through a couple of pages.

Jordy straightens his back and his eyes flicker from Hayley to Cormack. He's always so easy to read. Cormack jabs Jordy in the calf with the toe of his trainer but fortunately he's out of Dr Santini's sightline.

'Because it really helps with the diagnosis to know the exact circumstances of the first seizure.' He says the word 'first' slowly and emphatically. 'It's critical. Maybe you noticed symptoms that could help me work out what might have happened.' He snaps shut the biology book and contemplates Jordy. 'According to Lilly's notes, she received medical attention at a festival in the summer. Were any of you with her?' A current shoots through Lilly's body as if every nerve is receiving the same message at the same time. *He knows.*

'The only time it happened was at school. We were all

there.' Jordy nods and doesn't stop nodding until Hayley nudges him again. His lips, which look like a hastily drawn afterthought at the best of times, narrow into a cartoonish straight line.

'Actually, I wasn't there at the beginning, only the end,' mumbles Cormack.

'How come?' Dr Santini asks. 'Did someone tell you what was going on or did you happen to turn up by chance?'

'Pure chance,' says Cormack, giving him a dazzling smile. Dr Santini doesn't wait for him to expand and instead performs a sideways shuffle until the tips of his black Chelsea boots point at Hayley. He rocks slowly backwards and forwards waiting for her to say something.

'I couldn't really see,' says Hayley, with a smile. 'It's probably best to ask Jordy. He was sitting next to Lil at the back of the classroom.' Jordy, however, remains silent. 'We were in an English class, weren't we, Jordy? We were discussing *Beowulf*. You remember, don't you?' Hayley prompts him.

'That's right,' Jordy mumbles.

'Can you remember when you first noticed something was wrong with Lilly?' asks Dr Santini.

Jordy stares into the distance, like he's trying to recall something that happened centuries ago. He can't stop blinking. Lilly notices how the tips of his eyelashes are red, like his hair, while their roots are almost translucent. He looks so uncomfortable that eventually Dr Santini takes pity on him.

'I'm sorry if this is making you feel uneasy. But however awful it is for you to relive this experience, it is far worse for Lilly not knowing why it happened.'

'It's fine,' says Jordy. 'Really. It's all coming back. I was copying Lilly's notes on *Beowulf*. She doesn't mind me doing that and everyone knows she makes the best notes. I noticed her hand was shaking.'

'Did you say anything to her?'

'No. We're all terrified of the teacher and he'd been giving Lilly a hard time because she'd dropped a grade on some essays so it didn't seem strange that her hands were shaking. She cares a lot about her work.' He glances at Lilly as if to make sure he hasn't said anything out of turn. She smiles re-assuringly. The more detail he gives, the less likely the doctor is to be suspicious that she hasn't been entirely honest with him. Jordy pulls up the sleeves of his sweatshirt and shows Dr Santini the eczema running all the way up to his elbows. There are scabs everywhere. The bottom half closest to Jordy's wrist has open, weeping red sores that make Lilly's eyes water.

'That looks infected,' says Dr Santini. 'You should get it checked out with your GP.'

'It gets worse when I'm stressed,' Jordy says.

'Why are you frightened of your English teacher?' asks Dr Santini.

'Because if we don't hit the right grades, he won't let us stay in his class and the school might ask us to leave if we're under-performing. It affects their position in the league tables. That's what happened to Cormack. He got thrown out of the English class after his summer exams.'

Jordy glances anxiously at Cormack, who gives an almost imperceptible nod of approval.

'I see.' He writes this down and taps his notes with his pen.

Jordy continues: 'Mr Galveston asked Lilly a question. She's always been his favourite. He used to call her his heaven candle, which is an Anglo-Saxon kenning for a star, but then Freya turned up in the class and he became ob-sessed with her. He always has favourites.'

'Are they always girls?'

'They're always the cleverest students,' says Jordy. Then he apologizes to Lilly. 'I'm not saying that Freya is more intelligent than you.'

'She is,' says Lilly, with a shrug. 'She doesn't have to try. It's effortless for her.'

'He started pressurizing Lilly to address the question. It was something really basic. Even I knew the answer. I noticed she was getting sweatier and sweatier. She started drooling and then she slid off the stool, like she was melting.'

'I saw her having the fit,' Hayley chips in. 'It was so frightening. She was thrashing around on the floor, legs kicking out at anyone who went too close. It was like she was possessed. No one knew what to do. Freya called for an ambulance. I was too upset.'

'The only person who really knew what to do was Mr Galveston,' says Lilly. 'His beard scratched my face. And his breath smelt of cigarettes and biscuits.'

'You can remember that?' asks Dr Santini, almost pirouetting round to face Lilly. 'You didn't mention that before.'

'I can remember almost everything.'

Dr Santini's beeper sounds. There's an emergency in the ICU and he has to leave.

'Well, thank you all for your help.'

For an instant after he leaves no one speaks. Then Cormack leans towards Jordy. 'Ask her,' he says quietly. His words are like stepping on a nettle in the cotton grass. Jordy looks down at his flip-flopped feet. His toes are as long as Lilly's fingers.

'Ask her,' Cormack repeats.

'Ask me what?' Lilly says. For a wild moment she thinks that Jordy is going to ask her if she wants to go out with Cormack again because in years gone by that was how school relationships were negotiated.

'Ask her,' says Cormack again. This time there's more

menace in his tone. He nudges Jordy's ankle with the tip of his trainer, not hard enough to hurt, but hard enough for him to know he's not going to let this go. Jordy furiously scratches his wrists.

'Have you told anyone about what happened?' Jordy mutters. He can't look her in the eye. There is a long silence.

'No, I haven't,' says Lilly. 'Why would I do that?'

'And did you delete those Snapchat films?' asks Cormack.

'Yes,' she lies.

'Right,' says Cormack, thumping his hands against his thighs. 'We'd better split. Bye, Lil.'

Hayley gives her a quick hug and runs to catch up with Cormack.

'Is that why you came?' she asks Jordy. But she knows the answer to the question before she has even finished asking it. 'At least have the guts to look me in the eye.' Jordy stares up at her. His eyes have gone all cloudy. Lilly puts out her hand, runs her fingers gently through his thick red hair, down the side of his left cheekbone and tilts his pointy chin towards her. He's so familiar it hurts but she sees the treachery in his eyes.

'I almost forgot, Lil.' From his rucksack, he pulls out the notebook with 'The Certainties' written across the front and hands it to her. 'I thought you might not want anyone else to see this.'

'Thanks, Jords,' says Lilly.

Jordy gets up to go. It's their indifference that hurts the most. She watches as Cormack drapes his arm around Hayley. He's taunting her. Like he used to taunt Hayley. They saunter to the end of the ward and pull open the door as Grace pushes it from the other side.

To make it appear she doesn't care, she nonchalantly flicks through the notebook that Jordy brought in, pausing on a page that has the title 'Solid Words'. She skim-reads the list in her mum's tiny black handwriting: *weekly shop, swimming lessons, bedtime story, birthday treat, goodnight kiss*. When Lilly looks at the hands holding the notebook she has the strangest sensation that they don't belong to her. Her fingers are numb, as if she's just dived into the river at Earith. She watches as the notebook slips through her hands on to the bed, and when her fingers won't work to pick it up she uses her elbow to slide it under the pillow.

'How dare you?' Patrick hears Grace hiss at Cormack. Fortunately her voice blends with the hum of machines and the low murmur of conversation. 'Who gave you permission to come here?'

Patrick winces. He knows he should intervene but Grace's raw anger makes her ruthlessly decisive and he's floundering in the face of this unexpected encounter. He watches hopelessly as her eyes narrow and she presses her finger hard into Cormack's chest. Patrick finds himself focusing on tiny details: the fact that Grace has only put mascara on one eye; the way the buttons on her shirt are done up the wrong way; and the tattoo across Cormack's knuckles. He glances anxiously at Lilly, who stands stricken at the end of the ward tethered to the oxygen saturation monitor. Even if she can't hear Grace's words, her anger is obvious. When she finally stops prodding Cormack, Patrick finds himself fixated by the deep dimple her fingertip has left in the middle of his faded green T-shirt. The boy remains silent, his expression inscrutable, so Patrick can't decide whether he's scornful or scared.

'Aren't you going to do something, Patrick?' He suddenly realizes that although Grace is still prowling around Cormack she is actually talking to him. Now it's his turn to panic. What exactly does she expect him to do? Take a pop at Cormack? March him into the side room and interrogate him under the fluorescent lighting? Squeeze his balls until he confesses everything? He's not even sure what she wants to know. He runs through the facts. This is the boy who has had a secret relationship with their daughter for several months. They are both over the age of consent. Personally, Patrick would rather Lilly go for boys like Jordy, who would have treated her with respect, rather than Cormack, who apparently made lewd sexual comments about Lilly to show off in front of his friends. But there's nothing new in that dynamic. That's why Rob, who was all ruthless charm, got all the girls instead of him. And although Patrick would rather not think of his daughter having sex with anyone, in the age of hook-ups, sex-on-demand apps, live sex streamed to your phone, it strikes him as quaintly old-fashioned that Lilly and Cormack kept their relationship private. He should have tried to explain this to Grace.

'Not here. Not now, Grace,' he hears himself say. He tries to be assertive but his tone sounds ridiculously plaintive, like Mia when she won't get off the computer.

'We just wanted to visit Lil, to see how she is, Mrs Vermuyden,' Jordy politely interjects, clearing his throat a couple of times.

Patrick shoots him a quick smile that he hopes is both grateful and encouraging. Jordy scratches his arms and Patrick recoils when he sees the bloody weeping sores on his wrists.

'We've been so worried about her, Grace,' says Hayley. 'I was there when it happened and I've had nightmares ever since. It was terrible seeing my best friend go through something like that . . . but you're absolutely right. We should have checked with you first before visiting. It's not Cormack's fault. It's mine. I should have known.'

Grace doesn't stop staring at Cormack. Her tenacity is both admirable and terrifying. She steps towards him. 'I know your kind,' she says, pressing her finger into his chest again. 'Stay away from my daughter.'

'And I know yours,' says Cormack, smoothly moving her hand out of the way. He stares fixedly at Grace until she looks away, then turns his back on them to push his way through the double doors, like a cowboy leaving a saloon bar. Hayley rushes after him and he puts his arm around her. Only Jordy looks back and waves.

'What on earth are you thinking? How is having a go at Cormack in front of Lilly's friends going to help?' Patrick hisses at Grace. He feels a shimmer of nerves that this reckless impetuosity isn't a new quality and either he has ignored it or it has erupted after years of dormancy. He uneasily remembers the way she turned Lilly's bedroom inside out.

'I want him to know that his card is marked. I'm not going to let this go until I know the truth.'

'Calm down,' Patrick orders. He scans the ward to check if anyone is looking but one of the advantages of hospital life is that everyone is caught up in their own dramas. 'If people see us losing control, this thing is going to get bigger and bigger. Everyone watches us.' *Actually, what most people do now is steer a wide berth around them in case they're contagious*, Patrick thinks.

'You need to face up to what has been going on with Lilly. What kind of dad lets a boy treat his daughter like that?'

'You should deal with the facts rather than conjecture. Like a proper journalist, instead of someone who works for a two-bit newsletter.'

186

He's grateful when Juan herds them into an empty recovery room and brings them a cup of almost drinkable tea. Patrick scrolls through his phone and deletes the message from Marius, warning that he needs to be paid before the end of the week.

Lilly rolls on to her side and lies immobile, facing the window, nose touching the bedrails, imagining this is how it might feel to be in a prison cell. She dreamily wonders if the sickly smell drifting past her nose is coming through the gap in the window. She can't be certain if the tingling in her hands began when Cormack left or her parents arrived or during the horrendous interlude in the middle where they all collided and Grace's meltdown made the alarm on her heart monitor shriek so loudly that Dr Santini was called back to the ward. But it had definitely begun by the time Juan intervened. She doesn't want her parents to know. When she thinks about Grace, it is as if a great weight is pressing down so hard on her chest that she can take only the shallowest breaths.

She explains to Dr Santini how the tremor started in her fingers shortly after the sickly smell returned, and crept up through her wrists and into her arms. She expects to find saliva pooling in her throat like last time but instead her voice is clear: 'Please don't make me see my parents. Please. They make everything worse.'

'I'll tell them you need to rest. It's very important that you stay as calm as possible for the telemetry tests.' He tries to distract her by describing how twenty-four electrodes will be stuck to her scalp and these will read her brainwaves while a video records all of her movements. He looks serious and she feels bad that she has spoilt his day by having a relapse.

He prescribes a sedative and Lilly is grateful for the way it immediately muffles her feelings. Her leaden eyelids refuse to stay open. They remain tight shut when the nurse checks the oxygen monitor on her finger and dinner arrives on a trolley. Lilly thinks of her mother's anger, Hayley's euphoria, Cormack's hatred, Jordy's bloody wrists, the pregnancy test. *The world is nothing more than pure emotion and I don't want to feel any more.*

She can't believe that she is the same person who jumped into the lock by Earith Sluice to demonstrate her fearlessness to Cormack shortly after she'd started sleeping with him. She remembers how the four walls of the narrow coffin-like lock were filled to their uppermost limit and it felt like a mysterious force was sucking her to the bottom and keeping her captive there. When she looked up she couldn't see the light from the sun any more. Everywhere was darkness. She lost her bearings and held her breath until she was overtaken with a rapturous feeling, as if she was floating outside her body. This is how she feels now, except this time Cormack isn't waiting to grab her beneath her arms and pull her to the surface.

10

It's strange how sometimes the best and worst moments happen at exactly the same time, Mia thinks, as she tunes out of Miss Swain's latest attempt to explain the concept of fronted adverbials to her year-six English class the following day. When Tas sat down beside her out of the blue at the beginning of the lesson, Mia was filled with a rare sense of complete happiness that started in the middle of her stomach and spread outwards until her entire body felt held in a strange state of grace.

The week he was in hospital is the longest they have gone without seeing each other since they first met, and even looking at the broken zip on his battered red rucksack made her smile. However, the joy was short-lived as it became apparent that he was completely ignoring her. For the first time ever, he hasn't spoken a word to her the entire lesson. She can't even be certain that he has looked at her. Instead he focuses on useless tasks, like sharpening all his pencils and cleaning his fingernails with a compass.

When Miss Swain starts handing round worksheets Mia steals a furtive look at him. Tas stares at the piece of paper. She notes that his eyes are still bloodshot. She wants to tell him that she hopes they stay like this until Halloween because it's a really good look for trick or treating.

She turns to the worksheet and sighs deeply. They have

to come up with three examples of fronted adverbials. 'God help me!' mutters Mia, which is a phrase she has heard her dad use frequently over the past couple of weeks. She admires Miss Swain's determination to get them through their SATs but, frankly, if even Bea Vickers can't come up with an example of a fronted adverbial, what hope is there for the rest of them? Even her dad had never heard of them when she asked him last night.

She didn't bother consulting Grace. Her mum spends all her time on her computer either reading the latest news on the contagion or researching Lilly's symptoms and cross-checking them with what happened to Tas. The only time she speaks to Mia is when she wants to ask a question about how Tas felt before his seizure. *Did he say it was as if he was being dragged into a dark tunnel? Was the sensation in his hands more like pins and needles than stinging nettles?* Or she investigates what has been going on between Lilly and Cormack. Mia might as well be invisible.

Like Lilly's dead baby. Perhaps when they do the brain scan there will be a hole the shape of a foetus in the middle and people will finally understand what has happened. Mia is beginning to think that Lilly won't get better until her parents know the truth and half wonders if she should be the one to tell them. She thought her dad might realize when she showed him the picture in her Anglo-Saxon diary but he didn't even react.

'Any questions?' asks Miss Swain.

Mia's hand shoots into the air. 'Is this the kind of question they might ask you in a job interview?'

'No,' says Miss Swain, crisply, as she heads towards Bea's desk. Mia turns round to see that Bea is crying.

'I'm never going to understand,' she whimpers. 'I'm going to fail.'

'Tas,' Mia whispers, taking advantage of the diversion. 'Did you bring something for Show and Tell?' She wonders whether anyone has told him that Miss Swain has organized a competition to distract them from the hysteria over the contagion. He gives her a sideways glance but his head doesn't move. She notices that he has done up all of his shirt buttons to try to hide the bruising around his neck.

'Tas,' she hisses. 'Do you want to know what I'm going to talk about?' He continues to ignore her.

Mia starts to explain to him that she wanted to bring in Elvis, but she's worried he's not well. His skin has gone a mottly grey colour and there's a ridge on his back where his spine is starting to show. She knows that Tas loves her eel as much as she does. 'Maybe I should release him. What do you think? I'm going to build him up a bit with octopus so he has the strength to swim home to mate.'

'Where are you going to get octopus?' he suddenly asks.

'Sainsbury's,' she whispers back. His lower lip curls into a smile, although he still doesn't look at her. 'Shall I show you what I've brought in for Show and Tell?'

Tas finds secrets irresistible. Usually he would tickle her to death to get something like this out of her. 'It's something amazing that no one has ever brought in before. It's going to be unforgettable. Un-for-gettable.'

It has to be because there is a lot riding on this Show and Tell. Over the past week Mia has noticed that the same girls who were desperate to be her friend in the days immediately following Tas's seizure have stopped asking her to join in their games and have gone back to ignoring her, leaving her to eat lunch alone. One new friend who had asked her on a playdate on Monday told her the following day that she had made a mistake and couldn't invite her after all.

They haven't made mean comments like they used to

but their interest in her has definitely faded. This is worse than what happened before because for a brief, blissful period Mia had realized how it might feel to be popular like Lilly.

In the days after she'd saved Tas's life, Miss Swain had been really nice to her. She'd made her class monitor for the week and given her an A for her next entry in the Anglo-Saxon diary. But even Miss Swain has started to get impatient with her again. When her mum and dad forgot to pick her up because they were visiting Lilly a couple of days ago, the teacher had turned down her request for an ice cream and told her to go and sit in the school office until they arrived. When Mia tried to tell her again about how the archaeologists have caused the illness by angering the spirits of the dead, Miss Swain brusquely warned her 'to deal in facts not fiction'.

Mia puts her hand into her bag to feel for her Show and Tell object. 'I'm holding it in my hand, Tas. Don't you want to see what it is?'

When he doesn't respond, she throws her rubber at him. It hits him on the cheek but he doesn't flinch.

Miss Swain finishes circling the classroom and returns to her desk. 'Mia, perhaps you can remind the class what a fronted adverbial is,' she says. Mia gives a nonchalant shrug. 'Then, since you and Tas both find these difficult, can I suggest you stop trying to distract him?'

'Yes, Miss Swain.' She pronounces the teacher's surname 'swan' because this always makes Tas laugh.

'Tas, would you like to go and sit next to Bea?' suggests Miss Swain.

Tas nods. He picks up his belongings and moves to the row behind. Mia's breath catches in her throat. *What is wrong with him?* During first break he runs into the playground

192

before Mia has even got up from her desk. She stomps around looking for him. Eventually she finds Tas cowering in the corner of the sports cupboard, knees pulled tight against his chest, hands covering his face.

'Will you come back with me after school?' she asks him. He doesn't move.

'I can't, Mia,' he whispers.

'Why?' He doesn't reply. 'Why can't you?' Mia persists. Tas never refuses her anything. That's why she loves him. From the first day they met everything was so straightforward.

'I can't. I'm too scared.' He looks up at her.

'We need to go through with the final part of our plan,' Mia insists. He looks so frightened that she almost feels sorry for him.

'I don't want to hurt you,' he whispers.

'Don't worry, Tas, we're protected,' she tells him.

He gets up and pushes his way past her back into the playground. She'll never catch him. He's the fastest runner in the year.

Later that afternoon Miss Swain sits at the back of the classroom, waiting for Bea to finish her long-winded Show and Tell about a fossil she found in a Cambridgeshire field. It's an ammonite, which everyone knows are two a penny in these parts. Literally all you have to do is stick a spade in the ground and you'll dig one up. Mia impatiently taps her pencil on the desk until the lead finally snaps.

'Thanks, Bea. We've learnt so much,' Miss Swain interrupts, when it becomes apparent the girl might never stop. 'You must have put a lot of work into researching these fascinating fossils. Amazing!' The teacher checks the clock on the wall and asks Mia to go to the front. As she gets up, Mia notices that Miss Swain closes the notebook where she has been reviewing the different Show and Tell talks and pulls a mirror out of her handbag to check her lipstick.

Mia knows that school is meant to end in six minutes but she doesn't see why she should cut short her own speech just because Bea's talk dragged on, especially when she's spent the best part of a week researching and rehearsing in front of Elvis. Miss Swain is always going on about the importance of bloody resilience but then lets cry-babies like Bea off the hook.

She carefully positions herself behind Miss Swain's desk, clears her throat, straightens her back, and stands, feet splayed, her ankles pressed tightly together so that she can feel the ring. Her hand remains inside the rucksack clutching the object she is about to reveal. It's a technique to heighten anticipation and generate maximum tension that she learnt from watching David Blaine videos.

Still concealing the object, Mia starts to speak. 'In Egyptian times, when a woman thought she might be pregnant she urinated on a seed of wheat and a seed of barley. If the wheat grew it meant she was having a girl. If the barley grew she was having a boy. If neither sprouted she wasn't pregnant at all.'

Mia feels twenty-four sets of eyes bore into her. She knew this would get their attention. Ten-year-olds always find bodily functions irresistible. A couple of the boys snigger and nudge each other. She ignores them and continues.

'In the sixteenth century, specialists known as piss prophets would read a woman's urine like tea leaves, claiming to know by its appearance if the woman who supplied it was pregnant.'

The same boys are now giggling uncontrollably. She sees Tas staring at her. He is smiling broadly and shaking his head in disbelief. Next to him Bea has her hand over her mouth in shock and awe. She nudges Tas but he shifts away from her. He approves, Mia joyously realizes. His reaction gives her courage. She sees Miss Swain shift uncomfortably in her seat. She won't appreciate the subject matter but it's difficult for her to get angry because Mia is following Miss Swain's exact instructions to stick to the facts and use the correct terminology.

Mia slowly withdraws her Show and Tell object from the bottom of her rucksack. When it looks as if it is about to emerge she tantalizingly keeps it just out of view so that everyone cranes forward, desperate to catch the first glimpse. She has the confidence of someone who knows that no one else has pulled off such a great introduction to their talk this week or possibly ever in the history of Show and Tell. When finally she pulls out the small plastic cylinder everyone looks puzzled. Someone wonders whether it is a kazoo.

'This is a pregnancy test,' Mia announces in a serious tone. She holds it up above her head. A collective gasp ripples around the classroom. She waits for a second. This is definitely more enticing than Madani's talk on Indian sweets, which included a sample for everyone in the class; it's way more interesting than Reg's talk on Lionel Messi, even though he brought in a shirt signed by the footballer; and it's more engaging than Hope's talk on poisonous caterpillars. Everyone had agreed that these were the best talks so far. But Mia already knows she has trumped them all. She glances at Miss Swain to gauge her expression and is pleased to see that she looks surprised because there are lots of points for originality. The prize is surely within her reach and this gives her renewed confidence. She pulls the dipstick out of the box, removes the lid with an extravagant flourish and gives a small bow, like a magician's assistant.

She points out where a woman has to pee as well as the small window in the middle, which shows the result. Everyone is completely silent. She has them eating out of her hand.

'But this is more than a straightforward pregnancy test,' says Mia, lowering her voice for maximum effect. The entire class leans even further forward over their desks to scrutinize the dipstick. No one is laughing any more. 'You can tell from the blue line through the middle that it is a positive pregnancy test. Strictly speaking, this means that the person who urinated on it was going to have a real actual baby.'

Miss Swain looks flustered, as if she is trying to work out whether telling her to stop now will cause more disruption than letting her continue. Mia sidetracks into the modern history of pregnancy tests, explaining how before the blue line was invented a positive result came in the form of a baby's smiling face, a belly that looked pregnant and even a wriggling sperm. This had evolved over the years as people realized that getting pregnant isn't always cheery or good news for a woman. Then she mentions how half of Anglo-Saxon women died during childbirth, which probably explains why some women did everything they could to get rid of unborn babies and that perhaps this was what the girl at the burial site had done, which is why it's a terrible idea to dig up her grave.

The school bell indicating the end of the day rings in the background but no one moves. Mia speaks over the noise. 'This is why she was punished. Nowadays, in some countries, if a woman doesn't want to keep her baby, she can have an abortion. This is when you go to hospital and either take a pill or get a special doctor to suck out the baby with a Hoover so it is born dead. You can use a Dyson too.'

There is a collective intake of breath. Mia hopes no one

asks her exactly how this works. She walks round to the side of the desk. Twenty-four sets of eyes follow her. She explains how the history of abortion is as old as the history of pregnancy, and that the Egyptians used to coat a tampon in honey and crushed dates to induce miscarriages. Miss Swain's mouth hangs open.

'The girl who this test belongs to got pregnant very young. Her boyfriend loved someone else and she couldn't tell her parents what had happened because it wasn't part of their plans for her. And so, very sadly and tragically, she came to the conclusion that she couldn't bring another life into the world.' Miss Swain stands up and is about to speak when Mia starts up again. She addresses the whole class but really she's only speaking to one person. She fixes Tas with her gaze. She pauses for effect. 'I know this because she told me.'

I I

Grace warily eyes her phone as it silently blinks on the desk beside her. She doesn't recognize the number so she lets it drift to voicemail. She's exhausted by calls from well-meaning parents she's barely met enquiring about Lilly, especially when there's nothing new to tell them and they all ask the same questions. 'They can't find anything wrong with her . . . There's still no explanation . . . She's not infectious.' She understands that people are scared. Some are even refusing to let their children go to school. Others want her advice because they suspect their children might be developing similar symptoms. Did Grace notice a strange rash on Lilly's torso? Did she have headaches? An aversion to bright light? There have even been a couple of calls from journalists. One of them wanted to know if she had signed Catriona Vickers's petition against the wind farm the same day Lilly had her seizure because she thought it had something to do with her daughter's illness. What could she say? 'I signed without reading it to get Catriona off my back'?

Today is the first time she's been back to work since Lilly fell ill and she wants to savour the illusion of normality. She didn't have to come in: Tony is perfectly capable of putting the newsletter to bed on his own. But after another night of bad dreams and fitful sleep she'd woken up with an overwhelming urge to get out of the house.

Just before the weekend the builders had inexplicably told Patrick that they were downing tools, leaving everything half finished. The house is a total mess of loose wires, exposed brickwork and half-grouted tiles. Even worse, although the boiler had been broken all winter, when they got back from the hospital yesterday they discovered that, after months of inactivity, the radiators had mysteriously belched into action and couldn't be turned off. The air inside the house has been sucked dry and the red dust has baked to a hard crust.

There are dying insects everywhere. Grace's head feels full of them: buzzing wasps, wriggling centipedes and burrowing beetles. Patrick diagnosed an electrical fault after hitting the radiator with a hammer. She knows it's a half-baked theory but he treats any criticism as an affront to his masculinity so, rather than argue about getting in a plumber, it seemed easier to leave him and Mia asleep.

When Tony comes through the door and sees Grace at her desk he hugs her with such emotion that the middle buttons of his shirt pop open. She is immediately made to feel how chaotic and rudderless office life has become without her and how order will inevitably be restored now that she is here. It feels good to be wanted and even better to be seen as the fulcrum of self-control and stability when at home Patrick treats her as if she's unhinged. He even speaks differently to her, slowing down the syllables in each word so that by the time he reaches the end of a sentence she can no longer remember its beginning. 'You're indispensable,' Tony says chirpily, when finally he releases her. His smooth round face glistens in the heat and he smells of cheap aftershave and instant coffee but his familiarity induces the sweetest kind of happiness. For a brief and rare moment her worries about Lilly evaporate.

'I can't stay for long,' she reminds him.

'You've lost weight,' he observes, ignoring her comment. 'You're all skin and bone.' He offers her a piece of congealed chocolate biscuit that is stuck to the bottom of his editor's sign. When Grace turns it down he pops it into his mouth. 'Which leads me nicely on to our front-page story: the problem of obesity among local ducks that are fed too much white bread. Might win us a Pulitzer.'

It's a well-worn joke. Beyond a few perfunctory questions about Lilly, Tony shows no interest in the reason for Grace's absence, even though he must have seen the television and newspaper reports on the sick schoolchildren. 'If it can't go in the newsletter, it's not news,' is his general philosophy. Grace once joked that the reverse was true: if it was news it didn't go in. He had looked so hurt she had never mentioned the frothy content of the newsletter again.

Instead he positions himself on the edge of her desk and earnestly recounts his frustrations with printers changing deadlines, advertisers failing to pay bills and the broken photocopier that costs too much to mend. She's heard it all before but it's such a good distraction from thinking about Lilly that she wishes he would never stop. He pleads with her to write three short features for their next edition, even though she has told him she can do only half a day's work. When he finally stops speaking she notices her desk is covered with a fine film of biscuit crumbs.

She quickly pulls together a piece about a fire in a tinder-dry stubble-field, produces half a page on the overweight ducks, and finally turns to the regular back-page feature. It was her idea to do a question-and-answer with prominent members of the local community at the end of each newsletter and she savours these interviews because it gives her an inkling of how it might feel to be a proper journalist.

Grace looks at the schedule and sees that the next slot is due to be filled by the archaeologist running the dig on the Travellers' site. As she dials the number, she manages a smile as she remembers Mia's madcap theory that the archaeologists are responsible for Lilly's illness, which in turn reminds her of the missing ring. So at the end of the interview Grace casually explains she's a parent at the local primary school and asks whether it has been found. The archaeologist explains that the police have been called in to investigate its disappearance because it is a rare example of a ring with runic inscriptions and is worth tens of thousands of pounds, which means it was most likely stolen to order. After this, Grace emails her three stories to Tony, who grumbles about having to edit everything on screen because the printer isn't working, as if this has never happened before.

'You're so fast, Grace,' he compliments her.

While Tony is immersed in his edits, Grace pulls out Lilly's phone from her bag and turns it in her hand, as if she's examining a valuable relic of her own. Except instead of decoding runic inscriptions she has to get to grips with the even more enigmatic content of Lilly's social-media accounts.

It had been an impulsive decision to go to Lilly's bed to say goodbye after the confrontation with Cormack. Patrick fought hard to dissuade her, arguing that not only had the doctor said Lilly should be left to sleep but that any delay would mean she would break her promise to pick up Mia from school for the first time that week. But Grace was adamant. She wouldn't leave without seeing her daughter, even if Lilly was sedated. So she slipped out of his grasp and headed back to Lilly's cubicle, noticing the red imprint of his fingers around her forearm.

She had planted a kiss on Lilly's cheek, worrying how cold her skin felt against her lips before combing her daughter's hair through her fingers and dividing it into two neat sections either side of a perfect middle parting. Then she had held Lilly's hand in her own, stroking her long pale fingers, frowning uneasily when she saw the way the skin was shredded around her nails: it was something else she had failed to observe about her daughter. *How long have they looked like this?* she wonders. And why hadn't she noticed before?

She felt Lilly's breath on her cheek but it was as faint as the whisper of the leaves outside the open window. *Still as death.* For the first time Grace understood the meaning of the phrase. She couldn't believe how she had taken for granted the simple wonder of Lilly breathing for so many years. She had always prided herself on anticipating danger for her children. She had dragged Lilly to swimming lessons almost as soon as she could walk; she had pressed a glass on her skin at the first sign of any potential meningococcal rash; she had accompanied her on dummy runs to practise the route to secondary school. But it had never occurred to her that one day she might just stop breathing.

As she watched the shallow rise and fall of Lilly's chest, Grace closed her eyes to breathe in the essence of her daughter. But alongside the familiar scent of lemon, fresh cake and damp wood, there was the same sickly-sweet odour. She jerked around, almost expecting her mother to be standing there. *Stay away, Olwyn,* she warned. She slammed the window shut in case the smell was coming from outside. But it was too late. The same old worries wrapped themselves around her body like bindweed, until it felt as if she was the one who couldn't breathe. *She wasn't good enough. She would neglect her children. She had inherited bad blood.*

Then an idea took shape. Without thinking, she took Lilly's phone from her handbag and pressed her daughter's left thumb on the fingerprint sensor. Lilly didn't flinch. The password was accepted. Then it was a quick Google search to work out how to prevent the phone from locking again, and suddenly she was inside Lilly's world. *I won't let you down this time*, she whispered as she left.

She hasn't shared this development with Patrick because he would purse his lips and lock his jaw in the expression of hostile disapproval that has become his signature look over the past few weeks. He's even annoyed with her for researching Lilly's illness and her attempt to find commonalities with what happened to Tas and the girl from the secondary school. She hasn't had much luck with the latter. The girl's mother has stopped answering her calls.

She had overheard Patrick on the phone to his mother yesterday evening, describing Grace's behaviour as irrational and discussing whether he should encourage her to seek professional help. And she can tell he has been in contact with Nuala because he keeps coming out with words that only she uses, like 'pronto' and 'discombobulated'. He's so ridiculously transparent. If he bothered to talk to her, he might discover that she agrees with him: she is mad with worry about Lilly. But Patrick never expresses what he thinks. Instead he holds forth about Lilly's right to privacy and autonomy as if he's presenting evidence to a select committee. He's completely avoiding the fact their daughter has been leading some kind of double life. She knows Patrick will immediately dent any self-congratulatory pride in her aptitude for sleuthing.

Grace opens her notebook. When she began her research earlier today, she decided to approach it with detached professionalism, trawling through Lilly's social media, messages and photos with the same kind of methodical rigour she would apply if she were an investigative reporter. She imagines herself as one of those crusading journalists who have won prizes doing true-crime podcasts.

The only surprise so far has been the banality of Lilly's life on social media. *Digital communication really is the enemy of creativity*, Grace quickly concluded, after a long session scanning unimaginative adverts, pointless memes, birthday notifications and changes in profile pictures on Lilly's Facebook account. Now she turns her attention to Snapchat. It's less familiar and it takes her a while to work out the quickest way of getting through the hundreds of saved messages.

She knows what she's looking for, even if she's unsure how to find it. She skips the spike in unopened messages in the days after Lilly's first seizure and instead focuses on group chats with the most interesting names. But Highway to Hell turns out to be Lilly's English class exchanging messages about their stress over Mr Galveston's mood swings, and Waterbabes is her swimming team. It's like doing the cryptic crossword: the clues only make sense when you're given the answers. Grace checks the messages from Lilly's closest friends. Then, towards the end of the feed, she finds a thread called celestialcreatures. She remembers the tattoo on Cormack's knuckles and realizes straight away that this is Lilly and Cormack's thread. She pauses, then thinks of her mother again and presses enter.

There are no recent posts. The last messages Cormack sent were the day after Lilly's seizure. She scans through them noticing the change in tone from *please call me, please now, u okay lil* to *keep it on the down low, don't say a word* and finally *STFU*.

She scrolls all the way to the beginning of the chat and

sees that it started mid-July, just before the end of the summer term. At the bottom are dozens of videos. 'Yes,' she says triumphantly, gripping the phone. She's hit the jackpot. The first five are blurry clips of Lilly, Cormack, Hayley and Jordy hurtling down the same straight Fenland road in a truck. They end almost before they begin. Grace can tell from the potholes and the way the truck is wider than the road that they are most likely driving down one of the droves that bisect remote farms in the Middle Level.

Loud music plays in the background so you can't hear anything that is said. Cormack's tattoos make him clearly identifiable as the driver. There's an occasional glimpse of his right hand gripping the steering wheel. In the early videos the other arm is draped around Hayley. Just one week later Lilly has replaced her. Grace notes this date. Even though most of them are shot in slow motion, Grace can tell Cormack is always driving too fast. None of them wears a seatbelt. Jordy must be the cameraman because everything is filmed from the row of seats behind.

Grace scrolls in search of a longer clip. This one lasts a minute. It starts with Lilly standing on her own, staring down at something hidden off camera. At first she's so still that Grace thinks the phone has frozen. But then a wisp of hair blows into her face. The background colours are unnaturally bright: the sky is vivid blue and the long grass too green. Lilly's gaze is fixed on the ground so you can't see her eyes. At first it's difficult to tell what she's looking at. Then the camera pans down and Grace can see from the metal winding gear and the guillotine gates at each end that she's poised on the edge of a lock.

She's wearing her old blue and white striped bikini. She does a few stretches and reaches for the sky with her hands. In the background Grace hears Jordy's voice: 'Don't jump,

Lil, don't do it!' Cormack laughs and the camera shakes. He turns the lens towards Hayley, who looks at the ground sullenly, drilling her toe into the long grass. He asks her something and she looks up and sticks out her tongue and grins, but the smile has gone before it reaches her eyes. Lilly doubles over, legs slightly bent, hands resting on her feet, head flexed, staring at the inky black water, as if she's in a competition. Which, in a sense, she is. For a moment, she's caught on the edge of something that is bigger than the decision to dive into the lock. She smiles at Cormack and in her expression Grace notices a hardness and a softness that she hasn't seen before. She notes this too.

Then suddenly Lilly leaps from the edge and dives beneath the surface. The lock is narrow and she has no idea how deep the water is. 'No!' Grace cries out. Why on earth would she do this? It's so dangerous. Grace has warned Lilly endlessly about the mysterious currents, the weeds that wrap themselves around limbs, the underwater pumps and old machinery hidden in the Fenland waterways. The clip stops but the scene is picked up in the next video. It starts, art-student style, with the concentric circles in the water where Lilly dived in growing smaller and smaller as though the lock has swallowed her whole. Grace's hands shake so violently that she has to put the phone on the desk to watch the rest. She sees Jordy pacing up and down the edge of the lock, running his hands through his red hair until it stands on end. Ten, twenty seconds pass. It unexpectedly finishes. Grace feels nauseous. When she touches her face it is damp with tears.

In the next shot Hayley is lying flat on her stomach at the edge of the lock, repeatedly calling Lilly's name. Jordy strips to his underpants and drops down on his hands and knees to reverse clumsily towards the ladder attached to the side. But he's too scared to climb below the first few rungs. He hangs his head in shame. 'Lilly's the only one with *cojones*.' Cormack laughs in the background. Then, just as suddenly as she disappeared, Lilly's head bursts to the surface. 'Two minutes and ten seconds,' Cormack announces triumphantly. 'You win.' At that moment Grace doesn't recognize her own daughter.

Breathlessly she scrolls to a new set of videos. This time it's dark outside. In the background there's a hum of music. Grace checks the date. It's the weekend of the festival that Lilly wasn't meant to be attending. Lilly is wearing a floaty yellow dress. Her head is bowed and she sways from side to side with her eyes closed, one hand making circles in the air, the other holding what looks like a big fat joint to her lips so you can see the dress is armless and backless. It's no more than a piece of silk material. Grace quickly moves on to a series of shots taken later the same day.

It's now dusk. Lilly is running towards a wood, away from a field full of colourful tents pitched at chaotic angles. The person filming is so close to her that Grace can see not only is she barefoot but her calves are red and raw with scratches. As she runs she keeps glancing back over her shoulder. There's something wrong. She's so wild-eyed with fear she doesn't even seem to notice that she's barrelling through patches of nettles. There's none of the invincible recklessness of the previous clips. Instead Lilly looks terrified. The person holding the phone pants as he struggles to keep up. *Stop, you bastard*, Grace wants to tell Cormack. *You're frightening her*. Lilly reaches the edge of the wood. For a split second she stops and looks back. Then she scrambles over a bank and disappears between two poplars. The person holding the phone pans across the landscape in search of her. But she's gone. That's the last clip and now there's nowhere else to go.

'There are too many unanswered questions. *What is Lilly trying to escape from?* Grace has spent too much of her own life running away from things to consider that Lilly might be running towards something. She closes her eyes and feels herself being dragged backwards through time.

PART TWO

12

On 25 November 1991, shortly after she turned fifteen, Grace's father disappeared and her mother's new boyfriend moved in. The date was etched in Grace's memory not because it was the last time she saw her father but because Freddie Mercury had died the previous day and she had listened to 'Bohemian Rhapsody' on a loop in tribute. There was no emotional goodbye, no last-minute wrangling over custody arrangements and no promises to keep in touch. Her father didn't even leave a forwarding address. All Grace remembers is that two weeks after her birthday she went into her parents' bedroom with her little brother Luca, to remind them they had school, to find her mother in bed with a man she had never seen before.

They were both unapologetically naked. Neither Rudy nor Olwyn made any attempt to cover themselves. Grace instinctively put her hands over Luca's eyes and tried not to stare at the one-eyed snake lying prone in a thick forest of dark pubic hair. She had never seen anyone so hairy in her life. She traced a line from his groin, up his stomach to his chest and then down his legs. Even his fingers and toes had hair. Yet he was completely bald: the top of his head was shiny and dark like a conker.

'Where's Dad?' Grace asked, in a smooth tone as if she was enquiring about the whereabouts of a lost pair of nail clippers or a missing shoe. Luca hid behind her, so close that she could feel his breath on her arm. She put out her hand and he clung to it tightly.

'He's gone,' said Olwyn. 'Poof!' She waved her arm like a magic wand, as though she had made him disappear, which in a sense she had.

'But he's only just come back,' said Grace, with a puzzled frown. Their father had arrived home less than two months ago after living with an Amazonian tribe in Peru for a year. *Poor Amazonians*, Grace thought. *They had probably only just recovered from his last visit.*

'Has he gone to find himself again?' Luca asked, in confusion. 'Why does he keep getting lost?'

Olwyn ignored their questions. 'I have some wonderful news for you both,' she said, with a radiant smile. She was flushed a pale pink, as if she had been lightly steamed. 'Rudy is going to be your new dad.' Since Grace thought her mother was about to tell them she was pregnant, this almost came as a relief.

'So how will you get divorced from our old dad if he's lost?' she asked politely. 'I know a lawyer. He might be able to give you some advice.' She had recently discovered that her teacher's husband was a solicitor and her description of a world of rules and logic had left Grace wide-eyed with wonder. There was nothing predictable in her life. Not even the simple stuff. Like mealtimes. Or finding loo roll beside the toilet. The only constants in the house her mother rented on the edge of the Forest of Dean were damp, dust and the sickly-sweet smell of the candles she made from crystallized violet petals to sell on her stall at the Saturday market in Lydney.

'It's all very friendly,' said Olwyn. 'We're going to divide everything fifty-fifty.'

'How is it possible to divide nothing?' Luca asked. 'Grace always says if you divide zero by zero you get zero.' Since Olwyn and Rudy were lying on a mattress on the floor because the iron bedframe had been sold to a scrap merchant a couple of weeks earlier, it wasn't an unreasonable observation. 'Will you cut the fridge in half?'

'Good maths,' said Grace, squeezing his hand a little harder so he wouldn't say any more. She knew how quickly her mother could pivot from joy to anger.

'Come on, Luca, don't be so negative,' Olwyn pleaded, in her little-girl voice, all petulant lower lip. Grace hated it when she used that tone on Luca. 'Let's share in our joy.'

'I might cut you in half and leave half with your old dad and keep half for myself,' said Rudy to Luca, with an empty laugh. Olwyn giggled. Grace squeezed out a smile. She didn't like him but she knew instinctively that she mustn't let him know this.

'That's not very nice,' said Luca. 'I don't want . . .' Grace squeezed his hand again.

'So will you be getting married?' Grace asked, calculating that this would be her mother's fourth wedding. Although two had been to their father so perhaps they counted as one.

'Marriage, now there's a bourgeois concept,' Rudy drawled, rubbing the top of his head with his hand as if he was polishing an apple.

Grace had no idea what 'bourgeois' meant but she could hear the implied criticism in his tone, which meant it was probably a good thing. 'Bourgeois' sounded cosy and safe and exotic in the right way. She resolved to add the word to the list she kept in the back of a notebook she had started a couple of years ago when she had begun trying to make sense of her life. The notebook was titled 'The Certainties'.

The first word Grace wrote in 'The Certainties' was 'Luca' with a love heart around his name. Her little brother was utterly predictable and he made life bearable. For as long as they could remember, they knew they were blessed to have each other. She later gave this page the title 'SOLID WORDS'. She added to it each time she encountered nouns that made her feel safe. *Unconditional love, packed lunch, Lego.* On the following page she drew a fridge with its door open and shelves filled with products that she neatly labelled. It was difficult for her to make close friends at school because she couldn't invite them home, and there were whole expanses of her life that she couldn't share with anyone. But on the odd occasion that she went to someone's house, the first thing she did was to sneak a peek inside their fridge. One day she and Luca would have a fridge like the one she had drawn.

When she thought of the future, she always imagined them together, without Olwyn. She discovered that making lists of words and plans was the best way to feel in control and avoid thinking about the big questions, like why her mother didn't take care of them and her father kept disappearing. She knew a part of her heart had been hollowed out by their lack of love and that she would never feel like a normal person. But it would be different for Luca because he had her.

On another page she made lists of habits she had observed in other people's homes – *weekly shop, swimming lessons, bedtime story, birthday treat, goodnight kiss, bookshelf, football*. She tried as far as she could to do some of these for Luca. The only thing she couldn't manage were swimming lessons. Grace couldn't swim and lessons were too expensive. She put a lot of effort into observing how other people behaved and tried to teach what she had learnt to her brother. She wanted his life to be easier than hers. She wanted him to have proper friends and clean clothes with the right smell so that he wouldn't have to be an outsider. He wasn't yet old enough to internalize the deep sense of shame that Grace felt about her family. She lived in a state of terror that they might be found out, in case Luca and she were taken away and made to live apart.

Sometimes, when their parents were fighting, usually at the end of yet another party (although 'party' implied a degree of organization that was absent at these gatherings), Luca would come into her room and ask her to read 'The Certainties' out loud. She would stop only when their father fell silent, usually because he had passed out in the sitting room below. Grace wasn't sure why she collected words but she hoped some day, when she had more control over her life, they might come in useful.

'So what do you think will happen next?' Luca asked, as they retreated from the bedroom after meeting Rudy. He wasn't particularly worried because their life had never been predictable and as long as Grace was in charge he knew everything would be fine.

'I'm not sure,' Grace replied.

When Grace thinks about what unfolded over the following four months, she tries to focus on the facts rather than the feelings. Facts were safe, whereas you could drown in feelings. Rudy wasn't like the other men Olwyn usually took up with. They were almost exclusively stoners with a weekend interest in hallucinogens. In this respect, but only this respect, Olwyn demonstrated remarkable consistency. Most of them stayed in bed until late afternoon and then got up to discuss grandiose plans that never materialized: music festivals that evolved into a couple of their friends playing guitar; vegetable gardens that were never planted; jewellery that was never made. Just before he disappeared, their father had signed up to do a crystal-healing course but had had to abandon it when he lost his crystals on the bus on the way home from Gloucester.

Rudy was different. He got up at sunrise and went to bed at sunset and insisted they should all follow his example. He actually got things done and, to begin with, this was a welcome novelty. At first things changed for the better. He brought a washing machine with him that he plumbed in and allowed Grace to use twice a week as long as she washed his clothes too. Picking up his dirty underpants and T-shirts made her feel sick. They stank of incense and stale sweat and no matter how much she washed her hands after handling them the smell seemed to linger. But if she got herself organized she could rotate school uniforms so she and Luca had clean clothes every day. The first time they used the machine Luca sat cross-legged in front of the glass door, watching in wonder as their clothes embraced and did a slow dance. Before, she had washed everything in the kitchen sink. The nearest launderette was in Lydney, four miles away, and Olwyn's van broke down more often than it worked.

Rudy banned Olwyn from smoking weed and drew up a list of domestic tasks that she had to complete every day. He made her work in the garden, digging a vegetable patch, trimming overgrown hedges and clearing brambles. He gave her targets of how many candles she should produce in a week and the whole house filled with the scent of violets. For the first time since Grace could remember, Olwyn was actually awake when they left for school and when they got home. She even started making packed lunches, although the sandwich fillings were still too embarrassing to eat in public. Where other children had ham or cheese, theirs were filled with strange-coloured vegetable mush that Luca called slop.

Rudy culled some of Olwyn's wackier friends, like Jimmy the Scot and Mad Maria, who periodically moved in with them and created nothing but chaos and noise, and latterly a baby who had kept them awake at night. There was a ban on alcohol. Grace discovered she could get on with her homework undisturbed. There was food in the fridge and proper mealtimes. Rudy had some weird ideas. He insisted that Olwyn always sit opposite him, to balance the male and female energy by anchoring the rays of the Alpha and Omega, and talked non-stop on subjects that none of them could understand. But it seemed a small price to pay for routine.

After a few weeks, however, it became clear that Rudy had his own agenda and he expected unquestioning allegiance to its principles. His behaviour became more and more erratic and paranoid. He got rid of the old television and the radio because he said bad people could use them to communicate with them, which meant that Luca couldn't watch football any more. Rudy used the same argument to prevent them from visiting Mrs Sylvester, their neighbour up the road, who had been so kind to them over the years, making packed lunches for school when they were little and allowing Grace to use her kitchen table for homework while Luca played with Lego that had once belonged to her own children. But Mrs Sylvester was deemed 'negative' because not only did she have a television, she had a computer, which Rudy said made her even more dangerous: it meant she had the potential to communicate with other universes.

Every evening he delivered a lecture on anything from why consumerism was destroying the world to how to create a harmonious lifestyle through self-sufficiency. 'We live in a post-capitalist society that has no respect for primitive ancient life. There's pollution everywhere and this toxicity has invaded every cell of our life,' he would shout, banging his hand on the table. After a couple of weeks of these talks, people Grace had never met before started turning up to listen.

Rudy announced that he would be setting up a new business running self-enlightenment courses. Grace was initially optimistic about this development. When someone asked what her parents did she could say Rudy was a teacher, which back then was at the top of her list of safe words. It would also mean regular money for the first time since she could remember. He drew up budgets with projected income and expenses. The first students started to arrive. Olwyn was introduced as the cook and cleaner, which was probably the only honest thing Rudy told them.

To liberate his followers from worldly worries, Rudy insisted they gave him control of their finances during their stay. He encouraged some of them, especially the young girls, to write to their parents to say they had a new family. She saw how he tried to touch these girls and was ashamed to feel relieved because at last he had tired of pawing at her mum in public. After six weeks Rudy had two dozen disciples.

'Isn't he clever?' said Olwyn, who had taken to sitting on Rudy's knee after dinner, mainly to stop the female disciples from getting there first.

'We are creating the perfect community,' he declared. He started to wear white robes and grow a beard, which Olwyn was required to trim every morning. The sight of the dark hairs in the bathroom sink made Grace feel queasy. He imposed an increasingly strict diet that he told them would lead to heightened consciousness and long life. There were a lot of foods no one had ever heard of, like aubergine, filbert nuts and alfalfa sprouts. Certain products were deemed to be negative. A list of banned substances was pinned on the fridge and got longer and longer until it seemed there was almost nothing left that they could eat. Meat, fish, crisps and cheese were all banned. Anything with sugar was completely forbidden. But so were many vegetables, most fruit and almost all spices. When Grace asked him why ginger was negative, Rudy told her that it hindered energy flow. He had an answer for everything and evidence for nothing.

After a few weeks, Grace noticed that her bra was loose and her school skirt was hanging off her hips. Luca needed a belt to keep his shorts from falling down. He stopped kicking his football round the garden after school. His hamster cheeks disappeared. Doing homework became more and more of an effort, and going to bed at sunset was no longer a problem because they were both exhausted.

One afternoon when they got off the bus from school, Mrs Sylvester was waiting for them. She was visibly shocked at their appearance. 'Is your mum not feeding you?' she asked, in the jokey tone adults sometimes use when they are being deadly serious. 'Do you want me to do packed lunches like I used to when you were little?'

Grace told her that Rudy now made their packed lunches and that he had strict rules about what they could eat. She tried to explain the logic of his argument.

'You know that's a load of bloody nonsense, don't you?' Grace had never heard Mrs Sylvester swear.

'Yes,' said Grace. 'But please don't say anything to Mum. She has to tell him everything.'

After that Mrs Sylvester waited for them at the bus stop every afternoon to give them a sandwich, salad, fruit and home-made cakes. On Fridays she would pack a bag of treats that Grace carried home in her school bag and hid in her bedroom.

'If you need me, you know where I am.' Mrs Sylvester said the same thing every Friday and it helped them to get through the weekends.

Luca hugged her and only let go when she gave him a second piece of home-made flapjack. 'Don't tell Rudy,' he begged Mrs Sylvester, as he devoured it.

'What would he do if he found out?' Mrs Sylvester asked, narrowing her eyes.

There were bigger problems than being hungry. But Grace couldn't bring herself to share them with Mrs Sylvester. She wasn't sure she even possessed the language to articulate what was happening. One of Rudy's disciples, a man in his late twenties, had started coming into Grace's bedroom in the night and trying to touch her. She could recall the exact sensation of waking up to feel his hand snaking beneath the sheet and pushing between her legs. She started sleeping in all of her clothes and would push him away with her fists until eventually he fell on all fours beside her and furiously rubbed his groin as if he was polishing one of Rudy's Indian artefacts. She can still remember the way his mouth would droop open so she could see the slit of his tongue pressing against his teeth as his breath quickened.

When Grace told Olwyn what was going on, her mother shrugged and suggested she put a lock on the door. Luca took to sleeping in her bed every night and Grace no longer tried to persuade him back to his room.

Rudy became more and more controlling. To begin with, it was Olwyn who bore the brunt of his irrational demands and mood swings. Grace and Luca were used to their parents fighting downstairs at night, but although alcohol made their dad aggressive, it also meant he blacked out quickly. Rudy, however, was a teetotaller and had a manic energy that meant he could sustain his fury through the night. One evening Grace and Luca were upstairs in bed when they heard banging and shouting coming from the sitting room. Grace opened the bedroom window and the two of them leant out to listen. They weren't allowed to come downstairs after the sun had set, but now that it was autumn this meant they were confined to their bedrooms for most of the evening. Rudy had discovered that Grace had been hiding food in her bedroom. They could hear Olwyn begging for calm.

There was the sound of furniture crashing to the floor and then a scream. Olwyn scrambled upstairs and they heard her turning the handle of Grace's bedroom door. She thumped on it, imploring them to let her in. Luca started crying. 'He's going to kill her! He's going to kill her!' When Grace turned the key, it was Rudy who pushed his way in. Olwyn followed close behind. She had a deep gash across her forehead that was bleeding down her cheek so it looked like she was crying red tears.

Rudy marshalled them downstairs and made them sit at the kitchen table all night until they confessed. In the early hours of the morning he took them through his new regime, outlining 'behaviour modification techniques' that would help them to become better people. He introduced something called 'prophecy time' after dinner, where he claimed he could describe conversations that were taking place in other rooms. 'I know what you're thinking,' he would tell them, pursing his full red lips and narrowing his eyes to slits. Grace knew he was lying because her thoughts mostly involved ways of killing him. But it was easier to second-guess Luca because all he thought about was food. Luca was terrified and began wetting his bed every night.

Worst of all, he banned Grace and Luca from sharing a

bedroom, arguing that it was bad to mix male and female energy. He started interrupting his spiritual meetings several times an evening to come up and check that they were in separate rooms or he would send up one of his devotees to report back to him. The same man from before promised Grace he wouldn't say anything about Luca being in the room as long as she allowed him to get into bed with her and touch her breasts. When Grace refused and called him a creep, he told Rudy that he had found Luca under her bed and the next day Rudy put a lock on the outside of Luca's door. She tried to convince her mother Rudy was at best a fake and at worst insane but Olwyn gave the same stock answer to any criticism. 'Luca needs to learn how to deactivate his negative energy.'

Grace moved her bed so that it was parallel to Luca's on the other side of the wall. When he started crying, because he was scared to be alone in the dark, she would tap on the wall. When this stopped working she picked at the plaster-board until she had made a tiny hole so their fingers could touch.

Grace became increasingly suspicious of everything Rudy said. She found a letter showing that he had been declared bankrupt and owed money to lots of different people. Olwyn told him everything Grace had said. He slapped her and announced that he wanted them to stop going to school. 'Intellectualism is unspiritual,' he declared. 'It's tempting you from the righteous path.'

School was Grace's lifeline: there were snacks at break; free meals at lunchtime to supplement the disgusting sandwiches; a library where she could read books in peace; other people who could be relied on to look after Luca; and teachers who encouraged her to imagine a future where she might go to university. She was close to the top of the class in most subjects. Doing well at school was her main strategy for escaping home.

'He's right,' Olwyn agreed. 'We do everything for ourselves out here. We grow our own food and make our own clothes. Maybe I could home-educate you.'

'Social Services will notice. They will come here asking questions,' said Grace. 'They might take us away and then you won't get any child benefit.' It was possibly the most intelligent thing she had ever said.

In mid-March Rudy announced that he was starting preparations for the Celebration of the New Fire Ceremony. Grace was immediately apprehensive. It felt as if it was the end of something whose beginning she didn't fully understand.

'What does that involve?' she asked suspiciously. Rudy explained that it was his personal interpretation of an ancient Aztec ceremony to purify themselves before the beginning of spring. It would involve everyone carrying a lit torch into the River Lyd on the stroke of midnight during the spring equinox in five days' time. Everyone, apart from Olwyn, Grace and Luca, would be paying a thousand pounds to participate in the ceremony. As a special treat he would allow them to take part for free.

Rudy immediately began preparations: no one was allowed to work; Grace and Luca were banned from going to school; they could eat only after sunset; and everyone apart from Rudy had to be silent. He terrified Luca by repeatedly telling him how the energy in his body would turn from negative to positive when he immersed himself in the water. Luca clung to Grace's arm and refused to go anywhere without her.

'I'm scared of water. I can't swim.'

'We'll leave before it happens,' she promised him. But isolated from school, there was no one to turn to for advice.

'When?'

'We'll go the same evening. They'll be so busy they won't notice we've left.'

'But we don't have any money,' Luca whispered. She held his hand and noticed how his skin was mottled, his nails were covered with white spots and the cuticle almost transparent. His breath was quick and rasping.

'Don't worry. I've got it all sorted,' said Grace, trying to sound confident. She opened her notebook and showed him the plan. She had drawn it so that it would be easier for him to understand. There were five pictures, each with a number and arrows leading from one to the other: (1) Our house. (2) The log across the Scarrowbeck. (3) Mrs Sylvester's house. (4) School. (5) SAFETY. Safety was a house Grace had drawn with the two of them standing outside smiling.

'What's safety?' Luca asked.

'Safety is bedtime stories, mealtimes, packed lunches, clean clothes, a fridge full of food, plasters for cuts, toothpaste for teeth.'

'Is safety a particular place?'

'It's a place where we're heading but we don't know where it is yet,' said Grace, who was trying to conceal her own worries. He briefly fell quiet and Grace thought he had gone to sleep.

'Like Heaven?'

'Not exactly. Mrs Sylvester will help us get there.'

'Will they find somewhere we can live together?' He clung to Grace, like a monkey.

'Of course,' said Grace, although she knew it might be difficult to find foster carers who were willing to take in siblings.

'Do you think Mrs Sylvester could adopt us?'

'Sssh,' said Grace, putting her finger to his lips. She

could hear Rudy coming upstairs. He moved fast, like a shape-shifter. Olwyn called him from the kitchen where she was boiling vats of violets in big saucepans.

'I heard noises coming from Grace's room,' he shouted down to her.

'Rudy, come here and be with me,' Olwyn simpered.

In the version of the story where Rudy was a psychopath and Olwyn his victim, Grace liked to think that their mother was trying to lure him away from them. But there was a darker version where her mother was a straightforward narcissist who cared only about her own needs. Either way, Olwyn didn't protect them.

'The ceremony will purge him of his negative energy,' she heard Rudy say, as he turned back downstairs.

On the evening of the celebration everyone was given a bonfire torch to carry down to the river where the ceremony was going to take place. Rudy was sitting by a fire in the garden. He had burnt a piece of cork and was drawing strange patterns all over his face, which made him look even more menacing. Luca sat next to him. He looked at Grace and she could see tears streaming down his face. At this point she knew she hated Rudy. It was the purest, most visceral sensation she had ever felt. Even now she still carries that feeling inside her. The biggest regret of her life is not killing him at that moment. He made Luca sit beside him and told Grace to go back into the house to collect some blankets from the cupboard outside her bedroom so that Luca didn't get cold. When she came back they had all disappeared.

It was dark but Grace guessed they would head down the hill through the woods to the river. She dropped the blankets and started running. She was wearing jeans, a T-shirt and flip-flops, and the nettles stung her legs through the denim. She glanced back a couple of times in case Luca had appeared but there was no sign of him. Rudy had planned this.

'Luca! Luca!' Her voice pierced the night air. She remembered where the track started and to begin with it was easy to stay on it because the terrain was scrubby and flat. As the slope got steeper, however, it became less uniform, until it narrowed into a meandering series of switchbacks. The rhododendrons and camellias gradually gave way to ancient trees that became denser and denser. Their canopy stole the light of the moon and Grace became disoriented. She hugged her way around thick tree trunks and found her path blocked by brambles. She had to stop more and more frequently to listen out for Rudy and the rest of his group. She could hear laughter and Rudy's voice yelling instructions. Once when she shouted Luca's name she was almost certain she heard him call back. But the wind played tricks with the sound so that at one minute the voices seemed to come from one direction and the next they came from completely the opposite. Grace rationalized that as long as she kept going downhill she would surely reach the river. She realized she had strayed from the path because ferns and brambles were licking her thighs and it was spongier underfoot. It smelt of damp and decomposition. She tripped over a couple of times on tree roots and tumbled to the ground where she knelt on all fours sobbing while she tried to get her bearings.

As she got closer to the river, stones became boulders and she was forced to slow down. She could hear people singing but when she tried to move towards the noise the soft earth beneath gave way to a steep granite escarpment. In the distance she could see flames flickering from the torches. She got on to her hands and knees so that she didn't fall down the drop but the ground seemed to give way and she found herself uncontrollably rolling down a steep slope until she landed with a heavy thud. She was winded and took a moment to catch her breath but she had reached the river. To her left she could hear people shouting and knew that Luca must be close by. She called out for him again.

'Luca! Luca! Take deep breaths!' She guessed from the noise of frantic splashing that Rudy was submerging him in the water. She crawled towards the river and waded in. The water came up to her stomach. It was freezing. She couldn't swim so she half ran towards the noise but she was going upstream against the current and when it got too deep she had to head to the bank again, which slowed her down. She could hear Olwyn shouting and then the shouts turned to screams. By the time Grace got there Luca had disappeared.

Luca's body was found several days later in a tributary of the River Severn. Grace pleaded with the police to be allowed to hug her brother one last time but she was gently told it would be too distressing. The police liaison officer explained that when people drown the air sacs in their lungs act like a sponge, until their body is so heavy with water that it sinks to the riverbed: Luca was bloated out of all recognition. Grace wanted Rudy to be charged with murder. But the police said that if he had been killed before he drowned his body would have floated because his lungs would have been full of air. It would be impossible to prove Rudy meant to kill him and he could only be charged with manslaughter. It quickly became irrelevant because Rudy had already disappeared. He was never found and charged.

Grace was allowed to select which objects to put in Luca's coffin with him. She chose his favourite T-shirt and shorts, one of Mrs Sylvester's flapjacks and one of her lists from 'The Certainties'. At his funeral, when the time came to scatter the cold, dark lumps of earth on to the child-size coffin, Olwyn tried to throw herself into his grave. 'My baby, my baby,' she cried out, over and over again, as the vicar pulled her back.

Even at Luca's funeral Olwyn had to make it all about her. She was wearing a long, flowing floral dress in a stiff fabric that looked as though it was made from a pair of curtains. It kept slipping off her shoulder, revealing the bruising on her back. Grace felt no pity for her. She was as responsible for Luca's death as Rudy. What kind of mother fails to keep her child safe?

Mrs Sylvester kept a firm grip on Grace's hand throughout the funeral. Grace could feel people staring at her but they looked away whenever they caught her eye. She understood. There was only so much pain they could endure. Afterwards Grace stayed with Mrs Sylvester for a few months until she turned sixteen. But memories of Luca were everywhere and her mother was just up the road. So she went to London, found a room in a flat and got a job as a waitress.

Over the next three years she quickly spiralled into a pattern of self-destructive behaviour that she found terrifying because it reminded her of her mother. She drank too much, took too many drugs and had unprotected sex with men who weren't necessarily unkind but were similarly untethered.

She met Rob when she turned up for her first appointment with a therapist at the wrong time. By her early twenties Grace was beginning to grasp that she couldn't simply erase her past and, without change, she wouldn't survive it. There were days when she could bury the loss deeper than others, but it always came back in nightmares, self-recrimination, fear and regret. She remembered sitting in the waiting room, as far from Rob as possible, studiously avoiding his gaze. She preferred not to engage with people because they would inevitably ask a question she couldn't answer. She could tell, just by looking at him, that he was an extrovert. His shirt was too bright, his long hair too artfully tousled, and he had immediately started talking to her.

'What are you in for?' he asked, tapping the pointy toe of his cowboy boot.

She thought for a moment. She wasn't used to people being so direct. 'The loss of the most important relationship in my life, I guess,' she had finally responded. It was the first time she had ever mentioned the loss of Luca to anyone and she only said it because he had asked the question. Fortunately he was too wrapped up in himself to digest what she had said.

'What are the odds?' he had replied. 'Me too.'

'You've lost a sibling?' she asked, in surprise. The coincidence was too much.

'No, I've given up drugs,' he said, ashen-faced. 'I'm so sorry.' He was filled with remorse for his glib insensitivity and shallowness. For the first time in ages, however, Grace had laughed. They had become friends, but it was an offbeat, occasional friendship that flourished during a dark time in their lives when they were both all kinds of messed up. They understood intuitively that it wouldn't endure beyond their recovery because they would remind each other of what they were trying to forget.

Back then Rob wasn't well known as a music producer, but a couple of years after they met, he invited Grace to a gig played by the band that eventually made his name and his fortune: he was worried he wouldn't get a big enough audience. The venue was filled with his family and friends, including Patrick, who seemed to Grace like the antithesis of his wild younger brother.

Neither Rob nor she ever referenced where they had met. He didn't want his family to know about his problems with addiction. And she wanted a new beginning where no one asked awkward questions about her past. But there had always been an ease between them and a comforting sense of mutual responsibility for each other's wellbeing. It was a simple friendship: they wanted each other to be happy. They were both survivors. *People make too much of remembering*, Grace thought. Remembering can drive you crazy because some things are just too brutal. She carried Luca in her heart and that was enough. The rest had been buried. Until now.

13

It was Grace who insisted Patrick should go on a bike ride before their meeting with Lilly's consultant the following week. He would never have dared suggest it himself. Everything he did seemed to invoke the Wrath of Grace. Yesterday she had flown at him for his underwhelming reaction when she mentioned that the receipt she had found in Lilly's bedroom came from a grim pub in the Fens, notorious for drug-dealers. She had presented him with copies of newspaper articles, and he had made a flippant joke about how nothing changes because it was the same pub where Rob used to buy grass as a teenager. *It wasn't like she'd uncovered Watergate!*

When he casually mentioned that he'd promised to bring Lilly's phone to the hospital, she accused him of jeopardizing her recovery. And then five minutes later when he let her know that Mia's teacher had emailed to request an urgent meeting with them, she was furious with him for bothering her with trivia. He can't win. She can't focus on anything apart from Lilly. Of course he's distraught about her relapse earlier in the week. But in her frenzy Grace resembles a Fen Blow, a duststorm of black soil that occasionally comes in from the fields to turn even the perfectly sane mad. At least there have been no new cases of children falling ill.

She's been driving herself crazy keeping up with the chat on social media. There's a new conspiracy theory every day. Catriona's campaign has been taken up by a dystopian triumvirate of climate-change deniers (who blame the wind farm), anti-vaxxers (who blame childhood vaccines) and the far right (who think the deep state is involved in a cover-up). No one seems to deal in facts any more. When they take Mia into school they have noticed people crossing the street to avoid them, even though everyone has been officially informed that there is no evidence of infection and Tas has made a full recovery. Patrick laughs it off but Grace feels like they're shunning her. Even his mother wondered if it was 'safe' for someone of her age to risk visiting Lilly in hospital.

This morning, however, after checking in with the hospital to make sure Lilly hadn't had any more seizures during the night, Grace had not only helped him locate his helmet and cycling shorts, she had practically pushed him out of the door. As if he needed any persuasion to be reacquainted with his new Trek-Emonda. As he dusted down his bike, he also noticed that she didn't immediately switch on the news or compulsively check her social media. There was no sign of the blue book with her research into Lilly. She didn't even quibble when Mia announced she wanted to catch the bus to school with Tas. It makes no sense but, then, nothing has made much sense since the day Lilly fell ill.

As he pedals down the drove that leads past the Travellers' site towards Earith, he calls Nuala and they debate whether Grace might have turned a corner. 'Not that there's many of those in these parts,' he jokes, riding upright with no hands on the bars, wishing Nuala was there to appreciate his youthful sense of balance.

But halfway round his favourite circuit Patrick finds he's

totally lost fitness. After an hour in the saddle, his upper calves scream for mercy and he's developing an uncomfortable sore in the soft flesh around his scrotum because, like a complete amateur, he forgot to apply the chamois cream. And he's not using his diaphragm properly to breathe. Instead of doing six breaths a minute he's doing more like fourteen. Less than three weeks ago he completed the same thirty-nine-mile ride with ease, beating the youngest member of the cycling club in record-breaking time. Today he's hyperventilating like an old man. He keeps reciting his cycling mantra, 'The pain you feel today will be the strength you feel tomorrow,' but he can't even manage that in one breath.

In the distance he spots a track leading away from the drove towards one of the dykes. He decides to take a break so that he can call his brother, wondering whether his anxiety about this might explain his erratic breathing. He turns sharp right and swerves towards the edge of the track but forgets to twist his ankle to unclip from the pedal and ends up in a crumpled heap of metal on the ground. Patrick groans. It's the humiliation that hurts the most. He tentatively tests his limbs to make sure nothing is broken and examines his arms for asphalt burns. So much for the Shimano hydraulic braking system. He guiltily eyes the twisted carbon handlebar, hoping that no one ever discovers the money to buy it came from Rob's loan.

He climbs up a bank to get a mobile-phone signal and sits down on a comfortable clump of milk parsley overlooking the dyke. One of the issues his ancestors didn't anticipate when they drained the Fens was that, without water, the peaty soil would dry up and shrink until the land dropped below sea level, so this dyke now runs higher than the onion fields that surround it. He stares up at the vast expanse of sky above him and squints at a huge marsh harrier flying leisurely overhead. How is it that Rob has managed to escape so far from here while his own world has shrunk smaller and smaller, so he's still cycling the same route he did when he was a child? He used to find the endless repetition of the featureless landscape comforting, but now he feels exposed by it, as if he can't hide from himself any more.

He checks his messages. There's a missed call from the school office so he sends a quick email to confirm that he will come in to do his talk for the after-school Art Society on the Impressionists, even though their pastel-coloured sentimentality makes him feel queasy. But it's what parents want and he needs the extra cash. He has lost count of how many letters have arrived from credit-card companies about missed payments.

Bracing himself, he dials Rob's number. It can't be put off any longer. Marius had called him early this morning and ruefully explained that he had received three increasingly angry messages from Grace about the builders' disappearance, and that if Patrick didn't pay at least half of what he owed by the end of the week he would feel obliged to tell his wife what was going on. Rob's mobile phone goes straight to voicemail so Patrick calls his office and gets put through to his assistant.

'Vermuyden Productions,' she says smoothly. 'How can I help you?'

Patrick tries not to mind. So what if Rob has two assistants, an office in Soho with forty employees, plus a couple of Brit awards and Grammys on the mantelpiece at his house in the country? Patrick had always aspired to be the intellectual aesthete, not the ambitious entrepreneur. 'I was wondering if my brother is around.'

'I'll see if he's available,' she says. The tide of bitterness swells with every second he's kept on hold. An inane track by one of his brother's bands plays in the background. He bets that Rob is keeping him waiting on purpose, knowing this music will wind him up. Patrick imagines his blood pressure getting higher and higher until finally a vessel in his brain bursts, like the River Ouse in the winter rains.

'Patrick, what can I do for you?' says Rob, eventually. It's just a turn of phrase but it so perfectly encapsulates how the balance of power has shifted between them over the past few years that Patrick's breath catches in his throat. Rob sounds distracted, as if he's scrolling through emails at the same time as speaking to him.

'I was calling for a catch-up.'

'Are you in the middle of mowing the lawn?' Rob teases him. 'You sound out of puff.'

Don't rise to the bait, Patrick warns himself. 'Actually I'm in the middle of that cycle-ride up the drove towards Earith. It's a magical day.' He wants to make it sound like he's a free spirit while Rob is prisoner to the forces of capitalism, but even before he's finished speaking Patrick knows he sounds like a man with no direction and too much time on his hands.

'I was going to give you a call to see how Lil is doing but you know how it is . . .' Rob apologizes. 'I read the piece in *The Times* about a mystery illness.'

'There are no new cases and she seems much better. Thanks for asking. A little subdued, but that's to be expected. She's just spent three days in the same room having her brainwaves monitored to see if they can identify what's causing the seizures. Amazing what technology can do.' He sounds deliberately upbeat to establish the right mood for his request.

'Amazing,' Rob agrees. There's an awkward silence. In the background Patrick hears the click-click of the mouse.

'Was there something in particular that you wanted? Sorry, but I'm needed in a meeting in five minutes.'

Patrick looks up at the sky again. The marsh harrier hovers overhead, hunting for prey. He wishes it would swoop down and carry him away. He rubs the back of his neck. 'I was wondering if you could lend me some more money, please. Until the end of the month. I'm in a bit of a tight spot. The builder's walked off the project and we need to sort out the damp on the top floor before Lil comes home. Grace is worried about the mould.' It all comes out in a rush that makes him sound desperate. There's silence at the other end of the phone. 'Rob? Are you still there?'

'How exactly are you going to reimburse me by the end of the month when you haven't paid back any of the first loan?'

He wasn't expecting this. Patrick stands up and looks along the dyke as far as the horizon. Even the vegetation endlessly repeats itself. Sedge and reeds as far as the eye can see.

'Realistically it's not going to happen, is it?'

Patrick squirms. In the past Rob has unquestioningly acquiesced to these periodic requests. This time he's going to make him beg. He takes a couple of deep breaths. 'I got a letter from the developers guaranteeing the compensation should have come through by then.'

'Well, I'd quite like to see that letter before I give you any more money.'

'It's all a bit of a juggle until they cough up,' Patrick says, trying to find a deep belly-laugh, but making a hissing noise that sounds as if he's deflating. He covers it up with a cough.

'What I really don't understand is why you don't have any extra cash from selling Pretoria Road.'

Patrick's skin prickles with irritation. 'It's always more expensive than you think moving house, isn't it?' He attempts an even, convivial tone but his voice shows the strain.

'It shouldn't be when the house you're moving to costs less than the house you've moved from.'

'You know about all the problems we've had. We're not the only ones. It's been all over the newspapers. It's cost me a fortune.'

'You should never have bought that shitty little house. You know better than anyone that it's built on marshland.' Rob pauses. 'Why do you always make such crap decisions?'

He hears the contempt in his brother's voice and flails around, looking for excuses. 'My teaching hours were cut . . . I couldn't get a mortgage. I had to take out credit-card loans . . . There was no choice . . . You know how it is.'

'I don't, actually,' Rob says, his tone hardening.

How dare he? This is a man who didn't get out of bed before midday for most of his twenties, who paid other people to do his A-level English essays and whose idea of exercise was rolling a joint. Patrick reminds himself that his main objective is to secure money and the weight of this thought gives him renewed purpose. He's been holding the trump card all this time without even acknowledging it.

'I just want to put things right. For Grace's sake.'

It occurs to him that, over the years, Rob's affection for Grace has surpassed any feelings his brother might once have had for him. It's not surprising. She's guided Rob through most of his relationship woes. Grace was the person at the end of the phone who persuaded him not to call off his wedding the night before he married Ana. And she helped convince Ana to give Rob another chance after he was unfaithful to her for the second time. He remembers how Rob even went to the trouble of finding Grace an original poster for a 1979 Leonard Cohen concert at the Hammersmith Odeon on the day she was born as a thirtieth birthday present. Grace, it strikes him, is the only thing that Rob respects about him.

'Does she know anything about this?' Rob sighs.

Patrick can hear the defeat in his tone. He resists the urge to punch his fist in the air. His shoulders immediately start to relax. 'Obviously she knows but I don't want to bother her with trivia right now. She's got enough on her plate.' He almost laughs at the way he has subverted Grace's own words. 'She's been a bit off kilter, actually.'

'I'll give you half on condition that you agree to see someone who can help you draw up a debt-management plan.'

Patrick laughs off Rob's proposal.

'I'm being serious,' Rob cuts in. 'This is the last time I'm doing this.'

'Thanks,' says Patrick. His brother is a sanctimonious dick. But his fury is short-lived by necessity because he needs to work out where on earth he's going to come up with the rest of the money for Marius.

'Perhaps we should come and stay for the weekend,' Rob interjects. 'To help out. Maybe Ana could take Mia into Cambridge for the day. This can't be easy for her. Then I can sit down with you and help sort out your finances. And if I think we've made progress, I'll give you the rest of the money. How does that sound?'

What can he say? He knows the last thing Grace wants at the moment is Rob and Ana turning up on the doorstep. But he's cornered. 'Of course. We'd love that,' he says, reminding himself that Rob and Ana will cancel if a better offer comes their way.

'How about this weekend?'

'Sure.'

'Great,' Rob says. 'I've got to go. I'm being called into this meeting. We'll see you on Saturday.'

Patrick puts down the phone and calls the builder to tell him the news. 'Ten grand this week and another ten in two weeks' time.' Marius promises to be back on site the following week. Patrick is so relieved by this temporary reprieve that he texts Grace to tell her he'll cycle all the way to the hospital and meet her there.

Grace is nonplussed to find Lilly waiting in the side room, deep in discussion with Dr Santini. She had imagined that at least initially she and Patrick would be speaking to the consultant about the results of her tests on their own. It's strange to see her unencumbered by wires for the first time in almost three weeks. Grace knows she should be pleased that the doctor thinks Lilly is well enough to be liberated from all the monitors but instead it makes her stomach knot. *If the machines aren't watching out for her, how will anyone know if something's wrong?*

Lilly is no longer dressed in her hospital gown. She's put on the same grubby blue T-shirt she was wearing the day she was admitted and a pair of faded jeans with holes in the knees. Grace doesn't recognize either and somehow this makes her feel even more on edge. Not that she can complain about Lilly's outfit when Patrick has just turned up sweaty from cycling with a hole in the backside of his shorts and a bloody gash on his elbow.

'Good ride?' she asks, raising an eyebrow.

'Had a bit of a wipe-out but it all came good in the end,' he says, in the deliberately breezy tone he uses when he wants to fend off awkward questions. He kisses her cheek and his lips feel warm against her skin. The unexpected intimacy underscores the distance between them and she suddenly feels like crying.

Sensing her brittleness, Lilly gives a rigid smile through cracked lips. Grace sees the warning in her eyes. *Don't make a fuss, Mum.* Grace is grateful for the inherent selfishness of teenagers: Lilly thinks it's all about her.

As Lilly puts down her water bottle on the table, and accepts a hug from her parents, Grace notices how slowly her daughter moves. She pulls her close and the oversize T-shirt slips off Lilly's shoulder to reveal a bony ridge of vertebrae. Her skin is mottled and grey. Given that she's just spent the best part of three days in a windowless room in the basement having her brainwaves monitored, it shouldn't be surprising. But still Grace is shocked at how quickly she has faded. 'You look like a plant that hasn't had enough sunshine,' she says, attempting to sound upbeat.

'Elvis the eel springs to mind,' joshes Patrick.

'At least he gets to swim,' says Lilly.

'Only in a circle,' says Patrick.

They're all trying to find the right words and strike the right tone and not quite managing.

'I'd settle for a bucket right now.' Lilly sighs. 'I miss the water so much.'

Grace remembers the video of Lilly diving into the lock and the way she disappeared without a trace beneath the surface. She studies Lilly, searching for answers. *I don't know my own daughter.*

'Welcome, welcome,' says Dr Santini, getting up to shake their hands. 'Very good to see both of you again.' He thanks them for coming, as though they are the ones doing him a favour. They all sit down at the small round table, chatting about the heatwave, which is apparently about to end, as if they're at an airport waiting for a flight.

Grace looks at Lilly's face and all she can remember is the fear in her eyes in the video from the festival. She's spent the morning repeatedly watching the same clip in slow motion in case she had missed any clues. Cormack must have been so close to catching her. She is certain that Lilly was running for her life. *What did he do to you?* She feels a visceral need to be physically connected to her daughter and puts her hand on top of Lilly's. Lilly indulges her just long enough not to seem rude and then pulls away.

The doctor pretends he hasn't noticed and clears his throat, placing his palms on Lilly's notes. He starts to outline the results of all the tests they have conducted, explaining in his rich, melodious voice how these have been discussed with his colleagues in their morning meeting. He reveals that the lumbar puncture has proven there is no inflammation in her spinal fluid and reiterates that the MRI of her brain had come back normal, which means some of what he calls 'the real nasties', like brain tumours and multiple sclerosis, can be completely ruled out. Grace likes the way he intermingles medical terminology with the kind of language Lilly might use.

'This is all very positive, isn't it?' says Patrick, eagerly.

'I've been very lucky,' says Lilly, picking off bits of glue from where the electrodes were stuck to her scalp. Her courage makes Grace feel tearful again. Lilly has been through so much. Dr Santini goes on to explain how they have conducted electrical studies of Lilly's nerves because of the ongoing tingling in her fingers and that they can find nothing wrong with her neurological pathways. As he speaks, it dawns on Grace that, although she has spent the past three weeks desperate to get to the bottom of why Lilly has had these seizures, a diagnosis won't necessarily make anything better. The doctor might be about to tell them she has a lifelong condition that requires round-the-clock care at home. She finds herself constantly swallowing, as if she's trying to suppress the anxiety that hares uncontrollably around her body.

Dr Santini continues with a careful and precise account of the telemetry monitoring, explaining how Lilly has spent three days under constant video surveillance with twenty-four electrodes attached to her scalp to make round-the-clock recordings of her brainwaves, while a cardiac electrode took similar readings of her heart. He pulls out various bits of paper from Lilly's notes, outlining how this has been crucial in order to make sense of her symptoms.

'It might sound an odd thing to say, but we were very fortunate that Lilly had a seizure that first day.' He irons the computer read-out flat with his hand, even though there are no creases, and Grace understands that he is about to say something they may not want to hear. She turns her head from side to side, trying to make sense of the perfectly symmetrical peaks and troughs.

'It looks like something by Bridget Riley,' jokes Patrick, admiring how the white brainwaves stand out against the vivid blue background.

'The truth is we can see no changes to Lilly's brainwaves,' says Dr Santini, pushing the piece of paper towards them, tracing his long, elegant finger up and down the peaks and troughs. 'This pattern is precisely what we might expect to see in someone who is conscious.' He looks up at Grace and she can see that he is wondering whether she understands.

'I don't,' she says, anticipating his question. She can't work out from his expression whether this is a good or bad outcome.

'We were working on the assumption that Lilly might

have epilepsy, but this demonstrates conclusively that she doesn't,' says the doctor.

'How can you be so sure?' asks Patrick.

'It's quite simple, really. If Lilly had epilepsy, we would have seen a change in the pattern of her brainwaves when she had a seizure.'

'I still don't understand,' says Grace.

Dr Santini's gaze moves steadily between Patrick and Grace. He leans forwards towards them. 'There is really only one reason that a person can be unconscious with their brainwaves looking normal and that is if the loss of consciousness is caused by something psychological.'

'You've lost me there,' says Patrick. But Grace gets it.

'There is nothing physically wrong with Lilly,' the doctor confirms.

'Are you saying she's faking the seizures?' Grace asks, immediately regretting her choice of words because they sound faintly aggressive.

'The seizures are real but they aren't due to any disease,' the doctor reiterates.

'What about the increase in her white blood cells?' Patrick asks.

'That could easily have been caused by the stress of the seizures,' the doctor explains.

'Couldn't it be something contagious?' Grace asks, afraid of the implications of what he is saying. She suddenly wants Catriona to be right. 'A disease in the water out on the Fens? Or something to do with the wind farm? That's what people are saying. She's been swimming there a lot. Near where the archaeological dig is taking place. The little gypsy boy lives near there, too.'

'I can reassure you that if there was an infection it would definitely have shown up in Lilly's blood tests by now. And although I'm not at liberty to talk about other patients in detail, I can say that no physical cause has been found for their seizures either. In fact the girl admitted last week from the secondary school had a burst appendix that turned into peritonitis.'

'But our younger daughter witnessed the boy's seizure and it sounded just like Lilly's,' says Grace.

'Children can be very suggestible,' says Dr Santini, carefully. Later, Grace wished that she had asked him exactly what he meant. Her focus, however, was on Lilly, not Mia, and by the time she understood the implications of his comment it was too late.

'The doctor is saying I'm ill but I don't have a disease, Mum,' Lilly interrupts. Grace had almost forgotten that she was sitting between them.

Dr Santini turns towards her. 'I couldn't have put it more eloquently myself,' he says warmly.

'He's explained everything to me and I think he's right,' says Lilly, quietly. 'The seizures have an emotional cause.'

'Is this something you've seen before?' Patrick turns to the doctor.

'It is,' says Dr Santini. 'It's difficult to comprehend but sometimes people suffer from such overwhelming emotions they cannot bear to feel them. Rather than experience the anguish inside them, they develop physical disabilities such as seizures. We call this a conversion disorder.'

'Why would this happen to Lilly?' Grace cries out. 'She's never ill. She's hardly ever missed a day of school.'

'Emotion can have an enormous effect on the human body. If we're scared our hearts race, and when we're sad we cry. One extreme way the body can respond to upset is to produce blackouts and convulsions.' He leans towards Patrick and Grace. 'Sometimes there is a memory or an emotion that is so painful for someone to experience that it gets converted into something physical.'

'So if there's no disease, then what is the cure?' Grace asks.

'Lilly needs to talk to someone to try to work out what the trigger for these seizures may be. We have spoken at length about this and Lilly has agreed that it would be a good idea for me to refer her to someone who can help get to the bottom of what may be going on. You're very lucky that Lilly understands. Many patients take years to come to terms with such a diagnosis.'

Grace thinks of the video she found on Lilly's phone and wishes she could play it now. She glances across to her daughter, who stares fixedly at the table, and wonders if she has made the same connection.

'You mean a psychologist?' Patrick asks nervously.

Dr Santini nods. 'The most important thing is to get Lilly back into her old routine as soon as possible before she misses too much of normal life. She needs to get home and go back to school.'

'Do you have a time frame?' asks Grace.

'I think she should be able to come home within the next few days.'

'What happens if she has another seizure at home? What are we meant to do?' Grace anxiously asks.

'They're not dangerous,' says Dr Santini. 'Just let them happen. Sit with Lilly and speak to her calmly until it's over. Sometimes we find that when dissociative seizures are diagnosed they often disappear as soon as the diagnosis is made.'

'What sorts of triggers have you seen in other patients?' Patrick asks.

'A birth, a death. Being the victim of a crime, the breaking up of a relationship, or financial problems. Lilly tells me she has been under a lot of academic stress at school.'

'Maybe I shouldn't go back into Mr Galveston's class in case it was the pressure that caused the seizure,' Lilly interjects.

'If you're not in his class, you can't apply to do English at Cambridge,' Grace points out.

'I may not want to,' says Lilly. 'I may want to leave school and get a job.'

'I know what's caused all this,' says Grace, through gritted teeth. 'It's that boy, Cormack. Everything has gone wrong since you got involved with him and went to that festival. Nuala told me all about it.'

'Mum, please,' Lilly begs. She doesn't look up. 'Don't.'

'Grace,' Patrick warns her.

'You know nothing, Mum,' says Lilly. 'If you go on like this I won't even come home. I'm almost eighteen. I don't have to.' She gets up from the table and leaves the room.

'So where did you get it?'

Mia could tell from the moment she'd sat down beside Tas on the bus that morning that he had thought of little else since her triumph at Show and Tell. When they walked into the year-six classroom together he had even ignored Miss Swain's 'helpful suggestion' that he might work better if he sat next to Bea, and flopped into his old seat beside Mia.

'Who was going to have the baby, Mia? Please tell me.'

In the lessons before break he tried to persuade Mia to agree to a deal in which she would tell him who had got pregnant in return for him bunking off school to buy octopus for Elvis in the local supermarket. *He must think she's a candy ass if she's going to cave in like that.*

'Please can I see it one last time?'

Mia ignored him, like he had ignored her. Instead she focused on writing the most moving part of her diary, the account of how the girl's terror of dying during childbirth grew as her belly grew until all she felt was fear. It took her an entire class to get this down on paper. Just before the bell rang for lunch she couldn't resist showing it to Tas and asked him to imagine half the girls in the classroom dying.

'What about her boyfriend?' Tas asks. 'Won't he help?'

'He abandoned her. For another girl. Strictly speaking, that's what boys do,' Mia says fiercely. 'Apart from my dad.'

Tas shifts uncomfortably in his seat, but as soon as the bell rings for lunch he starts questioning her again, trailing after her into the dining room like a puppy. 'I'm sorry I didn't get in touch with you,' he says. 'It wasn't my fault. And I'm sorry I've been ignoring you at school.'

'Not good enough,' says Mia, angrily swishing her pigtail over her right shoulder so that it smacks against his cheek.

His lower lip trembles and she feels bad. He needs to toughen up and she needs to stop being such a soft touch.

'It's my mum's fault. She says I should stay away from you,' Tas suddenly blurts out.

'When did she say that?' Mia is genuinely surprised by this revelation. Rawnie has always been so kind to her. She thinks of the flaky biscuits that she makes especially for her and the way they melt in her mouth. If only Rawnie understood how much Mia was trying to help her.

'After what happened. She's suspicious.'

'I saved your life.'

'She don't see it that way.' She can tell he's upset because his accent thickens. 'Come on, Mia, we tell each other everything, don't we?'

'Well, we did until you didn't.'

She chews her lip and counts to ten. The urge to blurt out the truth is too tempting. They never used to play games with each other like this. But things have changed. *Nothing ever stays the same.* Mia feels stupid for not realizing this before. She swallows the lump in her throat. They've reached the edge of the playground where the old wooden Wendy house sits on the edge of the football pitch. She heads towards it and pushes the door. It hinges open.

'I don't want to go in there again,' says Tas, stopping outside. 'It's got bad memories for me.'

Tas is the bravest person she has ever met and it upsets her to see him being such a coward. His eyes do that thing when he panics where they turn down at the end so he looks like a puffin. Mia almost feels guilty for causing him so much stress. 'But you want to know who the pregnancy test belongs to, don't you?' Mia tempts him. He hesitates for a moment, then follows her inside, leaving the door open. Mia paces restlessly around, collecting up toys and books and putting them in boxes. Tas puts two plastic cups and saucers and a plastic jug on the small table.

'How do you take it?' he jokes, lifting the teapot.

'Just milk. No sugar,' says Mia. They sit down opposite each other at the table.

'Cake?' Tas asks, offering her a garishly multicoloured plastic triangle.

'That's pizza.' Mia giggles, pretending to take a bite.

'This is what it would be like if we lived together,' Tas says. He gently tugs her plait until her face is so close to his that she can smell the Haribos on his breath.

'We can't live together if you have to move away,' says Mia, firmly, noticing that one half of his right eye is still bloodshot while the other has returned to its usual colour. Tas lets go of her plait, leans back and vigorously stirs his pretend cup of tea with a plastic spoon.

'You know what you have to do,' says Mia.

250

'I don't want to hurt you.'

'I don't feel pain like other people.'

'I'm scared, Mia.'

'If you do it, I'll tell you who the pregnancy test belongs to.'

After a few seconds he nods. 'Okay,' he whispers. 'Okay.'

Mia gets up from the table and kneels on the floor in the middle of the Wendy house with her fingers interlaced behind her head, like a prisoner about to be executed, except she feels almost excited about what is to happen. Tas might have given up hope, but this could be their last chance to prevent him from having to leave his home. Her school skirt rides up over her thighs and the wooden slats dig into her shins. She thinks of her mum and dad and decides that people spend too much of their life being afraid. The door blows half open but it's only the wind. Outside they see a huge bird flying overhead.

'It's the marsh harrier,' murmurs Tas.

'He wants us to do it,' says Mia, confidently.

Together they start to recite the rhyme Tas taught her, like they did last time, because it helps to steady their nerves. 'Ekkeri, akai-ri, you kair-an, fillisin, follasy, Nicholas, ja'n . . .' Tas stands in front of her so close that she can see how the knees of his trousers are worn and his left shoe has a hole. He runs his finger tenderly over her forehead. He is trembling.

'You know what you have to do,' she tells him. When she looks up at him his cheeks are shiny and she realizes he is crying. In that moment she knows he loves her. Still staring at him she starts breathing in and out, faster and faster, panting with her mouth open like a dog, until she's built up so much momentum that her head starts to throb and her entire body tingles. She closes her eyes. Tas counts her breaths. When he reaches sixty, Mia dizzily drags herself upright and slumps against the wall, head lolling to the side.

'It's Lilly's,' she whispers. Then she breathes in as far as she can and holds her breath until she feels as if her lungs are going to burst. They had watched all the YouTube videos together until they were experts on the Choking Game. She trusts him completely. Tas leans into her, pushing his forearms as hard as he can into her chest, his head pressing into her neck. Everything blurs. He presses harder. Tas's features go out of focus. Fireworks go off in her head. He's pressing too hard. She shudders. Once he has finished he will go for help and tell the teachers that Mia had a seizure, like her sister. The archaeologists will be ordered to leave the site and Tas's family will be able to stay. Just a few more seconds and she will reach oblivion.

'What the hell is going on here?' *It's the voice of a screech owl.* For a few seconds Mia wonders if they have crossed into another world inhabited by woodland animals. She thinks of Mr Tumnus. Tas jumps away from her and Mia instantly feels lonelier than she ever knew was possible.

She staggers around the Wendy house like a drunken old man, crashing into the plastic cooker and sweeping the cups and saucers on to the floor before finally sliding on to the cold wooden slats. She feels someone leaning over her and recognizes Miss Swain's perfume.

'Open your eyes, Mia Vermuyden!' Miss Swain commands. Mia hadn't even realized they were still closed. She looks up at the teacher and sees that her face is tight with either anger or fear or perhaps both.

'What have you done?' Miss Swain shouts at Tas, pulling Mia into her arms. The wrong person is holding her but she doesn't have the power to resist Miss Swain's embrace. 'Tell me. Right now.'

'We had an argument,' says Tas. Mia tries to speak but her voice is too hoarse from the compression in her neck. Through the door, she sees other teachers and students standing in shocked silence outside. Miss Swain calls for someone to fetch the school nurse.

14

The word at school the following day is that the Vermuyden sisters have both gone round the bend. Grace could tell as much from the way no one could meet her eye when she walked through the playground with Patrick and Mia after their meeting to discuss 'the incident'. She could imagine what they were saying. *The younger girl almost killed her best friend by choking him until he had a convulsion, then forced him to do the same to her! Can you imagine! The elder girl is having seizures but there's nothing wrong with her! Fake seizures and faked seizures! What a family!* Any relief that the contagion wasn't real would have been tempered by anger at having been taken for fools. This morning there was only one newspaper piece with the headline 'Hysteria in the Age of Social Media' beside a picture of Catriona Vickers.

For an excruciating hour yesterday evening she knew exactly what other people were thinking because, in their frenzy of speculation, the parents in Mia's class had forgotten that Grace was part of the same WhatsApp group. She followed their discussion about how it could be possible that Mia had the strength to squeeze Tas's neck so tight that all the blood vessels in his eyes had burst. Someone suggested that maybe she stood on his neck in her oversized big black boots. Grace flinched at the casual cruelty.

Following an email from both schools, there was an

anxious debate about how you could tell if your child was playing the Choking Game. *Unexplained bruises. Headaches. Broken blood vessels in the eyes.* Someone wondered if there was something sexual about Mia and Tas asphyxiating each other. *Wasn't there a sense of euphoria as oxygen was cut off to the brain? And wasn't their relationship weirdly intense?* The blame game began. *Grace should have been keeping a closer eye on her daughter. Mia is always in the frame when something goes wrong. What about the missing ring? The weird Show and Tell? The way she hits children who disagree with her?*

Grace's face burnt with shame. *They are right. I am a bad mother,* she thought. *I am no different from my own mother.* Just as everyone was starting to get completely carried away, Misha Hemp pointed out that for a ten-year-old it was plain funny to make someone pass out and watch them stagger around as they came to, which was apparently why some children called the game The Funky Chicken. *Children do stupid things,* she wrote. It was obvious Mia was trying to copy what had happened to her sister because her parents were focused on their daughter's illness. People shouldn't rush to judge. Grace was grateful for the way she had shifted the mood.

Everyone agreed it was scandalous there were videos on YouTube showing children how they could make someone lose consciousness. Catriona proposed a new campaign, her crusade against the wind farm having been derailed by an email from the Department of Health confirming that reports of a mystery contagion were 'unfounded and mischievous' and that their investigation was suspended 'with immediate effect'. When no one showed any enthusiasm she misquoted Oscar Wilde: *To have something wrong with one child may be regarded as misfortune, to have something wrong with both looks like carlessness,* she wrote.

We still have a car, Grace wrote, to remind people she was part of the group chat. After a collective intake of breath, most of the messages were deleted. Some people even apologized and asked if they could help in any way. Grace responded by leaving the WhatsApp group.

It's almost midnight and Grace is still wide awake. She can't remember the last time she slept properly. She dreads the crawling hours between now and dawn and gets out of bed so that she doesn't disturb Patrick. *Same bed, different dreams.* She remembers the old Chinese proverb as she glances back at him. They have retreated into their own worlds.

The weather has finally broken and, for the first time in four months, it's raining. She hears the sound of water dripping on the floor above. But when she goes into Mia's room instead of a new leak she finds Elvis splashing around his bucket, trying to retrieve what look like chunks of rancid octopus from the surface. He smells of mud and fear and lost hope. Mia is sound asleep with all the lights on. She refuses to sleep in the dark or leave the windows open because she's scared of the bad spirits in the Fens. Grace tiptoes towards her. Her thick plait covers the side of her neck where Tas compressed her carotid artery. She gently lifts it and sees a perfect imprint of the boy's fingers on her neck. It reminds her of the handprint paintings Mia used to love to do at nursery when they were little. 'What on earth were you thinking?' she whispers, leaning over to kiss Mia's forehead.

Mia sleepily opens her eyes. 'Was I a wanted baby, Mum?' she murmurs. 'Did you want to get rid of me? Do you wish I didn't exist?'

'The most wanted,' says Grace, puzzled by her question.

She must be feeling guilty for causing them so much trouble. 'Today was a bad day but everything passes. We love you whatever. That's just how it is.'

Mia closes her eyes. Grace puts her hand on her chest to feel her heart beating beneath her fingers, like she used to when she was a baby. Her daughter is a riddle that no one can solve.

During the meeting at school this morning a lot of time was spent trying to work out exactly why Mia had done something so dangerous. No one doubted the Choking Game had been her idea and she didn't deny it. She explained that she had simply copied videos she found on YouTube, promised they had only played twice and that she had made up the description of Tas having a convulsion.

'You mean you lied,' Patrick growled. 'Don't make it sound like this was a creative-writing exercise.'

Mia gave a benign smile and went into great detail about the mechanics of asphyxiation, as if this knowledge somehow reduced the risk.

'Cutting off oxygen to someone's brain is not a game,' Grace interrupted sternly. Mia sat impassively between her and Patrick on the edge of a worn blue sofa in the corner of the headmistress's office. Grace lurched between blind fury with her for causing so much trouble when, for the first time in her life, Lilly needed all their attention, and the desire to hold her close and never let her go because she couldn't stop thinking about what might have gone wrong if Miss Swain hadn't chanced upon them in the playhouse. She feels sick with guilt for neglecting Mia.

The headmistress declared it was her professional view that Mia was disturbed by what had happened to her sister. Patrick said there was obviously a connection between Lilly's illness and her desire to fake a seizure but, beyond wanting attention, he couldn't understand her motivation. Grace admitted they had been preoccupied with Lilly and that Mia had slipped under the radar. 'It's all my fault.' The headmistress said she shouldn't blame herself and hinted that, in view of her sister's illness, perhaps Miss Swain's safeguarding of a vulnerable child wasn't as thorough as it might have been.

Miss Swain was less emollient. She saw Mia's behaviour as a case of extreme attention-seeking and said that, far from being vulnerable, Mia was one of the most resilient and manipulative children she had ever come across. She said that no matter how much support she had in class it would never be enough. They discussed methods for Mia to communicate her feelings. 'Perhaps she could draw them,' suggested Miss Swain, 'rather than interrupt the entire class the whole time.' Mia gave a quick eye-roll. 'My recommendation would be that she sees a child psychologist.' No one disagreed.

Patrick kept asking Mia why Tas allowed her to strangle him and pretend he had a fit. 'What purpose did that serve?' He couldn't articulate why he thought this was so important, just that there was something that didn't add up.

'That's easy. The Romany boy is caught up in her thrall. His mother has been worried about Mia's hold over him for some time. He would do anything for her,' Miss Swain explained. 'Anything.'

Grace saw a tiny smile curl on Mia's lower lip when the teacher said this. Otherwise she displayed barely any emotion.

'Do you have any questions, Mia?' the headmistress finally asked, after announcing that Mia and Tas would have to spend break-time indoors in separate classrooms until the end of term but would not be suspended from school.

Grace felt her shoulders relax. The idea that she might

have had Mia at home full time just as Lilly was about to leave hospital had filled her with guilt-inducing dread. She glanced at Mia, willing her to apologize or show some sign of contrition.

'Only one,' Mia said. 'For Miss Swain.' She turned to the teacher. 'If you died, what objects would you like to have in your burial pot? Apart from your lipstick, of course.'

It was only on the way home that it occurred to Grace that Mia had unquestioningly agreed with them all, which made everyone feel as if their own theory was borne out, yet left them no closer to a plausible explanation. Patrick had been right to press her on Tas's involvement. She tried to share her concerns with him but he was too distracted to focus. He drove erratically, either too slow or too fast.

As they turned into the road that led to Black Fen, an overturned lorry carrying onions blocked their way, and they had to wait for half an hour, eyes watering from the smell, while a local farmer cleared the road. Patrick gripped the steering wheel so hard that his knuckles were as white and shiny as the onions, raging against unreliable builders, climate-change deniers, cuts to schools, and disloyal siblings. The muscle in his left cheek twitched. Every sentence started with 'Can you believe?' It reminded Grace of memory games they used to play in the car when the children were little.

'Can you believe that Rob and Ana haven't been to visit Lilly all this time?'

'Can you believe there might be more cuts to the history of art department?'

'Can you believe they still haven't sent compensation for the damp?'

'Can you believe they allow these huge HGVs to transport onions?'

Mia hardly spoke during the journey. Instead she sat in the back of the car staring out of the window, pressing her nose so hard against the glass that she got a nosebleed.

Grace closes the door and goes into Lilly's room. She watches the rain beating down outside the window and sees that the drains have already overflowed, sending a cascade of water down the path towards the house. She remembers how the water lapped at the front door during the spring floods, and they had to put on wellington boots to get to the car every morning. *Thank God at least that will never happen again.*

She opens Lilly's cupboard and distractedly divides her tops into two piles, according to colour, and straightens the books on her shelf, making sure that they are in descending order of size. She smooths the cover of the bed where Lilly will be sleeping in two days' time and sits down at her desk, trying to arrange her files and books in the exact way she left them. Grace has spent many nights longing for Lilly to come home but now the prospect makes her feel sick with worry. *Who will keep an eye on her? What happens if that boy harms her again? Or if she has another fit?* It's all very well the doctor telling them to stand by and watch until it's over, but what if Dr Santini has got this wrong? After Lilly had gone off in a strop she'd pleaded with him to keep her in hospital until they had a true picture of the psychological reasons underpinning the seizures.

'Don't be ridiculous,' Patrick countered, before Dr Santini even had a chance to respond.

The doctor explained that it could take some time to get to the bottom of the problem because Lilly would have to confront the very emotions she wanted to avoid. He paused, as if weighing up heavy opposing thoughts before revealing that he wasn't sure Lilly had been entirely honest about the circumstances surrounding the first seizure.

'What do you mean?' Grace pressed him for more details.

'I think she might have had a seizure before the one in the English class,' he explained cautiously. 'It's a hunch. I have no evidence. But I do know that she received medical treatment at a festival in the summer. There's a note on her medical records.'

'Do you know what for?' asked Patrick.

'The details are a little sketchy. Dehydration. Uncontrollable shaking. Emotional distress.'

'That's the moment where everything went wrong,' said Grace, emphatically. 'I knew it!' She felt utterly vindicated by this revelation. 'I told you it had nothing to do with academic pressure,' Grace said to Patrick. 'Or unhealthy competition between her and Freya. She can handle all that.'

'I think we need to look at the facts before we draw any conclusions,' warned Patrick.

'You don't want to admit that Cormack did something bad to her at the festival,' said Grace.

The timeline made perfect sense: the video was shot at 5 p.m. and Lilly had visited the medical tent some time after that. All she had to do was work out what had happened in the gap between the two events. The fact that there are no conversations between Lilly, Cormack, Jordy and Hayley on social media the entire week after the festival made her theory even more credible. If she had had Lilly's phone in her pocket at that moment, she would have shown Dr Santini the clip to ask his opinion. He obviously suspected a cover-up. The festival has to be her main line of enquiry. She's convinced that if she can expose what happened, Lilly will begin to recover. And if she proves Cormack's role in all this, Lilly may want to bring charges against him. Then none of those smug, holier-than-thou parents who question her parenting skills can hold her responsible.

She opens the drawer of Lilly's desk and takes out her mobile phone. She's been restricting herself to checking it every couple of hours. She watches it come to life in her hand with new messages and notifications. At least now it takes her only a couple of minutes to navigate her way through Lilly's social media. There's a photo from Hayley of her diving topless into a river and three messages that all say the same thing, although the punctuation gets louder and louder. *Liiillllyyy?????!!!!* screams the third. Even when she writes, Hayley is larger than life. She now has a pretty comprehensive list of Lilly's circle of friends. She knows who is the funniest (Jordy), who is the most active, but never speaks (Emma Vickers), and who posts the most revealing photos (Hayley).

Grace scrolls down to Lilly's conversation with Cormack. He still hasn't been in touch. Yet again, she watches the video of Lilly running away from him at the festival even though she has seen it dozens of times. She hikes up the volume as loud as possible, closing her eyes so that she can concentrate. At the beginning there's the noise of live music playing in the background. But it quickly fades. Then all Grace can hear is the occasional crackle of twigs breaking underfoot and Cormack's jagged breathing as he hunts her down. She puts the phone to her ear, listens and hears his breath turn to a snarl. It's almost as if he's breathing in the room with her. There's no doubt in her mind that he's a predator. The video ends with Lilly's cry piercing the night air.

Grace once read somewhere that most decisions are taken seven seconds before people think they have made them because human behaviour is largely controlled by the subconscious. Each choice is a complex blend of everything an individual has ever thought, experienced, touched, seen and smelt through their life. *We are no more than our history.* This is the only way Grace can explain that when she looks down at the phone she sees she has sent a message to Cormack from Lilly's phone.

Hey.

She stares at the screen in disbelief, hoping he doesn't respond. After all, it's one o'clock in the morning and he has school the next day. But almost immediately the phone vibrates in her hand. Grace jumps and drops it on to the desk. It quivers again.

wats up?

She should stop now. She could delete the two messages. Lilly would never know and Cormack would never realize they'd come from her. She feels a shimmer of nerves. She reminds herself that she's doing this for Lilly. She needs to find out what he did to her. If she does nothing, Lilly won't get better.

u home?
no. got my phone back tho
still wearing my t shirt?
not right now.
wot u wearing now.
nothing.
send pics of nothing.

She takes a photo of the empty view of the night through Lilly's window and captions it *nothing.*

haha

For a while she channels her nervous energy into cleaning Lilly's room. She dusts surfaces and ferociously hoovers the carpet until there are deep furrows in the pile. But when she licks her finger and runs it along Lilly's desk a new layer of red dust has already appeared. So she starts all over again. She looks up at the ceiling and sees that even the damp patches have turned a rusty red. She notices how it now sags, as though something is pressing down on it from the roof space above. No matter what the builders do, the damp always comes back. The house oppresses her. All their problems have started since they moved here. *I feel as if I'm in a locked room that is slowly filling with water.* She thinks of Lilly diving into the lock and remembers Mia's crazy idea about bad spirits and wonders if there's something in it. The phone beeps again. She picks it up.

U still have feelings for me? he writes.

yeah

even after everything?

always

I'll make it up to u

I'll hold u to that

Many people ask the question 'How did I become this person?' but Grace doesn't have to. She knows exactly why she is the way she is. *I am my history.*

15

It's only twenty-three days since Lilly was last at home. Yet when she pushes open the door late on Thursday afternoon she feels like she's reconnecting with a previous life. Superficially, at least, nothing has changed. She still trips over Patrick's bicycle in the hallway, although she notices that its handlebars are bent out of shape; Mia's bag with the riot of key rings lies half open beside an unplastered wall; and the same red dust coats everything like icing sugar. She can taste its bland grittiness on her lips.

She follows her dad into the kitchen, squeezes her eyes shut for a moment, knowing that when she opens them she will find Grace stirring something in a saucepan and Mia doing her homework at the table, just as they do at the same time every evening. Their backs are turned to her. She feels like an intruder wandering into one of those oppressive Dutch paintings of family life that her dad loves so much, in which dogs symbolize fidelity and rough seas the turbulence of love. *It's strange how life goes on without you. How quickly you can be written out of other people's history.* She can't decide whether to be comforted or disturbed by this thought. The adaptability of human beings gives her hope that she might be able to get beyond her embarrassing illness that isn't an illness. But it also means other people will have adjusted to life without her. She anxiously scans the kitchen for her phone. Cormack is always prowling on the edge of her consciousness. She can't wait to check if he's been in touch and to let Hayley and Jordy know she'll be back in school tomorrow.

Lilly has imagined this moment so many times over the past few weeks that it almost feels as if she's lived it before. She's been desperate to get home. She's fed up with hospital food, the lingering smell of antiseptic and old mashed potato, the smears and stains of other people's bodily secretions. She wants to sleep in her own bed with a pillow that doesn't resemble a sanitary pad, have a hot bath instead of a lukewarm shower and sleep through the night without being woken up. But now she's here it dawns on her that she hasn't considered how exhausting it will be negotiating other people's emotions, especially her mum's. Whenever she thinks about Grace, her fingers start to tingle.

'Smells good, Mum,' Lilly says politely, dropping her bag on to the floor. It's not the sort of thing she would usually comment on but with Grace she needs to keep things on a level and her first question definitely can't be about the whereabouts of her phone.

'Lil!' shrieks Mia, leaping up so quickly that her chair tips backwards on to the floor.

Grace starts and drops the wooden spoon into the pan, spattering sauce on her shirt. She turns round to smile at Lilly, apparently unaware of the juice dripping down her front. 'Welcome back, darling. It's so good to have you here,' she says, smiling so earnestly that she looks like she's about to cry.

'I can't believe I'm back,' says Lilly. 'Do you know where my phone is?'

'There's a sign that she's fully recovered,' Patrick teases.

'On the desk in your bedroom,' Grace confirms brightly. 'Fully charged.'

Mia grabs a sheet of cardboard from the kitchen table and runs over to Lilly. 'I'm so glad you're back.' She presses a poster into her hands. 'Welcome Home Lilly!' reads the crooked handwriting. The line of the exclamation mark is drawn to look like Elvis's body, with gills and a fin, and the stop point is his smiling face complete with overbite. Lilly laughs and Mia hugs her tight, pressing her head into her sister's shoulder so that Lilly can clearly see the imprint of Tas's hand on her neck. She touches the mark and Mia flinches.

'What were you thinking?' Lilly whispers.

'Lots of things,' Mia whispers back, in an uncharacteristically wistful tone.

During the journey back from the hospital Patrick had casually dropped into the conversation that Mia was once again in 'Big Trouble' at school after playing something called the Choking Game. 'But when is Mia not in Big Trouble?' he had quipped, with an overworked laugh. Turning some thing serious into a joke has always been one of his most transparent diversionary techniques. Lilly knew straight away that he was holding something back. She pressed him for more details, weevilling in with questions until he capitulated, declaring she was turning into a bullish journalist like her mother.

'Bullshit not bullish,' said Lilly, dismissively. 'Mum's not a real journalist. She writes a newsletter.' She immediately regretted the accusation, less for its petty meanness than the way it betrayed emotion she didn't want to have to explain to him. Then she remembered the infuriating way he avoids unpacking tricky emotions and turned the spotlight of her fury on him, sitting in hostile silence until he gave a full account of what had happened. He reluctantly explained that Mia and Tas had played a game they had copied from the internet that involved choking each other until they passed out from oxygen deprivation. 'That doesn't sound much like a game,' Lilly said, in amazement. 'Why would they do that?'

'They were trying to make it look like they were having seizures.'

She noticed the muscle in his jaw twitching. 'Like me?' He was trying to protect her, which made Lilly feel even worse because it was a reminder of how everyone will tread warily around her when all she wants is for everything to be the same.

'Her teacher thinks she was attention-seeking because we've been so focused on you.'

'Well, I bet that got their attention.'

'For sure.' Her dad nodded. Then he started talking about how he would put good money on a northerly wind bringing a storm just in time for the weekend, and wondered if she knew that there were 286 pumping stations in the Fens working round the clock to force the water back to the sea. She stared out of the window as he talked, tracing a line along a dyke all the way to the horizon. It looked as if someone had drawn it in black ink. *One day the water will come for us all.*

'Lil, Lil.' She's suddenly aware of Mia tugging at her arm. 'So what do you think of my poster?'

'I love it,' Lilly says, ironing it out on the table to examine it more closely but also to turn away from Grace's feverish surveillance.

'Do you really?'

'One hundred per cent. You're very good at drawing.'

'It took her absolutely ages,' says Grace. She comes over to the table, puts her arms around Lilly and hugs her tight. 'I can't believe you're really here. It's like a miracle.'

Lilly counts to five, then untangles herself and peers at the strange hieroglyphics around the edge of Mia's drawing. 'What's with the spooky writing, Mimi?'

'It's your name in Anglo-Saxon letters,' Mia explains. 'We're doing them at school.'

'Shall we have supper?' asks Grace. Lilly wishes she would stop saying everything with such a hopeful look in her eyes. She reminds her of Hayley's Labrador. The emphasis is meant to be on restoring normality. But everything smacks of effort and a desire to please, which only makes her feel under more pressure. She remembers the psychologist's words: *Sometimes being in hospital is a release from an unhappy or pressurized home environment.* When they sit down she notices that the table is covered with a pale blue cloth that normally only comes out when her grandmother visits, and the vegetables have been decanted into bowls. The glasses and cutlery all match. Even Grace looks glossy.

'I've got you some of that juice you really like. The one with kale and cucumber,' Grace says, as she opens the fridge. It's packed with food. Every shelf is stacked with military precision. There are orderly columns of milk, juice and different types of probiotic yogurt, a battery of vegetables and salad, and a whole regiment of pickles. It's just like the picture of the fridge her mum had drawn in the notebook. Lilly feels an unexpected wave of emotion sweep over her as she observes Grace's futile search for the juice.

'Have you drunk it, Mia? I told you to save it for Lilly. It's got to be here somewhere.' She starts frenetically to remove everything from the top shelf.

'Actually, water is fine, Mum.'

Patrick pours Lilly a glass of water while Grace flutters up and down the kitchen, like a moth, opening and closing cupboards.

'Please, Mum, it doesn't matter,' begs Lilly. Grace finally sits down and peers into the jug of water.

'There's a red film. You didn't clean the jug properly, Patrick,' she says brusquely, seizing Lilly's glass just as she's about to drink from it.

'It's fine,' counters Patrick. 'There's nothing there.'

She washes out the jug and glasses before sitting down again.

'Bloody dust,' says Grace, breathlessly. 'Did Dad tell you? The builders have abandoned us.'

'It's all got a little weird here,' Mia warns apologetically from the opposite side of the table.

'Why has Marius stopped coming, Dad?' Lilly asks.

'They went on holiday,' says Patrick, vaguely.

'All of them? For three weeks?' Lilly asks.

'They'll be back next week.'

Grace asks questions without waiting for answers. 'Is the food okay for you? I've tried to use ginger and honey to marinate the chicken because it's meant to be good for maintaining calm. But maybe it's too spicy after all that bland hospital food. I should have done something simpler. Like carrot and parsnip soup. I'll do that for lunch tomorrow.'

'It's great, Mum. Thanks,' says Lilly, cutting the chicken into tiny slices to keep busy. She sees the knife shake in her hand. She's worried about going back to school in case she has another seizure, but she doesn't want to tell her parents because then they might prevent her from going. All her teachers have received precise instructions on what to do but, instead of reassuring her, it somehow makes a relapse seem inevitable. She worries that Dr Santini and the psychologist might have missed something and that she really is physically ill. *What if I have a seizure and die?* She remembers their advice and repeats it in her head. *Accepting the seizures are harmless is a key part to making them stop. Don't feed them with attention.*

'Is it too hot for you in here, Lil? We can't get the radiators to turn off but I can open the door into the garden.'

'Honestly, it's fine,' says Lilly. 'It was hot in the hospital.'

Her dad tries to lighten the atmosphere by pretending he can't find his glasses when they're on his head and telling a story they've all heard before about one of his students who was asked to illustrate his answer with examples in an exam on landscape painting and drew pictures of rabbits and birds instead.

Lilly longs to escape to her bedroom. When Dr Santini came to say goodbye this morning, he advised her to find space alone whenever she started to feel anxious or the tingling in her hands. He gave her a small leather-bound notebook as a present. 'Watch out for triggers. And write them down.' She should have told him she feels worst around her mum. She knew this from the start. But if she had, she might have ended up blurting out the whole story. However, she did admit to him that the seizure three weeks ago was not the first. The first one happened the last weekend of the summer term. She could pinpoint the exact date because it was the day her aunt and uncle came for lunch, just after Mia discovered the pregnancy test. One minute she had been standing in the garage, the next she had found herself lying on the floor, unable to remember what had happened. He looked puzzled and asked why there was a paramedic's report about her collapsing at a festival in the middle of the holidays. 'It wasn't me,' she told him. 'We gave my name to the paramedics so my friend wouldn't get into trouble.' He asked her if she could tell him any more and she shook her head. 'That's enough for the moment,' she said. He congratulated her for making such good progress.

'Can I just say how wonderful it is to have all four of us round the table again?' says Grace, reaching out to hold hands with Lilly and Mia. Patrick sees Lilly glance at the kitchen door and knows she's itching to escape. He does a sympathetic eye-roll but she doesn't respond. He senses a new steeliness in her demeanour but, unlike Grace, he feels no fear that she no longer bends to their will.

'Mum, please,' Lilly implores. 'You've seen me every day.'

'So what did you get up to today, Mia?' Patrick interjects, attempting to turn the spotlight away from Lilly and on to her younger sister.

'Not a lot,' says Mia, shovelling food into her mouth, seemingly unaware it is spilling on to her school skirt.

'Well, maybe that's no bad thing,' he teases. He wishes she would do up the top button of her shirt so he can't see the marks on her neck and hopes she didn't go to school exposing her craziness for the world to see.

'What are all those scratches on your hands and wrists?' Lilly asks.

Mia hides her hands so no one can examine them. 'I fell over during Netball Club.'

'You've joined Netball Club! That's great,' says Grace, who has been trying to persuade Mia to sign up all year. 'Sport is such a great way to make friends. Isn't it, Lil?'

'Well done,' Patrick loyally echoes in his most upbeat tone, even though he thinks they both sound like evangelical preachers.

'Does Bea do Netball Club? Maybe you should invite her

over and do some goal-scoring practice. We could put up a hoop outside,' suggests Grace.

'I'm playing a defensive position,' says Mia, her mouth full of rice. 'Bea's a natural attacker. And I don't want to be in the team.'

'It's sad not to be part of a team when you could be. Lilly has got so much out of swimming squad. Haven't you, Lil?'

'It's not that sad,' says Mia. 'There's far sadder stuff.'

'Like what?' asks Lilly.

'Like war and famine.' Mia pauses for a moment and rubs the tail of her plait above her upper lip. 'And when people who want to have babies can't have them and people who don't want them get pregnant. Like the Anglo-Saxon girl who is buried at the Travellers' site.'

'How do you know she didn't want to get pregnant?' asks Patrick, when what he really wants to ask is why her healthy interest in any subject always corrodes into unhealthy obsession, like her infatuation with Tas and her fixation with her teacher. He can understand why people find her intensity so offputting. It repels him too.

'She fell in love with a boy who didn't love her back and she knew she would die during childbirth so she wanted to be rid of the baby.'

'You can't know that,' says Grace. 'You're imagining what happened. You're projecting a false reality.'

Mia's gaze darts between the three of them. 'When you think about it, there's probably more reasons for not having a baby than for having one, aren't there? If you're too young to look after it or the father doesn't want to be involved. Or you don't have enough money.' Mia glances at Lilly, who glances at Grace and Patrick and sees them stiffen.

'I'd better get my stuff ready for school,' says Lilly. She's clock-watching, calculating whether she has spent enough time at the table to leave without causing either offence or worry.

'What do you mean?' Grace asks sharply.

'Grace . . .' Patrick warns. But he pulls back when he sees her expression.

'I don't know where anything is,' says Lilly, who is already halfway out of her chair. 'I've got to get all my files together. And my swimming kit. Do you know where my goggles are? And my biology textbook?'

'You can't go to school tomorrow,' says Grace, frantically. Her face is ashen.

'Why not?'

'It's too much too soon.'

'Too soon for who? You?'

'You need time to adjust. It's too risky.'

'What are you talking about, Mum? If I miss school I'll get even more behind with my work and Mr Galveston will definitely throw me out of his class. Isn't that what you care about most?'

'Maybe that's not such a bad idea,' Patrick jokes, but the mood has curdled.

'I've thought about it a lot. The sooner I go back, the better. Otherwise the pressure will just build up. Dr Santini and the psychologist both agree I should get back to normal life as quickly as possible.'

'Maybe we can go together on the bus,' suggests Mia. 'I know the route really well. I'll look after you.'

'I've had enough of your bad ideas, Mia,' says Grace savagely.

'I think it's a good plan,' Lilly counters. Mia smiles adoringly at her.

'What happens if it was something at school that caused

the seizure?' says Grace. She pauses for a beat too long. 'Or someone? What happens if you have another seizure and there's no one there to help?'

'Come on, Grace, the school has drawn up a ten-page contingency plan,' says Patrick, impatiently.

Grace bats his comment away with her hand, as if swatting a mosquito. 'If I were you, I'd stay at home for the next couple of weeks and let me help you. You can ask the teachers to set you assignments and I can oversee them. I can help you make a timetable and write up lists of quotes for you to learn.'

'But you're not me, Mum. I'm going and you can't stop me.' Lilly leaves the room and storms upstairs, closely followed by Mia. They hear her bedroom door slam shut at the top of the house.

'That went well,' says Patrick. 'You need to go back to work, Grace, and get on with your own life. For all our sakes.' He doesn't mention that they can't survive without her meagre salary.

Mia sits at the desk in her bedroom, composing her Anglo-Saxon diary. She's coming to the end of her story. They're starting a new topic next week and Miss Swain's written instructions for their final homework are to 'finish with a flourish' with a 'detailed and dramatic' conclusion using ten complex words they have never used before. Mia has made a list that starts with opium (she's got Dr Santini to thank for that one) and ends with abortion (following on from her Show and Tell). Anyone who does this is guaranteed the top grade, Miss Swain had promised, as she handed out the sheet in class, just after she had announced that Bea and Madani were joint winners of the Show and Tell. Miss Swain gave Mia the award for Best Effort. 'That's a real achievement,' she told Mia.

As soon as class finished, Mia got a pair of scissors and cut up the certificate into hundreds of tiny pieces and scattered them like confetti over Miss Swain's desk. Tas had skipped school again so there was no one to agree with her that she had been robbed of victory.

Although Miss Swain has instructed the class to focus on writing rather than drawing, Mia has dedicated the final page to a very detailed picture of her Anglo-Saxon girl floating above a field full of flowers, smiling serenely. Her uncomfortable pregnant stomach has disappeared. The ring is back on her finger. On her head Mia has drawn a flower crown with intricately sketched tiny flowers that she's colouring in.

She had started drawing it during a lunchtime detention yesterday. Bea had spent most of morning break pretending to have a seizure every time she saw Mia. If Tas had been there, they would have laughed it off together. 'If you don't shut up I'll strangle you until you pass out,' Mia had retaliated. 'I'm good at that.'

Bea had burst into tears and Mia was the one who ended up in detention. 'Do you often have thoughts about harming Bea?' Miss Swain had asked casually.

'Of course,' she had replied. Honestly, adults ask such stupid questions.

She hears Lilly's footsteps leave the bathroom and hesitate outside her bedroom door. *Please come in, Lil!* The door slowly opens.

'Shouldn't you be asleep?' Lilly asks. She goes over to the window.

'Don't,' says Mia.

'Don't what?'

'Don't open the curtains. Please.'

'Why?'

'I get scared of the bad spirits out there.'

'Funny how you're not afraid when someone half strangles you but the night air terrifies you. Makes no sense.' Lilly snaps the curtains shut. 'What exactly are you scared of?'

'Bad spirits that lead you into the water and leave you to drown.'

Lilly wanders over to her desk and looks over Mia's shoulder. 'Gosh, that's such a good picture.' She sounds genuinely impressed.

'Thanks,' says Mia, softly. She's always pathetically grateful for Lilly's praise.

'Why aren't her feet touching the ground?'

'She's floating above the earth,' says Mia, vaguely.

'Why?'

'She's come out the other side of a bad experience,' Mia explains.

There's a noise like bubbles bursting coming from Elvis's bucket. He pokes his head against the grille and Mia lifts it off so she can stroke his chin. His skin is still as smooth as liquid velvet. But it has turned from inky black to mottled green on top and silver underneath and his eyes look bigger.

'God, he stinks,' says Lilly, kneeling down beside the bucket.

'I cleaned him out yesterday. It's just his natural smell.' Mia shrugs.

'He looks like he's crying,' Lilly frowns as she gets closer to his face. 'His eyes are really watery.'

'Eels can't cry. They don't have eyelids,' says Mia.

'Maybe he's got an infection. Poor Elvis,' she says, stroking his head and speaking to him. 'To think of the freedom you had, catching all those currents underneath the Atlantic to get here, and now you're stuck in this disgusting bucket. No wonder you're so depressed.' She looks up. 'You should let him have his freedom, Mia. Give him back his life.'

'Are you talking about you?' Mia asks, in confusion. She can tell Lilly's doing that thing where people say one thing but mean another. She needs to be like Elvis and find the right current to swim along but she always gets it wrong.

'Maybe.'

'What's really wrong with you? Mum says your seizures come from your head. Does that mean you're faking them?' Mia chews the tail of her plait and runs the damp tip over her upper lip.

'Well, I haven't been playing the same game as you and Tas, if that's what you mean,' says Lilly, wryly. 'The seizures are real. But they're caused by emotional stress rather than something medical.'

'That's what I thought.'

'Well, you're quite the little doctor, aren't you?' says Lilly sarcastically.

She's prickly, like the burrs with hooks that Mia picks from her jumper after playing in Tas's yard. But she has to ask the question. 'Do you think they might have something to do with what happened between you and Cormack?'

'You mean us splitting up?' Lilly tensely circles the room. She picks up one of Mia's scented rubbers and smells it, then fiddles with some hair toggles and rearranges the empty perfume bottles that Grace has given her, putting them all back down in the wrong places.

'No. I mean what happened at the beginning of the summer.'

Lilly looks at her long and hard. 'What exactly are you talking about?'

'The pregnancy,' whispers Mia, knowing it's the wrong

thing to say but unable to rein in her curiosity. She still can't quite believe how Lilly sat opposite her at dinner every night for weeks without giving away that she had a baby growing in her stomach. She probably felt sick every morning and had interesting cravings. *Why didn't she tell her?* No one seems to want to share secrets with her any more. Not even Tas.

'I told you not to mention that ever again.' Lilly puts up her hand so close to Mia's face that she can see the criss-cross of lines on her palm.

Mia steps to the side. 'I just thought that maybe keeping all of that a secret might have made you ill. I've thought so much about you going to that clinic all by yourself and how lonely you must have felt. I wish you'd told me about it.' Mia feels her lower lip wobble.

'It was fine. I was fine.'

'Were you sick in the mornings? I feel so bad I never noticed.'

'God, Mia, please shut up about this, will you?' says Lilly.

'Did you tell the doctor? In case the abortion caused your seizures? Couldn't they tell when they were doing all those checks on you?'

'No.'

'Maybe you should tell Mum and Dad. I feel bad they don't know.'

Mia sees Lilly's hands start to shake and wonders if she's going to have a seizure right here right now in her bedroom and how, if she does, it will be her fault for asking too many questions. Lilly picks up her diary and aggressively flicks through it. She comes to the page with the drawing of the pregnant Anglo-Saxon girl with the photograph of her own face superimposed on top of it.

'What the fuck is this?' Mia tries to grab her diary but Lilly holds it in the air out of her reach.

'It's a story about the girl who gets pregnant during Anglo-Saxon times and thinks she's going to die during childbirth. The one I told at dinner!'

'Then why have you put a photo of my head on her body? God, you are out of your mind, Mia.' She tears out the page, rolls it into a ball and flicks it into the bin as she leaves the room, slamming the door behind her. Mia lies on her bed sobbing.

Grace drifts in and out of sleep, but it proves a slippery, elusive thing that she never quite manages to hold on to. She can't stop thinking about how this is the first night since the seizures started that Lilly has gone to bed without any machines watching over her. She stares at the ceiling. Lilly's room is directly above. For all they know, she could be having a seizure right now. She had suggested to Patrick that perhaps they should use the old baby monitor to listen out in case something went wrong in the night. He had looked at her as if she was crazy and refused to help search for it in the garage.

After Luca died, Grace didn't sleep properly for years. Sometimes she would go home with someone she had just met at one of the bars and clubs where she worked simply to avoid bumping into her little brother in her dreams. She had a recurring nightmare in which she could hear him calling out to her but could never find him. Some nights she would wake up, reach out for Luca and wonder how the tiny space he used to occupy in the crook of her arm could seem so vast now that he was gone.

At around three o'clock in the morning, when she can no longer fight back the dark thoughts, she goes upstairs to Lilly's room, gingerly turns the handle and edges into her bedroom, leaving the door ajar so the landing light illuminates the bed where she lies fast asleep.

She cautiously unfurls herself on the bed, close enough to feel the heat from Lilly's body without touching her, and watches the rhythmic rise and fall of her chest, like she used to when she was a baby, worrying about the prospect of her going to school the following day as if it was her first day at nursery, until finally it grows light outside. She might not have been there when Luca needed her, but she can be there for Lilly.

The next morning Lilly strides down the corridor towards Mr Galveston's classroom, absorbing the heat of other people's gaze. Students and teachers alike slow down to stare at her as they pass. She understands. Having read all the social-media and news reports about the hysteria provoked by her seizure, she's not surprised to have become the object of their curiosity. It's the same sense of voyeurism that makes cars on the motorway slow down to watch the aftermath of an accident. As she walks, she reassures herself by imagining the silence and muted tones of swimming underwater in the river at Earith. She just needs to catch the right current and she will keep moving forward.

Lilly heads past the lockers, past the sixth-form common room with its grubby sofas and broken microwave, and past the mural of inspirational figures. Nelson Mandela. Florence Nightingale. Malala Yousafzai. She stops beside Winston Churchill, because something looks different about him, and sees that someone has drawn a joint in his hand and a voice bubble coming from his mouth that says, 'I inhaled.' She finds Jordy's tag at the bottom and smiles.

When she goes into the classroom she's relieved to see that she has arrived before Mr Galveston. For an instant everyone freezes, as if Lilly has pressed the pause button on a video. Phones, conversations, last-minute changes to

283

homework all hang in mid-air. Then friends come over to say hello but they're not the right friends. Lilly goes to the back of the classroom and sits down in her old seat beside Jordy. He leans over and gives her a clumsy half-hug. He has the same wary look in his eyes as he had in the hospital.

'It's great to have you back, Lil,' he says, his cheeks flushing red. 'I've missed you.' She can tell he means it and regrets that she has become a complicating presence in his life.

'Did you miss me or the essays I lend you?' she teases. She has helped him out at school for as long as she can re-member, and she wants to remind him that they have more history together than he does with anyone else. Later she'll reinforce this by posting a picture of them together in a paddling pool as toddlers. He gives a quick smile. His face seems longer and thinner than ever.

'Actually, Freya has been helping me a bit,' he says, glan-cing across the row of desks to where Freya sits beside Hayley, giggling at something on her phone. 'She's been hanging out with us.' He's trying to be open with her. She'd seen pictures of the four of them on Instagram and liked them because she didn't want to appear salty but, still, it's a thump to the solar plexus to hear from Jordy how she has been so easily replaced.

'Hey, Lil.' Hayley insinuates herself between Lilly and Jordy and puts her arms around them both. She's wearing the same perfume as Freya, one of those cheap sweet body sprays that smell like jelly beans. She gives Jordy a kiss on the cheek that makes him blush again.

'God, Lilly, you must be so glad to be out of that hell-hole! I needed therapy to get over it and I was only there for a couple of hours.' Hayley speaks so loudly that the entire row in front turns round to look at them. Lilly waves, nervously greeting everyone by name to avoid appearing aloof or uncomfortable with their scrutiny. They all smile back but she knows they're probably remembering how Mr Galveston put his lips on hers and how her skirt hiked up so far you could see her knickers. At least no one posted photos or films of what had happened. It didn't take long to catch up with her social media last night. In fact, in social-media terms she was almost dead or at least in urgent need of resuscitation. Although lots of people had messaged after she went to hospital they pretty much gave up after the first week. It's like she had stopped existing. Her Snapchat group with Hayley, Cormack and Jordy has died, which makes her suspect they have probably set up another without her.

'Yeah. It's good to be back.'

Freya comes over and puts her arm around Jordy, who fits his angles into hers. 'I've missed you, Lil,' she says. 'Especially in class.'

'Thanks,' says Lilly, taken aback by Freya's warmth.

'It's too intense without you. Mr Galveston is relentless.'

'So what exactly is wrong with you?' Hayley asks. 'My mum told me that you're not ill or anything. She said it's all caused by stress.'

'I have a conversion disorder so the stress is in my head but it comes out through my body,' says Lilly. She'd practised how she was going to answer this question during her last session with the psychologist, but now she's here she can't remember the response she had rehearsed. 'They're caused by emotional stress.'

'Like my eczema,' says Jordy.

'Exactly,' says Lilly gratefully.

'The old mind-body connection,' quips Freya.

'So you weren't faking it?' Hayley asks. She's being

friendly but she hadn't messaged Lilly after she told her she was coming to school and she hadn't liked any of her photos or commented on anything. It's as if she's going through the motions in public but online she's totally ignoring her.

'Why would I fake something like that?' asks Lilly. She's been warned that this is the most common misconception about her illness but she didn't expect Hayley to be one of the doubters.

'Your sister did.'

'She's only ten years old,' says Jordy.

'What Mia did was nuts. Even by her standards,' says Lilly. Her desire to be part of the conversation shamefully overrides any loyalty to Mia.

'You might have done it to make Cormack feel bad about everything that happened so he gets back together with you?'

Lilly knows straight away that this is something Hayley has discussed with Cormack.

'You're talking shit,' Jordy warns Hayley.

'It's fine. I'm fine,' says Lilly, wondering if everyone is speculating about what caused her seizures.

'By the way, the four of us are having a party at my house this weekend. You can come if you like,' says Hayley. 'If your mum lets you.'

She says it casually but her intent is clear. She's showing off her closeness to Cormack, Jordy and Freya to underline Lilly's distance from them. She's like one of the animals in her biology A-level essay on demarcation of territory.

'She won't mind,' says Lilly, knowing full well that Grace will go bat-shit crazy if she says she's going to a party.

'You can pretend you're at mine and stay over afterwards,' says Jordy, quickly.

'Or mine,' Freya offers.

'Thanks,' says Lilly. 'That would be great.'

'I'll add you to the group, then,' Hayley says.

Lilly hates the idea that everyone will see she's been invited at the last minute but the thought of not being invited at all is worse. Luckily Mr Galveston comes into the room so Hayley can't gloat any more. When he sees Lilly back in her old seat he theatrically flings opens his arms. 'Lilly! Feeder of wolves! Tree of the fire of the sea! How are you feeling?'

In many ways it is the perfect welcome. She looks at his plump red lips and, instead of feeling embarrassed to think of them on her mouth, she's grateful that he tried to save her life. 'Relieved not to have had the sleep of the sword, Mr Galveston,' she quips. Everyone laughs. She's the best in the class when it comes to playing him at his own game.

'Very good. You've been much missed. Especially by Jordy, who must have been pining for you because his marks have gone into a steep decline in your absence.'

Because of the cuts, the school library is now open for only half a day. So at lunchtime, instead of going into the sixth-form common room, Lilly ignores the 'Closed' sign on the library door and slips inside. She heads to the far corner behind the history section, where there is a long window seat hidden from view by books on the First World War. It is one of her favourite places in the whole school. She lies down with her head resting on her rucksack and breathes in the familiar earthy smell.

The effort of pretending to everyone that everything is normal is exhausting. But she feels way more triggered at home than at school. In the class on *Beowulf* she was on fire, even winning the debate with Freya on whether it is an epic or a tragedy.

'You can talk to me about anything,' were Grace's parting words as she dropped her off.

'You listen without listening,' Lilly retorted. She wondered how Grace would have reacted if she'd told her that when Cormack was inside her she felt like the boundaries between them were so blurred that they actually became one person. Adults pay far too much attention to words when it's feelings that count for everything. But Lilly suspects her mum knows this better than anyone. She checks her body for signs of tingling or numbness at this thought but there is nothing, apart from the steady beat of her heart.

She pulls out the notebook Dr Santini gave her and notices that he has written something in his tiny spidery handwriting on the inside cover. *The truth will set you free but at first it will make you miserable.* She puts on her headphones and flits through her favourite new Spotify list without listening to any track to the end. *The truth may set me free but it will make everyone else miserable.* Next time she sees Dr Santini she will tell him this.

Lilly closes her eyes and practises the deep breathing the psychologist has taught her to help her slow down. Since what happened at the festival, even in her dreams, she's always running. When she opens them again, Cormack is standing beside the window seat staring at her. It's as if she has conjured him into being. She sits up and looks over his shoulder to see if Hayley and Jordy are with him but he's alone.

'Are you trying to avoid me?' he asks, cocking his head with a familiar half-smile.

She has devised a strategy of detached friendliness to deal with people on her first day back at school. It's a self-protecting mask that she can hide behind without anyone realizing. It has worked with Jordy and Hayley and her classmates, but as soon as Cormack smiles all resolve drains away. All she wants to do is win him over again. Desire trumps pride every time. Even after what he did at the festival. It doesn't frighten her because there's beauty in the simplicity of such pure emotional certainty. She would settle for the same fate as Mia's eel: one final entanglement, then death. *I would do anything for you*, she doesn't say.

'Not in a way that makes avoiding you central to my existence,' she says instead.

He laughs. 'Can I sit down?' She envies his certainty and the way he's so comfortable with himself. He always knows what he wants and that was why it felt so good when he wanted her. She makes a friendly but not intimate space for him beside her.

'So, how are you feeling, Lil?'

'Like I'm ten years older.'

'And ten years wiser?'

'No. Just older. Never wiser.'

He peers at her face. 'Well, you look exactly the same to me.' They stare at each other for a beat longer than is comfortable, before leaning back against the sign on the window that says 'Do Not Lean on the Window.' Lilly likes the way they are positioned symmetrically with their legs hanging over the edge of the seat, their shoulders slumped against the glass, almost touching.

'So what exactly did they see when they looked into your brain?'

'There was a whole area devoted to *Beowulf*. It took up so much space that my brain short-circuited. They think that was the trigger for the seizure.'

'For real?'

She snorts with derision.

'You get me every time.' He laughs, shaking his head from side to side so his long dark hair hides his face. His laughter is the best sound in the world. She imagines a university interview where the answer to every question is 'Making Cormack laugh'. *What is your best memory? What do you like doing to relax in your spare time? What makes you happiest? What is your greatest achievement? What are your plans for the future?* She's forgotten how good he is at playing with her feelings.

'Well, I'm glad you're better,' he says.

'I'm always better when I'm with you,' she says.

'I know,' he mumbles, looking away. It's an ambiguous response. Does he mean he feels the same? Or is he simply acknowledging that he realizes, despite everything that's happened, Lilly still loves him?

'So are you going to come to the party at the weekend?'

'You mean *your* party?' Lilly asks quizzically, cocking her head to one side. 'The one you're sharing with Hayley?'

'She's got the best house,' he says, all brazen cheek. 'And her parents are going out. That's two pretty strong arguments.'

'God, you're as shallow as the sluice at low tide,' says Lilly.

He laughs again, but this time it sounds more hollowed out. 'It won't be the same if you're not there, Lil. Will your mum let you come if she knows it's my party?'

'I won't tell her,' she says. 'I'm sorry about her going at you in the hospital. She's totally lost the plot.'

'Why does she hate me so much?'

'She has a particular type in mind for me and you're not it, I guess.' Lilly shrugs.

'Why not?'

'You're too wild. You're not going to uni and she blames you for my illness. And, before you ask, I haven't told anyone.' He lifts a strand of hair away from her cheek and his finger brushes her skin. She leans into his hand and he doesn't pull away. All she wants is the sensation of his skin against hers one last time.

'I'm really sorry about everything that's happened,' he says. 'Sometimes I wish we could go back in time.'

'Me too.'

'I'm really glad you got in touch,' he says. She's about to ask him what he means but the library door opens.

'Cormack, are you in here?' Hayley shouts.

'Yeah, just coming,' he yells back, quickly pressing his finger to Lilly's lips to indicate she should say nothing. She opens her mouth to kiss it but he has already pulled away, and within seconds of him leaving, it feels as if he was never there in the first place. That's how it always is with Cormack. Things only feel real when she's with him, and when they're apart it's as though their whole relationship was a figment of her imagination.

16

On Saturday morning they're woken by the noise of the wind chimes in the garden tinkling manically. Down in the kitchen the draught has blown the get-well cards for Lilly off the mantelpiece and the beads from Mia's friendship-bracelet kit are scattered all over the dusty floor. The wind whistles and moans through the gaps in the poorly fitted doors and windows at different pitches so it sounds as if someone is playing pan pipes.

The four of them peer through the patio doors to the end of the garden and the ploughed field beyond, watching in awed silence as leaves squall around the lawn and branches list until Grace feels almost seasick. In the distance the sky slowly turns the same colour as the field until finally the huge black cloud obliterates the horizon.

'What's happening?' asks Mia, apprehensively.

'It looks like a sandstorm,' says Grace. She takes advantage of the distraction to put her arm tentatively round Lilly, who flinches but at least doesn't immediately pull away.

'Close,' says Patrick. 'Except it's dust, not sand. It's a Fen Blow. We used to get them the whole time when we were children. The wind lifts the topsoil from the fields and turns it into a huge dust cloud.'

'Why does it do that?' asks Lilly.

Grace steals a glance and sees her face is flushed pink.

There's a sheen down the sides of her nose and above her upper lip. Compared to Mia, her skin feels hot and clammy. *Is it excitement or is she running a fever? What if she's picked up a hospital infection?* Grace hasn't paid such forensic attention to tiny physical changes in Lilly for years. It's only three days since she first came home but she's already exhausted with the effort of watching over her.

'The peat soil has lost so much water that it has dried out and eroded so it just blows away. One day these fields will probably disappear,' Patrick explains.

'So, strictly speaking, our family has caused an environmental disaster?' questions Mia.

'We can hardly be blamed for something our ancestors did three hundred years ago.' Patrick laughs. 'That really wouldn't be fair.'

'"The sins of the father are to be laid upon the children,"' says Lilly, doing her best imitation of Mr Galveston doing Shakespeare.

'What does that mean?' asks Mia, betraying her worry by chewing the end of her plait and running it over her top lip.

'That children are cursed for the bad things their parents do. It's a quote from *The Merchant of Venice*.' Lilly is talking to Mia but staring at Grace.

'Very impressive,' says Grace, simultaneously pleased that Lilly has re-engaged with her A-level English text and grateful that, despite everything, she still looks to her for approval. She wishes they could stay like this for ever, like the tiny smiling frozen family holding hands inside the snow globe on Mia's bookshelf.

'You've never done anything bad, Mum, have you?' Mia asks, leaning into Grace so intensely that her hipbone juts uncomfortably into her thigh.

If only it were Lilly rather than Mia who found comfort in being close to her. Lilly, however, remains implacably, inhumanly distant. She arrives home from school each day in a strange mood of exhausted euphoria but won't discuss anything, not even what classes she's attended, let alone who she's seen. Every time she leaves in the morning Grace thinks of the video and agonizes over what Cormack might have done to her and whether he will do it again.

Yesterday Grace went into work to write up her interview with the archaeologist, but when she read it back, the questions and answers were all in the wrong order. Her eyes prickled with tiredness, and when Tony emptied out his drawers until he found eye drops and offered to put them in, she had to press her lips together to stop herself crying. So, during her lunch break she composed a long email to Mr Galveston explaining that it was 'strongly suspected' Cormack was the underlying cause of the stress that had triggered Lilly's seizures. She hinted that he had 'almost certainly' done something illegal. *Please can you ensure they are kept apart at all times until our investigations are finished?* she requested. Mr Galveston had emailed back to suggest that she came in to speak to him as soon as possible. Grace noticed that not only did he fail to agree to her request, he also included Patrick in his response, which had led to a row last night during which Patrick accused her of being deranged.

'Mum!' says Mia, digging the sharp hipbone into her thigh again. 'I asked you a question.'

'Never. Nothing bad, ever,' says Grace, distractedly, kissing the top of Mia's head. She has a strange earthy smell, as if she's hewn from the same soil that blows outside the window.

'Unless being addicted to orange squash counts,' Patrick teases. 'Or stockpiling food. Those are about the worse things Mum ever does.'

Mia manages a smile. Lilly doesn't.

'Are you absolutely sure it's not bad spirits coming to get us?' Mia asks. 'I swear that dust cloud is hanging right over the archaeological site.'

'I've never been more certain about anything,' says Grace, draping her arm around Mia's bony shoulders, being careful to avoid the bruising and sores on her neck and chest. She's scrawny, like Luca was scrawny. Grace pulls away so the thought can't settle.

'Maybe it's come to carry the spirit of the dead girl and her baby up to Heaven,' says Mia, her gaze darting hopefully between the three of them.

'How do you come up with this stuff?' Patrick roars with laughter. 'You're wasted doing SATs. You should be writing episodes of *Game of Thrones*.'

'Don't indulge her, Dad!' Lilly rolls her eyes. She turns to Mia and squeezes the top of her shoulder with her hand. 'Give it a rest with the Anglo-Saxon girl,' she warns. 'It's getting really boring.'

'Well, I think it's great Mia is taking such an interest in her school work,' says Grace, praising Mia rather than criticizing Lilly in an effort to restore the fleeting harmony.

'No, it's not, Mum,' counters Lilly, testily. 'It's not normal. She's a total freak.'

Grace takes a deep breath. The composition of the air around them feels suddenly altered, as if she's now inhaling the tiny particles of bitterness, anger and resentment that Lilly has just breathed out. She can't cope with the way her temperament has become so mercurial. Sometimes she wonders if the seizures might have damaged the part of her brain that controls her emotions, even though Dr Santini had explained this was impossible. Lilly knows perfectly well that the reason Mia refused to go to school last year was because the other children in the class waged a Facebook campaign calling her a freak.

'That's enough, Lilly,' she says sharply. 'I don't care if you've been ill. There's no excuse for unkindness.'

'I'm not a freak, am I?' asks Mia, rubbing her upper lip with her hair over and over again.

'Of course you're not,' says Patrick, pulling her towards him and away from Lilly. He gently tugs the plait from her hand.

'What kind of person gets involved in some weird strangling game to copy their sister's illness, simply to get a bit of attention?' Lilly asks angrily. 'You caused complete hysteria and made people look like fools for believing in some contagion. Do you know that's why people think my seizures are fake? You've made everything so much more difficult for me.'

'You don't understand,' says Mia, who seems weirdly unfazed by Lilly's verbal onslaught.

'Too right I don't understand,' says Lilly. 'No one does.'

Mia looks up at her, with eyes as wide as saucers. 'I didn't do it for me. I did it for Tas,' she says, in an even tone.

'Why on earth did you think that Tas would be helped by you throttling each other?' Grace asks, in astonishment. 'Why does Tas need help anyway?'

'His whole family needs help,' says Mia.

'This got Tas into a whole heap of problems with his family,' Patrick points out. 'Do you realize his mum doesn't want him to go to school with you any more?'

Mia nods. A single big clumsy tear falls down her cheek. She ferociously wipes it away.

'I thought if people believed that children who visited the archaeological site were getting seizures they'd have to abandon the dig and Tas's family would be able to stay,' she explains solemnly. 'He's my one true friend in the world.' This is the only moment her voice wobbles.

'Why would digging up an archaeological site cause seizures?' asks Patrick, in bewilderment.

'Because it's a burial site and they disturbed the spirits of the dead, especially the deviant girl who had stones on her back so her spirit couldn't escape,' says Mia.

'Holy shit, Mia,' says Lilly. 'I swear you're the one that needs to see a psychologist, not me.'

'She's already seeing the school counsellor,' says Grace.

'Then why is she still so crazy?'

'That's enough, Lilly,' says Grace. She kneels down until she is at head height with Mia and strokes her cheek. She knows Mia is telling the truth because there is a mad logic to her explanation. She shudders inwardly as she thinks about the investigation by the Department of Health, and the fears of parents who thought their child might be the next one to fall ill. She remembers Catriona's campaign and the ensuing media circus. Mia had caused all of this.

'Why didn't you tell us before?' Grace asks. 'It would have saved you and everyone else a whole lot of trouble.' She holds Mia close and tells her that she loves her but the only truth Mia really wants to hear is that Tas won't have to leave.

'It's like the psychologist says. The truth sets you free, Mia,' says Lilly, sarcastically. 'It's a lesson all of us in this family could do with learning.'

'I thought I was helping him,' says Mia. 'But I've made everything worse.'

'The only person Tas needs saving from is you.' Lilly gives an empty laugh and slides from beneath Grace's arm while Mia shrinks further into her side.

'That's not true,' she whimpers. 'Tas loves me.'

Lilly turns her back on them and hurtles towards the

staircase, stopping at the bottom to face her parents. 'By the way, I'm going to Jordy's house this evening. He's going to help me catch up with all the work I've missed with Mr Galveston. I'm really behind on *The Merchant of Venice*.'

Grace's body stiffens. 'You can't do that,' she says, a little too quickly. 'The last bus home is at ten. Why don't you get Jordy to come here? It would be so nice to see him.'

'Back off, Mum. It's all organized. I'm going.'

Grace realizes she's being cloying. Before Lilly was discharged from the hospital, Dr Santini warned her against being over-protective, using phrases like 'adolescent autonomy', 'self-governance' and 'cognitive independence' to get across his message. But he didn't know what she knew. He hadn't seen that video. She might have failed with Luca but she's not going to fail with Lilly. One day she will try to explain how everything she feels and does as a mother is a response to her own childhood. She will tell them about her little brother and how in the years following his death she asked herself every day what might have happened if she had turned down Rudy's request to go and fetch a blanket. She will explain how life can pivot on a split-second decision. How love and loss are forever entwined. How she feels Luca's presence all around until it occupies the core of her being. She looks out of the window again and the vastness of the landscape is a reminder of the vast empty feeling of grief.

'Well, let's talk about it later,' suggests Patrick.

'Yeah. Let's always leave until tomorrow what you can do today. That's worked really well for you as a life strategy, hasn't it, Dad?' Lilly slams the door.

The doorbell starts ringing in a long, bronchial drone because the damp has crept into the wiring.

'I'll go,' says Grace, relieved to have an excuse to leave the kitchen. She tries to assemble her features into an expression of benevolent warmth, to convey a sense of domestic and personal harmony that she most definitely doesn't feel.

The bell wheezes again.

'Coming,' she cries, in her best sing-song voice. Because of the public nature of Lilly's illness, there has been a stream of well-wishers dropping in cards and flowers all week. The sitting room is starting to resemble a shrine. Grace is grateful for their thoughtfulness but the constant scrutiny saps her energy and the conversation inevitably becomes awkward when it turns to Lilly's diagnosis. 'She's had seizures, but she doesn't have epilepsy'; 'The seizures are real, but they don't have a physical cause'; 'There's no medical reason. They're psychological. Nothing to do with wind farms.'

Because of the hysteria generated by Lilly's illness, Grace feels she owes everyone an explanation, not least to try to break the cycle of endless speculation. But no one has heard of conversion disorder and most people leave with more questions than answers. She notices how some of them look over her shoulder into the house as if searching for hidden clues to Lilly's illness. *What secrets are concealed there?* she imagines them asking. *Sexual abuse? Domestic violence? Or some deviant version of pushy parenting?* Sometimes she catches them observing Mia in the background and sees the disquiet in their face if she turns and reveals the imprint of Tas's hand on her neck and the bruising on her shoulder. As she turns the key in the lock, Grace braces herself.

The wind works in her favour, blowing against the front door as she battles to push it open so she has a few seconds to adjust to the totally unexpected appearance of Rob and Ana on the doorstep.

'Oh!' she says, her relief at finding familiar faces not quite masking her surprise.

'Hi, Grace. We come bearing gifts!' says Rob, cheerfully, pushing sideways through the door, balancing a large pile of what look like professionally wrapped parcels in his arms. He stops for a moment to frown contemptuously at Patrick's new bike, then continues into the kitchen.

'How are you?' asks Ana, holding her in an extravagantly long embrace, her oversize scarf and coat smothering Grace's face. 'You poor things. It must have been horrendous!' Grace allows herself to be consumed by Ana, but as they unravel her sister-in-law must register the lingering surprise in her expression.

'Were you not expecting us?' Ana asks, cocking her head quizzically. She manoeuvres her suitcase on wheels exaggeratedly around the multiple obstacles in the hallway and sashays into the kitchen. It dawns on Grace with creeping dread that they are planning to stay the night. 'Did Patrick forget to tell you?'

'No, no, of course not,' bluffs Grace. She purses her lips tight to avoid betraying any irritation with Patrick, who has either forgotten he invited his brother and sister-in-law or, more likely, avoided telling her they were coming because he knew she would never agree to them staying on Lilly's first weekend home. For sure, Rob will take advantage if he senses antagonism between them, exposing any division for his own entertainment. 'You're just a touch earlier than anticipated.'

'I texted Patrick when we bypassed Cambridge,' says Rob, apologetically, as he arranges the gifts on top of each other for maximum impact on the kitchen table.

Patrick approaches Ana with open arms, carefully avoiding Grace's gaze. 'Ana, so nice of you to come all this way to see Lilly,' he says.

'Presents for the birthday girl. For Monday. Make sure

she saves the best till last,' says Rob, patting the smallest box. He begins a long-winded account of his desire to buy a really special present for his niece's birthday but Grace suspects it's an opportunity to underscore his globetrotting lifestyle. He describes searching in vintage shops on a work trip to Los Angeles and in the souk during a long weekend in Marrakech, then finally ending up going to a Sotheby's auction while in New York for the MTV music-video awards to pick up 'a little something' he had spotted in an online catalogue. Grace notices Patrick bristle at this particular detail. His first failed job interview out of university was at Sotheby's and he will see a barb in this apparent act of generosity, whether it was intended or not.

'It's a pair of 1960s earrings made from lapis lazuli,' Ana blurts out.

'The same colour as Lilly's eyes,' says Rob.

'How do you remember what colour her eyes are?' asks Patrick.

'Because they're the exact same shade as Grace's,' says Rob.

'And guess who had to go for a long weekend to New York to pick them up because he was so scared they would get lost if we shipped them?' asks Ana, who has an uncanny ability to dress up even the most selfish acts as self-sacrifice, as if her whole life has been put on hold to serve Rob.

'Well, it's really kind of you both,' says Grace. She means it. Rob has always been an exemplary uncle and Lilly will be thrilled. But she can tell they are there for some other undeclared purpose. She feels it in the way they begin and finish each other's sentences and the looks of mutual support they exchange at regular intervals. It's the harmony between them that makes her most suspicious.

'Where's Lil?' asks Rob, scanning the kitchen for her.

'Up in her bedroom. Resting,' Grace responds. 'She rests a lot.'

'How is she?' he asks. 'We wanted to come sooner . . .'

'But you know how it is,' says Ana. 'Life is just so full.'

'She's doing great, all things considered. Went back to school this week. And enjoyed it!' says Patrick. 'She's amazing.'

'And are you any closer to finding out what actually caused these seizures?' asks Ana.

'They're stress-induced,' says Grace, nodding emphatically.

'How could stress cause something so dramatic?' Rob asks.

'Sometimes when the brain gets overloaded it just shuts down,' Patrick explains. 'Like a computer when it freezes.'

'Surely Lilly's life isn't that full of anxiety,' Rob asks.

'The doctors say it's either down to a single traumatic event or an accumulation of stress over time,' says Patrick.

'Do you think she felt under a lot of academic pressure?' asks Ana.

'We really can't be certain,' says Grace, who knows this is probably the theory favoured by most people who know her.

'She's trying to work it out with the psychologist,' says Patrick.

'But you must have some idea?' Rob persists.

'It all started after she went to a music festival in the summer,' says Grace. 'She won't discuss any of it with us.'

'Maybe she took some dodgy pills,' suggests Rob. 'That generation spend more time worrying about whether they're eating a free-range egg than considering what might be in a shitty little pill they've bought on the Dark Net.'

'Lilly's not into that kind of stuff,' says Grace. 'We think it's more likely connected to some problems she had with an ex-boyfriend.'

'I didn't even know Lilly had a boyfriend,' says Ana.

'Well, neither did we,' says Grace. 'And therein lies the problem.'

'I knew,' says Mia, popping up from behind the sofa at the end of the room where she's been making friendship bracelets. 'He's called Cormack and he goes to the same school as Lilly.'

Patrick continues to talk with a false brightness of purpose, herding them towards the sofa where Mia is sitting and offering to make cups of tea. Grace sees Rob look around the kitchen, digesting the cupboards with missing doors, the unplastered walls, the floorboards piled in the corner and the cardboard boxes covered with dustsheets. 'Bit of a war zone in here, isn't it, Grace?' He looks genuinely concerned. 'It can't be good for Lilly's health. And what's that horrendous noise? It sounds like someone playing a mutant pan pipe.'

'This house has more holes than a Swiss cheese. And the bloody builders went on holiday,' says Mia, so obviously repeating something she has heard Patrick say that everyone starts laughing. At least her mood has been transformed by Rob and Ana's arrival.

'Come here, most favoured niece,' says Rob, as Mia throws herself into his arms.

'I'm so glad you're here. You can't imagine how difficult it has all been!' says Mia, dramatically.

'You sound like a little old lady,' Rob teases, as he throws her over his shoulder. 'Did someone try to kill you?' he asks, touching the handprint on her neck.

'Only because I asked them to,' says Mia.

'Then why didn't they finish you off? That's exactly what

I would have done.' He starts to tickle Mia, who wriggles and squeals.

Grace sees Rob and Ana looking at the marks on her neck and shoulders. Rather than expressing shock, as people usually do when they see her injuries for the first time, Grace notices them exchange an almost imperceptible nod, like they're ticking off another item on a checklist. It dawns on Grace that Beth has probably instructed them to visit to check what is going on and report back to her. Ana approaches Mia, shaking a large box from side to side like a maraca. 'For you,' she says to Mia. Rob throws Mia on to the sofa beside the present.

She opens it slowly, carefully peeling back the Sellotape so it doesn't ruin the paper, and whoops as she unveils a huge Lego Elves set. 'Oh, my God,' she says. 'The Elemental Guardians. How did you find these? Thank you so, so much.'

She starts unpacking plastic packets and lining them up on the coffeetable while Rob and Ana settle down either side of her on the sofa. Ana sheds her coat and jumper. 'It's pretty warm in here,' she says.

'It's a house of microclimates,' Patrick riffs. 'We go from desert to rainforest in less than three floors. In the attic it's positively temperate.'

'The radiators won't turn off,' Grace explains. 'It's as simple as that.' She's less annoyed with Ana for complaining than with Patrick's desperate attempts at jocularity. She follows him back into the kitchen. 'I can't believe you didn't tell me,' she hisses.

Patrick turns on the kettle and Grace switches it off. He turns to face her. 'You wouldn't have agreed,' he replies, with a nonchalant shrug.

'I don't want them here,' says Grace, belligerently.

'Maybe it will do us all good to be diluted.' He turns on the kettle again.

'You need to tell them to leave right now,' Grace says. 'They can't stay the night. It means Lilly will have to share her room with Mia.'

'I can't do that,' says Patrick, adamantly.

'Why?'

'Not when they've come all this way and brought all these presents.'

'Lilly doesn't want them here.'

'What's your evidence for that?'

'She's been upstairs in her room since they arrived.'

'Lilly left long before she knew it was Rob and Ana at the door,' says Patrick.

'She needs space. And they'll end up having a row.'

'The atmosphere wasn't exactly peace and love before they got here.'

'I haven't even got lunch for them.'

Patrick pauses and scratches his head. 'Well, what if I take Rob to the pub and you chill here with Ana?'

Grace weighs up his proposal. The good thing about Ana is she's never happier than when talking about herself, which at least means Grace won't have to discuss Lilly.

'Ana will be good at repelling the unwanted well-wishers,' he adds, knowing that will be the clincher.

'Okay,' she reluctantly concedes. 'On condition they leave before lunch tomorrow.'

When they had spoken earlier in the week Patrick was relieved that his brother understood the discussion about his finances could not take place at home, although he was equally infuriated when Rob followed this up with an email entitled 'Conditions of Loan', outlining the documents he

306

wanted him to get together before they met. It was the bullet points that really got to him. 'Bank statements dating back three years; details of mortgage debt and payments; credit-card debt; County Court summons.' *Who the fuck does he think he is?* It all sounded oddly formal, as though the PA with the husky voice might have written it.

When Patrick tells Rob he's going to take him to the pub for lunch, as if the idea has just occurred to him, and he will be the one paying, Rob responds by sending a text to remind him to put his papers in a couple of plastic bags and deposit them in the boot of his car 'to avoid any embarrassment'. Sometimes Patrick regrets they are no longer children and he can't simply rugby-tackle his younger brother to the ground and pummel him in the stomach until he begs him to stop. Instead he texts back a terse *tks*.

'We're going out for a quick pint,' Rob tells Ana, kissing the top of her head. 'Patrick could do with a change of scene.'

Patrick waits for Ana to object. Instead she somewhat implausibly insists she can think of nothing she would rather do than build a Lego Elves house with Mia, which makes him paranoid that Rob has told her what's going on and she might let something slip to Grace while they're away.

Patrick recommends a gastro-pub in the centre of Cambridge where he sometimes hangs out marking essays in between classes. Rob, however, wants to head north, deeper into the Fens, to the Edith Tavern, a grungy pub where they used to go as teenagers, and where Grace discovered Lilly had been with Cormack. Patrick offers to drive but Rob says he'd rather go in his car, which isn't surprising considering he's arrived in an old E-type Jag with customized seats made from vintage leather that probably cost triple the amount of Patrick's debts.

'Not sure I like the idea of used leather,' says Patrick, delicately wrinkling his nose as he pours himself into the front seat. 'You don't really want to imagine what it might have been used for.'

'Yeah, it's a bit gimmicky, isn't it? But it was a present from a client so I can't complain,' says Rob, distractedly. He's too busy trying to find the right playlist for the journey to rise to the sneer in Patrick's tone. He flits between Nick Cave and P. J. Harvey before settling on Manic Street Preachers. Patrick is heartened that it's the exact album they used to listen to on their way to this pub when they were younger. He's hoping that evoking some kind of nostalgia might make Rob more benevolent towards him, then realizes the album is *This Is My Truth, Tell Me Yours* and gets paranoid that Rob is actually taking the piss.

They head away from the main road. But as soon as they hit the backroads, the wind picks up until all is roar and bluster. The road bisects two enormous fields and is totally exposed to the elements. The gusts are so strong that Patrick feels them pushing the car off the road. Soon they are immersed in a cloud of black dust blowing from the fields. It's so difficult to see that Rob has to turn on the headlights and crunch down gears until the car is crawling. He starts worrying what the peaty dust cloud might do to his engine. *Choke it to death, hopefully*, thinks Patrick, bitterly. Then he feels a twinge of guilt because Rob is here to help him: he's the only person standing between him and potential bankruptcy.

If someone asked him to put a price on the cost to his pride of this forthcoming discussion there wouldn't be any figure big enough.

He remembers Lilly talking about the modals of lost opportunity. *Would have, should have, could have.* He *would* have avoided this if he hadn't got into debt on four different credit cards two years ago; he *could* have been saved if he'd come clean with Grace and told her he was no longer working full time as soon as his hours were cut; he *should* have faced up to the situation before they moved house. But it wouldn't have fitted with the script she had written for him, just as what had happened to Lilly didn't match the life she had mapped out for her.

The only time he truly feels shame is when he thinks of Lilly. Sometimes he sees the pity in her eyes and he is convinced that she knows and that this knowledge has contributed to the stress that caused her illness. With Mia it's different. It's not that she deserves less, it's that so little matters to her. She doesn't care whether her boots have holes or her hand-me-down school skirt is several sizes too big or her bedroom walls are black with damp. All she cares about is the little boy from the Travellers' site. He remembers what she told them this morning and is simultaneously chilled by her misguided compulsion to put things right and proud of her loyalty to Tas.

'God, it's years since I've experienced a Fen Blow,' says Rob, squinting over the steering wheel. 'There's something magnificent about its power.'

'It looks like a painting by Gerhard Richter,' shouts Patrick, over the noise of the wind as the pylons, sheep and occasional tree slowly blur into indistinguishable shapes. A huge lorry carrying vegetables suddenly emerges from the cloud on the other side of the road and forces them into the verge. When they finally drive into the empty pub car park and Rob gets out of the car, the wind almost dislocates the door from its hinges.

'Wild weather,' shouts Patrick.

They go into the pub. It's virtually empty. On the counter is a huge pot of pickled eggs that Rob jokes must have been there since they last visited in 1996. The same posters still hang on the walls. 'I haven't spoken to my wife in years – I don't want to interrupt her'; 'The cost of living's going up and the chance of living's going down.' Everything is coated in a layer of grease. Rob orders a couple of pints at the bar and pays without even waiting for Patrick to get out his wallet. They sit together at a table in the corner, away from the draught blowing in dust through the gap at the bottom of the door.

'I really can't understand why you wanted to move back here,' says Rob. 'It makes me feel like I'm suffocating. That empty landscape chews you up and spits you out whole.'

'You're implying there was a choice,' says Patrick, who has already decided that honesty combined with self-pity might generate the best leverage to secure a full loan.

'What do the children make of it all?'

'Lilly hates it. She much preferred being in the city centre with all her friends. Mia doesn't mind. Her best friend lives on the Travellers' site up the road.'

'The one who strangled her?'

'Yep.'

Rob takes a deep gulp of beer, turning the frayed beer mat round with his hand. 'And what about Grace? Is she happy?'

'The house is a fucking nightmare. Every day there's a new problem. And now, after everything that's happened to Lilly and Mia, I wouldn't be surprised if she told me she wanted to start anew somewhere. But she doesn't realize we're trapped. I looked at the value of the house on Zoopla and it's worth way less than we paid for it.'

Rob shreds the beer mat into tiny pieces, then tries to put it together again, like a puzzle. There's a sense of expectancy, as if he's about to say something of vital importance. 'She deserves more.'

'She does,' says Patrick, relieved that he has misread Rob's mood. He nods fervently in agreement. The barman comes over with some complimentary pickled eggs and takes their lunch order, explaining it has to go in quickly because the chef is knocking off early.

'I'll have the chicken and chips,' says Rob.

'We're out of chicken,' says the barman. 'Sorry, mate.'

'How about a couple of prawn cocktails with chips on the side?'

'We're good for that.'

A few minutes later prawns in a sauce made of tomato ketchup mixed with salad cream arrive, with genuine white sliced bread and margarine. Rob is totally seduced by its authenticity. Patrick decides coming here might have been a master stroke.

'God, I miss eating crap,' Rob says. 'It's all quinoa and curly kale in our house.'

'Well, you both look good on it.'

'Don't do that.'

'Do what?'

'Try to flatter me. Doesn't work. It's inauthentic. Unlike the prawn cocktail.'

They both fall silent for a minute, nursing their beers. Then Rob holds up a prawn and pretends to interview it about how long it has been since it was actually in the sea. Patrick isn't sure whether or not to laugh, so he tries a snort of approval but it ends up sounding like a groan.

'Any progress with the IVF?' he asks, hoping fraternal warmth will make Rob generous, then kicking himself for reminding his brother about something that is probably haemorrhaging his savings.

'Ana wants to try again. I'm not so keen. The hormone injections make her even more volatile.'

'Have you considered it might be you firing blanks?' Patrick asks. 'All that stuff in your twenties could have played havoc with your sperm.'

'My sperm are in very good shape, thanks,' says Rob.

Patrick feels his impatience. It occurs to him that Rob sees him as a problem that needs solving, in much the same way that he and Grace view Mia.

'So where's it all gone, Patrick?'

'Where's all what gone?' responds Patrick, trying to strike a languid pose, cocking his head almost coquettishly and resting it against an uncomfortable nodule on the back of the wooden bench.

'Come on, Patrick, we don't have time to fuck about.'

He's being kind because, of course, Patrick has all the time in the world: his pared-down role at school barely qualifies his job as part time.

'Well, as the character who goes bankrupt in *The Sun Always Rises* said, It happened "gradually, and then suddenly",' says Patrick, glibly.

'Why do you always do that?' asks Rob, throwing his arms into the air in frustration so that the confetti of torn-up beer mat floats to the floor.

'Do what?' asks Patrick, turning a pickled egg in his hand as if he's examining an ancient relic.

'Try to deflect serious questions. It probably explains how you've ended up in this mess in the first place.'

'I've explained it all before. The house is a nightmare. It eats money.'

'But it's not just the house, is it, Patrick? One of the

reasons you ended up moving here is because you were already up to your neck in debt.'

Patrick gets up to go to the toilet. He needs to clear his head so that he doesn't end up saying something he'll regret. As he pees, he looks at himself in the mirror, but he can't even hold his own gaze. So he stares at the signs on the wall telling customers what not to throw into the toilet. He notices there are pictures, too, for people who can't read or don't speak English. Condoms. Cigarette butts. Nappies. He gives a grim laugh. When he goes back Rob has joined the adjacent table to theirs and started laying out all of Patrick's papers in neat rows.

'You need to prioritize your debts,' advises Rob. 'Pay off the ones that have most serious consequences first. How far behind are you on mortgage payments?'

'Four months,' says Patrick, wondering how he knew this.

'So how much do you owe?'

'Four and a half thousand pounds.'

'Well, that's where you need to focus your attention.'

He makes a separate pile for all the builders' bills, utility bills and credit-card loans. He suggests that he find a company where he can put all his debts into one loan at a lower interest rate. He's methodical and precise. Neither are adjectives Patrick would conventionally have associated with his brother. Once everything is laid out, Rob gets out his calculator and adds up the total. It comes to more than fifty thousand pounds.

'Maybe that new bicycle was a bit of a stretch. What do you think?' says Rob, caustically.

'Well, it helped me achieve my PB on the Black Fen ride,' jokes Patrick, wishing his brother didn't have to overlay everything with his disapproval. 'I'm sure I don't owe as much as that.' It seems absurd to him that he doesn't have enough money to fill his car with a full tank of petrol whenever it runs low, to live in a nice house in a decent area, unthinkingly to buy Mia sets of Lego Elves. He remembers Rob in his early twenties, sofa-surfing at friends' houses because he couldn't keep down a job, taking drugs that dulled his brain and made him lazy, and their parents' despair that he would never make anything of himself. He cannot reconcile his brother back then with the person sitting in front of him now. Even worse, he doesn't recognize himself.

'Hope isn't a strategy,' says Rob, dispassionately. 'You've just watched me doing the sums.'

'I've picked up a couple of hours' work doing art-history evening courses for adults,' says Patrick, trying to sound calm. 'There's a huge appetite for culture in Cambridge.'

'You need to get another job that pays better.'

And then comes the twist. Rob offers to pay the money he owes the builder but he wants to transfer it to their joint account.

'You can't do that,' Patrick roars. 'Grace will find out.'

'She needs to know.' Rob's eyes narrow. 'You're going to have to sell the house. You can see that, can't you? You can't even scratch the surface of your regular payments with the salary you earn. Every month you'll be further in debt.'

Patrick hesitates. His sense of desperation momentarily eclipses his sense of shame. 'What about if you buy the house? As an investment? Maybe we could carry on living there but pay you rent.'

'Why would I want to own a damp house in the middle of the Fens?' He says it gently, more gently than Patrick deserves.

Patrick reaches out to him and touches his hand. It's a gesture that lasts no more than a few seconds. But it reveals that, despite the imbalance between them, there is still a gap in Rob's life between what he wanted and what he got. 'For Grace. You could do it for Grace.'

17

At the same time as Patrick is cutting his deal with Rob, Lilly heads out to catch the bus into the centre of Cambridge. Although the wind has dropped, the half-hearted drizzle has turned to rain. She realizes as soon as she reaches the bus stop that it was a mistake to leave without a coat but in the distance she sees the blurry outline of headlights approaching. If she goes back she'll have to wait another hour for the next one to arrive. It's an easy decision: she would rather get soaked and run the risk of hypothermia than go home and face Grace again.

Lilly understands that her illness has come as a shock to her mum. She just wishes she could tone down the anxious hyper-vigilance. Her every word, gesture and expression is forensically audited and Grace treats any trip she makes outside the house like a mission into enemy territory. She sees threats everywhere, which simultaneously makes Lilly more anxious about going out, but also more determined to follow through with her plans, which, to quote Ana, who had waded into the row, is 'doubly counterproductive'. *I really can't see that much danger in revising Shakespeare at a friend's house*, Ana had teased Grace. *Sounds like a pretty nineteenth-century dilemma to me.* When Lilly said goodbye, Grace still held her close as if she might never see her again.

Once she's on the bus Lilly checks her phone. There's

nothing, apart from a few likes for the pictures she took of the duststorm. So she turns on Snap Map and sees four smiling cartoon images of Hayley, Cormack, Freya and Jordy inside Hayley's house in De Freville Avenue. Lilly feels her courage leach away. She can't believe they're all getting ready for the party without her. Even worse, she can see that although Hayley was last on Snapchat an hour ago, she hasn't bothered to respond to any of her messages.

Lilly quickly makes sure she's on ghost mode so no one can see she's travelling on her own through the middle of nowhere to get to the party. She plays Jordy's Snapchat story, knowing it will kill her mood, then feels even more ridiculous when it does just that. Sure enough, there's a video of him smiling at the camera as he swigs from two bottles of Captain Morgan and then, with a flourish, simultaneously pours the contents into a big plastic bowl to make mojitos.

She knows he's making cocktails because, until their falling-out, Lilly and Hayley were meant to be sharing this party. They had spent hours after their summer exams planning a joint 1970s-themed eighteenth birthday where they would wear identical Abba outfits and serve rum cocktails. She hears Cormack's voice in the background and sees Freya and Hayley standing on chairs, draping fairy lights around the sitting room, dressed in identical Abba outfits. It's the first time ever she can remember going to a party without her and Hayley getting ready together. She wonders if they consciously decided not to invite her or if they had forgotten that she was ever part of their group in the first place. Either way, it hurts like hell.

She's tempted to go home. But her premature arrival would surely trigger as much anxiety as her early departure. Besides, she doesn't fancy spending an evening watching her dad and uncle fighting for dominance: it's an uneven contest that her dad is destined to lose. Neither does she want to overhear Ana confide in Grace that she cries every time she gets her period, because it makes Lilly think about the pregnancy test. Even if she couldn't admit it to Dr Santini, she knows the moment of discovery in the garage three months earlier triggered the first seizure that day.

The only good reason for going home is to say sorry to Mia. She feels guilty for upsetting her, especially when she's so sad about Tas. But Lilly can't cope with her little sister's dramas until she's sorted out her own. And Mia scares her because sometimes her witchy intuition and unhinged imaginings make her accidentally stumble upon essential truths. She remembers the photo of her head superimposed on the pregnant body of the Anglo-Saxon girl in the diary and shivers. Mia is obviously traumatized by what Lilly told her about the abortion, but while Lilly is determined to keep her feelings private, Mia wants to reinforce their closeness by discussing everything. She won't ever understand that Lilly is protecting her. The truth is that although Mia needs her, Lilly doesn't want to be needed.

When she was Mia's age, Lilly remembers, she naively assumed that everyone's need for each other was the same, like a balanced equation. Now she understands that most people live in a state of want for something or someone they can't have, and all life's drama is contained in that gap. When she's with Cormack, every atom in her body is drawn to him, yet he's indifferent. Then she considers her family: Patrick needs Grace more than Grace needs Patrick; Grace needs Lilly more than Lilly needs Grace; Ana wants Rob more than Rob wants Ana. She can tell that from the way he's so lukewarm about having a baby. *It's all so messed up.*

When she gets off at her stop beside Maid's Causeway, Lilly decides it's too early to go to Hayley's house. Instead she heads across Midsummer Common and strikes out on the path that leads to the Fort St George Bridge, relishing the freedom of being out alone at night in the city, even in the rain. When she sniffs the damp night air she feels euphoric. She starts listing everything she misses about Cambridge: 'The noise, the street lights, the road markings, the way there are always people around, the Red Poll bullocks on Midsummer Common, the trill of bicycle bells.' Articulating it all out loud somehow makes her feel better, as if she's still in a relationship with the city she loves. Then she does the same for Cormack: 'The smell of his hair, the chickenpox scar above his left buttock, the way he makes me feel anything is possible . . .' How his breath on her neck renders her inchoate. But when she stops all that's left is the painful ache of unfulfilled desire. She remembers the tenderness of their encounter in the library and it gives her hope that maybe their story hasn't ended and their distance is just an interlude.

On the other side of the bridge she decides spontaneously to deviate from her usual route to Hayley's house and visit her old home. She hasn't been back since they moved, not even in the summer when she came in every day to work at the punting company upriver. Turning into Pretoria Road feels like coming home in a way she knows Black Fen Close never will. She even remembers the position of uneven paving stones and the exact number of steps from the turning to the front gate. When she reaches the house she stares up at the window of her old bedroom and sees the light is on. She wishes she could go up there, fall asleep and wake once Cormack has decided their interlude is over.

The front of the house has changed. It looks smarter. The turquoise front door has been painted black and the scruffy hedge has been replaced with a couple of small, elegant miniature trees. Lilly tentatively goes through the gate, up the path and bears right towards the sitting-room window. The curtains are half open. She peers in through the gap and sees a couple sitting on a sofa watching *My Little Pony* with two small children. One child sits, eyes closed, on his dad's knee chugging down a bottle of milk while an older boy zooms around the room in a red and yellow plastic car just like the one Mia used to have. *When did everything go so wrong for us?* Lilly wonders, as she observes the scene of domestic harmony inside her old house. She thinks about the pregnancy test, Mia's crazy flights of fantasy and her own seizures. Then she goes back further in time and considers how Grace's controlling behaviour and Patrick's financial recklessness started years ago. Then she realizes everything didn't go wrong because it was never really right in the first place. She hears thunder rumbling in the distance and decides it's her cue to head to the party.

Hayley's parents own a big Edwardian villa a couple of blocks away in one of the most expensive streets in the city. Everyone agrees it is the perfect party venue because there's enough room for a hundred people to dance in the enormous ground-floor sitting room, and a garden terrace with tables, chairs and sunloungers that stretches the entire width of the house. Lilly hears the party before she sees it. By the time she reaches the front door, the music is so loud that it feels as if the ground is throbbing beneath her feet. She's surprised that Hayley's dad hasn't had a meltdown.

Turning up on her own without any alcohol makes her feel like a loser twice over. Fortunately the door is ajar so Lilly slinks in without anyone noticing and goes straight to the toilet just off the hallway to put on her costume. She locks the door behind her. The toilet is already a mess. The basin is smeared with black eyeliner, and damp tissue clogs the plughole. She puts on a pair of psychedelic flared trousers and the suede waistcoat with tassels that she found in one of the boxes in the garage and manages to create a pretty cool 1970s eye-make-up look with kohl and blue sparkly eyeshadow. Finally she ties a scarf around her head and drapes the tail down her right shoulder. She looks in the mirror and doesn't really recognize herself. *I'm happy not to be you for a while*, she decides, blowing a bitter kiss at her reflection. Then she texts Grace to tell her she has arrived at Jordy's and to warn she might be back a little later than anticipated because Mr Galveston has set an extra essay that she didn't know about. *Might have to stay over*, she warns. Then she switches off her phone. She knows exactly how to throw Grace off the scent.

As she comes out of the toilet Emma Vickers arrives and Lilly ends up walking into the party with the least cool girl in the year. At least it beats going in completely alone. She scans the room for her friends but can't find them. There are disco balls hanging from the ceiling and flashing lights that make it feel like everything is happening in fast forward. Emma pours her a mojito from a jug and they sit down on one of the enormous white sofas. Lilly winces as she sees that there are already stains on the arm.

'Aren't the flashing lights bad for you?' Emma asks.

'What do you mean?'

'Don't they cause epilepsy?'

'I haven't got epilepsy,' says Lilly, trying not to sound impatient with Emma, who has the unfortunate air of someone who lives in a constant state of fear about saying the wrong thing.

'How are you feeling?' Emma asks.

'Good,' Lilly says, sipping the cocktail. It's the first time she has drunk alcohol for weeks and it tastes delicious.

'Very good, actually.' Dr Santini had warned her off alcohol for the next three months but she needs something to blunt her mood, which swings wildly from feeling too much to feeling nothing at all. She keeps half an eye on the dance floor, hoping Cormack will emerge from the crowd.

'What is it that's actually wrong with you?'

Lilly had placed a bet with herself over how long it would take for someone to ask this question (twenty minutes). Emma, however, has managed to exceed even her most pessimistic expectations.

'I have stress-related seizures,' says Lilly, vaguely. 'I'm working with a psychologist to try and get to the bottom of them. They're kind of mysterious.'

'What have you got to be so stressed about, Lilly Vermuyden?' Emma asks, fiddling with the zip of her pale pink jumpsuit. 'You're the golden girl. Top in the class. Heading for Cambridge. Got with the best-looking boy in the school.'

Lilly searches for traces of bitterness in her tone but Emma just sounds sad. 'That's only how it looks from the outside,' says Lilly, surprised by how Emma perceives her situation. 'Nothing is that easy.'

'If it's not easy for you, can you imagine how difficult it is for me?'

Lilly isn't sure how to respond. She barely notices Emma when she's in school. She tries to name her friends or who she sits with at lunch and draws a blank. Emma operates on the edge of everything. Lilly suddenly feels guilty for ignoring her all these years. 'Well, it's not like that any more,' says Lilly, putting her hand on Emma's. 'I was top of the class. But I'm not any longer. I can't work because my head feels so fuzzy, and in getting with the boy I ended up losing my best friend.'

'That's very honest of you,' says Emma.

'And that's not all,' says Lilly. 'There's problems in my family. Big problems.'

'To do with Mia, you mean?' Emma asks. 'My little sister told me she did the craziest Show and Tell last week. My mum emailed to complain that it was inappropriate. Everything my mum does is so embarrassing.'

'I didn't hear about that one,' says Lilly, taking another swig of her drink. 'Mia does a lot of crazy things and I was still in hospital.' She's getting bored hearing about Mia running at windmills all the time.

Apparently sensing she's losing Lilly's interest, Emma swiftly continues. 'Get this. Your sister brought a used positive pregnancy test into class and spoke without stopping for twenty minutes about contraceptives and abortion from the ancient Egyptians to modern times. Then when the teacher cut it short she physically attacked my sister for speaking for too long.' She pauses. 'I don't mind. My little sister probably had it coming. She's a total pain.'

'Shit,' says Lilly, floored by this revelation. 'That *is* crazy.' She anxiously casts her mind back to that hot afternoon in the garage when Mia found the pregnancy test in the tin box in the garage. She distinctly remembers hiding it in a plastic bag. Then Lilly recalls how she had been distracted by another discovery in the same tin: the torn-up remnants of the old postcard and the notebook. Mia must have taken the pregnancy test while she was trying to piece the postcard back together without her noticing. *Lest you forget*, it read. There were two crucial bits missing: the top left corner that said who it was written to and the bottom right corner that said who it was from.

She drums on the arm of the sofa with her fingers. She should have known that Mia would keep the pregnancy test. She thinks of all the eccentric collections hidden in her sister's bedroom: pencil shavings from her favourite crayons; her baby teeth; the tissue from her first nosebleed; the skin that Elvis has shed. Why wouldn't she keep the dipstick with the blue line in the little window? The first thing she will do when she gets home is force Mia to hand it over and make sure she hasn't told anyone who it belongs to.

'Are you okay, Lilly?' Emma asks. 'Did I say the wrong thing?'

'I'm fine,' says Lilly, with a quick smile, finishing off her drink. 'It's a good story.'

Fortunately, at that moment, a compilation of the best moments from 1970s children's programmes starts playing on a screen erected by the doors leading into the garden. Lilly gets up to move closer and is transfixed by the sight of a dog with a long, shaggy coat and hippie fringe bustling around, and a hyperactive yellow and red snail in hot pursuit of a pink cow chewing flowers.

'Lil, you came,' yelps Jordy, excitedly. He waves at her and dances over, all cocky swagger. He's wearing an open-necked Ziggy Stardust costume in lurid stripes that clash with his hair, red platform boots and lightning-bolt make-up across his face. 'I'm so pleased you're here.' He hugs her for a beat too long. The weed and alcohol have softened his edges. He points at the screen, 'Trippy, huh?'

'What is it?'

'It's a really cool programme called *The Magic Roundabout*. Wait till you get to *The Clangers*, though. I put it all together as a present for Hayley.' He takes a deep drag of a joint and Lilly watches the hot red ash fall on to the wooden floor.

'Have Nuala and George gone out?' Lilly asks, rubbing the floor with the toe of her trainer so the ash doesn't burn the oak.

'They're away,' says Jordy.

'Do they have any idea Hayley's having a party?'

'Nope,' he says, with a wide smile, not mentioning that Lilly was meant to be sharing the party. 'They think she's staying at mine.'

'So do my parents,' says Lilly. She doesn't have to pretend with Jordy. He knows what Grace is like.

'All roads lead to me,' he booms, throwing his arms wide open, so his shoulder pads wilt. 'Although we'll all end up staying here, of course. The night is long.'

'Of course,' Lilly agrees, although she hasn't really given much thought to where she will spend the night, other than that she's not going home and is hoping she might end up sharing a bed with Cormack. Jordy steers her towards the music with his hand in the small of her back and they start dancing to 'Creature Comforts', his all-time favourite Arcade Fire track.

'That's not very 1970s,' she shouts.

'The music was shite.'

She calculates that she has been dancing with Jordy at parties for close to fifteen years and that his technique hasn't really evolved since he was three. 'You're good at dancing in heels,' she says. He spins round in response with his hands in the air and for the first time in ages Lilly really lets go.

More guests pour into the room until it is so heavy with sweat that even the walls seem to shine. She glances over and sees Emma sitting by herself on the sofa, like she's the loneliest person in the world. Lilly looks away. Jordy plays air guitar and pretends that his fist is a microphone. He offers her his joint. 'I think I actually prefer the smell of skunks to skunk,' says Lilly, pulling a face. He throws back his head and laughs longer than the joke deserves.

Someone turns up the volume on the speakers and opens the doors into the garden to let in some air. The wind has picked up again and is now so strong that they repeatedly bang against the wall. Lilly isn't sure how long they dance but when she looks back at the sofa Emma has disappeared.

After a few more tracks, Lilly tells Jordy she's going to get a drink. She wants to find Emma and tell her there are few things in life that dancing doesn't make better and since Jordy is currently doing the robot she doesn't need to worry about making any dud moves. She heads towards the kitchen past the doors into the garden and sees the trees throwing wild shapes of their own in the wind. There's a low howl that can be heard even over the music. In the kitchen she finds Hayley crouched beside the door of the fridge, catching ice cubes from the dispenser in one of Nuala's expensive copper saucepans. Except the fridge isn't co-operating and coughs out the ice in fits and starts so that every few seconds Hayley resorts to rhythmically thumping the stainless-steel door. Even in the mellow dimmed light, Lilly can see shadowy dents around the ice-dispenser. *Oops,* she thinks. *Nuala won't like that.*

'Hey.' Lilly waves nervously at Hayley.

'Hey,' yells Hayley over the noise, glancing briefly at Lilly before returning to the temperamental ice-dispenser.

Does she look away because she's trying to focus on creating ice? Or is it that she's still punishing Lilly for what happened with Cormack?

She feels a gnawing in the centre of her stomach that she puts down to a mixture of nerves and hunger. She needs re-assurance that Hayley, her best friend since year seven, really wants her to be at her eighteenth birthday party. Even four months ago such a scenario would have been inconceiv-able. Lilly weighs this up as tiny chunks of crushed ice start cascading from the fridge.

'It's a cool party,' says Lilly.

'Yeah, thanks.' Hayley turns to the fridge and thumps it again. 'Fucking thing.'

Maybe they didn't put her on the original list because she realized Lilly was in hospital and didn't want her to get FOMO. She knows in her heart that Hayley couldn't simply have forgotten her. Almost everyone from their year is here, even Emma, who Hayley generally can't stand.

Hayley shrieks as proper full-size ice cubes start to pour uncontrollably out of the ice-dispenser, filling the saucepan. 'Quick, Lil! Get me a bowl!' Lilly knows her way round this kitchen. She grabs a couple of Tupperware containers from the cupboard beside the sink and rushes back to help Hayley. Ice has already spewed over the edges of the saucepan and the floor is now slippery with ice cubes.

'Oh, my God, how am I going to make it stop?' Hayley squeals, as she slips and slides around.

Lilly kneels beside her and attempts to catch ice in her empty container but she's now laughing so much that it compromises her accuracy. Jordy comes into the kitchen and stands by the door, chuckling at the hopelessness of the situation. Then he runs and drops on to his knees to slide over towards them, bumping into Hayley, which makes her drop the saucepan so that more ice tips on to the floor.

'Please make it stop! Please make it stop!' screams Hayley, breathless with laughter as Jordy rolls in the ice.

He thrashes around on the floor singing 'Ashes To Ashes' from beginning to end and giggling wildly when it comes to the line about wanting an axe to break the ice.

'I always done good things, I always done bad things,' he yells, mashing up the lyrics. Lilly laughs so hard that her eyes water.

Then, suddenly, Cormack is there, dressed in a moth-eaten

Afghan coat, a low-cut cheesecloth shirt that Lilly could swear she has seen his mother wear, and a pair of cowboy boots. He smells as if he's been marinated in patchouli oil. He gives her a hug but it's of the 'I love you as a friend' kind, where there's more hyperbolic backslapping than genuine connection. For an exquisite moment her cheek presses against the bare skin of his chest. She thinks of the Louise Bourgeois poster that hangs in her parents' bedroom of the couple stitched together and wishes she could be surgically attached to him in the same way.

'I'm so happy you're here, Lil,' he says, pulling away even before he's finished speaking. The intimacy of their moment in the library has vanished.

'Me too,' says Lilly. They stand awkwardly in front of each other. Then they both speak at exactly the same time. She feels Hayley observing them. Lilly knows she's living on borrowed time. There's a countdown taking place. Like when they waited in the summer for the winner of *Love Island* to be announced or watched the space shuttle take off from NASA in a biology class. *T minus seventeen seconds and counting.* Of course she'd theorized but she had chosen not to admit it to herself because, as long as there was no certainty, she could live in the hope that he would still change his mind. Hayley leans into Cormack. She's a little taller than Lilly and her head doesn't fit quite so neatly into his shoulder. *So this is it*, thinks Lilly, scrutinizing his response as if she's going to write it up in a lab report.

Cormack puts his arm around Hayley in the same easy way he used to drape it around her and pulls her in front of him, like a human shield, carefully avoiding Lilly's gaze. Hayley smiles as the fur on the Afghan coat tickles her nose. Then she pivots towards him and presses her lips to his mouth. For a split second Lilly sees Cormack glance at her. All the complexity of human emotion is contained in that look: regret, lust, anger, joy, fear. Then he closes his eyes and kisses Hayley back, pulling her in a kind of slow dance towards the garden door.

Lilly feels a physical pain in her chest. Her heart starts to race and she wonders if she's about to have another seizure. *For a sensitive person, a series of short, sharp shocks can be all it takes,* Dr Santini had told her. As Hayley waltzes backwards towards the door, she lifts her hand and gives her the finger. Lilly reels. She understands that Hayley has been planning this moment, or at least a version of it, since she barged into the tent and caught her with Cormack on the last night of the festival. To avoid making a fool of herself by crying, she forces herself to think of all the English essays she has ever written on revenge. Shylock avenging Antonio. Beowulf's revenge against Grendel. *It's practically the oldest theme in the world.*

'Let's go dance again, Lil,' says Jordy, quickly, holding out his arm so Lilly can pull him up from the floor. As they go back into the sitting room, her hand starts to feel numb and her fingers tingle. She realizes with relief that it's because Jordy is holding on to her so tightly. He turns the music up as loud as the amp can tolerate until it's impossible to talk or even think and hands her a bottle of Prosecco that he has liberated from Nuala's larder. She closes her eyes and gulps it down, eyes shut, like the baby drinking the milk in her old house. Freya comes over to join them and gives Lilly a sympathetic hug. Everyone knows.

Feeling drunk, but the kind of drunk where she's filled with restless energy, Lilly looks at her phone and sees it's almost eleven. She needs to find somewhere quiet to check in with her parents. Downstairs is a mess so she heads to the first floor, eyeing the muddy footprints on the cream stair carpet as she goes up. She finds Emma asleep on a sofa on the landing outside the closed door of Hayley's bedroom, a tiny slug of drool dripping from her mouth. She assesses her breathing, rolls her on to her side and heads up another flight of stairs to Nuala and George's bedroom at the top of the house. She locks herself into their en suite bathroom and rests her cheek on the cool marble sink unit. She can't imagine ever feeling how she does about Cormack with anyone else. Even as she has this thought, she pokes fun at herself for committing what Mr Galveston would call the Cardinal Sin of Cliché. She imagines spending the rest of her life without anyone touching her like Cormack did and feels terrified that the best isn't to come because it's already happened. Then she turns to the toilet, leans over and vomits with commendable elegance for a couple of minutes.

Feeling marginally renewed, Lilly looks at herself in the mirror and squeezes toothpaste on her finger to get rid of the acidy bile on her teeth and gums. Then she washes the make-up off her face. It's blissfully quiet. She sits on the toilet seat and calls Patrick because he won't pose any awkward questions. When he doesn't pick up she reluctantly calls Grace. Lilly has done the maths: if Grace insists she wants to pick her up she could be at Jordy's house within twelve minutes. Neither of them answers. So she sends a text explaining that their essay plan on revenge is going so well that Jordy's parents have suggested she should stay the night. Then she turns off her phone.

Ironically, there's a big part of her that now wishes she could escape home. Jordy isn't close to peaking and she can't imagine he'll want to leave before daybreak. Worst of all, she'll have to endure sleeping under the same roof as Cormack and Hayley. Earlier today she had loudly complained about having to move into Mia's room for the night to make way for Rob and Ana. Now she can't think of anything better than being curled up in bed beside her little sister. She might even tell Mia about Hayley's treachery. It would make Mia so happy to think that Lilly was confiding in her. It could be the trade-off for handing over the pregnancy test.

She wanders back down to the kitchen to look for Jordy. The party has entered a new phase. The MDMA crew are loved up, thirsty and trying to fill their bottles with water from the tap at the double sink, which seems to be permanently turned on so the water slops over the edge and on to the floor. In an attempt to clear surfaces, someone enterprising has even filled the dishwasher with cans and bottles. The stoners have got the munchies and a saucepan with spaghetti in it has boiled dry on the cooker. Lilly turns off the flame. No one seems aware that the smoke alarm is ringing. Everyone is loaded. At least no one notices what anyone else is doing any more. So she sits down at the kitchen island because it's the best vantage point to observe the scene.

Freya comes over and sits beside her. The zip of her Abba suit has broken so she's tied the arms round her waist and has put on a shirt that possibly belongs to Hayley's dad.

'Feels like we're in a saloon bar,' says Lilly, drinking a large glass of water. Freya drunkenly explains that she wanted to warn her about Cormack and Hayley. Apparently he had insisted he had told her the first day she came back to school.

'Well, he didn't,' says Lilly, without mentioning their encounter in the library. She knows there's some significance to his duplicity and decides to explore the issue when she's feeling more sober.

'It's not right, Lil,' Freya says. 'It's just not right.' Lilly appreciates her sympathy although it too closely resembles pity to make her feel any better. Freya focuses on trying to soak up red wine stains on the marble surface with the edge of George's shirt but they won't shift. 'I've applied for Oxford,' she says apologetically, rubbing the kitchen island with renewed vigour.

'Marble is a porous rock,' Lilly responds, tapping the kitchen worktop. 'It's made of calcium carbonate so it reacts with acids. So you won't get that stain out.' Her non-sequitur makes both of them laugh.

'This isn't a kitchen island, anyway. It's a runway,' Freya observes, which sets them off again.

'Looks like there's a plane coming in to land,' Lilly warns as Jordy stands at the opposite end of the island and throws himself on his stomach to slide towards them at full pelt, sending bottles, plastic glasses, fruit and crisps flying to the floor.

'"I have a tender spot in my heart for cripples, bastards and broken things,"' he says, quoting from *Game of Thrones*, as he lands beside them, which makes them start laughing all over again. *This could be worse. This could be worse,* Lilly thinks.

Jordy slips on to the stool the other side of her. 'You deserve so much better, Lil,' he says.

'He's right,' says Freya.

'I can't get him out of my head.' Lilly sighs.

'Couldn't you pretend I'm him and kiss me and see what happens?' Jordy suggests.

'We tried that before, Jords. There was no chemistry,' says Lilly, laughing. 'But thanks for offering to sacrifice yourself.'

'It would have been my very great pleasure,' says Jordy, giving a little bow. 'Truly.'

'You need a plan of distraction,' says Freya. 'Why don't we hang out, just the three of us, next weekend? To celebrate your birthday. We can go clubbing.'

'Let's go to Fez,' says Jordy. 'You won't need a fake ID any more.'

'That would be great,' says Lilly. For the first time in ages she feels a sense of possibility.

The kitchen and the garden outside are momentarily illuminated as lightning forks across the sky. For a moment everyone is frozen in time. Lilly thinks she catches sight of Cormack standing by the door of the sitting room. The lights in the kitchen flicker and a collective cheer breaks out that is almost instantly drowned by a clap of thunder so loud the earth vibrates beneath them. She searches the room for Cormack but he's disappeared, if he was even there in the first place.

Lilly uses her dad's fail-safe method for working out if a storm is overhead by counting to seven. Just as she reaches seven there is another clap of thunder that is so loud it sounds like a bomb exploding. There are yells and screams. She drifts towards the kitchen window to watch the electrical storm. The boom of thunder is still echoing when another flash of lightning claws the sky. At least Hayley's neighbours can't complain about the noise any more.

Jordy has put on 'Blinded By Your Grace', which everyone agrees perfectly matches the epic nature of the weather event outside. Lilly stares out of the window with Freya by her side. She's grateful for the way Mother Nature has stolen the limelight.

'Beats fireworks,' says Freya.

'Beats everything,' says Lilly.

After the next bolt of lightning the electricity surges

and flickers again, then dies along with Stormzy. There are shouts and screams of exhilaration and then an uncanny silence that is filled by a new barrage of thunder. Like dominoes falling, the lights go out in every house in the street until the city is as dark as any field in the middle of the Fens. The sober few scramble to find their phones and some manage to turn on the torch. Most are too wasted to do anything except sit down and wait for it all to pass.

The wind buffets the house, emitting a low howl, but it can't muster the same strength as it does back home, where the landscape is empty apart from the new housing estate. The rain is a different story. It's more like a tropical downpour. A few thrill-seekers go out on to the terrace. Whenever the lightning flashes Lilly catches sight of them throwing wild dance moves or opening their mouths to drink the rain. They are soaked but no one cares. She spots Jordy in the middle of them. His Ziggy Stardust make-up has washed down the side of his face. A few of the boys and girls take off their T-shirts and wave them in the air. Jordy removes his entire costume apart from the red boots and runs naked around the garden, shaking his fist and yelling at the sky.

Lilly turns on her phone so that she can film him. It starts vibrating with messages. Predictably enough, there's a text from her dad saying that, after several hours of risk assessment, her mum has decided that it is safer for Lilly to stay with Jordy than to venture home. She smiles. Then she notices a Snapchat notification had popped up ten minutes ago. When she opens it, there's a message from Cormack. *Where r u?* During the next flash of lightning she looks around to see if she can spot him but neither he nor Hayley seems to be in the room. She messages him back *where r u?* He messages back: *Look outside.* She presses her nose to the window and sees a light blinking. He's in the cabin at the end of the garden.

She waits for the next battery of lightning to burn itself out and slips on to the terrace, past Jordy and his friends, and on to the lawn. The grass is parched from months of drought and the bald patches have turned into pools of mud. Her trainers are instantly waterlogged. In between the lightning strikes, it's so dark that she has to use her hands to feel her way past the rose beds, so by the time she gets to the end of the garden not only is she soaked and muddy but her arms and hands are scratched and bleeding.

Using her phone as a torch Lilly tentatively pushes open the cabin door and shines the light around the room, taking in the kitchenette on the left, the sheepskin rugs on the floor and the shelves of yoga mats. Nuala and George never do anything by halves. She finds Cormack sitting on the sofa and walks towards him, shining the torch in his face, noticing how pale his skin is and the dark rings around his eyes. 'You look like a raccoon,' she says.

'Is it a good look?' he asks, raising an eyebrow.

It dawns on her that he flirts with her only when they're alone. He never does it in front of other people. She can't believe it's taken her so long to notice this. 'How did you get in?' she asks.

'The window,' he says, pointing to a broken latch.

He begins a complicated explanation of how he used his penknife to jimmy the lock but Lilly isn't listening. Instead she's thinking of all the things they have never done to-gether: they never spent a whole night watching a Netflix series and waking up in the same bed in the morning; they never shared a meal in Wagamama's; they never double-dated with friends. When she thinks about it, she realizes that most of their communication is via private message. He never once publicly acknowledged their relationship. It existed in the shadows. Mostly in the musty darkness of the back of his truck.

She sits down beside him on the sofa. The rain has glued her hair to her scalp. He leans over and lifts a wet strand that has stuck to her cheek. She feels short of breath but it's different from how he usually makes her feel. It's the prelude to more caution rather than less. He doesn't appear to notice.

'I've been thinking a lot about what we did at the festival,' she says suddenly. She wasn't planning to say this but she doesn't want to talk about him and Hayley yet, and she's fed up with the way he closes down discussion on what happened while expecting her never to reveal the truth to anyone else.

'Come on, Lil, don't be a Debbie Downer,' he cajoles her. 'That's ancient history. There's nothing to be gained from revisiting it now. Let's just enjoy the moment.' He puts out his hand to fiddle with the tassels of her leather waistcoat and slides his finger on to the bare flesh of her back.

'I want you to know how I see it, and I want to know if this is how you see it too,' says Lilly, moving away from him.

'Okay,' he says, but it's the sort of okay that comes with strings attached.

Lilly still wakes up in the night thinking about what happened on their second day at the festival. It was meant to be the climax of the summer holidays, and in a sense it was, just not in the way it was meant to be. The four of them had planned every aspect of the trip together. They had secured fake IDs, decanted vodka into plastic bottles, borrowed sleeping bags and bought enough biscuits and bread rolls to keep them going for three days. Unbelievably, Jordy and Hayley had no idea anything was happening between Cormack and Lilly, still less that it had started before the beginning of the summer holidays. Jordy's blindness wasn't surprising: he never focuses on anything long enough to notice what's going on beneath his nose. But Hayley's historical sense of superiority meant it didn't occur to her that Cormack might have chosen Lilly over her.

When eagle-eyed Hayley had noticed an unused packet of condoms in Lilly's washbag, she had joked that she was hoping to get lucky. Hayley had said that, judging from the vibe emanating from Cormack, something was almost certainly going to happen between them and that she might end up raiding Lilly's supply. Lilly now wonders if Cormack was playing them off against each other right from the start.

By the end of the second day, Lilly and Cormack were getting frustrated that they couldn't carve out any time alone together. At night they all shared a tent, and during the day Hayley kept trying to find excuses to be alone with Cormack, sending Lilly and Jordy on futile errands to fetch water or charge mobile phones. Whatever they did, Hayley or Jordy stuck with them. So Cormack decided it would be 'jokes' to slip a double dose of the Xanax he had scored at the Edith Tavern into Hayley's water bottle, and sent her with Jordy to the stage in the woods with the promise that he and Lilly would catch up. At the time it had seemed an inspired solution to get them out of the way. Lilly didn't encourage Cormack but neither did she try to talk him out of the plan. Sitting on the fence has always been her biggest flaw.

Cormack and Lilly then had the kind of sex that made her realize why people can go mad when they fall in love. It felt as if they had made some unique discovery about the point of existence that transcended ordinary life. A couple of hours later she turned on her phone to check if it was time to go back to the floating stage for Waze and Odyssey and saw six missed calls from Jordy. When he picked up on the first ring, Lilly knew something was wrong. She couldn't remember him ever answering his phone before.

Jordy was hysterical. They were somewhere in the woods and Hayley was out of it. 'I don't understand what's happened,' he kept saying. Cormack was indifferent. He seized Lilly's phone. 'Don't worry, mate. Hayley's always out of it,' he told Jordy dismissively, instructing him to put her in the recovery position. 'We'll catch you later.'

Jordy called again and Lilly could hear the fear in his voice. 'She's talking shit and when she's not talking shit she's lying on the ground twitching.'

Lilly tried to persuade Cormack they should go and look for them but he kept patting the tempting space beside him on top of the sleeping bag. 'She's always been a drama queen,' he whispered.

'I think I'm losing her, Lil,' Jordy sobbed down the phone. 'Help me. She's not breathing right. I need you.' Lilly frantically pulled on her floaty yellow dress, crawled out of the tent and started running barefoot towards the woods.

By the time she arrived Hayley had come round and was vomiting into a bush.

Cormack treated the whole incident as a joke, filming everything on his phone, until the medics in the first-aid tent started asking what pills Hayley had taken and who had given them to her. A rogue batch of Xanax was doing the rounds. No one had said anything. They gave the first-aid team Lilly's name to throw them off the scent in case the police followed up. No one would ever believe that Lilly would be involved in anything to do with drugs.

*

'It was a bad decision. She could have died.' Lilly is almost crying.

'Yeah, but she didn't,' says Cormack. 'You're just feeling bummed out because of what you found out tonight about Hayley and me. I'm sorry you had to discover it like that. I kept wanting to tell you. Then whenever I'm with you, I start to doubt if I've made the right decision.'

He puts his hand around her waist and inside her tasselled suede waistcoat to touch the dimple above her right buttock. 'God, I love that dimple,' he says. She moves his hand away. He leans in to kiss her neck and she looks away.

'What's wrong, Lilly?'

'I don't want to do this any more.' Lilly gets up and leaves. You can't be afraid of losing something that you never had. He never loved her like she loved him.

'If you're not interested, then why did you send me all those messages when you were in hospital?' he asks.

'I didn't send you any. I didn't have my phone with me.'

'Come on, Lil,' he chides her. 'I know you're annoyed with me but you have to see it from my point of view. I thought I had a chance with you again. You got pretty flirty.'

'Maybe it was one of your other girlfriends,' says Lilly, trying to sound sassy rather than bitter.

He gets out his phone.

'I kept them,' he says. It takes a while to read their conversation because there are so many messages. She can see right away that they were sent from her Snapchat and that they cover the period she was in hospital. For a split second, she wonders if it has been hacked. But the content reveals that whoever was impersonating her knew intimate and even confidential details of her life, including the results of hospital tests and that something had gone wrong at the festival in the summer. It sounds eerily like her until

340

the tone gets flirty. There's a phrase she's seen before. *Lest we forget*, it says. She frowns. It's the same phrase that was on the back of the postcard she found in the garage.

'That isn't me,' she says. 'It's my mum. She must have taken my phone. She's been pretending to be me.'

'That's fucked,' he says.

Lilly leaves the cabin. She walks through the garden and out of the gate on to the street. She feels the familiar tingling start in the tips of her fingers and creep up her arms. She practises the breathing exercises and manages at least to contain the sensation just below her elbow. She can't get the bus home because it's too late, and she can't call a cab because her purse is in the bag she has left at Hayley's house and she doesn't want to go back to the party. It has stopped raining and the urge to keep moving is overwhelming.

So she carries on walking through the familiar streets where she used to live, past the roundabout, heading north until the houses thin out and finally she is in open country-side. She wants to plunge into the river at Earith and hold her breath until her lungs burst. She's caught on that dangerous edge where rage and sadness converge. Her phone is in her hand. She doesn't want to message Grace. On some level, in spite of everything, she feels sorry for her mum because she is a damaged person and her behaviour is unhinged. But her anger far outweighs her pity. And there is a stronger feeling: a need for self-preservation. She's spent months being the keeper of the worst kind of secret. For both their sakes, she needs to leave home and create a life separate from Grace. Sometimes being loved too much is too close to suffocation.

18

It's ten o'clock on Sunday morning and still no word from Lilly. Mia doesn't need to go downstairs to appreciate there's trouble brewing because she can hear it all from her bedroom. There has been a flurry of phone calls. So far Jordy's parents have confirmed they are 'utterly certain' that no *Merchant of Venice* revision took place at their house on Saturday because Jordy had spent the entire day with Cormack and Freya at Hayley's house getting ready for the party they were all sharing. Not only are they 'totally unaware' that Lilly was meant to be staying the night at their house, they have 'absolutely no idea' whether Jordy spent the evening with Lilly at all because he 'most definitely' isn't home either. *Miss Swain would tell them they are relying too much on emphatic adverbs.*

They offer to get in touch with Jordy while Grace and Patrick wait on the line but predictably enough he doesn't pick up his phone. 'He's a very sensible lad, so I'm sure he'll call back,' says Jordy's dad, reassuringly. He asks awkwardly after Lilly's health and says how pleased they are that she is back at school because Jordy had gone into a decline without her. 'He was missing her so much that he dropped two grades in English,' his mum chips in.

How can parents have so little idea what their children are really like when they share the same genes and have lived with them for

343

so many years? Mia wonders, in amazement. Off the top of her head, she recalls three totally, utterly, compellingly unsensible things Jordy did when he was at their house in the summer: (a) he broke the kettle by poaching an egg in it; (b) he burnt his groin trying to bleach his pubic hair blond; and (c) he drove Cormack's truck into the gate. But then she reverses this logic. *Do children ever really know their parents?*

The notion makes her uneasy. She would like to discuss it with Grace who has just raced upstairs, two steps at a time, and darted into Lilly's bedroom. 'Mum, can I try and guess what you would put in your burial pot if you were to die?' Mia asks, as she sidles into Lilly's room. She's guessing nail clippers, black mascara, orange squash, Lilly's GCSE certificates. If she gets half right, at least it will prove that she half knows her mum.

'Not now, Mia,' says Grace, frantically. She's going through the files and books on Lilly's desk. 'Can't you see I'm busy?' She flings a copy of *The Merchant of Venice* on top of a couple of files and rushes back downstairs. There's a thump as she throws them down on a hard surface. *How can she be back in the kitchen so quickly? Maybe she's a shape-shifter.*

'See? She never even intended to go to Jordy's,' Mia hears Grace shout. 'Otherwise she would have taken these.'

'Perhaps she forgot them,' Ana suggests.

'Lilly never forgets anything when it comes to her school work. She's always organized,' says Grace, fiercely. 'I know my daughter.'

Except you don't.

'Her bag looked pretty full to me,' says Rob.

'Well, it wasn't full of school work.' Grace's voice is as tight and as quivery as a stretched elastic band.

'Don't worry. I'm sure there'll be some logical explanation,' says Rob.

344

'Something bad has happened.' Grace starts to panic. 'I can feel it in my bones. What if she went to meet that boy? What if he's done something to her again?'

'What boy?' asks Ana, who can generally be relied upon to ask the wrong question at the wrong moment, particularly when the conversation isn't focused on her.

'Look, it's obvious she went to this party,' says Patrick. 'And it's obvious that Cormack was at the party because he was hosting it with Hayley.'

Well said, Dad.

'We can't be sure.'

'Let's give Nuala a call,' Patrick suggests. 'Go straight to the horse's mouth.'

'She never knows what's going on,' says Grace, with a contemptuous snort. 'She's completely irresponsible. She lets Hayley do whatever she likes.'

Mia hears the dial tone as they attempt to contact Nuala. When she doesn't answer they call George, who picks up straight away and proudly confirms they are in Italy for a 'dirty weekend' to celebrate their twentieth wedding anniversary. He's on speakerphone so everyone can hear. Mia is unsure what a dirty weekend is but the way George says it makes her think it's related to something Elvis might do when he reaches the Sargasso Sea.

'Well, congratulations on reaching the big two-oh,' says Patrick, flatly. 'Where are you staying?'

Mia knows her dad's casual approach will wind up her mum who is completely wired. She counts to seven. Just as she reaches six, sure enough Grace interrupts, which means a storm is directly overhead.

'George,' says Grace, abruptly.

'Hello, gorgeous!' says George.

Mia puts two fingers into her mouth and pretends to

vomit. She can't stand the way he always slithers around her mum.

'We were wondering if you know if Lilly went to Hayley's party last night?'

There's a long pause.

'What party?' asks George. 'Hayley's not even at home. She's staying at Jordy's for the weekend.'

'That's not what Jordy's parents are saying,' says Grace. 'They told us that Hayley invited the entire school year to a party at your house last night. Jordy even sent them a picture of himself dressed up as Ziggy Stardust standing on your kitchen island.'

'I do not like the sound of this,' says George, several times, as he chews over this information. Mia hears him waking up Nuala and apprising her of the situation. Nuala evidently doesn't realize she is on speakerphone because she sleepily warns her husband that Grace overreacts about everything. 'She's completely uptight. Practically Amish. She'd have Lilly wearing a long dress and bonnet if she could.'

'And I do not like the sound of that,' Mia sings to Elvis. She puts the wire grille back on top of Elvis's bucket and half wonders if she went downstairs whether Ana might agree to help her finish the Lego Elves treehouse.

'Let me call Hayley and we'll get back to you as soon as we hear anything,' says George.

The phone call is abruptly cut off.

'Join the Amish, huh?' says Rob. 'I can see you in one of those bonnets, Grace.'

Mia feels a surge of affection for her uncle for always trying to make things better for her mum. She hears Grace try to call Lilly again. Her dad makes a weak joke to Rob and Ana about teenagers never answering their phones

346

when you need them to. They try to muster a laugh but it's all a bit half-hearted. She bets they wish they had never come for the weekend. Then the phone rings again.

'Whatever next?' She addresses Elvis with a world-weary sigh.

Nuala's panicked voice cuts through her thoughts. 'You're right about the party – the neighbours called dozens of times. The house is a total mess – ruined carpets, stained sofas . . . There were lots of tears from Hayley –'

'Any news on Lilly?' Grace interrupts.

'Lilly was there the whole night,' Nuala confirms. 'Hayley said she left in the early hours after a big row with Cormack. We're catching the next flight home. I'll keep you posted if I hear any more. Don't worry about Lil. She's a sensible girl.'

The phone call ends. Mia assumes that at least Grace will now stop worrying because she's had confirmation that Lilly was at the party. She waits expectantly on the edge of her bed for Grace and Patrick to call her downstairs to ask her for advice as the only other member of the family who actually knows Cormack. Instead her mum starts going on and on about how he caused Lilly's seizures, which he did, just not in the way her mum thinks.

'We should call the police and tell them she's ill and has gone missing,' sobs Grace.

Mia sighs. She longs to be taken seriously by someone apart from Tas. But they seem to have forgotten her very existence. Even Ana and Rob haven't asked where she is. In Mia's opinion, this is a big mistake because they're overlooking the one person in the world who holds the key to unlocking the whole mystery.

A few days ago her parents had sat her down and carefully explained how Lilly is meeting a 'special doctor' twice a week to get to the bottom of what has caused her seizures, as if she hadn't realized this already. She's heard them having the same circular argument about the possible causes all week. It goes something like this: Grace insists that she is 'certain beyond certainty' that Cormack did something bad to Lilly at the music festival. *How can you be certain beyond certainty when certainty is so certain?* Mia wonders, whenever her mum says this.

'Like what?' her dad then demands.

'Maybe he spiked her drink or forced her to do something sexually that she didn't want to do. Or raped her,' her mum replies.

Each time the offence gets more horrific. So her dad says she's wasted as a journalist and should be writing fiction. 'There's no empirical evidence for any of this, Grace,' he usually yells at this point.

Strictly speaking, her mum blames her dad for encouraging Lilly to go to the festival and her dad blames her mum for putting Lilly under so much pressure at school. One evening she overheard her mum crying as she told Patrick that he didn't understand like she did that there are bad people out in the world. Their rows are like the wildfires in the stubble fields during harvest: just when you think they've dampened down, they start raging all over again.

Increasingly when they disagree, Mia has the feeling that really they are arguing about something completely different. Like when she tussles with Miss Swain about using a pencil for maths instead of a pen. In fact the dispute is about how much the teacher and she hate each other. She's beginning to think that if Lilly doesn't tell them the true reason for her seizures very soon, her parents will get divorced over it. She understands what divorce means. It means her dad will move into a flat where he has to dry his underpants on a radiator and eat Pot Noodle. And Mia will move even further away from the Travellers' site with her mum, who will get even madder about school work and end up making her do Kumon maths with Bea Vickers. *This cannot be allowed to happen!*

She knows exactly what the bad thing was that caused Lilly's stress and the likely reason for the argument between Lilly and Cormack at the party. She goes over to the bedroom window and notices that it has now rained so much that the pond at the end of the garden has come back. *Perfect conditions to release an eel,* she thinks. She puts her hand down the back of the radiator, removes the pregnancy test from its hiding place and puts it into the pocket of her dressing gown. Then she heads downstairs. As she goes into the kitchen she thinks they will immediately notice that she is aglow with the knowledge of a secret about to be released. The pregnancy test actually feels hot against her thigh. But no one takes any notice of her because they're too busy bickering.

'Why isn't she picking up her phone?'

'It's either run out of battery, turned off or there's no signal,' says Rob. 'Try not to catastrophize, Grace. Think about the most likely outcomes, not the least.'

'She's ill. What if something happens to her? What if she's on her own and has a seizure and there's no one to help?' Her mum's voice sounds sad and anguished, like the red kite's. 'We should call the hospital in case she's been taken there.'

'You're overreacting,' yells Patrick.

'And you're underreacting,' Grace yells back. 'Lilly could be in real danger.'

'You need to calm down, Grace,' Ana advises. 'You're jumping to conclusions.'

'Who are you to tell me to calm down?' Grace snaps.

'How many hours have I spent trying to sort out your problems?'

'Look, having great sex with your first boyfriend isn't a known trigger for stress, Grace,' Rob says, trying to introduce some levity into the situation. 'Not in my experience, at least.'

Mia thinks of how the eels that go back to the Sargasso Sea mate just once, then die, and how that could be pretty anxious-making. 'Well, it could be,' she interrupts them.

They all turn round in surprise.

'Sorry,' says Rob, guiltily. 'I didn't realize you'd come down, Mia. That wasn't appropriate.'

Mia walks towards the table and stands in front of them, straight-backed, as if she's finally coming on stage to deliver a speech she's been rehearsing for weeks. This is her moment.

'Well, it could be stressful having sex with your first boyfriend if you end up getting pregnant,' she says vehemently.

'Can we try not to make this about you for once?' Grace warns. 'We've all heard enough about the bloody Anglo-Saxon girl.'

'What Anglo-Saxon girl?' Rob asks, in bemusement.

'I'm not talking about her,' says Mia, putting her hand into her dressing-gown pocket. 'I'm talking about Lilly.' She feels four sets of eyes bore into her and clears her throat. 'I've tried to tell you without telling you so many times. To give you clues so that you can work out what's been going on without me betraying Lilly. But everyone ignores me,' Mia says, her voice trembling.

'To be honest, I think you do a pretty good job of getting attention, Mia,' says Patrick, dismissively.

She pulls the pregnancy test out of her pocket, takes the dipstick out of the box and points to the little window with the blue line. 'This. Belongs. To. Lilly.' She leaves a full stop between each word, for emphasis, and waves the dipstick, like a wand. It's an unnecessary flourish. She has their complete attention.

'What are you talking about?' asks Grace. Mia explains that Lilly told her at the beginning of the summer, the same day that Rob and Ana last visited, that she had got pregnant with Cormack's baby and had an abortion all on her own. She feels very grown-up saying the word 'abortion' and, judging by Rob and Ana's slack-jawed expressions, unlike Miss Swain they're very impressed with her use of complex vocabulary. 'Her argument with Cormack last night was probably because she decided to confess to him and he obviously got upset. Otherwise she didn't tell a single soul. Apart from me.'

'Why on earth did she tell you?' Grace can't disguise the disbelief in her tone.

'Because I'm her sister and we share everything.' She hesitates as it occurs to her that, *strictly speaking*, this isn't completely accurate. 'And I was the one who found the pregnancy test.' She hands it over to Ana, simply because she's sitting closest. Ana stares at it as though it might explode in her hand.

They pass the box and the dipstick around the table to each other as if they're playing Pass the Parcel, except there's no music, just the rasping noise of Grace's breath getting faster and faster. When it reaches Patrick he squints at the end of the cardboard packaging for so long that Mia wants to grab it from his hand and tell him to either say something or give it to the next person. Ana and Rob look shell-shocked. For a moment she regrets involving them. It must be tough for her aunt and uncle to discover that Lilly got pregnant so easily. She hopes their admiration for the

351

way that she has managed to solve the riddle of Lilly's seizures where everyone else has failed might ease their pain.

'This is what caused Lilly's stress. The answer was here all the time but no one bothered to ask me the question. It's a shame I didn't know earlier because then maybe Lilly could have given Rob and Ana her baby.'

Ana's face crumples.

'Where did you find this, Mia?' Grace asks. She sounds deadly serious, like the words are too heavy. She probably feels guilty that Lilly didn't confide in her and for all the horrible things she has said about Cormack, who seemed perfectly nice the few times Mia had met him.

'It was in a box in the garage,' says Mia, proudly. 'Strictly speaking, it was in a box, inside a box, inside a box. So I did well to find it at all.' She waits for them to congratulate her.

'Give it to me right now,' Grace snaps at her. Mia refuses. Grace turns to Rob and Ana and smiles so hard the edges of her mouth twitch. 'Mia spins stories out of nothing. Even her teacher says she's a fantasist.'

Mia reels back as if her mum has hit her. 'Not true! Lilly asked me to look after it!'

'Give it to your mum,' barks Patrick. 'This isn't a game.'

'Aren't you grateful I've managed to sort all of this out for you?' Mia says plaintively. She doesn't understand what she's done wrong.

Patrick clears his throat. 'Look at the date,' he says, aggressively tapping the end of the box. 'It doesn't add up.'

It's so typical of her dad to focus on the most boring detail. Mia hadn't even noticed a date. *It's so obviously the dipstick that's interesting, not the box.* She had almost thrown the packaging away. Rob takes the box from Patrick. *'Expiry March 2007.'* He reads it out loud. Twice.

'That's twelve years ago. When Lilly was five.' His

forehead furrows like he's grappling with a complex equation. *Even I can work out that maths*, thinks Mia.

'Two years before Mia was born,' says Patrick, finally. His head slumps as if it's buckling with the weight of a particularly heavy thought. There's another long silence that Mia can't decipher.

'Obviously it doesn't belong to Lilly,' says Grace, eventually.

'How can you be so sure?' asks Mia.

'Upstairs, now, Mia,' barks Patrick.

'Because it belongs to me,' says Grace.

In the garage Grace searches frantically for the packing box with the old tin container where Mia found the pregnancy test. When the builders had arrived at the beginning of the summer to put right all that was wrong with the house, she must have unthinkingly stored it away in one of the boxes now stacked in the garage, along with the rest of the contents of their wardrobe. She's furious with Lilly and Mia for snooping through her belongings, even though she recognizes the hypocrisy in her attitude.

The carved Peruvian tin had belonged to her father. She liked to pretend it was a present from him but the truth was that he had left it at the house in Lydney the same day he abandoned her and Luca. She remembers telling her little brother she was looking after it until their dad came home and Luca wondering why on earth anyone would come back to collect an empty tin. It occurs to her that this is precisely the sort of question Mia would ask. And then she realizes that the moments she gets angriest with Mia are the moments when she reminds her most of Luca.

She remembers the exact contents of the tin: the pregnancy test, the newspaper report about Luca's body being found in the river, the letter from Mrs Sylvester, 'The

Certainties' and the torn-up postcard. Right now it's the postcard that really matters. Even back then she had the insight to realize its explosive potential and had torn it into six pieces, separated the identity of sender and recipient and hidden them in the pocket of an old suede waistcoat that had belonged to Olwyn.

Grace curses herself for keeping these memories of the past. But their existence has given her a vital sense of connection between the person she used to be and the person she has become: they are the bridge from the past to the present. Everyone needs a sense of their own history, a narrative that informs where they have come from and points to where they are going, especially those who have no loving witnesses to help them write their own.

That's why she is always the parent in the front row at school plays and assemblies, taking photos and making videos, so Lilly and Mia could look back on their childhood and know it was happy and secure. There is a record of every significant milestone in their lives: framed pictures on every mantelpiece, photo montages of family holidays; Lilly's triumphs at swimming competitions; and at least a dozen big leather albums with handwritten captions. Grace has dedicated herself to filling her children's lives with schedules and plans to compensate for the vacuum of her own childhood. In creating their history, she had hoped to obliterate her own and inoculate them against the unhappiness of her upbringing. And by keeping secret what had happened to her, she hoped to protect them from repeating history. Her father was an addict and her mother was delusional, narcissistic, and likely suffered from borderline personality disorder. She would do everything in her power to ensure that nurture trumped nature. What she had failed to take into account was that she couldn't write her children's history. They have to write their own.

It occurs to her that, far from escaping her childhood, she has allowed it to infect every decision she has ever made. Patrick was the antithesis of her father: one of the main reasons that she had attached herself to him was the promise of security. Patrick was even-tempered and reliable. He didn't touch drugs, exercised religiously and restricted his alcohol consumption to a couple of beers at the weekend. He even self-regulated the amount of coffee he drank. In Patrick, Grace thought she had found someone who could insulate her from life's uncertainties.

She had spent the years after Luca's death running away and when she met Patrick she had stopped. Within six months she was married, pregnant and had moved to Cambridge, a city she had never even visited. She went from total uncertainty to total certainty and thought she had managed to bury her past. They had good sex rather than remarkable sex. But she had lived too close to her mother's unhealthy sexual relationships and the predatory pawing of Rudy's sleazy acolytes to feel like she was missing out. It was enough.

She rooted herself in his family, adopting their customs and rhythms until they became her own. She remembered once telling Patrick he was her life raft. She could tell from his embarrassed laugh that he knew without wanting to know. She remembered waking up one morning, shortly after Lilly was born, lifting Lilly out of her crib and looking at them both in the mirror. 'This is who I am,' she said, without taking on board that Lilly was a separate entity.

She finds a half-open soggy cardboard box on the floor by the door that leads from the garage into the garden. The Peruvian tin, with the llamas embossed on the lid, is there.

Grace remembers how Lilly had described the scent of violets before each seizure. She should have realized she had found the box with the few belongings she had brought from the house where her mother boiled up violets to make candles. Her first notebook and the suede waistcoat were saturated with their sickly-sweet odour.

'The Certainties' is inside. She starts flicking through it. On the final page, just after the newspaper cutting about Luca's death, she finds the six pieces of postcard stuck together. Lilly has got here before her. *She knows. She knows everything.* On the back page, after the newspaper article about Luca's death, Lilly has written something: 'There's no right way to grieve, Mum. There's no right way to love. I get it. Your secret is safe with me. You have what you need to get through most situations. And so do I.'

Grace understands that Lilly has been trying to protect her and that is the load she has been carrying. In seeking to protect her children she had unwittingly burdened them with her past. She also knows that although Lilly might not be aware of the circumstances of what happened all those years ago, she is almost certainly aware of who else is involved. Tears pool in her eyes. It was all a terrible mistake. And yet it was also utterly inevitable.

In the autumn of 2006, when Lilly was five years old, Grace received a letter from Mrs Sylvester telling her that Olwyn had died six months earlier. The letter had taken three months to arrive because it had been sent to their old address. *Their home before the last one, before the last one, before the last one*, as Lilly used to say, sounding like a Dr Seuss story. Patrick, it turned out, had not been such a reliable choice after all. His career never really took off and they were always short of money. At the end of Mrs Sylvester's letter,

356

almost as a footnote, she asked Grace if she could please let her know what she wanted her to do with her mother's ashes, which she had been given after the funeral, 'a simple affair, poorly attended'. The way she worded the question made Grace bite her lip because it perfectly encapsulated both Mrs Sylvester's practical nature and her sensitivity, to her mind a perfect combination of qualities. *You only need one person to love you as a child to learn how to love.*

She understood that Grace might not want to have anything to do with scattering her mother's ashes and wanted to give her an elegant right of refusal. In the event, Grace went to collect them, primarily because she wanted to see Mrs Sylvester to thank her properly for all the help she had given her and Luca as children. She hadn't been back to Lydney since Luca's death. She had never visited his grave. There was no need. She carried him in her heart. She never spoke of her loss to anyone. There were no photos because Olwyn wasn't the kind of mother who made family scrapbooks. Grace had, as she explained to Mrs Sylvester, taken a scalpel to her old life and surgically excised it because it was the only way she could keep on living. She explained that she couldn't look backwards very often because it felt like getting vertigo. 'I feel like I could get dragged over the edge,' she said, and Mrs Sylvester nodded in silent assent.

Mrs Sylvester listened more than she spoke. She didn't judge Grace for not telling Patrick about her past. She said that people have to find their own path to learn to live alongside tragedy. She simply expressed regret that she hadn't intervened more forcefully earlier. Only then did the words start to get stuck in her throat. Grace started to tell Mrs Sylvester that she had done way more than she had to in a very difficult situation. Mrs Sylvester put up her hand and said that everyone had lost, but Grace had lost the most and shouldn't waste words trying to comfort her.

Grace left with the urn in her bag. She didn't know where she would take the ashes, just that she wanted them to be as far from Luca as possible. At some point during the journey, the train carriage started to fill with the sickly smell of violets so at the next station she took the urn and shook them out of the window on to the track. It was somewhere between Swindon and Bristol. She didn't want to remember exactly where.

When she got to London it was too late to get the last train to Cambridge. She called Patrick and he suggested she ring his brother to see if she could stay at his flat.

She could hear from the noise in the background when Rob picked up the phone that he was at a party. He explained that he was at the tail end of an awards ceremony and offered to send a car to fetch her. 'I'm wearing jeans,' she warned him.

'The woman next to me is wearing a wolf mask,' he responded drily. 'No one will notice.' He didn't ask any awkward questions because he knew where Grace had been.

'Was it awful?' Rob had asked, as she sat down opposite him in the club. She nodded. 'But it was also cathartic.'

He understood. They sat in comfortable silence for a while, observing a man and a woman on the next-door table lean into each other in a way that suggested they were attracted to each other but hadn't yet had sex, a state of affairs that Rob called the Prelude. They laughed at how the couple mirrored each other's body language, tilting their heads to the same side, and licking their lips at the same time, and agreed it was like the birds-of-paradise mating dance on David Attenborough's show.

It started as a game. By this stage both of them were

emphatically drunk. 'Let's imagine what they're saying to each other,' suggested Rob, enthusiastically. They were used to playing games at family events so it didn't seem strange.

'Isn't that a bit cruel?' Grace asked. 'They might notice.'

'God, you're always so hung up about what other people think of you,' he said. It was his favourite critique of her. That decided it. They turned to face each other at the table. Rob tilted his head so far to one side that his ear almost touched his shoulder and she copied him. They looked ridiculous.

'I'm going to crick my neck,' she said.

'You go first,' he replied.

'Would you rather know or not know?' she asks. It was a good question because it encapsulated all the uncertainty and enquiry of the head-tilting ritual going on at the table beside them.

'Know what?' He frowned, copying the facial expression of the young guy on the next-door table.

'Know how everything is going to end before it begins?'

'God, I love it when you get all philosophical on me.' They glanced at the couple, who were so besotted with each other that they had no clue Rob and Grace were mimicking them. The man had leant forward to pull a stray hair away from the woman's eye. Rob leant over and did the same to Grace. Then when the man ran his finger down the woman's cheek, Rob copied the gesture.

'Too intimate,' Grace said drunkenly, pushing his hand away. Rob put his finger to his lips to tell her to be quiet and then she blew the game apart by doing the same, forgetting that she wasn't meant to be copying him.

'We're losing impetus.' Grace giggled.

'Let's play I Love It When,' said Rob. She looked puzzled.

'I love it when you look at me with those cold blue eyes,' he said. 'Your go.'

'I'm not sure I like cold.'

'Periwinkle blue, to be precise,' he said. He pointed at the couple, who were leaning towards each other but forming a barrier to complete intimacy by crossing their arms on the table. Rob and Grace copied their position.

'I love it when you make me feel that there is no past and no future and only the present exists,' she said.

He conceded that she was much better at the game than him and had a way with words. He offered to recommend her to a friend of his who wrote advertising copy. 'Thanks,' said Grace, copying the way the girl at the next table ran her finger around the rim of her wine glass. When the man got up to go and get a drink, Rob stood up.

'So do you want to get another drink?'

'I want,' she said.

The two men came back and sat down at exactly the same time.

'I'm getting really drunk,' said Grace.

'I love it when you get drunk,' he said. 'Okay, Grace, if you were to turn on the radio and your five favourite tracks played one after the other, what would they be?'

'You'll tell me I've got this all wrong,' she replied.

'I won't. There's no such thing as wrong. It's just your opinion. Reverse order.'

She thought for a moment. 'Number five, Psychedel-ic Furs "Pretty In Pink". Number four, the Verve "Bitter Sweet Symphony", Number three, Cranberries "Linger".'

'God, you are so post-punk.'

'I said you'd tell me I got it wrong,' she said triumphantly.

The man at the table next door reached for the wom-an's hand and squeezed his fingers around hers, pressing his thumb along her wrist. Rob reached out for Grace's hand and she felt his thumb circle the sensitive area on the inside of her wrist. She closed her eyes, and when she opened them he was staring at her. He leant over the table and they kissed even though the couple on the table next door hadn't. And that was just the Prelude. It was really bad luck to fall pregnant after a one-night stand. Really bad luck. But if anyone had ever asked if she regretted that night she wouldn't have been able to say.

19

Mia is totally confused. She thought they would all be so pleased with her for telling the truth, but not only is she being shut out of everything again, she is being blamed for revealing Lilly's secret, which turns out to be her mum's secret, and somehow also involves Rob. She stares at the enigmatic expression of the matryoshka doll on her window-sill. *Human beings are nothing more than layers and layers of secrets*, she decides.

Berating herself for her inability to read situations, Mia stretches her skinny arm down the back of the piping hot radiator to retrieve the ring from its hiding place on the ledge of the bracket. She holds it tight in her fist, closes her eyes and prays for everything to go back to how it used to be. When she opens her fingers there is a painful circular welt where the ring has burnt the palm of her hand. She doesn't understand that metal conducts heat and instead views this as a warning. *Perhaps the ring isn't simply a force for good. It is also a force for evil.* Apprehension grows as it occurs to her that, *strictly speaking*, everything started to go wrong from the moment she borrowed the ring from the archaeological site: Lilly's first seizure happened the same day; the plague of the red dust began; her parents' arguments started; her friendship with Tas got complicated; and Elvis became ill. *Why does it take me so long to understand these obvious truths?* It dawns on her with growing dread that, far from helping Tas, taking the ring could create serious problems for his entire family.

She's seized by the conviction that she needs to return the ring to its rightful owner as soon as possible. *At least she can put this right.* Mia kneels on the floor beside Elvis to inform him of her plan, resting her chin on the edge of his bucket to stare into his wise beady black eyes. They look cloudier than usual and he doesn't move or flop on his side for his belly rub. Instead he gives her a regretful look that seems to express how happy he has been to get to know her but that the time has come for him to go home. *The biggest gift you can give someone is their freedom,* she remembers Tas once telling her, when he was describing why his family struggled so much to be able to carry on with their life on the road. She decides that after she puts the ring back she will collect Tas from his caravan so they can release Elvis together. The goodbye will be less painful if Tas is with her and he will love her all the more for letting her eel go wild again. It will be a cross between an episode of David Attenborough and *The Durrells.* 'I have ruined everyone's lives. And I'll ruin yours too if I don't let you go,' she whispers to Elvis.

She's looked up details about Elvis's journey back to the Sargasso Sea online with her dad. So she knows that even if he manages to make the 3000-mile journey she will never see him again because he will have sex and die. 'At least he will die happy,' Patrick had quipped. She finds it really annoying the way adults joke about sex when all it seems to bring is Big Trouble. She thinks about her mum and dad. And Lilly and Cormack. And Rob and Ana. And the Anglo-Saxon girl. She puts the ring on her finger, throws on her red anorak, and creeps downstairs, carrying Elvis's bucket in one hand, her Anglo-Saxon diary in the other. There's too much noisy discussion coming from the kitchen for anyone to notice the front door open and close behind her.

The bad weather means there isn't anyone on the bus to stare at a small girl travelling alone with a heavy bucket of murky water containing a curious eel pressing his nose against the grille. Mia is pleased to see that Elvis already seems more animated. As the bus pulls up by the track that leads to the Travellers' site, she shivers and hesitates on the bottom step with her bucket. An early-morning mist stalks the Fens, but instead of thinking about the cold, Mia is worrying about the evil spirits that might be lurking in the fog. She touches the ring and twists it round until the garnet faces her palm and clenches her fist so the stone digs into the burn. The pain helps her summon courage for what lies ahead.

Sensing her hesitation, and no doubt wondering why such a young girl is travelling alone, the driver asks if she is 'completely certain' this is the correct stop and 'why exactly' she wants to be left in the middle of nowhere. Mia is tempted to argue that there is no such thing as nowhere because everywhere is in the middle of somewhere. But she doesn't want to draw attention to herself so she explains that she is visiting a friend who lives in one of the caravans. 'You might know him. He's called Tas,' she adds.

The bus driver gives a relieved smile and offers Mia a peppermint, which she turns down. 'I pick him up to bring him to school every day. Nice boy.'

One thing she has learnt over the past month is that to be a really good liar it's best to stick close to the truth. That's what Lilly does and she is the best liar Mia has ever come across. 'I'm taking my pet eel to visit him.' She points at Elvis.

'Well, send him my best,' the driver calls out. 'And don't get cold, will you? The weather's on the turn.'

The bus pulls away. Mia has never felt more completely alone. No one knows where she is or what she is doing. It's not a frightening feeling, in part because it's so familiar, but mostly because out here in the Fens, if you know how to look and listen, you're surrounded by life. Tas has taught her all about the orchestra of birds: the bittern playing the horn, the drumming of the snipe and the wood pigeons singing a cappella. She knows the difference between a rabbit and a hare, a falcon and a marsh harrier. He has shown her how to skin a rabbit so the fur peels off like a banana skin and how to trim a horse's hoof. He has allowed her into his world and she will not let anyone take it away from her.

Now that she is on the track Mia can see that the mist hovers above the earth, like a shroud, without actually touching the ground. She doesn't realize that this is because the earth is warmer than the air above it and instead assumes it has something to do with the magic conducted by the angry spirits from the graves the archaeologists have disturbed. She hears a noise and falls on her knees to hide behind a clump of spiky sedge growing on the bank of the dyke that runs parallel to the field, one arm wrapped protectively around Elvis's bucket. But when she peers through the sedge beneath the veil of mist there is nothing more threatening than a hare racing away from her along a furrow between rows of leeks.

The mist has lifted to thigh height. Mia stomps purposefully up the drove in the direction of the Travellers' site, trying to calm her nerves by pretending she is the Dauntless Girl, who isn't scared of anything. *If a will-o'-the-wisp or boggle tries to tempt me into a dyke, I'll just shout it down.* She feels for the ring on her finger and imagines the Anglo-Saxon girl wandering through this landscape, unafraid of the devils and ghosts lurking in the same damp mist that wraps itself around her now. She pictures her living in a hut on stilts and the terror of watching her stomach grow and grow, knowing that the father of her child didn't love her and the chances were that she and her baby would die during childbirth. Except now it is no longer Lilly's face she sees. It is Grace's. *Mia is a fantasist.* The words hurt, like the sedge lacerating her legs.

She can't believe how Lilly has lied to her, but the sense of betrayal helps her understand how her dad might be feeling right now. She will never forget the way his face collapsed when he saw the date on the pregnancy test. *I could have had another older sister or a brother.* She bites her lip hard so she doesn't cry and blames the wind for the tears streaming down her cheeks.

It takes twice as long as usual to reach the end of the drove. She has to keep swapping hands because the bucket containing Elvis is so heavy and she's walking into an easterly wind that her dad once told her blows straight in from Russia. The Travellers' site is half as big as it used to be before the archaeologists came and stole their land. She heads left through the field where Guit used to graze. It now contains three portable cabins where all the coins, pottery and jewellery are stored and cleaned before being catalogued. This was where she had first seen the ring.

Head down, she crab walks towards the burial site with her bucket. Mia doesn't consider herself a natural rule-breaker. After a brief internal tussle, however, she concludes that if the archaeologists really don't want people trampling over their work then they should install tighter security. She heaves Elvis over the orange plastic fencing, then tries to climb over herself. But her foot gets caught in the seam at the top and she loses balance and lands on her back in a puddle atop earth baked hard by drought. Her stomach lists into her mouth and for a moment breathing out is impossible and she can only inhale the tiniest breaths. She wonders if this is what it is like for Lilly when she has a seizure. She shivers and quickly blames it on the cold.

'There's work to be done,' she tells Elvis, who eyes her anxiously from his bucket.

She has come on to the site beside the grave of the lady who was buried with her cow. She recognizes it instantly because you don't forget something like seeing the skeleton of a fully grown Anglo-Saxon cow, and it's by far the biggest grave. She remembers the archaeologist telling them how there were hundreds of amber beads in the woman's grave and that only the most important people were buried with animals. Mia had made Tas laugh by referring to the woman as 'Miss Swain' because she shared a similar need to be worshipped. Miss Swain would probably demand at least an elephant in her grave, Mia had whispered to Tas.

The memory makes her smile and gradually the pain in her stomach fades.

She gets up, dusts herself down and pulls out her Anglo-Saxon diary from her bag. For their homework the week before their trip, Miss Swain had instructed the class to draw a map of the archaeological site with a key that had to be stuck with glue in the middle of the notebook. Mia examines her map. Everything is marked: the graves, the archaeologists' office, the shed where the tools are kept and the river that runs behind the site. At the bottom of the page Miss Swain had written *Good effort, B minus* in her neat, uptight handwriting, and suggested that next time Mia should use more complex words from the SAT practice vocabulary.

Holding the map, she picks up Elvis and heads to Plot No. 3 where the girl and the baby are buried. *How horrible to be remembered as a number! No wonder the archaeologists have angered the spirits of the dead. They should have some respect.*

The grave is covered with black tarpaulin held down by six stones that a ten-year-old girl in heavy black leather boots doesn't have any problem lifting. She remembers with distaste the archaeologist's excited description of how difficult it had been to remove the ring from the girl's finger because the bones had been so horribly disfigured from too much heavy work.

She kneels down and touches the edge of the tarpaulin. Being alone with her Anglo-Saxon girl is very different from being here with her class. Mia tentatively lifts the edge of the plastic. The girl's skull is immediately visible. Although she was buried face down because she was viewed as a sinner, her head rests sideways, left cheekbone to the ground, so her jaw is clearly visible. Mia notices again how her mouth hangs open in an agonized half-scream.

Why is it always women who are made to suffer for having sex and getting pregnant? It's so bloody unfair. Spurred on by this thought, she carefully folds back the rest of the tarpaulin to reveal the tiny, perfect skeleton of the girl's baby between her legs. *Poor little baby!* She clambers down into the grave and kneels beside the skeleton. Her hands are shaking but she blames it on the cold.

There are heavy stones along the girl's spine that the archaeologist said were placed there to prevent her spirit from coming back to haunt the village. Mia impulsively removes each one and throws them over her shoulder. She gently touches the skull of the girl. Without this weight on her back, her spirit will finally be given the chance to escape from the dark, claustrophobic grave, where she has spent more than a thousand years, to roam freely across the Fens with her baby.

It's the next part of the plan, however, that is most important to Mia. She holds the girl's hand in her own. The bones feel hard and cold. She removes the ring and slips it on to the skeleton's finger. On Monday morning the archaeologists will come back and see the ring has been returned.

She scrambles out of the grave and covers it with the tarpaulin. Although the fog has lifted, the sky has turned an ugly grey. Another storm is coming.

'Our work here is done, Elvis,' she says dramatically. 'Let's go and find Tas.'

Mia doubles back down the drove to the Travellers' site. It's divided into two-dozen pitches around a dingy building where the showers and toilets are housed. Scrawny hedges and fences give each plot the illusion of privacy. Mia knows the site as well as anyone who lives there. She weaves in and out of the trailers towards Rawnie's, her arm aching with cramp from carrying the heavy bucket.

As she reverses into Tas's pitch through a hole in the hedge she calls his name in excitement. 'Tas! Tas! You'll never guess who I've got with me!' She picks off the burrs from her T-shirt and turns round, lifting the bucket triumphantly in the air. But there is nothing there. She closes her eyes in disbelief and counts to ten before opening them again. For a second Mia wonders if she has made a mistake. Then she recognizes the frayed lengths of blue rope where the dogs used to be tied up.

Her heart starts to pound as she frantically spins round. The trailer and the touring caravan are no longer there, although there are rectangles of brown grass where they once stood. The cockerel that struts his stuff has disappeared, as has Guit, the piebald pony that grazes on the grass growing in the gaps where the concrete has cracked. The chickens have gone. The leather seat where they imagined travelling around the world has vanished, as has all the scrap metal, the tyres and tiles. It's like they were never here. All that is left is a pile of black bin liners flapping loudly in the breeze. *Horses are family*, Tas always says. If Guit has gone, he has gone. She's too late. She spots one of Tas's elderly relatives on the other side of the hedge and asks what has happened to Rawnie.

'There was trouble,' he says vaguely.

'What kind of trouble?' Mia asks.

'The police was here. About a missing ring. They thought Tas had taken it.'

She understands straight away. 'It's all my fault,' she says, chewing her lower lip so she doesn't cry.

'Of course it's not your fault,' he responds kindly. 'Don't worry, lass. We're always on the move. And they've a good pitch waiting in Lincolnshire with family. Tas will have as much freedom and fresh air there as he did here.'

Mia falls on to her knees. She can't believe that Tas would have left without telling her. Her chest tightens as if it is being slowly compressed by a great weight. Then she realizes that it is because she is crying so much, she can't catch her breath in between sobs.

She weeps for the lost baby, the half-sibling she will never know; she cries for the deviant girl; she cries for her dad and her mum, who will surely get divorced because of her; she cries for the baby that Rob and Ana will never have; but mostly she cries for Tas because it is too late to save him. She can put up with everything else as long as Tas is with her. She can endure the hurtful comments from other children at school, Miss Swain's hatred, the way she

371

disappoints her parents, and the feeling that Lilly doesn't want to be close to her, if Tas is by her side. Without him there is no one left who believes in her. She thinks of all the nasty things that people have said about her being stupid over the years. And for the first time she thinks that they are right because it is her fault that he has gone. Elvis looks up at her and opens and closes his mouth in sympathy.

'We're on our own now, Elvis,' she sobs, as she strokes his head through the grille. She picks up the bucket and leaves the Travellers' site to head up the track to Earith Sluice.

Her biggest worry now is how Elvis is going to make his way through the sluice. She has had nightmares about him getting stuck in a lock. In her dreams she sees him swimming round in ever-decreasing circles, unable to escape before finally dying of hunger and decomposing in a rancid watery grave. She knows that she has to release him the other side of the sluice where the river is tidal and will carry him to the sea. She lifts the heavy bucket and starts walking. She owes it to Tas to honour her promise to free her eel. And she owes it to Elvis to make sure that at least he has a chance of a better life.

It isn't far from the Travellers' site to the sluice, but the burn on her palm now stings so much that she can only carry the bucket in her left hand. It keeps bumping against her calf and the water slops into her leather boots so her feet are quickly soaked. Elvis is thrown around as if he's caught in a storm at sea.

The temperature has dropped after the storm the previous night and it's now pouring with rain. Mia shivers and zips up her anorak. Elvis helps her to keep going. He looks up at her, totally trusting. Even though she might have messed up everything else, she's going to get this right. *Strictly speaking, this is a life-and-death issue.*

'My only friend in the world,' she says to him. She starts to cry again.

She remembers the day she found Elvis in the pool of mud at the end of the garden at the start of the spring floods. She was with Grace, who was driving stakes into the ground beside the garden shed to monitor water levels. At first she didn't notice him. He was completely still, luxuriating in the mud. But then she saw a pair of small beady eyes looking up at her. She peered back, and for two minutes they played the staring game, until finally she blinked first. She didn't realize back then that he had no eyelids. He tipped his big ugly snout towards her. Even then on that first encounter Mia knew that Elvis was the wisest, funniest and most loyal creature she had ever come across. She traced a line along his back and he felt like liquid velvet. She picked him up and he slid between her fingers and when she dropped him again her hand was slippery with slime.

When at last she reaches the sluice, she doesn't recognize the landscape from the last time she was here in the summer. Streams have turned into rivers, and rivers into lakes. She imagines this is what it might have looked like before her relatives drained the land.

The concrete sluice is cold and forbidding. The gates strain against the weight of the water that is being held back. Last time she was here Patrick had explained how the sluice is meant to direct the water from the River Ouse into the Old Bedford River and the Hundred Foot Drain when the levels rise. But it had rained so much last night that the sluice is overwhelmed and all three rivers have burst their banks. Even the road is flooded.

'Ely eels,' trills Mia, as she splashes across the road,

remembering how the city got its name. The flooding is good for Elvis. But not so good for her. The water almost reaches the tongue of her boots and it's difficult to get her bearings. She climbs over the stile opposite the sluice and starts walking along the riverbank.

It gets boggier underfoot. The sky and water turn the same slate grey and it's heavy going in the muddy terrain. Whenever she thinks about turning back she looks at Elvis in his bucket and forces herself onwards. Maybe it would be best for everyone if she just sank in a bog. Lilly is going to be furious with her for revealing the secret it turns out she was keeping for their mum. It will be a terrifying kind of double fury. Judging by her dad's face, he obviously had no idea about Grace's pregnancy.

When she gets to the water's edge she sees that the river is raging. There are hungry black whirlpools and the usually quiet surface looks as if it's boiling. She knows right away she can't release Elvis here. He won't stand a chance of finding a good current to take him to the ocean and he'll exhaust himself before he even begins his journey.

So she walks further upstream along the bank, hoping the river will be less unforgiving where it's allowed to follow its natural course. She slips on the rough terrain a couple of times and tumbles into the sedge, losing her Anglo-Saxon diary in the process. Miraculously, the bucket remains upright. It's becoming clear she can't get much further. She cuts a path down to the river's edge. The water now reaches Mia's calves. It's cold but bearable. The mud, on the other hand, sucks her boots into the ground and it becomes more and more difficult and exhausting to pull them out. When the water reaches her knees she realizes that she can't go much further. She stops but she can't put the bucket down because it's too deep.

'This is where we say goodbye, my friend,' she breathlessly tells Elvis. She removes the grille from the top of his bucket. He swims in a circle and flips on his back to allow her to tickle his tummy one last time. Then she gently tips the bucket on its side, imagining that he knows she is giving him permission to leave.

'Swim up to the Wash and turn right,' she instructs him. He will know this because his instinct to go home to reproduce is older than time itself. Her dad had told her it's probably in his genes. He slips out of the bucket and stretches himself out and turns his head back towards her so he looks like a question mark. 'I'll miss you so much.' He stays.

'Go,' she tells him, pushing him away. She is crying so hard that the outline of his little face goes all fuzzy. Then, with a couple of switches of his tail, he is gone. She stands for a moment, sobbing, as the ripples on the surface disappear.

Then she turns round to attempt to locate the sluice. However, land and sky have turned the same colour so it's difficult to make out exactly where one begins and the other ends. She tries to wade away from the river towards the bank on the right but to her surprise it gets deeper. She lets go of the bucket and can tell how strong the current is because of the speed at which it floats away. She holds on to the reeds and sedge for balance even though they cut her hands. The water is now up to her thighs so Mia decides she has nothing to lose by swimming. At least then the mud can no longer hold her prisoner. Her mum has taken her to lessons ever since she can remember, and although Mia lacks Lilly's co-ordination, she isn't a bad swimmer. However, as soon as she plunges in, she realizes that there is a new enemy. The current immediately carries her back to where she released Elvis. Her teeth chatter from fear and cold. She half wonders if he might still be there and could surface to help her in some way. Perhaps she could cling on to him like the foam noodle she used as a float during swimming lessons.

She looks over to the right, sees a light in the distance and knows it is one of the bog creatures come to get her. She imagines it pressing her face down into the mud until she suffocates like the deviant girl and hears herself scream. The wind and the rain carry her cries away. Mia stands still and her boots sink deeper. The water level is rising fast and has reached her hips. She understands that she will have to swim again. The thought of being carried into the river and upstream to the sea terrifies her. She tries to lift her feet but they are stuck fast in the mud. *This is how people used to die in these parts*, she remembers her mum telling her. *It's like quicksand.* She struggles against the mud sucking her down into the riverbed, but the more she struggles, the deeper she sinks.

The water is now around her shoulders. She's crying so much that her chest rises and falls like one of the pumps. She should have taken off her anorak because it adds to the weight of her. She ducks underwater and frantically tries to release her feet from the boots. As usual, the laces are knotted tight around her ankles. When she comes up again she is coughing up muddy river water. She can feel the grit in her mouth and nose.

The light is getting closer to her and the water is now at mouth level. Mia breathes through her nostrils in terror, then feels a fire in her nose and throat as the muddy water forces its way into her very being. She sees her plait floating beside her and wishes it were Elvis. *I'm a goner*, she thinks. Her lungs start to fill with water. She hears a voice above the surface and knows it's one of the marsh creatures. She

feels it put its arms around her to embrace her and its tenderness is welcome.

Grace guessed that Mia had gone to Earith as soon as she
saw the bucket had disappeared from her bedroom. Just last
week Mia had announced that she thought Elvis had heard
the call of the wild and needed to go back to his homeland.
'Dad says he needs to fulfil his historical destiny,' she had
explained, before asking Grace what her historical destiny
might be and if she didn't know what it was, how could she
possibly ever fulfil it? 'Is it to reproduce?' she kept asking.
'I'm not sure I want to reproduce. It causes too many
problems.'

At first Grace had laughed. Then, as the questioning
continued, she had grown impatient because she was wast-
ing time that could have been better spent helping Lilly
catch up with her school work.

Grace grips the steering wheel as she drives through the
middle of yet another flooded road. The rain is so heavy
that it beats down on the car roof in a single roar. The
wipers neurotically slice backwards and forwards, and in
the blink where the landscape momentarily reveals itself,
she searches frantically for Mia but sees only Luca. 'He's
wearing his blue T-shirt, jeans and flip-flops,' she hears
herself say, over and over again. It was what she told the
police after he disappeared in the river. Olwyn, it turned
out, had given them a completely inaccurate description of
his clothes. Not surprising, since she never got him dressed.

Grace's heart beats so fast that her chest hurts. There is
no right way to grieve, the therapist had reassured her all
those years ago. Some people look for clarity in the past, to
the life they shared before their loss, and hold on to those
memories. But the five years she shared with Luca was a

period of such darkness and chaos that she could make no more sense of their life together than she could of his death. So Grace had chosen silence, hoping that if she squeezed the memory of his death hard enough, eventually it would disappear. Until Lilly's illness, she'd thought she had managed to hold the past at bay.

It doesn't take much rain for the road into Earith to flood. When the water starts to seep through the bottom of the doorframe, Grace abandons the car and sets out on foot. She wades across the road and looks out across the fields. There is water as far as the eye can see. The perfectly straight lines and geometric patterns have vanished. Gates, trees, fences are all submerged. It has become, as it once was, an aquatic landscape. The three rivers have merged to become one. The only remaining straight line is the path that runs parallel to the Hundred Foot Drain, which was built above sea level.

She sets off along this path at a half-jog. Every so often she stops to wipe her eyes. She can't tell any more if it's rain or tears. After ten minutes she stoops over her phone to see if there are any messages from Ana, who volunteered to stay at home in case Lilly or Mia came home, or Patrick and Rob, who have gone to search for the girls on the north side of the washes. There is one message from Rob. *Was it mine?* Grace doesn't respond. He will infer the answer from her silence. She will never see him or Ana again. She thinks of Patrick. Even if he doesn't admit it to himself, he knows. She has always accepted the limits of their marriage and so, she suspects, has Patrick. But their story is over.

She calls Mia's name, just as she had once called Luca's, but her voice dissolves in the wind. In the distance she sees something floating in the river. She climbs down from the path and wades into the water until she is close enough to see that it is Elvis's bucket. She knows what this means. She tries to get closer. The water is now thigh-deep and the bucket has already disappeared in the current behind a patch of half-submerged sedge that obscures her view.

She sees her teenage self, running down the hill towards the Lyd, calling Luca's name, and remembers the exact sensation of falling. Her whole life has been built around this moment, when her failure to anticipate danger meant that she wasn't there for Luca. It would seem history is a turning wheel and there is no escape from her past. She screams Mia's name.

When all the air has left her lungs she stops but still the noise continues and when she looks back across the water she sees that this time she isn't alone.

'Mia! Mia!' Lilly bellows, over and over again. When she first spotted her little sister in the water from the ridge overlooking the river, Lilly's first instinct was to flash the torch on her phone in the hope it would guide Mia towards her. Thank God she was wearing her red anorak because at least it made her visible in the sea of grey.

But the more she flashed the torch across the water, the more Mia tried to get away from it. Lilly cursed Mia's imagination, knowing she would probably think it was some monster of the marshes come to get her. She keeps remembering her dad's words whenever Mia gets into a scrape. *Mia is in Big Trouble*. This time, however, it's really true. She can tell from the way Mia's arms are flailing that she is completely disoriented. She's drowning, just like her mum's brother drowned. Luca. The uncle she never knew.

She remembers what Grace says about split-second decisions and throws off her trainers and peels off the flared jeans. Her swimming coach has taught her everything she needs to know about hydrodynamic drag. She runs towards the water. Someone must have opened the sluice because it is getting deeper by the second. Half swimming, half wading, she fights the current towards the swollen red anorak billowing around the surface. When Lilly reaches her little sister she stands behind her and tries to pull her out of the water but quickly realizes that her feet are stuck fast in the mud. She curses her great big boots. Mia might as well have a lump of concrete tied to her legs.

She takes a deep breath and dives underwater, holding on to Mia's legs so the current doesn't carry her away. The visibility beneath the surface is terrible. Lilly, however, is used to swimming in the murky depths of the sluice. She pulls and tugs at the laces of the boots. Her lungs feel as if they are bursting, but she knows if she goes up to catch another breath it might be too late. Then, suddenly, one of the laces breaks and she manages by degrees to unthread it from the eyelets to release Mia's foot from the left boot. Lilly swims up to the surface and lifts Mia's head out of the water. She's half choking and vomiting river water but at least she is breathing. 'Look at me, Mimi,' she commands, tilting her chin towards the sky. 'Follow my breath.'

'Lil,' Mia repeats on every out-breath. She tries to speak and Lilly urges her to save her energy and instead focus on keeping her head above water, then dives again to work on the other boot. The longest she had ever managed underwater at the sluice was three minutes and ten seconds and that was without the kind of challenges she now faces from the weather. Mia has tied this lace in a double knot but she has managed to unpick some of the threads, which makes it easier to pull it apart. Lilly's brain feels sluggish as if all its energy is focused on pulling out this second lace, one eyelet at a time. She imagines she is her mum and it is Luca in the water and it gives her strength to know that if she can pull this off she is saving the lives of two people, not one.

When Mia is released, Lilly bursts to the surface, gulping for air. Her lungs feel as if they're imploding, blood pulses in her head and she hears a noise in her ears, like whales singing. She clasps her arm firmly around Mia's waist, so the current can't steal her away. Mia chokes and retches as Lilly lists towards the figure waving frantically at them from the riverbank. Lilly is grateful to the empty landscape for giving her a clear sightline and to the sky for reflecting light off the water to illuminate their passage.

Grace lies flat on her stomach on a bed of reeds, arms extended ready to pull them both from the river. When finally they reach her she drags them out of the water and they lie beside each other, all three of them, trying to catch their breath beneath the rain. Grace looks up, searching for the ghost of Luca's absence, but it has disappeared. She has a rare sense of belonging in the moment and of being surrounded by everything that matters. She will go forward, like the water. 'I understand, Mum,' says Lilly. She offers her hand and Grace takes it.

Acknowledgements

This does not happen alone. I am indebted to my agent, Jonny Geller, for his impeccable advice and support, and the wider Curtis Brown team. No thanks big enough to my editors, Maxine Hitchcock and Matilda McDonald, at Penguin for their flawless editorial advice and for caring about the book as much as I do. Thanks also to copy-editor Hazel Orme for her meticulous professionalism, and to Emma Henderson and Ellie Hughes for all their hard work and dedication.

Growing up in Norfolk, the bleak Fenland landscape always seemed a mystical place. Thanks to Marina Allpress, my guide to the Fens, and to Patrick Mahoney, lock keeper at Hermitage Lock. I'm very grateful to Dr Carolyn Gabriel for her advice on conversion disorder, to Suzanne O'Sullivan for allowing me to quote from *It's All in Your Head*, and to Dr Rowan Burnstein at Addenbrooke's Hospital.

Special thanks to Phil Robertson and to other involved friends and family (an understatement): Helen Baker, Lucy Fergusson, Sarah Harrison, Charlotte Simpson-Orlebar, Helen Townsend, and Henry Tricks. To Ed and Maia for their ruthless edits, and to Felix and Caspar.